Scarlet Wilson wrote her first story aged eight and has never stopped. She's worked in the health service for twenty years, trained as a nurse and a health visitor. Scarlet now works in public health and lives on the West Coast of Scotland with her fiancé and their two sons. Writing medical romances and contemporary romances is a dream come true for her.

New York Times bestselling author **RaeAnne Thayne** finds inspiration in the beautiful northern Utah mountains where she lives with her family. Her books have won numerous honours, including six RITA® Award nominations from Romance Writers of America and Career Achievement and Romance Pioneer awards from RT Book Reviews. She loves to hear from readers and can be reached through her website at www.raeannethayne.com

Marie Ferrarella is a *USA Today* bestselling and RITA® Award-winning author and has written more than two hundred books for Mills & Boon, some under the name Marie Nicole. Her romances are beloved by fans worldwide. Visit her website at www.marieferrarella.com

One Autumn Proposal

**SCARLET WILSON
RAEANNE THAYNE
MARIE FERRARELLA**

MILLS & BOON

First Published in Great Britain 2019
by Mills & Boon, an imprint of HarperCollins*Publishers*
1 London Bridge Street, London, SE1 9GF

ONE AUTUMN PROPOSAL © 2019 Harlequin Books S. A.

Her Christmas Eve Diamond © 2012 Scarlet Wilson
The Holiday Gift © 2016 RaeAnne Thayne
Christmastime Courtship © 2017 Marie Rydzynski-Ferrarella

ISBN: 978-0-263-27943-6

1119

MIX
Paper from
responsible sources
FSC® C007454

This book is produced from independently certified FSC™ paper to ensure responsible forest management.

For more information visit: www.harpercollins.co.uk/green

Printed and bound in Spain
by CPI, Barcelona

HER CHRISTMAS
EVE DIAMOND

SCARLET WILSON

PROLOGUE

30 September

CASSIDY raised her hand and knocked on the dilapidated door. Behind her Lucy giggled nervously. 'Are you sure this is the right address?'

Cassidy turned to stare at her. 'You arranged this. How should I know?' She glanced at the crumpled piece of paper in her hand. 'This is definitely number seventeen.' She leaned backwards, looking at the 1960s curtains hanging in the secondary glazed double windows that rattled every time a bus went past. 'Maybe nobody's home?' she said hopefully.

This had to be the worst idea she'd ever had. No. Correction. It hadn't been her idea. In a moment of weakness she'd just agreed to come along with her colleagues to see what all the fuss was about.

'Where did you find this one, Lucy?'

Lucy had spent the past year whisking her friends off to as many different fortune-tellers as possible. By all accounts, some were good, some were bad and some were just downright scary. Cassidy had always managed to wriggle out of it—until now.

'This is the one my cousin Fran came to. She said she was fab.'

Cassidy raised her eyebrows. 'Cousin Fran who went on the reality TV show and then spent the next week hiding in the cupboard?'

Lucy nodded. 'Oh, great,' sighed Cass.

'I wonder if she'll tell me how many children I'll have,' murmured Lynn dreamily. She stuck her pointed elbow into Cassidy's ribs. 'She told Lizzie King she'd have twins and she's due any day now.'

'I just want to know if Frank is ever going to propose,' sighed Tamsin. 'If she doesn't see it in the future then I'm dumping him. Five years is long enough.'

Cassidy screwed up her nose and shook her head. 'You can't dump Frank because of something a fortune-teller says.'

But Tamsin had that expression on her face—the one that said, *Don't mess with me.* 'Watch me.'

There was a shuffle behind the door then a creak and the door swung open. 'Hello, ladies, come on in.'

Cassidy blinked. The smell of cats hit her in the face like a steamroller.

She allowed the stampede behind her to thunder inside then took a deep breath of clean outside air, before pulling the door closed behind her. A mangy-looking cat wound its way around her legs. 'Shoo!' she hissed.

'Come on, Cassidy!'

She plastered a smile on her face and joined her colleagues in smelly-cat-woman's front room. The peeling noise beneath the soles of her feet told her that the carpet was sticky. She dreaded to think what with.

Her three friends were crowded onto the brown sofa. Another cat was crawling across the back of the sofa behind their heads. Cassidy's eyes started to stream and she resisted the temptation to start rubbing them.

Once she started, she couldn't stop. Cat allergies did that to you.

'So who wants to go first?'

Cassidy glanced at her watch. How had she got roped into this?

'You go first, Cass,' said Lucy, who turned to smelly-cat woman. 'You'll have to do a good job, Belinda. Our Cassidy's a non-believer.'

The small, rotund woman eyed Cassidy up and down. Her brow was as wrinkled as her clothes. 'This way, dear,' she muttered, wandering down the hallway to another room.

Cassidy swallowed nervously. Maybe it would be easier to get this over and done with. Then at least she could wait outside in the car for the others.

The room was full of clutter. And cats.

As Belinda settled herself at one side of the table and shuffled some cards, Cassidy eyed the squashed easy chair on the other side. A huge marmalade cat was sitting in pride of place, blinking at her, daring her to move him.

Her gorgeous turquoise-blue velvet pea coat would attract cat hairs like teenage girls to a Bieber concert. She should just kiss it goodbye now.

'Move, Lightning!' Belinda kicked the chair and the cat gave her a hard stare before stretching on his legs and jumping from the seat, settling at her feet.

Cassidy couldn't hide the smile from her face. It had to be the most inappropriately named cat—ever.

Belinda fixed her eyes on her. How could such a soft, round woman have such a steely glare? Her eyes weren't even blinking. She was staring so hard Cass thought she would bore a hole through her skull.

She looked around her. Books everywhere. Piles of

magazines. Shelves and shelves of ornaments, all looking as though they could do with a good dust. Another
allergy to set off. One, two, no, three…no, there was
another one hiding in the corner. Four cats in the room.
All looking at her as if she shouldn't be there. Maybe
they knew something that she didn't.

'So, what do we do?' she asked quickly.

Belinda's face had appeared kindly, homely when
she'd answered the door. But in here, when it was just
the two of them, she looked like a cold and shrewd
businesswoman. Cassidy wondered if she could read
the thoughts currently in her head. That would account
for the light-sabre stare.

Belinda shuffled the cards again. 'We can do whatever you prefer.' She spread the cards face down on
the table. 'I can read your cards.' She reached over and
grabbed hold of Cassidy's hand. 'I can read your palm.
Or…' she glanced around the room '…I can channel
some spirits and see what they've got to say.'

The thought sent a chill down Cassidy's spine. She
wasn't sure she believed any of this. But she certainly
didn't want to take the risk of channelling any unwanted
spirits.

The TV special she'd watched the other day had
claimed that all of this was based on reading people.
Seeing the tiny, almost imperceptible reactions they had
to certain words, certain gestures. Cassidy had come
here tonight determined not to move a muscle, not even
to blink. But her cat allergy seemed to have got the better of her, and her eyes were a red, blinking, streaming
mess. So much for not moving.

She didn't like the look of the cards either. Knowing
her luck, she'd turn over the death card—or the equiva-
lent of the Joker.

'Let's just do the palm, please.' It seemed the simplest option. How much could anyone get from some lines on a palm?

Belinda leaned across the table, taking Cassidy's slim hand and wrist and encapsulating them in her pudgy fingers. There was something quite soothing about it. She wasn't examining Cassidy's palm—just holding her hand. Stroking her fingers across the back of her hand for a few silent minutes, then turning her hand over and touching the inside of her palm.

A large smile grew across her face.

The suspense was killing her. Cassidy didn't like long silences. 'What is it?'

Belinda released her hand. 'You're quite the little misery guts, aren't you?'

'What?' Cassidy was stunned. The last she'd heard, these people were only supposed to tell you good things. And certainly not assassinate your character.

Belinda nodded. 'On the surface you're quite the joker with your friends at work. On the other hand, you always see the glass half-empty. Very self-deprecating. All signs of insecurity.' She took a deep breath. 'But very particular at work. Your attention to detail makes you hard to work with. Some of your colleagues just don't know how to take you. And as for men…'

'What?' Right now, men were the last thing on her mind. And the word 'insecurity' had hit a nerve she didn't want to acknowledge. It was bad enough having parents who jet-setted around the world, without having a fiancé who'd upped and left. The last thing she wanted was some random stranger pointing it out to her.

'You're a clever girl, but sometimes you can't see what's right at the end of your nose.' She shook her head. 'You've got some very fixed ideas, and you're not very good at the art of compromise. Just as well Christmas is coming up.'

Cassidy was mad now. 'What's that got to do with anything? Christmas is still three months away.'

Belinda folded her arms across her chest, a smug expression on her face. 'You're going to be a Christmas bride.'

'What?'

The woman had clearly lost her cat-brained mind.

'How on earth can I be a Christmas bride? It's October tomorrow, and I don't have a boyfriend. And there's nobody I'm even remotely interested in.'

Belinda tapped the side of her nose, giving her shoulders an annoying little shrug. 'I only see the future. I don't tell you how you're going to get there.' She leaned over and touched the inside of Cassidy's palm. 'I can see you as a Christmas bride, along with a very handsome groom—not from around these parts either. Lucky you.'

Cassidy shook her head firmly. It had taken her months to get over her broken engagement to her Spanish fiancé—and it had not been an experience she wanted to repeat. 'You're absolutely wrong. There's no way I'm going to be a Christmas bride. And particularly not with a groom from elsewhere. I've had it with foreign men. The next man I hook up with will be a true fellow Scot, through and through.'

Belinda gave her *the look*. The look that said, *You've no idea what you're talking about.*

'That's us, then.'

Cassidy was aghast. Twenty quid for that? 'That's it?'

Belinda nodded and waved her hand. 'Send the next one in.'

Cassidy hesitated for a second, steeling herself to argue with the woman. But then the fat orange cat brushed against her legs and leapt up onto the chair beside her, determined to shed its thousands of orange cat hairs over her velvet coat. She jumped up. At least she was over and done with. She could wait outside in the car. It was almost worth the twenty quid for that alone.

She walked along the corridor, mumbling to herself, attempting to brush a big wad of clumped cat hair from her coat.

'Are you done already? What did she tell you?'

Cassidy rolled her eyes. 'It's not even worth repeating.' She jerked her head down the corridor. 'Go on, Tamsin. Go and find out when you're getting your proposal.'

Tamsin still had that determined look on her face. She stood up and straightened her pristine black mac— no orange cat hairs for her. 'You mean *if* I'm getting my proposal.' She swept down the corridor and banged the door closed behind her.

Lucy raised her eyebrows. 'Heaven help Belinda if she doesn't tell Tam what she wants to hear.' She turned back to Cassidy. 'Come on, then, spill. What did she say?'

Cassidy blew out a long, slow breath through pursed lips. She was annoyed at being called a 'misery guts.' And she was beyond irritated at being called insecure. 'I'm apparently going to be a Christmas bride.'

'What?' Lucy's and Lynn's voices were in perfect tandem with their matching shocked expressions.

'Just as well Tamsin didn't hear that,' Lucy muttered.

'Oh, it gets worse. Apparently my groom is from foreign climes.' She rolled her eyes again. 'As if.'

But Lucy's and Lynn's expressions had changed, smiles creeping across their faces as their eyes met.

'Told you.'

'No way.'

Cassidy watched in bewilderment as they high-fived each other in the dingy sitting room.

'What's with you two? You know the whole thing's ridiculous. As if *I'm* going to date another foreign doctor.'

Lynn folded her arms across her chest. 'Stranger things have happened.' She had a weird look on her face. As if she knew something that Cassidy didn't.

Lucy adopted the same pose, shoulder to shoulder with Lynn. Almost as if they were ganging up on her.

Her gaze narrowed. 'I'm willing to place a bet that Belinda could be right.'

Cassidy couldn't believe what was happening. The crazy-cat-woman's disease was obviously contagious. A little seed planted in her brain. She could use this to her advantage. 'What's it worth?'

Lucy frowned. 'What do you mean?'

Cassidy smiled. 'I'll take that bet. But what's it worth?'

'Night shift Christmas Eve. Oh.' The words were out before Lucy had had time to think about them. She had her hand across her mouth. It was the most hated shift on the planet. Every year they had to draw straws to see who would take it.

'You're on.' Cassidy held out her hand towards Lucy, who nodded and shook it firmly. She had no chance of losing this bet. No chance at all.

CHAPTER ONE

1 October

CASSIDY pulled the navy-blue tunic over her head. These new-style NHS uniforms were supposed to be made from a revolutionary lightweight fabric, designed for comfort and ease of fit. The reality was they were freezing and not designed for Scottish winters in a draughty old hospital. She pulled a cardigan from her locker and headed for the stairs. Maybe running up three flights would take the chill out of her bones.

Two minutes later she arrived in the medical ward. She took a deep breath. There it was. The hospital smell. Some people hated it and shuddered walking through the very doors of the hospital. But Cassidy loved it—it was like a big security blanket, and she'd missed it. It was just before seven and the lights were still dimmed. Ruby, the night nurse, gave her a smile. 'Nice to see you back, Cassidy. How was the secondment?'

Cassidy nodded, wrapping her cardigan further around her torso. Her temperature was still barely above freezing. 'It was fine, but three months was long enough. The new community warfarin clinic is set up—all the teething problems ironed out. To be honest, though, I'm glad to be back. I missed this place.'

And she had. But at the time the three-month secondment had been perfect for her. It had given her the chance to sort out all the hassles with her gran, work regular hours and get her settled into the new nursing home—the second in a year. Her eyes swept over the whiteboard on the wall, displaying all the patient names, room numbers and named nurses. 'No beds?' She raised her eyebrows.

'Actually, we've got one. But A and E just phoned to say they're sending us an elderly lady with a chest infection, so I've put her name up on the board already. She should be up in the next ten minutes.'

Cassidy gave a nod as the rest of the day-shift staff appeared, gathering around the nurses' station for the handover report. She waited patiently, listening to the rundown of the thirty patients currently in her general medical ward, before assigning the patients to the nurses on duty and accepting the keys for the medicine and drugs cabinets.

She heard the ominous trundle of a trolley behind her. 'I'll admit this patient,' she told her staff. 'It'll get me back into the swing of things.'

She looked up as Bill, one of the porters, arrived, pulling the trolley with the elderly woman lying on top. A doctor was walking alongside them, carrying some notes and chatting to the elderly lady as they wheeled her into one of the side rooms. He gave her a smile— one that could have launched a thousand toothpaste campaigns. 'This is Mrs Elizabeth Kelly. She's eighty-four and has a history of chronic obstructive pulmonary disease. She's had a chest infection for the last seven days that hasn't responded to oral antibiotics. Her oxygen saturation is down at eighty-two and she's tachy-

cardic. The doctor on call wanted her admitted for IV antibiotics.'

For a moment the strong Australian accent threw her—she hadn't been expecting it. Though goodness knows why not. Her hospital in the middle of Glasgow attracted staff from all over the world. His crumpled blue scrubs and even more crumpled white coat looked as though he'd slept in them—and judging by his blond hair, sticking up in every direction but the right one, he probably had.

She didn't recognise him, which meant he must be one of the new doctors who had started while she was away on secondment. And he was too handsome by far. And that cheeky twinkle in his eye was already annoying her.

After three months away, some things appeared to have changed around the hospital. It was usually one of the A and E nurses who accompanied the patient up to the ward.

Cassidy pumped up the bed and removed the headboard, pulling the patslide from the wall and sliding the patient over into the bed. The doctor helped her put the headboard back on and adjusted the backrest, rearranging the pillows so Mrs Kelly could sit upright. Cassidy attached the monitoring equipment and changed the oxygen supply over to the wall. The doctor was still standing looking at her.

For a second she almost thought he was peering at her breasts, but as she followed his gaze downwards she realised her name and designation was stitched on the front of her new tunics.

She held out her hand towards him. 'Cassidy Rae. Sister of the medical receiving unit. Though from the way you're staring at my breasts, I take it you've gathered that.'

His warm hand caught her cold one, his eyes twinkling. 'Pleased to meet you, Dragon Lady. I hope your heart isn't as cold as your hands.'

She pulled her hand away from his. 'What did you call me?'

'Dragon Lady.' He looked unashamed by the remark. 'Your reputation precedes you. I've been looking forward to meeting you, although from what I hear it's usually you who does the name-calling.'

She folded her arms across her chest, trying to stop the edges of her mouth turning upwards. 'I've no idea what you're talking about.' She picked up the patient clothing bag and bent down, starting to unpack Mrs Kelly's belongings into the cabinet next to her bed.

'I heard you called the last lot Needy, Greedy and Seedy.'

She jumped. She could feel his warm breath on her neck. He'd bent forward and whispered in her ear.

'Who told you that?' she asked incredulously. She glanced at her watch. Ten past seven on her first morning back, and already some smart-alec doc was trying to get the better of her.

'Oh, give me a minute.' The mystery doctor ducked out of the room.

It was true. She had nicknamed the last three registrars—all for obvious reasons. One had spent every waking minute eating, the other hadn't seen a patient without someone holding his hand, and as for the last one, he'd spent his year sleazing over all the female staff. And while the nursing staff knew the nicknames she'd given them, she'd no idea who'd told one of the new docs. She'd need to investigate that later.

She stood up and adjusted Mrs Kelly's venturi mask, taking a note of her thin frame and pale, papery skin. Another frail, elderly patient, just like her gran. She altered the alarms on the monitor—at their present setting they would sound every few minutes. With a history of COPD, Mrs Kelly had lower than normal oxygen levels.

'How are you feeling?' She picked up the tympanic thermometer and placed it in Mrs Kelly's ear, pressing the button to read her temperature then recording her observations in the chart. Mrs Kelly shook her pale head.

She sat down at the side of the bed. 'I need to take some details from you, Mrs Kelly. But how about I get you something to eat and drink first? I imagine you were stuck down in A and E for hours. Would you like some tea? Some toast?'

'Your wish is my command.' The steaming cup of tea and plate of buttered toast thudded down on the bedside table. 'See, Mrs Kelly? I make good on my promises.' He shook his head at Cassidy. 'There was *nothing* to eat down in A and E and I promised I'd get her some tea once we got up here.'

'Thank you, son,' Mrs Kelly said, shifting her mask and lifting the cup to her lips, 'My throat is so dry.'

He nodded slowly. Oxygen therapy frequently made patients' mouths dry and it was important to keep them hydrated.

Cassidy stared at him. Things had changed. She couldn't remember the last time she'd seen a doctor make a patient a cup of tea. It was almost unheard of.

She smiled at him. 'Makes me almost wish we could keep you,' she said quietly. 'You've obviously been well trained.'

His blue eyes glinted. 'And what makes you think you can't keep me?'

'I imagine A and E will have a whole load of patients waiting for you. Why did you come up here anyway? Was it to steal our chocolates?' She nodded towards the nursing station. The medical receiving unit was never short of chocolates, and it wasn't unknown for the doctors from other departments to sneak past and steal some.

He shook his head, the smile still stuck on his face. He held out his hand towards her. 'I forgot to introduce myself earlier. I'm one of yours—though I dread to think what nickname you'll give me. Brad Donovan, medical registrar.'

Cassidy felt herself jerk backwards in surprise. He looked too young to be a medical registrar. Maybe it was the scruffy hair? Or the Australian tan? Or maybe it was that earring glinting in his ear, along with the super-white teeth? He didn't look like any registrar she'd ever met before.

Something twisted inside her gut. No, that wasn't quite true. Bobby. For a tiny second he reminded her of Bobby. But Bobby's hair had been dark, not blond, and he'd worn it in a similar scruffy style and had the same glistening white teeth. She pushed all thoughts away. She hadn't thought about him in months. Where had that come from?

She focused her mind. This was a work colleague—albeit a cheeky one. She shook his hand firmly. 'Well, Dr Donovan, if you're one of mine then maybe I should tell you the rules in my ward.'

His eyebrows rose, an amused expression on his face. 'You really are the Dragon Lady, aren't you?'

She ignored him. 'When you finally manage to put

some clothes on, no silly ties. In fact, no ties at all and no long sleeves. They're an infection-control hazard.' She ran her eyes up and down his crumpled scrubs, 'Though from the look of you, that doesn't seem to be a problem. Always use the gel outside the patients' rooms before you touch them. And pay attention to what my nurses tell you—they spend most of their day with the patients and will generally know the patients ten times better than you will.'

His blue eyes fixed on hers. Quite unnerving for this time in the morning. His gaze was straight and didn't falter. The guy was completely unfazed by her. He seemed confident, self-assured. She would have to wait and see if his clinical competence matched his demeanour.

'I have been working here for the last two months without your rulebook. I'm sure your staff will give me a good report.' She resisted the temptation to reply. Of course her staff would give him a good report. He was like a poster boy for Surfers' Central. She could put money on it that he'd spent the last two months charming her staff with his lazy accent, straight white teeth and twinkling eyes. He handed her Mrs Kelly's case notes and prescription chart.

'I've written Mrs Kelly up for some IV antibiotics, some oral steroids and some bronchodilators. She had her arterial blood gases done in A and E and I'll check them again in a few hours. I'd like her on four-hourly obs in the meantime.' He glanced at the oxygen supply, currently running at four litres. 'Make sure she stays on the twenty-eight per cent venturi mask. One of the students in A and E didn't understand the complications of COPD and put her on ten litres of straight oxygen.'

Cassidy's mouth fell open. 'Please tell me you're joking.'

He shook his head. The effects could have been devastating. 'Her intentions were good. Mrs Kelly's lips were blue from lack of oxygen when she was admitted. The student just did what seemed natural. Luckily one of the other staff spotted her mistake quickly.'

Cassidy looked over at the frail, elderly lady on the bed, her oxygen mask currently dangling around her neck as she munched the toast from the plate in front of her. The blue tinge had obviously disappeared from her lips, but even eating the toast was adding to her breathlessness. She turned back to face Brad. 'Any relatives?'

He shook his head. 'Her husband died a few years ago and her daughter emigrated to my neck of the woods ten years before that.' He pointed to a phone number in the records. 'Do you want me to phone her, or do you want to do that?'

Cassidy felt a little pang. This poor woman must be lonely. She'd lost her husband, and her daughter lived thousands of miles away. Who did she speak to every day? One of the last elderly patients admitted to her ward had disclosed that often he went for days without a single person to speak to. Loneliness could be a terrible burden.

The doctor passed in front of her vision again, trying to catch her attention, and she pushed the uncomfortable thoughts from her head. This one was definitely too good to be true. Bringing up a patient, making tea and toast, and offering to phone relatives?

Her internal radar started to ping. She turned to Mrs Kelly. 'I'll let you finish your tea and come back in a few minutes.

'What are you up to?' She headed out the door towards the nursing station.

He fell into step beside her. 'What do you mean?'

She paused in the corridor, looking him up and down. 'You're too good to be true. Which means alarm bells are ringing in my head. What's with the nice-boy act?'

She pulled up the laptop from the nurses' station and started to input some of Mrs Kelly's details.

'Who says it's an act?'

Her eyes swept down the corridor. The case-note trolley had been pulled to the end of the corridor. Two other doctors in white coats were standing, talking over some notes. She looked at her watch—not even eight o'clock. 'And who are they?'

Brad smiled. 'That's the other registrars. Luca is from Italy, and Franco is from Hungary. They must have wanted to get a head start on the ward round.' He gave her a brazen wink. 'I guess they heard the Dragon Lady was on duty today.'

She shook her head in bewilderment. 'I go on secondment for three months, come back and I've got the poster boy for Surfers' Paradise making tea and toast for patients and two other registrars in the ward before eight a.m. Am I still dreaming? Have I woken up yet?'

'Why?' As quick as a flash he'd moved around beside her. 'Am I the kind of guy you dream about?'

'Get lost, flyboy.' She pushed Mrs Kelly's case notes back into his hands. 'You've got a patient's daughter in Australia to go and phone. Make yourself useful while I go and find out what kind of support system she has at home.'

He paused for a second, his eyes narrowing. 'She's not even heated up the bed yet and you're planning on throwing her back out?'

Cassidy frowned. 'It's the basic principle of the receiving unit. Our first duty is to find out what systems are in place for our patients. Believe it or not, most of them don't like staying here. And if we plan ahead it means there's less chance of a delayed discharge. Sometimes it can take a few days to set up support systems to get someone home again.' She raised her hand to the whiteboard with patient names. 'In theory, we're planning for their discharge as soon as they enter A and E.'

The look on his face softened. 'In that case, I'll let you off.' He nodded towards his fellow doctors. 'Maybe they got the same alarm call that I did. Beware the Dragon!' He headed towards the doctors' office to make his call.

Dragon Lady was much more interesting than he'd been led to believe. He'd expected a sixty-year-old, grey-haired schoolmarm. Instead he'd got a young woman with a slim, curvy figure, chestnut curls and deep brown eyes. And she was feisty. He liked that.

Cassidy Rae could be fun. There it was, that strange, almost unfamiliar feeling. That first glimmer of interest in a woman. That tiny little thought that something could spark between them given half a chance. It had been so long since he'd felt it that he almost didn't know what to do about it.

He'd been here a few months, and while his colleagues were friendly, they weren't his 'friends'. And he didn't want to hang around with the female junior doctors currently batting their eyelids at him. Experience had taught him it was more trouble than it was worth.

Distraction. The word echoed around his head again as he leaned against the cold concrete wall.

Exactly what he needed. Something to keep his mind from other things—like another Christmas Day currently looming on the horizon with a huge black storm-cloud hovering over it. He'd even tried to juggle the schedules so he could be working on Christmas Day. But no such luck. His Italian colleague had beat him to it, and right now he couldn't bear the thought of an empty Christmas Day in strange surroundings with no real friends or family.

Another Christmas spent wondering where his little girl was, if she was enjoying her joint birthday and Christmas Day celebrations. Wondering if she even remembered he existed.

He had no idea what she'd been told about him. The fact he'd spent the last eighteen months trying to track down his daughter at great time and expense killed him—especially in the run-up to her birthday. Everyone else around him was always full of festive spirit and fun, and no matter how hard he tried not to be the local misery guts, something inside him just felt dead.

Christmas was about families and children. And the one thing he wanted to do was sit his little girl on his knee and get her the biggest birthday and Christmas present in the world. If only he knew where she was…

There was that fist again, hovering around his stomach, tightly clenched. Every time he thought of his daughter, Melody, the visions of her mother, Alison, a junior doctor he'd worked with, appeared in his head. Alison, the woman who only liked things her way or no way at all. No negotiation. No compromise.

More importantly, no communication.

The woman who'd left a bitter taste in his mouth for the last eighteen months. Blighting every other relationship he'd tried to have. The woman who'd wrangled over every custody arrangement, telling him he was impinging on her life. Then one day that had been it. Nothing. He'd gone to pick up two-year-old Melody as planned and had turned up at an empty house. No forwarding address. Nothing.

The colleagues at the hospital where Alison had worked said she'd thought about going to America—apparently she'd fallen head over heels in love with some American doctor. But no one knew where. And he'd spent the last few years getting his solicitor to chase false leads halfway around the world. It had taken over his whole world. Every second of every day had revolved around finding his daughter. Until he'd finally cracked and some good friends had sat him down firmly and spoken to him.

It had only been in the last few months, since moving to Scotland, that he'd finally started to feel like himself again. His laid-back manner had returned, and he'd finally started to relax and be comfortable in his own skin again.

While he would still do everything in his power to find his daughter, he had to realise his limitations. He had to accept the fact he hadn't done anything wrong and he still deserved to live a life.

And while the gaggle of nurses and female junior doctors didn't appeal to him, Cassidy Rae did. She was a different kettle of fish altogether. A fierce, sassy woman who could help him make some sparks fly. A smile crept over his face. Now there was just the small matter of the duty room to break to her. How would she react to that?

Cassidy went back to Mrs Kelly and finished her admission paperwork, rechecked her obs and helped her wash and change into a clean nightdress. By the time she'd finished, Mrs Kelly was clearly out of breath again. Even the slightest exertion seemed to fatigue her.

Cassidy hung the IV antibiotics from the drip stand and connected up the IV. 'These will take half an hour to go through. The doctor has changed the type of antibiotic that you're on so hopefully they'll be more effective than the ones you were taking at home.'

Mrs Kelly nodded. 'Thanks, love. He's a nice one, isn't he?' There was a little pause. 'And he's single. Told me so himself.'

'Who?' Cassidy had started to tidy up around about her, putting away the toilet bag and basin.

'That handsome young doctor. Reminds of that guy on TV. You know, the one from the soap opera.'

Cassidy shook her head. 'I don't watch soap operas. And anyway...' she bundled up the used towels and sheets to put in the laundry trolley '...I'm looking for a handsome Scotsman. Not someone from the other side of the world.'

She walked over to the window. The old hospital building was several storeys high, on the edge of the city. The grey clouds were hanging low this morning and some drizzly rain was falling outside, but she could still see some greenery in the distance.

'Why on earth would anyone want to leave all this behind?' she joked.

Mrs Kelly raised her eyebrows. 'Why indeed?'

Cassidy spent the rest of the morning finding her feet again in the ward. The hospital computer system had been updated, causing her to lose half her patients at the touch of a button. And the automated pharmacy delivery seemed to be on the blink again. Some poor patients' medicines would be lost in a pod stuck in a tube somewhere.

Lucy appeared from the ward next door, clutching a cup of tea, and tapped her on the shoulder. 'How does it feel to be back?'

Cassidy gave her friend a smile. 'It's good.' She picked up the off-duty book. 'I just need to get my head around the rosters again.' Her eyes fell on the sticky notes inside the book and she rolled her eyes. 'Oh, great. Seven members of staff want the same weekend off.'

Lucy laughed. 'That's nothing. One of our girls got married last weekend and I had to rope in two staff from the next ward to cover the night shift. Got time for a tea break?'

She shook her head and pointed down the corridor. 'The consultant's just about to arrive for the ward round.'

Lucy crossed her arms across her chest as she followed Cassidy's gaze to the three registrars at the bottom of the corridor. 'So what do you make of our new docs?'

Cassidy never even lifted her head. 'Funky, Chunky and Hunky?'

Lucy spluttered tea all down the front of her uniform. She looked at her watch. 'Less than two hours and you've got nicknames for them already?'

Cassidy lifted her eyebrows. 'It wasn't hard. Although Luca is drop-dead gorgeous, he's more interested in his own reflection than any of the patients. And Franco has finished off two rolls with sausages and half a box of chocolates in the last half hour.'

'So none of them have caught your eye, then?'

Cassidy turned her head at the tone in her friend's

voice. She looked at her suspiciously. 'Why? What are you up to?'

Lucy's gaze was still fixed down the corridor. 'Nothing. I just wondered what you thought of them.' She started to shake her behind as she wiggled past, singing along about single ladies.

Cassidy looked back down the corridor. Her eyes were drawn in one direction. Brad's appearance hadn't improved. He was still wearing his crumpled scrubs and coat. His hair was still untamed and she could see a shadow around his jaw.

But he had spent nearly half an hour talking to Mrs Kelly's daughter and then another half hour talking Mrs Kelly through her treatment for the next few days. Then trying to persuade her that once she was fit and well, she might want to take up her daughter's offer of a visit to Australia.

Most doctors she worked with weren't that interested in their patients' holistic care. Their radar seemed to switch off as soon as they'd made a clinical diagnosis.

There was the sound of raucous laughter at the end of the corridor, and Cassidy looked up to see Brad almost bent double, talking to one of the male physios.

She shook her head and scoured the ward, looking for one of the student nurses. 'Karen?'

The student scuttled over. 'Yes, Sister?'

'Do you know how to assess a patient for the risk of pressure ulcers?'

The student nodded quickly as Cassidy handed her a plastic card with the Waterlow scale on it. 'I want you to do Mrs Kelly's assessment then come back and we'll go over it together.'

Karen nodded and hurried off down the corridor. Cassidy watched for a second. With her paper-thin skin, poor nutrition and lack of circulating oxygen, Mrs Kelly was at real risk of developing pressure sores on her body. For Cassidy, the teaching element was one of the reasons she did this job. She wanted all the students who came through her ward to understand the importance of considering all aspects of their patients' care.

There was a thud beside her. Brad was in the chair next to her, his head leaning on one hand, staring at her again with those blue eyes. He couldn't wipe the smile from his face. 'So, which one am I?'

Cassidy blew a wayward chestnut curl out of her face. 'What are you talking about now?'

He moved closer. 'Hunky, Chunky or Funky? Which one am I?' He put his hands together and pleaded in front of her. 'Please tell me I'm Hunky.'

'How on earth did you…?' Her eyes looked down the corridor to where Pete, the physio, was in conversation with one of the other doctors. He must have overheard her. 'Oh, forget it.'

She wrinkled her nose at him, leaning forward wickedly so nobody could hear. 'No way are you Hunky. That's reserved for the Italian god named Luca.' Her eyes fell on Luca, standing talking to one of her nurses. She whispered in Brad's ear, 'Have you noticed how he keeps checking out his own reflection in those highly polished Italian shoes of his?'

Brad's shoulders started to shake.

She prodded him on the shoulder. 'No. With that excuse of a haircut and that strange earring, you're definitely Funky.' She pointed at his ear. 'What is that anyway?'

Her head came forward, her nose just a few inches off his ear as she studied the twisted bit of gold in his ear. 'Is it a squashed kangaroo? Or a surfboard?'

'Neither.' He grinned at her, turning his head so their noses nearly touched. 'Believe it or not, it used to be a boomerang. My mum bought it for me when I was a teenager and I won a competition.' He touched it with his finger. 'It's a little bent out of shape now.'

Her face was serious and he could smell her perfume—or her shampoo. She smelled of strawberries. A summer smell, even though it was the middle of winter in Glasgow. He was almost tempted to reach out and touch her chestnut curls, resting just above her collarbone. But she was staring at him with those big chocolate-brown eyes. And he didn't want to move.

If this was the Dragon Lady of the medical receiving unit, he wondered if he could be her St George and try to tame her. No. That was the English patron saint and he was in Scotland. He'd learned quickly not to muddle things up around here. The Scots he'd met were wildly patriotic.

Her face broke into a smile again. Interesting. She hadn't pulled back, even though they were just inches from each other. She didn't seem intimidated by his closeness. In any other circumstances he could have leaned forward and given her a kiss. A perfect example of the sort of distraction he needed.

'Come to think of it, though…' She glanced up and down his crumpled clothes. How could she ever have thought he reminded her of Bobby? Bobby wouldn't have been seen dead in crumpled clothes. He'd always been immaculate—Brad was an entirely different kettle of fish. 'If you keep coming into my ward dressed like that, I'll have to change your name from Funky to Skunky.'

Brad automatically sat backwards in his chair, lowering his chin and sniffing. 'Why, do I smell? I was on call last night and I haven't been in the shower yet.' He started to pull at his scrub top.

She loved it. The expression of worry on his face. The way she could so easily wind him up. And the fact he had a good demeanour with the patients and staff. This guy might even be a little fun to have around. Even if he was from the other side of the world.

She shook her head. 'Stop panicking, Brad. You don't smell.' She rested her head on her hands for a second, fixing him with her eyes. Mornings on the medical receiving unit were always chaotic. Patients to be moved to other wards, new admissions and usually a huge battery of tests to be arranged. Sometimes it was nice just to take a few seconds of calm, before chaos erupted all around you.

He reached over and touched her hand, resting on top of the off-duty book. The invisible electric jolt that shot up her arm was instantaneous.

'I could help you with those. The last place I worked in Australia had a computer system for duty rosters. You just put in the names, your shift patterns and the requests. It worked like a charm.'

Her eyes hadn't left where his hand was still touching hers. It was definitely lingering there. She'd just met this guy.

'You're going to be a pest, aren't you?' Her voice was low. For some reason she couldn't stop staring at him. It didn't help that he was easy on the eye. And that scraggy hair was kind of growing on her.

He leaned forward again. 'Is that going to be a problem?' His eyes were saying a thousand different words from his mouth. Something was in the air between them. She could practically feel the air around

her crackle. This was ridiculous. She felt like a swoon-
ing teenager.

'My gran had a name for people like you.'

He moved even closer. 'And what was that?' He tilted
his head to one side. 'Handsome? Clever? Smart?'

She shook her head and stood up, straightening her
tunic. 'Oh, no. It was much more fitting. My gran would
have called you a "wee scunner".'

His brow wrinkled. 'What on earth does that mean?'

'Just like I told you. A nuisance. A pest. But it's a
much more accurate description.' She headed towards
the duty room, with the off-duty book in her hand. She
had to get away from him. Her brain had taken leave
of her senses. She should have taken Lucy up on that
offer of tea.

Brad caught her elbow. 'Actually, Cassidy, about your
duty room…'

He stopped as she pushed the door open and automatically stepped inside, her foot catching on something.

'Wh-h-a-a-t?'

CHAPTER TWO

CASSIDY stared up at the white ceiling of her duty room, the wind knocked clean out of her. Something was sticking into her ribcage and she squirmed, causing an array of perilously perched cardboard boxes to topple over her head. She squealed again, batting her hands in front of her face.

A strong pair of arms grabbed her wrists and yanked her upwards, standing her on the only visible bit of carpet in the room—right at the doorway.

Brad was squirming. 'Sorry about that, Cassidy. I was trying to warn you but…'

He stopped in mid-sentence. She looked mad. She looked *really* mad. Her chestnut curls were in complete disarray, falling over her face and hiding her angry eyes. 'What is all this rubbish?' she snapped.

Brad cleared his throat. 'Well, actually, it's not "rubbish", as you put it. It's mine.' He bent over and started pushing some files back into an overturned box. They were the last thing he wanted anyone to see.

Her face was growing redder by the second. She looked down at her empty hand—obviously wondering where the off-duty book she'd been holding had got to. She bent forward to look among the upturned boxes then straightened up, shaking her head in disgust.

She planted her hands on her hips. 'You'd better have a good explanation for this. No wonder you were giving me the treatment.'

'What treatment?'

She waved her hand in dismissal. 'You know. The smiles. The whispers. The big blue eyes.' She looked at him mockingly. 'You must take me for a right sap.'

All of a sudden Brad understood the Dragon Lady label. When she was mad, she was *mad*. Heaven help the doctor who messed up on her watch.

He leaned against the doorjamb. 'I wasn't giving you the *treatment*, as you put it, Cassidy. I was trying to connect with the sister of the ward I work in. We're going to have to work closely together, and I'd like it if we were friends.'

Her face softened ever so slightly. She looked at the towering piles of boxes obliterating her duty room. 'And all this?'

He shot her a smile. 'Yes, well, there's a story about all that.'

She ran her fingers through her hair, obviously attempting to re-tame it. He almost wished he could do it for her. 'Please don't tell me you've moved in.'

He laughed. 'No. It's not that desperate. I got caught short last night and was flung out of my flat, so I had to bring all my stuff here rather than leave it all sitting in the street.'

She narrowed her eyes. 'What do you mean, you got caught short? That sounds suspiciously like you were having a party at five in the morning and the landlord threw you out.'

Brad nodded slowly. 'Let's just say I broke one of the rules of my tenancy.'

'Which one?'

'Now, that would be telling.' He pulled a set of keys from his pocket with a brown tag attached. 'But help is at hand. I've got a new flat I can move into tonight—if I can find it.'

'What do you mean—if you can find it?' Cassidy bent over and read the squiggly writing on the tag.

Brad shrugged his shoulders. 'Dowangate Lane. I'm not entirely sure where it is. One of the porters put me onto it at short notice. I needed somewhere that was furnished and was available at short notice. He says its only five minutes away from here, but I don't recognise the street name.'

Cassidy gave him a suspicious look. 'I don't suppose anyone told you that I live near there.'

'Really? No, I'd no idea. Can you give me some directions?'

Cassidy sighed. 'Sure. Go out the front of the hospital, take a left, walk a few hundred yards down the road, take a right, go halfway down the street and go down the nearby close. Dowangate Lane runs diagonally off it. But the street name fell off years ago.'

Cassidy had a far-away look in her eyes and was gesturing with her arms. Her voice got quicker and quicker as she spoke, her Scottish accent getting thicker by the second.

'I have no idea what you just said.'

Cassidy stared at him—hard. 'It would probably be easier if I just showed you.'

'Really? Would you?'

'If it means you'll get all this rubbish out of my duty room, it will be worth it.'

'Gee, thanks.'

'Do you want my help or not?'

He bent forward and caught her gesturing arms.

'I would love your help, Cassidy Rae. How does six o'clock sound?' There it was again—that strawberry scent from her hair. That could become addictive.

She stopped talking. He could feel the little goose-bumps on her bare arms. Was she cold? Or was it something else?

Whatever it was, he was feeling it, too. Not some wild, throw-her-against-the-wall attraction, although he wouldn't mind doing that. It was weird. Some kind of connection.

Maybe he wasn't the only person looking for a Christmastime distraction.

She was staring at him with those big brown eyes again. Only a few seconds must have passed but it felt like minutes.

He could almost hear her thought processes. As if she was wondering what was happening between them, too.

'Six o'clock will be fine,' she said finally, as she lowered her eyes and brushed past him.

Brad hung his white coat up behind the door and pulled his shirt over his head. He paused midway. What was he going to do with it?

Cass stuck her head around the door. 'Are you ready yet?' Her eyes caught the tanned, taut abdomen and the words stuck in her throat. She felt the colour rush into her cheeks. 'Oops, sorry.' She pulled back from the door.

All of a sudden she felt like a teenager again. And trust him to have a set of to-die-for abs. Typical. There was no way she was ever taking her clothes off in front of Mr Ripped Body.

Where had that come from? Why on earth would

she ever take her clothes off in front of him? That was it. She was clearly losing her marbles.

Almost automatically, she sucked in her stomach and looked downwards. Her pink jumper hid a multitude of sins, so why on earth was she bothering?

Brad's hand rested on the edge of the door as he stuck his head back round. 'Don't be so silly, Cassidy. You're a nurse. It's not like you haven't seen it all before. Come back in. I'll be ready in a second.'

She swallowed the huge lump at the back of her throat. His shoulder was still bare. He was obviously used to stripping off in front of women and was completely uninhibited.

So why did that thought rankle her?

She took a deep breath and stepped back into the room, trying to avert her eyes without being obvious. The last thing she wanted was for him to think she was embarrassed. With an attitude like his, she'd never live it down.

He was rummaging in a black holdall. Now she could see the muscles across his back. No love handles for him. He yanked a pale blue T-shirt from the bag and pulled it over his head, turning round and tugging it down over his washboard stomach.

'Ready. Can we go?'

Cassidy had a strange expression on her face. Brad automatically looked down. Did he have a huge ketchup stain on his T-shirt? Not that he could see. Her cheeks were slightly flushed, matching the soft pink jumper she was wearing. A jumper that hugged the shape of her breasts very nicely. Pink was a good colour on her. It brought out the warm tones in her face and hair that had sometimes been lost in the navy-blue tunic she'd been wearing earlier. Her hair was pulled back from her face in a short ponytail, with a few wayward curls escaping. She was obviously serious about helping him move. No fancy coats and stiletto heels for her. Which was just as well as there were around fifty boxes to lug over to his new flat.

'Will you manage to carry some of these boxes down to my car?'

'I'll do better than that.' She opened the door to reveal one of the porters' trolleys for transporting boxes of equipment around the hospital. The huge metal cage could probably take half of his boxes in one run.

'Genius. You might be even more useful than I thought.'

'See, I'm not just a pretty face,' she shot back, to his cheeky remark. 'You do realise this is going to cost you, don't you?' She pulled the cage towards the duty room, letting him stand in the doorway and toss out boxes that she piled up methodically.

'How much?' As he tossed one of the boxes, the cardboard flaps sprang open, spilling his boxers and socks all over the floor.

Cassidy couldn't resist. The colours of every imagination caught her eyes and she lifted up a pair with Elmo from *Sesame Street* emblazoned on the front. 'Yours?' she asked, allowing them to dangle from one finger.

He grabbed them. 'Stop it.' He started ramming them back into the box, before raising his eyebrows at her. 'I'll decide when you get to see my underwear.'

When. Not if. The thought catapulted through her brain as she tried to keep her mind on the job at hand. The boxes weren't neatly packed or taped shut. And the way he kept throwing them at her was ruining her precision stacking in the metal cage.

'Slow down,' she muttered. 'The more you irritate me, the more my price goes up. You're currently hovering around a large pizza or a sweet-and-sour chicken. Keep going like this and you'll owe me a beer as well.'

The cheeky grin appeared at her shoulder in an instant. 'You think I won't buy you a beer?' He stared at the neatly stacked boxes. 'Uh-oh. I sense a little obsessive behaviour. One of your staff warned me about wrecking the neatly packed boxes of gloves in the treatment room. I can see why.'

'Nothing wrong with being neat and tidy.' Cassidy straightened the last box. 'Okay, I think that's enough for now. We can take the rest downstairs on the second trip.'

Something flashed in front of his eyes. Something wicked. 'You think so?'

He waited while she nodded, then as quick as a flash he shoved her in the cage, clicking the door behind her and pushing the cage down the corridor.

Cassidy let out a squeal. For the second time today she was surrounded by piles of toppling boxes. 'Let me out!' She got to her knees in the cage as he stopped in front of the lifts and pushed the 'down' button.

His shoulders were shaking with laughter as he pulled a key from his pocket for the 'Supplies Only' lift and opened the door. 'What can I say? You bring out the wicked side in me. I couldn't resist wrecking your neat display.'

He pulled the cage into the lift and sprang the lock free, holding out his hands to steady her step. The lift started with a judder, and as she was in midstep—it sent her straight into his arms. 'Ow-w!'

The lift was small. Even smaller with the large storage cage and two people crammed inside. And as Brad had pressed the ground-floor button as he'd pulled the cage inside, they were now trapped at the back of the lift together.

She was pressed against him. He could feel the ample swell of her breasts against his chest, her soft pink jumper tickling his skin. His hands had fallen naturally to her waist, one finger touching a little bit of soft flesh. Had she noticed?

Her curls were under his nose, but there was no way he was moving his hands to scratch the itch. She lifted her head, capturing him with her big brown eyes again.

This was crazy. This was madness.

This was someone he'd just met today. It didn't matter that he felt a pull towards her. It didn't matter that she'd offered to help him. It didn't matter that for some strange reason he liked to be close to her. It didn't matter that his eyes were currently fixed on her plump lips. He knew nothing about her.

Her reputation had preceded her. According to her colleagues she was a great nurse and a huge advocate for her patients, but her attention to detail and rulebook for the ward had become notorious.

More importantly, she knew nothing about him. She had no idea about his history, his family, his little girl out there in the world somewhere. She had no idea how the whole thing had come close to breaking him. And for some reason he didn't want to tell her.

He wanted this to be separate. A flirtation. A distraction. Something playful. With no consequences. Even if it only lasted a few weeks.

At least that would get him past Christmas.

'You can let me go now.' Her voice was quiet, her hands resting on his upper arms sending warm waves through his bare skin.

But for a second they just stood there. Unmoving.

The door pinged open and they turned their heads. His hands fell from her waist. She turned and automatically pushed the cage through the lift doors, and he fell into step next to her.

The tone and mood were broken.

'Are you sure you don't mind helping me with this? You could always just draw me a map.'

She stuck her elbow in his ribs. 'Stop trying to get out of buying me dinner. What number did you say the flat was? If I find out I've got to carry all these boxes up four flights of stairs I *won't* be happy.'

They crossed the car park and reached his car. She blinked. A Mini. For a guy that was over six feet tall.

'This is your car?'

'Do you like it?' He opened the front passenger door, moved the seat forward and started throwing boxes in the back. 'It's bigger than you think.'

'Why on earth didn't you just leave some stuff in the car?'

Brad shrugged. 'Luca borrowed my car last night after he helped me move my stuff. I think he had a date.' And some of his boxes were far too personal to be left unguarded in a car.

Cassidy shook her head and opened the boot, trying to cram as many of the boxes in there as possible. She was left with two of the larger ones still sitting on the ground.

She watched as he put the passenger seat back into place and shrugged her shoulders. 'I can just put these two on my lap. It's only a five-minute drive. It'll be fine.'

Brad pulled a face. 'You might need to put something else on your lap instead.'

She felt her stomach turn over. What now?

'Why do I get the distinct impression that nothing is straightforward with you?'

He grabbed her hand and pulled her towards the porter's lodge at the hospital gate, leaving the two boxes next to his unlocked car. 'Come on.'

'Where on earth are we going?'

'I've got something else to pick up.'

He pushed open the door to the lodge. Usually used for deliveries and collections, occasionally used by the porters who were trying to duck out of sight for five minutes, it was an old-fashioned solid stone building. The front door squeaked loudly. 'Frank? Are you there?'

Frank Wallace appeared. All twenty-five stone of him, carrying a pile of white-and-black fur in his hands. 'There you are, Dr Donovan. He's been as good as gold. Not a bit of bother. Bring him back any time.'

Frank handed over the bundle of black and white, and it took a few seconds for Cassidy to realise the shaggy bundle was a dog with a bright red collar and lead.

Brad bent down and placed the dog on the floor at their feet. It seemed to spring to life, the head coming up sharply and a little tail wagging furiously. Bright black eyes and a pink panting tongue.

'Cassidy, meet Bert. *This* is the reason I lost my tenancy.'

Cassidy watched in amazement. Bert seemed delighted to see him, jumping his paws up onto Brad's shoulders and licking at his hands furiously. His gruff little barks reverberated around the stone cottage.

He was a scruffy little mutt—with no obvious lineage or pedigree. A mongrel, by the look of him.

'Why on earth would you have a dog?' she asked incredulously. 'You live in Australia. You can't possibly have brought him with you.' Dogs she could deal with. It was cats that caused her allergies. She'd often thought about getting a pet for company—a friendly face to come home to. But long shifts weren't conducive to having a pet. She knelt on the floor next to Brad, holding her hand out cautiously while Bert took a few seconds to sniff her, before licking her with the same enthusiasm he'd shown Brad.

'I found him. A few weeks ago, in the street outside my flat. He looked emaciated and was crouched in a doorway. There was no way I could leave him alone.' *And to be honest, I needed him as much as he needed me.* Brad let the scruffy dog lick his hands. Melody would love this little dog.

'So what did you do?'

'I took him to the emergency vet, who checked him over, gave me some instructions, then I took him home.'

'And *this* is why you got flung out your flat?' There was an instant feeling of relief. He hadn't been thrown out for non-payment of rent, wild parties or dubious women. He'd been thrown out because of a dog. She glanced at his face as he continued to talk to Bert. The mutual admiration was obvious.

The rat. He must have known that a dog would have scored him brownie points. No wonder he'd kept it quiet earlier. She would have taken him for a soft touch.

She started to laugh. 'Bert? You called your dog Bert?'

He shrugged his shoulders. 'What's wrong with Bert? It's a perfectly good name.'

'What's wrong with Rocky or Buster or Duke?'

He waved his hand at her. 'Look at him. Does he look like Rocky, Buster or Duke?'

He waited a few seconds, and Bert obligingly tipped his head to one side, as if he enjoyed the admiration.

Brad was decisive. 'No way. He's a Bert. No doubt about it.'

Cassidy couldn't stop the laugh that had built up in her chest. Bert wasn't a big dog and his white hair with black patches had definitely seen better days. But his soft eyes and panting tongue were cute. And Brad was right. He looked like a Bert—it suited him. She bent down and started rubbing his ears.

'See—you like him. Everyone should. He's a good dog. Not been a bit of bother since I found him.'

'So how come you got flung out the flat? And what about the new one? I take it they're happy for you to have a dog?'

Brad pulled a face. 'One of my neighbours reported me for having a dog. And the landlord was swift and ruthless, even though you honestly wouldn't have known he was there. And it was Frank, the porter, who put me onto the new flat. So I'm sorted. They're happy for me to have a dog.'

Cassidy held out her arms to pick up the dog. 'I take it this is what I'm supposed to have on my lap in the car?'

Brad nodded. 'Thank goodness you like dogs. This could have all turned ugly.'

She shook her head, still rubbing Bert's ears. 'I'm sure it will be fine. But let's go. It's getting late and I'm starving.'

They headed back to the car and drove down the road past Glasgow University and into the west end of Glasgow. Lots of the younger hospital staff stayed in the flats around here. It wasn't really designed for kids and families, but for younger folks it was perfect, with the shops, restaurants and nightlife right at their fingertips.

'So what do you like best about staying around here?'

Cassidy glanced around about her as they drove along Byres Road. She pointed to the top of the road. 'If you go up there onto Western Road and cross the road, you get to Glasgow's Botanic Gardens. Peace, perfect peace.'

Brad looked at her in surprise. 'Really? That's a bit unusual for someone your age.'

'Why would you think that? Is it only pensioners and kids that can visit?' She gestured her thumb over her shoulder. 'Or if you go back that way, my other favourite is the Kelvingrove Art Gallery and Museum— as long as the school trips aren't there! There's even a little secret church just around the corner with an ancient cemetery—perfect for quiet book reading in the summer. Gorgeous at Christmastime.'

Brad stared at her. 'You're a dark horse, aren't you? I never figured you for a museum type.'

She shrugged her shoulders. 'It's the peace and quiet really. The ward can be pretty hectic. Some days when I come out I'm just looking for somewhere to chill. I can be just as happy curled up with a good book or in the dark at the cinema.'

'You go to the cinema alone?'

She nodded. 'All the time. I love sci-fi. My friends all love romcoms. So I do some with my friends and some on my own.' She pointed her arm in front of them. 'Turn left here, then turn right and slow down.'

The car pulled to a halt at the side of the road next to some bollards. Cassidy looked downwards. Bert had fallen asleep in her lap. 'Looks like it's been a big day for the little guy.'

Brad jumped out of and around the car and opened the passenger door. He picked up the sleeping dog. 'Let's go up and have a look at the flat before I start to unpack the boxes.'

'You haven't seen it yet?'

He shook his head. 'How could I? I was on call last night and just had to take whatever I could get. I told you I'd no idea where this place was.'

Cassidy smiled. 'So you did. Silly me. Now, give me the key and we'll see what you've got.'

They climbed up the stairs in the old-style tenement building, onto the first floor, where number five was in front of them. Cassidy looked around. 'Well, this is better than some flats I've seen around here.' She ran her hand along the wall. 'The walls have been painted, the floors are clean, and...' she pointed to the door across the hallway '...your neighbour has some plants outside his flat. This place must be okay.'

She turned the key in the lock and pushed open the door. Silently praying that she wouldn't be hit with the smell of cats, mould or dead bodies.

Brad flicked the light switch next to the door and stepped inside. He was trying to stop his gut from twisting. Getting a flat that accepted dogs at short notice— and five minutes away from the hospital—seemed almost too good to be true. There had to be a catch somewhere.

The catch was obvious. Cassidy burst into fits of laughter.

'No way! It's like stepping back in time. Have we just transported into the 1960s?' She turned to face him. 'That happened once in an old *Star Trek* episode. I think we're just reliving it.'

Brad was frozen. The wallpaper could set off a whole

array of seizures. He couldn't even make out the individual colours, the purples and oranges all seemed to merge into one. As for the shag-pile brown carpet...

Cassidy was having the time of her life. She dashed through one of the open doors and let out a shriek. 'Avacado! It's avocado. You have an avocado bathroom! Does that colour even exist any more?' Seconds later he heard the sounds of running water before she appeared again, tears flowing down her cheeks. 'I love this place. You have to have a 1960s-style party.'

She ducked into another room then swept past him into the kitchen, while Brad tried to keep his breathing under control. Could he really live in this?

He set down the dog basket on the floor and placed the sleeping Bert inside. His quiet, peaceful dog would probably turn into a possessed, rabid monster in this place.

He sagged down onto the purple sofa that clashed hideously with the brown shag-pile carpet. No wonder this place had been available at a moment's notice.

He could hear banging and clattering from next door—Cassidy had obviously found the kitchen. He cringed. What colour was avocado anyway? He was too scared to look.

Cassidy reappeared, one of her hands dripping wet, both perched at her waist. 'Kitchen's not too bad.' She swept her eyes around the room again, the smile automatically reappearing on her face. She walked over and sat down on the sofa next to Brad, giving his knee a friendly tap. 'Well, it has to be said, this place is spotlessly clean. And the shower's working.' She lifted her nose and sniffed the air. 'And it smells as if the carpets have just been cleaned. See—it's not so bad.'

Not so bad. She had to be joking.

And she was. He could see her shoulders start to shake again. She lifted her hands to cover her face, obviously trying to block out the laughter. His stomach fell even further.

'What is it?'

He could tell she was trying not to meet his gaze. 'Go on. What else have you discovered in this psychedelic temple of doom?' He threw up his hands.

Cassidy stood up and grabbed his hand, pulling him towards her. For a second he was confused. What was she doing? Sure, this had crossed his mind, but what did she have in mind?

She pulled him towards the other room he hadn't looked at yet—the bedroom. Surely not? He felt a rush of blood to the head and rush of something else to the groin. This couldn't be happening.

She pushed open the door to the room, turning and giving him another smile. But the glint in her eyes was something else entirely. This was no moment of seduction. This was comedy, through and through.

He stepped inside the bedroom.

Pink. Everywhere and everything. Pink.

Rose-covered walls. A shiny, *satin* bedspread. Pink lampshades giving off a strange rose-coloured hue around the room. Pink carpet. Dark teak furniture and dressing table. He almost expected to see an eighty-year-old woman perched under the covers, staring at them.

Cassidy's laughter was building by the second. She couldn't contain herself. She spun round, her hands on his chest. 'Well, what do you think? How's this for a playboy palace?'

His reaction was instantaneous. He grabbed her around the waist and pulled her with him, toppling onto the bed, the satin bedspread sliding them along. He couldn't help it. It was too much for him and for the next few minutes they laughed so hard his belly was aching.

They lay there for a few seconds after the laughter finally subsided. Brad's eyes were fixed on the ceiling, staring at yet another rose-coloured light shade.

He turned his head to face Cassidy's. 'So, tell me truthfully. Do you think this flat will affect my pulling power?'

Cassidy straightened her face, the laughter still apparent in her eyes. She wondered how to answer the question. Something squeezed deep inside her. She didn't want Brad to have pulling power. She didn't want Brad to even consider pulling. What on earth was wrong with her? She'd only met this guy today. Her naughty streak came out. 'Put it this way. This is the first time I've lain on a bed with a man, panting like this, and still been fully dressed.'

His eyebrows arched and he flipped round onto his side to face her. 'Well, Sister Rae, that almost sounds like a challenge. And I like a challenge.'

Cassidy attempted to change position, the satin bedspread confounding her and causing her to slide to the floor with a heavy thud.

Brad stuck his head over the edge of the bed. 'Cass, are you okay?'

She held up her hand towards him and shook her head. 'Just feed me.'

Fifty boxes later and another trip back to the hospital, they both sagged on the sofa. Brad pulled a bunch of take-away menus from a plastic bag. 'I'd take you out for dinner but I don't think either of us could face sitting across a table right now.'

Cassidy nodded. She flicked through the menus,

picking up her favourite. 'This pizza place is just around the corner and it's great. They don't take long to deliver. Will we go for this?'

'What's your favourite?'

'Thin crust. Hawaiian.'

'Pineapple—on a pizza? Sacrilege. Woman, what's wrong with you?'

She rolled her eyes. 'Don't tell me—you're a meat-feast, thick-crust man?'

He sat back, looking surprised. 'How did you know?'

'Because you're the same as ninety per cent of the other males on the planet. Let's just order two.' She picked up the phone, giving it a second glance. 'Wow, my parents had one of these in the seventies.' She listened for a dial tone. 'Never mind, it works.' She dialled the number and placed the order.

'So, what do you think of your new home? Will you still be talking to Frank in the morning?'

Brad sighed. 'I think I should be grateful, no matter how bad the décor is. I needed a furnished flat close by—it's not like I had any furniture to bring with me—so this will be fine.' He took another look around. 'You're right—it's clean. That's the most important thing.' Then he pointed to Bert in the corner. 'And if he's happy, I'm happy.' The wicked glint appeared in his eyes again. 'I can always buy a new bedspread—one that keeps the ladies on, instead of sliding them off.'

There it was again. That little twisting feeling in her gut whenever he cracked a joke about other women. For the first time in a lifetime she was feeling cave-woman primal urges. She wanted to shout, *Don't you dare!* But that would only reveal her to be a mad, crazy person, instead of the consummate professional she wanted him to think she was.

He rummaged around in a plastic bag at his feet. 'I'm afraid I can't offer you any fancy wine to drink. I've got orange or blackcurrant cordial.' He pulled the bottles from the bag. 'And I've got glasses in one of those boxes over there.'

Cassidy reached over and opened the box, grabbing two glasses and setting them on the table. 'So what's your story? What are you doing in Scotland?' *And why hasn't some woman snapped you up already?*

'You mean, what's a nice guy like me doing in a place like this?' He gestured at the psychedelic walls.

She shrugged. 'I just wondered why you'd left Australia. Do you have family there? A girlfriend?' She couldn't help it. She really, really wanted to know. She'd wanted to ask if he had a wife or children, but that had seemed a bit too forward. He wasn't wearing a wedding ring, and he hadn't mentioned any significant other. And he'd been flirting with her. Definitely flirting with her. And for the first time in ages she felt like responding.

'I fancied a change. It seemed like a good opportunity to expand my experience. Scottish winters are notorious for medical admissions, particularly around old mining communities.' He paused for a second and then added, 'And, no, there's no wife.' He prayed she hadn't noticed the hesitation. He couldn't say the words 'no children'. He wouldn't lie about his daughter. But he just didn't want to go there right now. Not with someone he barely knew.

Cassidy nodded, sending silent prayers upwards for his last words, but fixed her expression, 'There's around two and half thousand extra deaths every winter. They can't directly link them to the cold. Only a few are from hypothermia, most are from pneumonia, heart disease or stroke. And last year was the worst. They estimated nine pensioners died every hour related to the effects of the cold. Fuel payments are through the roof right now. People just can't afford to heat their homes. Some of the cases we had last year broke my heart.'

Brad was watching her carefully. Her eyes were looking off into the distance—as if she didn't want him to notice the sheen across her eyes when she spoke. He wondered if she knew how she looked. Her soft curls shining in the dim flat light, most of them escaping from the ponytail band at the nape of her neck. It was clear this was a subject close to her heart—she knew her stuff, but as a sister on a medical receiving unit he would have expected her to.

What he hadn't expected was to see the compassion in her eyes. Her reputation was as an excellent clinician, with high standards and a strict rulebook for the staff on her ward. But this was a whole other side to her. A side he happened to like. A side he wanted to know more about.

'So, what's the story with you, then?'

She narrowed her eyes, as if startled he'd turned the question round on her. 'What do you mean?'

'What age are you, Cassidy? Twenty-seven? Twenty-eight?' He pointed to her left hand. 'Where's your other half? Here you are, on a Monday night at…' he looked at his watch '…nearly nine o'clock, helping an orphaned colleague move into his new flat. Don't you have someone to go to home to?'

Cassidy shifted uncomfortably. She didn't like being put on the spot. She didn't like the fact that in a few moments he'd stripped her bare. Nearly thirty, single and no one to go home to. Hardly an ad for Mrs Wonderful.

'I'm twenty-nine, and I was engaged a few years ago,

but we split up and I'm happy on my own.' It sounded so simple when she put it like that. Leaving out the part about her not wanting to get out of bed for a month after Bobby had left. Or drinking herself into oblivion the month after that.

His eyebrows rose, his attention obviously grabbed. 'So, who was he?'

'My fiancé? He was a Spanish registrar I worked with.'

'Did you break up with him?'

The million-dollar question. The one that made you look sad and pathetic if you said no. Had she broken up with him? Or had Bobby just told her he was returning to Spain, with no real thought to how she would feel about it? And no real distress when she'd told him she wouldn't go with him.

Looking back she wondered if he'd always known she wouldn't go. And if being with her in Scotland had just been convenient for him—a distraction even.

She took a deep breath. 'What's with the questions, nosy parker? He wanted to go home to Spain. I wanted to stay in Scotland. End of story. We broke up. He's back working in Madrid now.' She made it sound so simple. She didn't tell him how much she hated coming home to an empty house and having nobody to share her day with. She didn't say how whenever she set her single place at the table she felt a little sad. She didn't tell him how much she hated buying convenience meals for one.

'Bet he's sorry he didn't stay.'

Cassidy's face broke into a rueful smile and she shook her head. 'Oh, I don't think so. He went home, had a whirlwind romance and a few months later married that year's Miss Spain. They've got a little son now.'

She didn't want to reveal how hurt she'd been by her rapid replacement.

He moved a little closer to her. 'Didn't that make you mad? He left and played happy families with someone else?'

Cassidy shook her head determinedly. She'd had a long time to think about all this. 'No. Not really. I could have been but we obviously weren't right for each other. When we got engaged he said he would stay in Scotland, but over time he changed his mind. His heart was in Spain.'

Her eyes fell downwards for a few seconds as she drew in a sharp breath, 'And I'd made it clear I didn't want to move away. I'm a Scottish girl through and through. I don't want to move.'

Brad placed his hand on her shoulder. 'But that seems a bit off. Spain's only a few hours away on a plane. What's the big deal?'

Cassidy looked cross. He made it all sound so simple. 'I like it here. I like it where I live. I don't want to move to…' she lifted her fingers in the air '…*sunnier climes. I want to stay here…*' she pointed her finger to the floor '…in Scotland, the country that I love. And I have priorities here—responsibilities—that I couldn't take care of in another country.' She folded her arms across her chest.

'So I made myself a rule. My next other half will be a big, handsome fellow Scot. Someone who wants to stay where I do. Not someone from the other side of the planet.'

The words hung between them. Almost as if she was drawing a line in the sand. Brad paused for a second, trying to stop himself from saying what he really thought. Should he say straight away that he would never stay in Scotland either? That he wanted his life to be wherever his daughter was—and he was prepared to up sticks and go at a moment's notice?

No. He couldn't. That would instantly kill this flirtation stone dead. And that's all this would ever be—a mild flirtation. Why on earth would what she'd just said bother him? He was merely looking for a distraction—nothing more. Something to take his mind off another Christmas without his daughter.

'Just because someone is from Scotland it doesn't mean they'll want to stay here. There have been lots of famous Scots explorers—David Livingstone, for example.' He moved forward, leaning in next to her. 'Anyway, that's a pretty big statement, Cassidy. You're ruling out ninety-nine per cent of the population of the world in your search for Mr Right. Hardly seems fair to the rest of us.' He shot her a cheeky grin. 'Some people might even call that a bit of prejudice.'

'Yeah, well, at least if I think about it this way, it saves any problems later on. I don't want to meet someone, hook up with them and fall in love, only to have my heart broken when they tell me their life's on the other side of the planet from me.' *Been there. Done that.* 'Why set myself up for a fall like that?'

'Why indeed?' He'd moved right next to her, his blue eyes fixed on hers. She was right. Cassidy wanted to stay in Scotland. Brad wanted to go wherever in the world his little girl was. A little girl he hadn't even told her about. Anything between them would be an absolute disaster. But somehow he couldn't stop the words forming on his lips.

'But what happens if your heart rules your head?' Because try as he may to think of her as a distraction, the attraction between them was real. And it had been a long time since he'd felt like this.

She could see every tiny line on his face from hours in the Australian sun, every laughter line around the corners of his eyes. His hand was still resting on her arm, and it was making her tingle. Everything about this was wrong.

She'd just spelled out all the reasons why this was so wrong. He was from Australia. The other side of the planet. He was the worst possible option for her. So why, in the space of a day, was he already getting under her skin? Why did she want to lean forward towards his lips? Why did she want to feel the muscles of his chest under the palms of her hands? He was so close right now she could feel his warm breath on her neck. It was sending shivers down her spine.

She didn't want this to be happening. She didn't want to be attracted to a man there was no future with. So why couldn't she stop this? Why couldn't she just pull away?

Ding-dong.

Both jumped backwards, startled by the noise of the bell ringing loudly. Even Bert awoke from his slumber and started barking.

Cassidy was still fixed by his eyes, the shiver continuing down her spine. A feeling of awakening. 'Pizza,' she whispered. 'It must be the pizza.'

'Saved by the bell,' murmured Brad as he stood up to answer the door. At the last second he turned back to her. A tiny little part of him was feeling guilty—guilty about the attraction between them, guilty about not mentioning his daughter, and completely irritated by her disregard for most of the men in the world.

Her mobile sounded, and Cassidy fumbled in her

bag. 'Excuse me,' she murmured, glancing at the number on the screen.

She stepped outside as he was paying for the pizzas and pressed the phone to her ear. 'Hi, it's Cassidy Rae. Is something wrong with my grandmother?'

'Hi, Cassidy. It's Staff Nurse Hughes here. Sorry to call, but your gran's really agitated tonight.'

Cassidy sighed. 'What do you need me to do?' This was happening more and more. Her good-natured, placid gran was being taken over by Alzheimer's disease, at times becoming confused and agitated, leading to outbursts of aggression that were totally at odds with her normal nature. The one thing that seemed to calm her down was hearing Cassidy's voice—whether over the phone or in person.

'Can you talk to her for a few minutes? I'll hold the phone next to her.

'Of course I will.' She took a deep breath. 'Hi, Gran, it's Cassidy. How are you feeling?' Her words didn't matter. It was the sound and tone of her voice that was important. So she kept talking, telling her gran about her day and her plans for the week.

And leaving out the thoughts about the new doctor that were currently dancing around in her brain.

Brad sat waiting patiently. What was she doing? Who was she talking to outside in that low, calm voice? And why couldn't she have taken the call in here?

More importantly, what was *he* doing?

Getting involved with someone he worked with hadn't worked out too great for him the last time. He'd had a few casual dates in the last year with work colleagues, but nothing serious. He really didn't want to go down that road again.

So what on earth was wrong with him? His attraction to this woman had totally knocked him sideways. Alison had been nothing like this. A few weeks together had proved they weren't compatible. And the pregnancy had taken them both by surprise. And although his thoughts had constantly been with his daughter, this was the first time that a woman had started to invade his mind.

His brain wasn't working properly, but his libido was firing on multiple cylinders. Which one would win the battle?

CHAPTER THREE

11 October

CASSIDY's fingers hammered on the keyboard, responding to yet another bureaucratic email.

'What's up, girl?' As if by magic, Brad was leaning across the desk towards her. 'You've got that ugly frown on your face again. That usually spells trouble for the rest of us.'

Cassidy smiled. For the last ten days, every time she'd turned around he'd been at her elbow. His mood was generally laid-back and carefree, though a couple of times she'd thought he was going to steer a conversation toward something more serious. She turned the computer monitor towards him. 'Look at this. According to "customer care" principles, we've got to answer the ward phone on the third ring.'

'Since when did our patients become "customers"?'

'Oh, don't get me started. I just replied, pointing out that patients are our first priority on the medical unit and I won't be leaving a patient's bedside to answer the phone in three rings.'

'Are you still short-staffed?' Brad looked around the ward, noting the figures on the ward and trying to work out if everyone was there.

Cassidy pointed to the board. 'There were seven staff sick last week, but they should all be back on duty either today or tomorrow.' Her frown reappeared. 'Why, what are you about to tell me?'

Brad walked around to her side of the desk and wheeled her chair towards him. 'I was going to invite you to breakfast. It's Saturday morning, the ward's pretty quiet, so it seemed like a good time.' He pulled a face. 'Plus, those five empty beds you've got are about to be filled. I've got five patients coming into A and E via the GP on-call service who will all need to be admitted.'

Cassidy stood up. 'So what's this, the calm before the storm?'

'Something like that. Come on.' He stuck his elbow out towards her. 'You'll probably not get time for lunch later.'

Cassidy handed over the keys to one of her staff nurses and headed down to the canteen with Brad.

There was something nice about this. The easy way they'd fallen into a friendship. She'd mentioned her front door was jamming and he'd appeared around at her flat to fix it. Then they'd walked to the Botanic Gardens a few times on days off and taken Bert out in the evenings. Even though they were tiptoeing around the edges of friendship, there was still that simmering 'something' underneath.

'I see you actually managed to put some clothes on today.' She ran her eyes up and down his lean frame, taking in his trousers and casual polo shirt. 'I was beginning to wonder if you actually owned any clothes.'

They'd reached the canteen and Brad picked up a tray. 'It's a deliberate ploy. If I live my life in scrubs then the hospital does my laundry for me. And I haven't got my washing machine yet.'

Cassidy nodded. 'Ah…the truth comes out.' She walked over to the hot food and lifted a plate. 'Why didn't you just say? You could have used my washing machine.'

'You'd do my washing for me?'

Cassidy shuddered. 'No. I said you could *use* my washing machine. I didn't say *I* would do it for you. Anyway, that's one of my rules.'

He watched as she selected a roll, put something inside and picked up a sachet of ketchup.

'What do you mean—one of your rules?'

She lifted a mug and pressed the button for tea. 'I have rules. Rules for the ward, rules for life, rules for men and rules for Christmas.'

He raised his eyebrows. 'Okay, now you've intrigued me. Either that, or you're a total crank—which is a distinct possibility.' He picked up his coffee. 'So, I'm interested. I know about the rules for the ward but tell me about these rules for men.'

She handed over her money to the cashier and sat down at a nearby table. 'They're simple. No overseas men.'

'Yeah, yeah. I've heard that one. And I'm not impressed. What else?'

'No washing. No ironing. No picking up after them. I'm not their mother. Do it a few times and they start to expect it. I get annoyed, then I start picturing them as Jabba the Hut, the fat, lazy monster from *Star Wars*, and yadda, yadda, yadda.' She waved her hand in the air.

'I was right. You *are* a crank.' He prodded her roll. 'And what is that? Everyone around here seems to eat it and I've no idea what it is.'

'It's slice.'

'Slice? A slice of what?'

'No. That's what it's called—slice. It's square sausage. A Scottish delicacy.'

'That's not a sausage. That looks nothing like a sausage.'

'Well, it is. Want to try a bit?' She held up her roll towards him.

He shook his head. 'That doesn't look too healthy. Apart from the pizza the first night I met you, you seem to spend your life eating salads or apples. I've never even seen you eat the sweets on the ward.'

'But this is different. This is Saturday morning. This is the bad-girl breakfast.' She had a twinkle in her eye as she said it.

Brad moved closer, his eggs abandoned. 'Should I keep a note of this for future reference?'

There it was again—that weird little hum that seemed to hang in the air between them. Making the rest of the room fall silent and fade away into the background. Making the seconds that they held each other's gaze seem like for ever.

But he kind of liked that. He kind of liked the fact that she didn't seem to be able to pull her gaze away any more than he could. He kind of liked the fact that once he was in the vicinity of Cassidy, his brain didn't seem to be able to focus on anything else. And from right here he could study the different shades of brown in her eyes—some chocolate, some caramel, some that matched her chestnut hair perfectly.

Whoa! Since when had he, Brad Donovan, ever thought about the different shades of colour in a woman's eyes? Not once. Not ever. Until now. Where had his brain found the words 'chocolate', 'caramel' and 'chestnut'?

'Maybe you should.' The words startled him. There it was again, something in the air. The way at times her voice seemed deeper, huskier, as if she was having the same sort of thoughts that he was.

But what did she think about all this? Was he merely a distraction? After all, she didn't want a man from the other side of the world; she wanted a Scotsman. And he clearly wasn't that. So why was she even flirting with him?

But now her eyes were cast downwards, breaking his train of thought. There was a slight flush in her cheeks. Was she embarrassed? Cassidy didn't seem the bashful type. Maybe she was having the same trouble he was—trying to make sense of the thoughts that seemed to appear as soon as they were together.

He didn't like silence between them. It seemed awkward, unnatural for two people who seemed to fit so well together.

He picked up his fork and started eating his eggs. 'So, tell me about the Christmas rules?'

Cassidy sat back in her chair, a huge smile appearing on her face in an instant. Her eyes went up towards the ceiling. 'Ah, Christmas, best time of year. I love it, absolutely love it.' She counted on her fingers. 'There are lots of rules for Christmas. You need to have a proper advent calendar, not the rubbish chocolate kind. You need the old-fashioned kind with little doors that open to pictures of mistletoe and holly, sleighs, presents and reindeer. Then your Christmas tree needs to go up on the first of December.' She pointed her finger at him. 'Not on the twelfth or Christmas Eve, like some people do. You need to get into the spirit of things.'

'Should I be writing all this down?'

'Don't be sarcastic. Then there's the presents. You don't put them under the tree. That's a disaster. You bring them out on Christmas Eve.'

Brad was starting to laugh now. The enthusiasm in her face was brimming over, but she was deadly serious. 'Cassidy, do you still believe in Santa Claus?'

She sighed. 'Don't tell me you're a Christmas Grinch. There's no room for them in my ward.'

The Christmas Grinch. Actually, for the last few years, it would have been the perfect name for him. It was hard to get into the spirit of Christmas when you didn't know where your little girl was. Whether she was safe. Whether she was well. Whether she was happy. Cassidy did look literally like a child at Christmas. This was obviously her thing.

He tried to push the other thoughts from his mind. He was trying to be positive. This year he wasn't going to fall into the black hole he'd found himself in last year, dragged down by the parts of his life he couldn't control.

'Any other Christmas rules you need to tell me?'

'Well, there's all the fun stuff. Like trying to spot the first Christmas tree someone puts up in their window. I usually like to try and count them as I walk home from work every day. Then trying to guess who has got your name for the secret Santa at work. And the shops—I love the shops at Christmas. The big department store on Buchanan Street has the most gorgeous tree and decorations. They'll be up in a few weeks. You have to go and see them. And there will be ice skating in George Square. We have to go to that!'

'But it's still only October. We haven't had Hallowe'en

yet.' Brad took a deep breath. He had an odd feeling in the pit of his stomach.

'We celebrate Christmas in Australia, too, you know. It might be a little different, but it's every bit as good as it sounds here. Where I live in Perth, everyone has Christmas lights on their houses. We have a huge Christmas tree in Forrest Place that gets turned on every November. Okay—maybe the temperature is around forty degrees and we might spend part of the day on the beach. But it's still a fabulous time. I'm gutted I won't be there this year.'

He was pushing his Christmas memories aside, and curiosity was curling at the bottom of his stomach. Little pieces of the puzzle that was Cassidy Rae were clicking into place. 'Have you ever celebrated Christmas anywhere else?'

Cassidy shook her head fiercely. 'I couldn't for a minute imagine being anywhere other than here at Christmas. Sometimes it even snows on Christmas Eve and Christmas Day. Then it's really magical.'

Brad frowned. 'Didn't you even celebrate Christmas in Spain with your fiancé?'

Cassidy looked at him as if he had horns on his head. 'Absolutely not.'

He folded his arms across his chest. 'Surely it doesn't matter where you celebrate Christmas—it's about who you celebrate with. It's the people, Cass, not the place.' He willed his voice not to break as he said the words. She would have no idea how much all this hurt him.

Cassidy was still shaking her head, and Brad had the distinct feeling he'd just tiptoed around the heart of the matter. She didn't want to move. She didn't want to leave. She wouldn't even consider moving anywhere else.

In some circumstances it might seem fine, patriotic even. But it irritated Brad more than he wanted to admit. How could Cass be so closed-minded? Was this really why she wouldn't even consider a relationship with him? Not that he'd asked her. But every day they were growing closer and closer.

Why hadn't he told her about Melody yet? The most important person in his life and he hadn't even mentioned her existence. He'd heard from his lawyer yesterday. Still no news. Still no sign. America was a big place. They were searching every state to see if Alison had registered as a doctor, though by now she could be married and working under a different name. If that was the case, they might never find her. And that thought made him feel physically sick.

His brain was almost trying to be rational now. Trying to figure out why Alison hadn't contacted him.

He was a good father—committed to Melody and her upbringing. He'd wanted a say in everything and that had kind of spooked Alison, who liked to be in control. And if she'd really met someone and fallen in love, he could almost figure out why she'd done things this way.

If she'd told him she wanted to move to the US, there would have been a huge custody battle. But to steal his daughter away and let eighteen months pass with no contact? That, he couldn't understand—no matter what.

He almost wanted to shout at Cassidy, *It's the people, Cass—always the people.* He couldn't care less where he was in this world, as long as he was near his daughter.

His mind flickered back to the four tightly packed boxes stuffed in the bottom of the wardrobe in his bedroom. Eighteen months of his life, with a private investigator in Australia and one in the US. Eighteen months when almost all his salary had gone on paying their fees and jumping out of his skin every time the phone rang.

No one could keep living like that. Not even him. It destroyed your physical and mental health. So he'd tried to take a step back, get some normality back into his life. He was still looking for his daughter and still had a private investigator in the US. But now he didn't require a daily update—an email once a week was enough. And the PI was under strict instructions to phone only in an emergency.

He looked at the woman across the table. He still couldn't get to the bottom of Cassidy Rae. She'd received another one of those phone calls the other day and had ducked out the ward, talking in a low, calm voice.

What on earth was going on?

Cassidy stared across the table. Maybe she'd gone a little overboard with the Christmas stuff. She always seemed to get carried away when the subject came up. It looked as if a shadow had passed across Brad's eyes. Something strange. Something she didn't recognise. Was it disappointment? She drew her breath in, leaving a tight feeling in her chest. She didn't like this.

But she didn't know him that well yet. She didn't feel as if she could share that it was just her and her gran left. And she wanted to hold on to what little family she had left. Of course Christmas was about people—even if they didn't know you were there.

She reached across the table and touched his hand. Every single time she touched him it felt like this. A tingle. Hairs standing on end. Delicious feelings creeping down her spine. The warmth of his hand was spreading through her.

He looked up and gave her a rueful smile, a little sad maybe but still a smile.

'Let's talk about something else. Like Hallowe'en. We usually have a party for the staff on the ward. I had it in my flat last year, but I think yours would be the perfect venue this time.'

Brad's smile widened. He looked relieved by the change of subject. 'I guess a Hallowe'en party wouldn't be out of the question in the House of Horrors.'

'It's not a House of Horrors. Why don't we just tell people we've got a theme for the year? It could be Hallowe'en-slash-fancy-dress, 1960s-style?'

He nodded slowly. 'I suppose we could do that. Are you going to help me with the planning?'

'Of course.' Cassidy stood up and picked up her plate and mug, 'Come on, it's time to go back upstairs. We can talk about it as we go.'

He watched her retreating back and curvy behind. One thing was crystal clear. This woman was going to drive him crazy.

30 October

Brad opened the door as yet another party reveller arrived. Bert had retreated to his basket, now in Brad's pink bedroom, in sheer horror at the number of people in the small flat. It seemed that inviting the 'medical receiving unit' to a party also included anyone who worked there, used to work there or had once thought about working there.

It also included anyone who'd ever passed through or seen the sign for the unit.

'Love the outfit!' one of the junior doctors shouted at Brad. He looked down. Cassidy had persuaded him to go all out, and his outfit certainly reflected that. The room was filled with kipper ties, psychedelic swirls, paisley patterns, and mini-skirts and beehives. For the men, stick-on beards seemed to be the most popular choice, with lots of them now sticking to arms, foreheads and chests.

Brad pushed through the crowd to the kitchen, finding an empty glass and getting some water. It was freezing outside, but inside the flat he almost felt as if he were back in Perth. He'd turned the cast-iron radiators off, but the place was still steaming, even with the windows prised open to let the cold air circulate.

He felt someone press at his back. 'Sorry, it's a bit of a squash in here.' He recognised the voice instantly.

'Where have you been? Wow!' Cassidy had helped him carry all the food and drink for the party up to the flat. Then she'd disappeared to get changed. His eyes took in her short red *Star Trek* dress, complete with black knee-high boots and gold communicator pinned to her chest. She pressed the button. *'How many to beam aboard?'*

'You didn't tell me we were doing TV. Not fair. How come you get to look smart and sexy and I get to look like some flea-bitten wino?'

She laughed and moved forward. 'I'm still in the sixties. The first episode of *Star Trek* was screened in 1966. I'm in perfect time.'

Someone pressed past her and she struggled to keep her glass of wine straight, moving so close to Brad that their entire bodies were touching. Her eyes tilted upwards towards him. 'I kind of like your too-tight shirt and shaggy wig. It suits you in a funny way.'

'Well, that outfit definitely suits you. But I feel as if you've fitted me up. I bet you had that sexy fancy-dress outfit stashed somewhere and were just looking for an excuse to give it an outing.' His broad chest could feel her warm curves pushing against him.

'You think I look sexy?' Her voice was low again and husky. Her words only heard by him. Someone else pushed past and she moved even closer in the tiny kitchen. *'How many to beam aboard?'*

They jumped. Startled by the noise. Brad grabbed her hand and pulled her through the door, past the people in the sitting room dancing to Tom Jones and the Beatles, and into the pink bedroom, pushing the door closed behind them.

Cassidy let out a little gasp. The pink shiny bedspread was gone, replaced by a plain cotton cream cover and pillowcases. But the dark pink lampshades hadn't been replaced, leaving a pink glow around the room. 'Too many people falling off your bed?'

He pulled the wig from his head, revealing his hair sticking up in all directions. 'Now, why would you think that?' There was a smile on his face as he stepped closer, pushing her against the door. His eyes were fixed on hers. His hand ran up her body, from the top of her boot, touching the bare skin on her legs, past the edge of her dress to her waist.

'Why would something like that even occur to you, Cass? Why would it even enter your mind? Because you keep telling me that we're friends. Just friends. You don't want anything more—not with someone like me, someone from Australia.' *Or someone with a missing child.*

Cassidy's heart was thudding against the inside of her chest. From the second he'd closed the door behind them she'd been picturing this in her head. No. Not true. From the first day that she'd met him she'd been picturing this in her head. It had taken her two glasses of wine to have the courage to come back to his flat tonight.

The tension had built in the last few weeks. Every lingering glance. Every fleeting touch sending sparks fluttering between them. It didn't matter how much her brain kept telling her he was the wrong fit. Her body didn't know that. And it craved his touch.

This wasn't meant to be serious. Serious had been the last thing on her mind—particularly with a man from overseas. But even though she tried to push the thoughts aside, Brad was rapidly becoming more than just a friend. She loved the sexual undercurrent between them, and the truth was she wanted to act on it. Now.

She leaned forward, just a little. Just enough to push her breasts even closer to him. If he looked down, all he would be able to see now was cleavage. *'How many to beam aboard?'* The noise startled both of them, but Brad only pulled her closer. She reached up and pulled the communicator badge from her dress, tossing it onto the bed behind them. 'I hate it when the costume takes away from the main event.'

She could see the surprise in his eyes. He'd expected a fight. He'd expected her to give him a reason why he shouldn't be having the same thoughts she was.

She smiled, her hand reaching out and resting on his waist. 'Sometimes my body sends me different messages from my brain.'

Brad lifted a finger, running it down the side of her cheek. The lightest touch. Her response was immediate. Her face turned towards his hand, and his fingers caught the back of her head, intertwining with her hair. She leaned back into his touch, letting out a little sigh. Her eyes were closed, and she could feel his stubble scraping her chin, his warm breath near her ear. 'And which message are you listening to?' he whispered as his other hand slid under her dress.

'Which one do you think?'

She caught his head in her hands and pulled his lips towards hers. This was what she'd been waiting for.

His lips touched hers hungrily, parting quickly, his tongue pushing against hers. She wrapped her arms around his neck.

This was it. Stars were going off in her head. If he didn't keep doing this she would explode. Because everything about this felt right. And it was just a kiss—right? Where was the harm in that?

'I've waited a whole month to kiss you,' he whispered in her ear.

'Then I've only got one thing to say—don't stop.'

CHAPTER FOUR

2 November

'WHAT are you doing here?'

It was three o'clock in the morning, and the voice should have startled her, but it didn't; it washed over her like warm treacle.

She turned her head in the darkened room where she was checking a patient's obs, an automatic smile appearing on her face. 'I got called in at eleven o'clock. Two of the night-shift staff had to go home sick, and it was too late to call in any agency staff.' She wrinkled her nose. 'Sickness bug again. What are you doing here? I thought Franco was on call.'

Brad rolled his tired eyes. 'Snap. Sickness bug, Franco phoned me half an hour ago with his head stuck down a toilet.'

Cassidy nodded. 'Figures. This bug seems to hit people really quickly. Loads of the staff are down with it. Let's just hope we manage to avoid it.' She finished recording the obs in the patients chart and started walking towards the door. Brad's arm rested lightly on her waist, and although she wanted to welcome the feel of his touch, it just didn't seem right.

'No touching at work,' she whispered.

His eyes swept up and down the dimly lit corridor. 'Even when there's no one about? Where's the fun in that?' His eyes were twinkling again, and it was doing untold damage to her flip-flopping stomach. She stopped walking and leaned against the wall.

'It's like this, Dr Donovan.' She moved her arm in a circular motion. 'I'm the master of all you can survey right now, and it wouldn't do to be caught in a compromising position with one of the doctors. That would give the hospital gossips enough ammunition for the rest of the year.' She looked down the corridor again, straightening herself up, her breasts brushing against his chest.

'I may well be the only nurse on duty in this ward right now, but I've got a reputation to maintain.' She tapped her finger on his chest. 'No matter how much men of a dubious nature try to waylay me.'

Brad kept his hands lightly resting on her waist. 'Hmm, I'm liking three o'clock in the morning, Cassidy Rae. It sounds as if there might be a bit of a bad girl in there.' He had that look in his eye again—the one he'd had when he'd finally stopped kissing her a few nights ago. The one that suggested a thousand other things they could be doing if they weren't in the wrong place at the wrong time. 'We really need to improve our timing.'

He was grinning at her now. The tiny hairs on her arms were starting to stand on end. This man was infectious. Much more dangerous than any sickness bug currently sweeping the ward.

She could feel the pressure rising in her chest. How easy would it be right now for them to kiss? And how much did she want to? But it went against all her principles for conduct and professional behaviour. So why did they currently feel as if they were flying out the window?

No matter how she tried to prevent it, this man had got totally under her skin. She was falling for him hook, line and sinker. No matter how much her brain told her not to.

She tried to break the tension between them. 'What do you want, anyway? I didn't page you. Shouldn't you be in bed?' The irony of the words hit her as soon as they left her mouth, her cheeks automatically flushing. Brad and bed. Two words that should never be together in a sentence. The images had haunted her dreams for the last few nights. And she had a very *active* imagination.

His fingers tugged her just a little closer so he could whisper in her ear. 'Bed is exactly where I'm planning on being. But not here. And not alone.'

Cassidy felt her blush intensify. Was she going to deny what had been on her mind? She wasn't normally shy around men. But something about Brad was different. Something was making her cautious.

And she wasn't sure what it was. She couldn't quite put her finger on it yet. But as long as she had the slightest inclination what it was, she didn't want to lose her heart to this guy. No matter how irresistible he was.

'I've got two patients coming up. Two young guys who've—what is it you call it here?—been out on the lash?'

Cassidy laughed and nodded at his phrasing. He really was trying to embrace the Scottish words and phrases around him. She raised her eyebrows, 'Or you could call them *blootered*.'

Brad shook his head. 'I think you all deliberately wait until I'm around and start using all these words to confuse me.' He looked out the window into the night at the pouring rain. 'One of the other nurses down in

A and E called the two young guys *drookit* and *mauchit*. I have no idea what she was talking about.'

Cassidy laughed even harder. 'Look outside, that will give you a clue. *Drookit* is absolutely soaking. *Mauchit* means really dirty. I take it the guys were found lying on the street?'

Brad nodded. 'I'm getting the hang of this, though. It's…' he lifted his fingers in the air '…going like a fair down there.'

She laughed. 'See—you're learning. Bet you hadn't heard that expression before you came to Scotland.' Her brow wrinkled. 'Hang on, where is it going like a fair? In A and E?'

'The short-stay ward is full already. That's why you're getting these two. They'll need Glasgow coma scale obs done. Are you okay with that?'

Cassidy smiled. 'Of course I am. We're used to getting some minor head injuries on the ward on a Saturday night.' She walked over to the filing cabinet and pulled out the printed sheets, attaching them to two clipboards for the bottom of the beds. She turned to face him. 'You know a group of doctors at one of the local hospitals invented this over thirty years ago.' She waved the chart at him. 'Now it's used the whole world over. One of the doctors is still there. He's a professor now.'

Brad raised his eyebrows. 'Aren't you just the little fund of information at three in the morning?' He looked around again. 'Haven't you got some help? I'm not happy about you being here alone with two drunks. There's no telling how they'll react when they finally come round.'

Cassidy pointed to a figure coming down the corridor. 'Claire, the nursing auxiliary, is on duty with me.

She was just away for a break. And if I need help from another staff nurse, I can call through to next door.'

She turned her head as she heard the lift doors opening and the first of the trolleys being pulled towards the ward. 'Here they come.' She scooted into the nearby six-bedded ward and pulled the curtains around one of the beds.

Five minutes later a very young, very drunk man was positioned in the bed, wearing a pair of hospital-issue granddad pyjamas. Cassidy wrinkled her nose at the vapours emanating from him. 'Phew! He smells like a brewery. I could get anaesthetised by these fumes.' She spent a few moments checking his blood pressure and pulse, checking his limb movements and trying to elicit a verbal and motor response from him. Finally she drew her pen torch from her pocket and checked his pupil reactions.

She shook her head as she marked the observations on the chart. 'At least his pupils are equal and reactive. He's reacting to pain, but apart from that he's completely out of it.' She checked the notes from A and E. 'Any idea of a next of kin?'

Brad shook his head. 'Neither of the guys had wallets on them. This one had a student card in his pocket but that was it.'

He raised his head as the rattle of the second trolley sounded simultaneously to his pager going off. He glanced downwards at the number. 'It's A and E again. Are you sure you're okay?'

Claire had joined her at the side of the bed. 'We'll be fine, but just remember, there are no beds left up here.'

Brad nodded. 'I'll try to come back up later,' he said as he walked down the corridor towards the lift.

* * *

Cassidy spent the next hour doing neurological observations on the two patients every fifteen minutes. Both of them started to respond a little better, even if it was belligerently. It was four o'clock in the morning now—that horrible time of night for the night shift where the need to sleep seemed to smack them straight in the head. Her eyes were beginning to droop even as she walked the length of the corridor to check on her patients. Sitting down right now would be lethal—she had to keep on the move to stay awake.

A monitor started pinging in one of the nearby rooms. 'I'll get it,' she shouted to Claire. 'The leads have probably detached again.'

She walked into the room of Mr Fletcher, a man in his sixties admitted with angina. Every time he'd turned over in his sleep tonight, one of the leads attached to his chest had moved out of place.

Cassidy flicked on the light, ready to silence the alarms on the monitor. But Mr Fletcher's leads were intact. His skin was white and drawn, his lips blue and his body rigid on the bed. The monitor showed a rapid, flickering electrical line. Ventricular fibrillation. His heart wasn't beating properly at all. Even though the monitor told her what she needed to know, she took a few seconds to check for a pulse and listen for breathing.

'Claire!' She pulled the red alarm on the wall, setting off the cardiac-arrest procedure as she released the brake on the bottom of the bed and pulled the bed out from the wall. She removed the headrest from the top of the bed and pulled out the pillows. Claire appeared at her side, pulling the cardiac-arrest trolley behind her. 'I've put out the call.' She was breathing heavily.

Cassidy took a deep breath. Brad was the senior doctor carrying the arrest page tonight. If he was still down in A and E, it would take him at least five minutes to get up here. Glasgow City Hospital was an old, sprawling building, with bits added on over time. It hadn't been designed with emergencies in mind, like some of the modern, newly built hospitals were. The anaesthetist would probably take five minutes to get here, too.

It didn't matter what the monitor said. Cassidy took a few seconds to do the old-fashioned assessment of the patient. Airway. Breathing. Circulation. No pulse. No breathing.

'Start bagging,' she instructed Claire, pointing her to the head of the bed and handing her an airway as she connected up the oxygen supply to the ambu-bag. She turned the dial on the defibrillator, slapping the pads on Mr Fletcher's chest and giving it a few seconds to pick up and confirm his rhythm.

'Stand clear,' she shouted to Claire, waiting a few seconds to check she'd stood back then looking downwards to make sure she wasn't touching the collapsed metal side rails. She pressed the button and Mr Fletcher's back arched upwards as the jolt went through his body.

Her adrenaline had kicked in now. She didn't feel sleepy or tired any more. She was wide awake and on alert, watching the monitor closely for a few seconds to see if the shock had made any impact on his heart rhythm. Nothing. Still VF.

The sound of feet thudded down the corridor as Brad appeared, closely followed by one of the anaesthetists. Brad's eyes widened as he realised who the patient was. 'VF,' she said as they entered the room. 'I've shocked him once at one hundred and twenty joules.'

Even though she had only been back on the ward for a month, she was on autopilot.

'What happened?' asked Brad. 'He was pain free earlier and we had him scheduled for an angiogram tomorrow.'

'Alarm sounded and I found him like this,' she said. 'He hadn't complained of chest pain at all.' She raised her knee on the bed and positioned her hands, starting the chest compressions. The anaesthetist took over from Claire and within a few seconds inserted an endotracheal tube. Cassidy continued the cycles of compressions as Brad pulled the pre-loaded syringes from the crash cart. After five cycles she stopped and their heads turned to the monitor again to check the rhythm.

'I'm giving him some epinephrine,' Brad said as he squirted it into the cannula in the back of Mr Fletcher's hand. 'Let's shock him again.' He lifted the defibrillator paddles. 'Stand clear, everyone. Shocking at two hundred joules.'

Everyone stood back as Mr Fletcher's body arched again. Cassidy went to resume the compressions. They continued for the next ten minutes with cycles of compressions, drugs and shocking. Cassidy's arms were starting to ache. It was amazing how quickly the strain of doing cardiac massage told on shoulders and arms.

'Stop!' shouted Brad. 'We've got a rhythm.' He waited a few seconds as he watched the green line on the monitor. 'Sinus bradycardia.'

He raised his eyes from the bed. 'Cassidy, go and tell Coronary Care we're transferring a patient to them.'

She ran next door to the coronary care unit, and one of their staff members came back through with her, propping the doors open for easy transfer. They wheeled the bed through to the unit and hooked Mr

Fletcher up to the monitors in the specially designed rooms. In a matter of a few moments, he was safely installed next door.

Cassidy nodded at Brad as she left him there to continue Mr Fletcher's care. Claire gathered up his belongings and took them next door while Cassidy quickly transferred him on the computer system.

She took a deep breath and heaved a sigh of relief. The adrenaline was still flooding through her system, her arms ached and her back was sore.

Claire appeared with a cup of steaming tea, which she put on the desk in front of her. 'Okay, Cassidy? I nearly jumped out of my skin when that alarm sounded. He'd been fine all night.'

Cassidy nodded. 'I hate it when that happens. Thank goodness he was attached to a cardiac monitor. I dread to think what would have happened if he hadn't been.'

A loud groan sounded from the room opposite the nurses' station. Cassidy stood back up. 'No rest for the wicked. That will be one of our head-injury patients.'

Sure enough, one of the young men was starting to come round. Cassidy started checking his obs again, pulling her pen torch from her pocket to make sure his pupils were equal and reactive. His score had gradually started to improve as he could obey simple instructions and respond—albeit grudgingly. Hangovers didn't seem to agree with him.

She moved on to the patient next door, who still appeared to be sleeping it off. As she leaned over to check his pupils, his hand reached up and grabbed her tunic. 'Get me some water,' he growled, his breath reeking of alcohol and his eyes bloodshot.

Cassidy reacted instantly, pushing him backwards

with her hands to get out of his grasp. 'Don't you dare put a hand on me,' she snarled.

'Cass.' The voice was instant, sounding behind her as Brad sidestepped around her, filling the gap between her and the patient.

The sunny surfer boy with cheerful demeanour was lost. 'Don't you dare touch my staff.' He was furious, leaning over the patient.

The drunken young man slumped back against the pillows, all energy expended. 'I need some water,' he mumbled.

Brad grabbed hold of Cassidy's hand and pulled her beyond the curtains. He ran his fingers through his hair. 'He still requires neuro obs, doesn't he?'

Cassidy nodded. 'That's the first time he's woken up. His neuro obs are scheduled to continue for the next few hours.'

Brad marched over to the phone and spoke for a few moments before putting it back down. 'I don't want you or Claire going in there on your own. Not while there's a chance he's still under the influence of alcohol and might behave inappropriately. Somebody from Security will be up in a few minutes and will stay for the rest of the shift.'

He walked into the kitchen and picked up a plastic jug and cup, running the tap to fill them with water. 'I'll take him these. You sit down.'

Cassidy didn't like anyone telling her what to do, especially in her ward. But for some reason she was quite glad that Brad had been around. It wasn't the first time a patient had manhandled her—and she was quite sure it wouldn't be the last. But there was something about it happening in the dead of night, when there weren't many other people around, that unsettled her.

And as much as she wanted to fly the flag for independence and being able to handle everything on her own, she was quite glad one of the security staff was coming up to the ward.

Brad appeared a moment later, walking behind her and putting his hands on her taut neck and shoulders. He automatically started kneading them with his warm hands. 'You okay, Cass?'

For a second she was still tense, wondering what Claire might think if she saw him touching her, but then relaxing at his touch. Her insides felt as tight as a coiled spring. What with the cardiac massage and the reaction of her patient, this was exactly what she needed. She leaned backwards a little into his touch.

'Right there,' she murmured as he hit a nerve. 'How's Mr Fletcher doing?'

Brad's voice was calm and soothing. 'He's in the right place. The staff in Coronary Care can monitor him more easily, his bradycardia stabilised with a little atropine and his blood pressure is good. We've contacted his family, and he'll be first on the list in the morning. He'll probably need a stent put in place to clear his blocked artery.'

'That's good. Mmm…keep going.'

'Your muscles are like coiled springs. Is this because of what just happened?'

She could hear the agitation in his voice.

'I hate people who react like that. How dare they when all we're trying to do is help them? He could have died out there, lying on the street with a head injury, getting battered by the elements. It makes my blood boil. If I hadn't come in when I did…' His voice tailed off then he leaned forward and wrapped his arms around her neck—just for a second—brushing a light kiss on her cheek.

It was the briefest of contacts before he straightened up, reaching for the cup of tea Claire had made a few minutes earlier and setting it down on the desk in front of her. 'Drink this.' He folded his arms and sat down in the chair next to her, perching on the edge. 'I need to go back to Coronary Care. What are you doing on Sunday? Want to grab some lunch?'

Cassidy hesitated, her stomach plunging. She had plans on Sunday. Ones she wasn't sure about including Brad in. After all, he was just a fleeting moment in her life, a 'passing fancy', her gran would have said. She wasn't ready to introduce him to her family yet. Especially in her current circumstances.

But the hesitation wasn't lost on Brad. 'What's up? Meeting your other boyfriend?' he quipped.

Her head shook automatically. 'No, no.' Then a smile appeared. 'What do you mean, my *other boyfriend*? I wasn't aware I had a boyfriend right now.' Why did those words set her heart aflutter? This wasn't what she wanted. Not with a man from thousands of miles away. Not with someone who would leave in less than a year. So why couldn't she wipe the smile off her face?

He could see the smile. *Distraction.* Was that all that Cass was? What about how'd he had felt a few minutes ago when that drunk had touched her? The guy was lucky there hadn't been a baseball bat around. Cass was getting under his skin. In more ways than one. And it was time. Time to tell her about Melody.

It would be fine. He'd tell her on Sunday. She would understand. She would get it. He had other priorities. He wanted to find his daughter, and that could take him anywhere in the world. Cassidy would be fine about it. She didn't want a serious relationship with an Australian. She obviously didn't mind the flirtation and distraction. Maybe she wouldn't even mind a little more. Something more inevitable between them.

This wasn't anything serious—she would know that. But he just didn't want anyone else near her right now.

Brad stood back up. 'Well, you do. So there.' He planted another kiss firmly on her cheek. 'And whatever you're doing on Sunday, plan on me doing it with you.' And with those words he strode down the corridor, whistling.

7 November

'We seem to be making a habit of this.' Brad smiled at Cassidy, his mouth half-hidden by the scarf wrapped around his neck, as she turned the key in the lock of the little terraced house in the East End of Glasgow.

His leather-gloved hand was at her waist and his body huddled against hers. It was freezing cold and the pavements already glistening with frost. Cassidy pushed the door open and stepped inside. 'I'm afraid it's not much warmer inside. Gran hasn't lived here for over a year, and I have the heating on a timer at minimum to stop the pipes from freezing.'

Brad pushed the door shut behind him, closing out the biting wind. 'I can't believe how quickly the temperature's dropped in the last few days. I've had to buy a coat, a hat and a scarf.'

Cassidy stepped right in front of him, her chestnut curls tickling his nose. 'And very nice you look, too.'

He leaned forward and kissed the tip of her nose, before rubbing his gloved hands together. 'So what happens now?'

She led him into the main room of the house and pointed at some dark teak furniture. 'The van should be here any time. It's taking the chest of drawers and sideboard in here, the wardrobe in Gran's bedroom and the refrigerator from the kitchen. The furniture goes to someone from the local homeless unit who's just been rehoused.'

'I take it there's no chance your gran will ever come home.'

Cassidy shook her head fiercely, and he could see a sheen cross her eyes. 'No. She fell and broke her arm last year. It was quite a bad break—she needed a pin inserted. She's already suffered from Alzheimer's for the past few years. I'd helped with some adaptations to her home and memory aids, but I guess I didn't really understand how bad she was.'

Cassidy lifted her hands. 'Here, in her own environment, she seemed to be coping, but once she broke her arm and ended up in hospital...' Her voice trailed off and Brad wrapped his arm around her shoulders.

'So where is she now? Was there no one else to help her? Where are your mum and dad?'

'She's in a nursing home just a few miles away. And it's the second one. The first?' She shuddered, 'Don't even ask. That's why I agreed to the secondment. It meant I could spend a bit more time helping her get settled this time. Her mobility is good, but her memory is a different story—some days she doesn't even know who I am. Other days she thinks I'm my mother. I can't remember the last time she knew I was Cassidy. And now she's started to get aggressive sometimes. It's just not her at all. The only thing that helps is hearing my voice.'

The tears started to spill down her cheeks. 'I know

I'm a nurse and everything but I just hate it.' Brad pulled his hand from his glove and wiped away her tears with his fingers.

He nodded slowly. So that's what the telephone calls had been about. No wonder she'd wanted some privacy to take them. 'So where's your mum and dad? Can't they help with your gran?'

Cassidy rolled her eyes. 'My mum and dad are the total opposite of me. Sometimes I feel as if I'm the parent and they're the children in this relationship. Last I heard, they were in Malaysia. They're engineers, dealing with water-pumping stations and pipelines. They basically work all over the world and hardly spend any time back here.'

His brow furrowed. He was starting to understand Cassidy a little better. Her firm stance about staying in Scotland was obviously tied into feeling responsible for her gran. 'So you don't get much support?'

She shook her head.

'Is there anything I can do to help?'

Cassidy looked around her. The pain was written all over her face. 'Everything in this house reminds me of Gran. I packed up her clothes last month and took them to the Age Concern shop.' She walked over to a cardboard box in the corner of the room, filled with ornaments wrapped in paper, crinkling the tissue paper between her fingers. 'This all seems so final.'

The knock at the door was sharp, startling them both. Ten minutes later almost all the heavy furniture had been loaded onto the van by two burly volunteers. 'The last thing is in here.' Cassidy led them into the bedroom and pointed at the wardrobe. She stood back as the two men tilted the wardrobe on its side to get it through the narrow door. There was a clunk and a strange sliding noise.

Brad jumped forward. 'What was that? You emptied the wardrobe, didn't you, Cassidy?'

She nodded. 'I thought I had.'

He pulled open the uptilted wardrobe door and lifted up a black plastic-wrapped package that had fallen to the floor. 'You must have missed this.'

Cassidy stepped towards him and peered inside the wardrobe. 'I can't imagine how. I emptied out all the clothes last month. I was sure I got everything.' She turned the bulky package over in her hands. 'I don't know how I managed to miss this.' She gave the men a nod, and they continued out the door towards the van.

Brad thanked the men and walked back through to the bedroom. Cassidy was sitting on the bed, pulling at the plastic wrapper. There was a tiny flash of red and she gave a little gasp.

'Wow! I would never have expected this.' She shook out the tightly wrapped red wool coat and another little bundle fell to the floor. Cassidy swung the coat in front of the mirror. The coat was 1940s-style, the colour much brighter than she would have expected, with black buttons and a nipped-in waist.

'This coat is gorgeous. But I can't *ever* remember Gran wearing it. I don't even think I've seen a picture of her in it. Why on earth would she have it wrapped up at the back of her wardrobe? It looks brand new.'

Brad knelt on the floor and picked up the other package wrapped in brown paper. 'This was in there, too. Maybe you should have a look at them?'

Cassidy nodded and then gave a little shiver.

'Let's go to the coffee shop at the bottom of the road. It's too cold in here. We'll take the coat with us,' he said.

She headed through to the kitchen and pulled a plastic bag from under the sink, carefully folding the red coat and putting it inside. 'This coat feels gorgeous.' She held the edge of it up again, looking in the mirror at the door. 'And I love the colour.'

'Why don't you wear it?' Brad could see her pupils dilate, just for a second, as if she was considering the idea.

She shook her head. 'No. No, I can't. I don't know anything about it. I don't even know if it belonged to Gran.'

'Well, I think it would look perfect on you, with your dark hair and brown eyes. Red's a good colour for you. Did you inherit your colouring from your gran?'

Cassidy still had her fingers on the coat, touching it with a look of wistfulness in her eyes. 'I think so. I've only ever seen a few photos of her when she was a young girl. She was much more glamorous than me.'

Brad opened the front door as the biting wind whirled around them. He grabbed her hand. 'I've got a better idea. Why don't we get a coffee to go and just head back to my flat? It's freezing.'

Cassidy nodded as she pulled the door closed behind them and checked it was secure. They hurried over to the car and reached his flat ten minutes later, with coffee and cakes from the shop round the corner from him.

Although it was only four o'clock, the light had faded quickly and the street was already dark. 'Look!' screamed Cass. 'It's the first one!'

Brad dived to rescue the toppling coffee cups from her grasp. 'What is it?' His head flicked from side to side. 'What on earth are you talking about?'

'There!' Her eyes were lit up and her smile reached from ear to ear. He followed Cassidy's outstretched finger pointing to a flat positioned across the street above one of the shops. There, proudly displayed in the window, was a slightly bent, brightly lit-up Christmas tree.

'You have got to be joking. It's only the seventh of November. Why on earth would someone have their Christmas tree up?'

He couldn't believe the expression of absolute glee on her face. She looked like a child that had spotted Santa. 'Isn't it gorgeous?'

And there it was. That horrible twisting feeling inside his stomach. The one he was absolutely determined to avoid this year. That same empty feeling that he felt every year when he spent the whole of the Christmas season thinking about what he'd lost, what had slipped through his fingers.

He felt the wind biting at his cheek. Almost like a cold slap. Just what he needed. This year was going to be different. He'd done everything he possibly could. It was time to try and get rid of this horrible empty feeling. He'd spent last Christmas in Australia, the one before that in the US, following up some useless leads as to Alison and Melody's whereabouts.

This year would be different. That was part of the reason he'd come to Scotland. A country that had no bad memories for him. A chance to think of something new.

Cassidy's big brown eyes blinked at him in the orange lamplight. She'd pulled a hat over her curls and it suited her perfectly. 'I really want to put my tree up,' she murmured. 'But it's just too early.' She looked down at the bustling street. 'Only some of the shops have their decorations up. I wish they all had.'

This was it. This was where it started. 'Christmas means different things to different people, Cass. Not everyone loves Christmas, you know?'

He saw her flinch and pull back, confusion in her eyes. There was hesitation in her voice. 'What do you mean? Is something wrong? Did something happen to you at Christmas?'

He hesitated. How could he tell her what was currently circulating in his mind? He wasn't even sure he could put it into coherent words. Melody hadn't disappeared at Christmas, but everything about the season and the time of year just seemed to amplify the feelings, make them stronger. Most importantly, it made the yearning to see his daughter almost consume him. He blinked. She was standing in the dimmed light, her big brown eyes staring up at him with a whole host of questions.

He should tell her about Melody, he really should. But now wasn't the time or the place. A shiver crept down his spine as the cold Scottish winter crept through his clothes. A busy street filled with early festive shoppers wasn't the place to talk about his missing daughter.

And no matter how this woman was currently sending electric pulses along his skin, he wasn't entirely sure what he wanted to share. He wasn't sure he was ready.

'Brad?' Her voice cut through his thoughts, jerking him back to the passing traffic and darkened night.

He bent forward and kissed the tip of her nose, sliding his arm around her shoulders. 'Don't be silly, Cass. Nothing happened to me at Christmas.' He shrugged his shoulders as he pulled her towards him, guiding her down the street towards his flat. 'I'm just mindful that lots of the people we see in the hospital over Christmas don't have the happy stories to share that you do.'

She bit her lip, cradling the coffee cups and cakes in her arms as she matched his steps along the busy street. 'I know that. I didn't just materialise onto the medical unit from a planet far away. I've worked there a long time.'

But her words seemed lost as his steps lengthened and he pushed open the door to the close ahead of them.

Cassidy took off her bright blue parka and put it on the sofa. She'd seen something in his eyes. Almost as if a shadow had passed over them, and it had made her stomach coil. Was there something he wasn't telling her?

She pulled the coffee cups from their holder and opened the bag with the carrot cake inside. This was exactly what she needed right now. The sofa sagged next to her as Brad sat down. He was still rubbing his hands together.

'I can't believe how cold it is out there.'

She smiled at him. 'Get used to it—this is only the start. Last year it was minus twelve on Christmas Day. My next-door neighbour is a gas engineer and his phone was ringing constantly with people's boilers breaking down.' She picked up the cup and inhaled deeply. 'Mmm. Skinny caramel latte. My favourite in the world. I haven't had one of these in ages.' She took a tiny sip then reached for the moist carrot cake.

'So I take it the fact you have a *skinny* caramel latte counteracts the effects of the carrot cake?'

She winked at him. 'Exactly.' She raised her eyes skywards. 'Finally, a man on my wavelength. They cancel each other out. And it's a skinny caramel latte with sugar-free syrup. Which means I can enjoy this all the more.' She licked the frosting from the carrot cake off the tips of her fingers.

'With this...' she nibbled a bit from the corner. '...a girl could think she was in heaven.'

'I can think of lots of other ways to put a girl in heaven,' the voice next to her mumbled.

Cassidy froze. Her second sip of coffee was currently stuck in her throat. You couldn't get much more innuendo than that. Should she respond? Or pretend she hadn't heard?

There was no denying the attraction between them. But did she really want to act on it? After a month in his company, what did she really know about Brad Donovan? She could give testimony to his medical skills and his patient care. He was amenable, well mannered and supportive to the staff.

But what did she really know about him? Only little snippets of information that he'd told her in passing. Stories about home in Australia, living in Perth and his training as a doctor. Passing remarks about childhood friends. He'd told her he had no wife or girlfriend.

So what else was it? What had made that dark shadow pass in front of his eyes? Why had he hesitated before answering the question? Or had she just imagined it all? Maybe there was nothing wrong, maybe something had caught his eye at the other side of the road, momentarily distracting him and stopping him from answering the question.

In the meantime, she could still feel that underlying buzz between them. Whenever he was near, she had visions of that night in his flat, pressed up against the wall in her sci-fi costume, wishing things could go further than they had.

Every time he touched her at work, even the merest brush of a hand was enough to set off the currents between them. It didn't matter that her head told her this wasn't sensible—he came from the other side of the world and would likely return there; her body was telling her something entirely different. Her imagination was telling her a whole host of other things…

He gave her a nudge, passing her the package he'd wedged under his jacket.

She stared down at the still-wrapped parcel in her hands, turning the brown paper package over and over.

'Are you going to open it?'

She picked at the tape in one corner. It was old, the stickiness long vanished, and it literally fell apart in her hands, revealing some white envelopes underneath. She pulled them out. Only they weren't white, they had yellowed with age, all with US postal stamps.

Her eyes lifted to meet his. Brad leaned forward, touching the pile of envelopes and spreading them out across the table. 'There must be at least twenty of them,' he said quietly. His fingers stopped at something. There, among the envelopes, was something else. A photograph. Brad slid the envelope that was covering it away and Cassidy let out a little gasp.

She leaned forward and picked up the black-and-white print. 'It's my gran!' she gasped. His head met hers as they stared at the photograph of a beautiful young woman with a smile that spread from ear to ear, wearing a beautiful coat with a nipped-in waist. Her head was turned to the side and her eyes were sparkling as she looked at the man standing next to her in a US army uniform.

Cassidy was stunned. There were a million thoughts that crowded into her mind. A million conclusions that she could jump to. But one thing stood out above all the rest. 'I've never seen her look so happy,' she whispered. 'Gran never looked like that.'

She turned to face Brad. 'I don't mean she was miserable—she was fine.' She pointed at the photograph. 'But I can't ever remember her looking like *that*.'

She didn't want to say anything else. She didn't know what to think. She'd just glimpsed a moment from the past, and it almost seemed sacred. The coat and letters had been hidden a long time ago by a woman who obviously hadn't wanted to throw them away but hadn't wanted them to be found. In a way, it almost felt like a betrayal.

She ran her finger over the photograph. 'I don't think I can even ask Gran about this. She's too far gone. I can't even remember the last time that she recognised me.'

Brad's arm wrapped around her shoulder. She could feel his breath at her neck. What would he be thinking? The same kind of thing that she was? That her gran had lost her heart to some US soldier?

She didn't want to think like that. It seemed almost judgemental. And it seemed wrong that Brad's first glimpse into her family was revealing something she hadn't known herself.

And she couldn't pretend that it didn't hurt a little. It had been just her and Gran for the last ten years but she'd never told Cassidy anything about this. She'd been a modern woman, liberal-minded and easy to talk to. Why had she kept this to herself?

His voice was quiet and steady as he whispered in her ear. 'Don't even think about asking her about it, Cass.' He lifted the photograph from her hand and sat it back down on the table. 'Take it as it is. A happy memory from your gran's life. She's beautiful in that picture. You can see the happiness in her eyes. Why shouldn't she have had a time like that?' His finger ran down the side of her cheek. 'She looks a lot like you.'

Cassidy turned to face him. His mouth was only

inches from hers and she subconsciously licked her lips. This was it. The moment she'd been waiting for.

It had taken him so long to kiss her again after the party. She didn't want to wait any longer. She didn't want to imagine any longer. She wanted to feel.

Her hands slid up around his neck as she pulled him closer. His mouth was on hers instantly, just the way she'd imagined. He pushed her backwards on the sofa, his hands on either side of her head as he kissed her, gently at first, before working his way down her neck, pushing her shirt open.

His body was warm, heating hers instantly. She could feel his whole length above her, and her hands moved from around his neck, down his back and towards his hips, pulling him closer to her.

This time there was no one else in the flat. This time they wouldn't need to stop. This time they could do what they wanted.

She pushed aside the rational side of her brain that was clamouring to be heard. She could worry about all that later. Her body was responding to him with an intensity she'd never experienced before. She'd already had a glimpse of the washboard abs when he'd changed in the doctors' office. Now she didn't just want to look—she wanted to touch, to feel, to taste.

He lifted his head, pushing himself back a little. His voice was little above a groan. 'Cass?'

The question only hung in the air for a fraction of a second. She didn't want to think about this. Right now she didn't care that he was from Australia and would probably go back there. Right now all she cared about was that he was here, *now*, with *her*.

A slow smile appeared on his face. 'Wanna stay over?'

He had no idea how sexy he was right now. His clear blue eyes were hooded with desire. She could feel his heart thudding against his chest. All for her.

She pressed herself against him again. 'I thought you'd never ask.'

He pulled her to her feet and led her towards his bedroom door, undoing the buttons on her shirt as they went. Her legs were on autopilot and she couldn't wipe the smile from her face.

He pressed her against the wall. 'I seem to remember being in this position with you before, Cassidy Rae.' His voice was deep, throaty, turning her on even more.

'I was playing hard to get,' she whispered in his ear. 'Did it work?'

He turned her around and pushed her onto the bed. 'Oh, yes.' He crawled towards her, poising himself above her. Her shirt was open now, leaving her breasts exposed in their black satin push-up bra. He bit at the edge with his teeth. 'Now, this doesn't look like ordinary underwear.' His fingers dug around her hips, sliding down the back of her jeans and finding the edge of her matching black g-string. 'Did you have something in mind when you got dressed this morning, Cass?' His low, sexy laugh sent shivers of delight down her spine.

It wasn't her normal underwear. But she could hardly even remember getting dressed this morning. Had she done this subconsciously, hoping she would end up in this position?

'Let's just say I'm a girl of many secrets.' She pulled his T-shirt over his head, revealing his pecs and tanned abdomen. If she hadn't been so turned on, she might have pulled in her stomach and worried about him seeing her curves. But from the look on his face, he liked what he was seeing. 'I have lots of gorgeous sets of underwear. If you're lucky, I'll let you see the red set,' she moaned as he started to kiss her neck, 'or the blue set...' Her hands were dipping lower on his body, to the front of his jeans where she could feel him throbbing against her. 'Or, if you're really lucky, I'll let you see the green set.'

He let out a groan. 'I can guarantee I'll love the underwear—no matter what colour. But what I love most is what's underneath. He traced his fingers down her throat as she arched her back in response. Then slid his hand underneath her, unfastening her bra strap and leaving her breasts exposed. 'Now, what can I do with these?' he murmured.

Cass pushed herself upwards, her breasts towards his mouth. 'You can start by getting rid of the rest of these clothes,' she commanded as she undid the buttons on his jeans, before wriggling out of her own. She waited as he discarded his jeans and underwear, before pushing him down on the bed and setting her legs astride him.

'I like this,' he murmured. 'A woman who likes to be in charge.'

'Oh, I'm always in charge,' she breathed in his ear as she ran her hands down his chest. 'And anyway, I'm examining your skin. You're way too tanned.' Her hands stopped at his nipples, brushing around them onto the fine hair on his chest. 'I feel it's my duty to check you for any areas of concern.' She lifted her hips and rubbed against him again.

He groaned. 'Anywhere in particular you'd like to start?'

She smiled and leaned over him again, her hardened nipples brushing against the skin on his chest. She swayed against him. 'I'll need to think about that.'

Brad let out a primal roar. He grabbed her and

flipped her around on the bed so he was poised above her. 'Enough teasing. You're going to be the death of me.'

His fingers reached down and dispensed with her g-string. She could feel the heat rise inside her. She was aching for him. He touched her and she gasped, tilting her hips upwards to him. 'Oh...this is going to be so good.'

'You bet it is,' he whispered in her ear, the stubble on his jaw scraping her shoulder.

'Mmm... Where else am I going to feel that?'

'Wherever you like.'

He moved for a second, reaching into the nearby drawer, and she heard the rustle of a condom wrapper being opened. Ten seconds later he was above her again. 'Are you ready?' he whispered.

'Oh, yes...' She opened her legs further and gasped as he plunged inside her.

He stopped, just for a second. 'Okay?'

She took a deep breath, while the full sensation surrounded her. Then she pulled his hips even closer, taking him deeper inside. 'Don't you dare stop,' she groaned. 'I've got you just where I want you.'

'Ditto.' He smiled again as he moved slowly, building momentum between them as he trailed a line of kisses down the side of her face and throat.

And there it was—the fever that had been building between them for weeks. All the looks and lingering glances. All the brief touches. All the electricity buzzing around them like fireflies. The first kiss, with its strained finish. All building to this crescendo, where nothing and no one could get between them.

Cassidy could feel her skin start to tingle. Nothing else was more important than this. Nothing else had ever felt as good as this. Nothing else had ever felt this *right*. This was perfect.

She let herself go, throwing her head back and crying out his name, as she felt him stiffen at the same time.

She felt her body turn to jelly, the air whooshing out from her lungs. Brad was still above her, his whole body weight now resting on her, his heart thudding against her chest.

She let out a laugh. Sweat slicked them together as she gave him a playful push. 'Move, mister, I can hardly breathe.'

He pushed himself up and sagged down beside her. 'Wow.'

Cassidy was breathing heavily, her eyes staring up at the ceiling and fixing on the still-pink light shade above her. She turned to the sandy-blond head on the pillow beside her, a smile creeping across her face. 'Yeah, wow,' she murmured.

CHAPTER FIVE

8 November

THE early-morning Scottish light crept across the room.
Even on the greyest days the sun's rays sneaked through
the clouds and scattered this room with light. Brad's
brain was fuzzy. Something was different. Something
had changed.

Then he felt a movement beside him, and the memories of the night before crowded into his brain. Cassidy.
Wow.

Then something else hit him, charging from the dark
recesses of his brain, and he stifled the groan in his
throat. Melody. He hadn't told her about Melody.

He turned around in the bed, resting his hand on
his arm, staring at the sleeping figure beside him. Her
chestnut curls spilled across the pillow that she had
wedged half under her arm as she slept on her side,
facing him.

She looked beautiful. Her fair skin was smooth and
unlined. Cassidy. His distraction. The woman he'd
lusted after for the last month.

But his stomach clenched. He was cringing. Things
in his brain just didn't add up. If Cassidy was only a

distraction, why should he tell her about Melody? There should be no need.

But he knew better than that. No matter how many times he tried to use the word 'distraction' for Cassidy, she was much more than that.

In the last few weeks she had crept under his skin. Hearing her voice brought a smile to his face. Knowing she was working the same shift made his whole day seem brighter. And spending time with her outside work made the days speed past. He knew her habits—she liked to take her shoes off at the door, she sat on the left-hand side of the sofa, she only watched the news on one TV channel. His mood had lifted just by being around her.

His thoughts were always with his daughter but they didn't consume every spare second of every day.

She made him happy. Cassidy made him happy. And he was about to jeopardise all that. He knew he should have told her about Melody. He'd meant to but just hadn't found the appropriate time.

And now, after he'd slept with her, it seemed like a dirty secret. He almost wished he'd put a photo in the doctors' office in the ward as soon as he'd started there. But the truth was that office was used by lots of doctors and it wasn't appropriate to put a family picture in there. And he just hadn't been ready to answer any difficult questions about his daughter.

But now? He sagged back against the pillows. It looked as though he was hiding something. It looked as though he deliberately hadn't trusted Cassidy enough to tell her about Melody. How awkward was this conversation going to be?

He turned his head sideways to look at her again, to look at that perfect face before he ruined everything.

A tiny part of him hoped that she wouldn't be annoyed at all. Maybe she would shrug her shoulders and tell him that it was fine?

Who was he kidding? How would he feel if the shoe was on the other foot? If Cassidy had a child she hadn't told him about? The thought was unimaginable. He could feel himself automatically shaking his head at the idea.

Things would be perfect if he could just freeze this moment in time. Keep everything just the way it was right now. Or, even better, just the way they'd been last night. That thought sent a smile across his face. If only…

A frown appeared on Cassidy's brow then her eyelids flickered open. Those big brown eyes that pulled him in every time. A smile appeared on her face instantly. 'Morning,' she whispered.

Relief flooded through him. She hadn't woken up and panicked. She seemed happy and comfortable around him. She obviously had no regrets about the night before. Not yet, anyway.

'Morning,' he whispered back. He couldn't help it. He was immediately drawn to her. He wanted to touch her, taste her skin again. He dropped a kiss on the tip of her nose.

A glint appeared in her eyes. Memories of last night? 'Wow,' she whispered again, her soft breath on his face.

Brad couldn't hide the smile. Her memories were obviously as good as his. If only every morning could be like this.

Her hand crept around his neck, and as much as he wanted to pull her closer and forget about everything else, he just couldn't. He had to get this over and done with.

He shifted backwards in the bed. 'How about I make you some breakfast?' His legs hit the floor before she had a chance to answer, and he pulled his underwear and jeans on rapidly. 'What would you like? Toast? Eggs? Bacon?'

Cassidy looked confused. She pushed herself upwards in the bed and adjusted the pillows behind her. 'I'll have whatever you're making,' she said quietly.

'Great. Give me five minutes and I'll give you a shout. Feel free to take a shower and freshen up.' He leaned forwards and planted another kiss on her forehead before disappearing out of the door.

Cassidy sat for a few minutes, taking deep breaths. What just happened? They'd had a fabulous night, and he'd asked her to stay over. And for a few seconds this morning when she'd woken up, everything had seemed fine. So what had made him jump out of bed like a scalded cat?

She flung back the duvet and swung her legs out of bed, wincing at the cold air in the room. There was a navy-blue dressing gown hanging up behind the bedroom door, and she wrapped it around herself, then headed to the bathroom.

She flicked the switch for the shower, grabbing an elastic band that was sitting on top of the bathroom cabinet and twisting her hair back from her face as she sat at the edge of the bath for a few moments, trying to fathom what was going on.

Was Brad regretting their night together? The thought almost made her belly ache. She couldn't imagine anything worse. Maybe he was only interested in the thrill of the chase and once that was over...

No. No, it couldn't be that. She'd got to know him over the last few weeks, and he didn't seem to be like that at all. Maybe he just felt awkward because it was the first time they'd woken up together?

Yes, that could be it. Her eyes fell to the sink. Brad had obviously been in here first as he'd left her a new toothbrush and toothpaste and a huge white soft towel. She stuck her hand under the shower. It had heated up perfectly, so she stepped into the steaming water.

There was almost a tremor on her skin. Her insides were coiling, to the point of almost feeling pain. She couldn't bear the thought of Brad wanting to walk away after their night together. And it wasn't about the humiliation or about being used. Although those things would be bad enough.

It would be the fact he didn't feel the same connection that she did. The fact that his thoughts didn't wander to her about a million times a day—the way hers did to him. It would be the fact he didn't feel the constant zing between them. Those were the things she couldn't bear.

She could still smell him on her skin and almost regretted having to wash it away, but the blue shower gel with its ocean scent reminded her of him again. She rubbed it into her body even harder, then a few minutes later stepped out of the shower and dried herself rapidly. It only took a few moments to realise she'd nothing to wear, so she padded back through to the bedroom and rummaged in a few of his drawers.

'Cassidy! Breakfast!'

The smell was drifting through the house. Eggs, bacon and tea. Perfect.

'Hey.'

She was standing in the doorway dressed in a pair of his grey jogging trousers and an oversized pale blue

T-shirt. His clothes had never looked so sexy. Her hair was ruffled, some little strands around her neck still wet from the shower.

He pulled out a chair for her. 'Have a seat.' All Brad could think about right now was getting this over and done with. He had to come clean. Easier said than done.

He put the plates on the table and poured the tea while Cassidy watched him carefully. She wasn't stupid. She knew something was going on.

She took a sip of her tea, chasing her eggs around the plate with her fork. Watching. Waiting.

Brad pressed his lips together. He reached across the table and took her hand. 'Cass, there's something I need to tell you.'

He could see the tiny flare of panic in her eyes that she was trying to control. She set her tea back down on the table. Her voice was steady. 'So, what is it you want to tell me "the morning after the night before", Brad?'

He winced. There was no getting around this. Cassidy didn't even know what 'it' was—but the implication was there. If this was something important, he should have told her before he'd taken this relationship to the next level.

'I have a daughter.' The words were blurted out before he had a chance to think about it any longer.

'What?' The shocked expression on her face was very real. This was the last thing she'd expected to hear.

Brad took a deep breath. 'I have a daughter, Melody. She's nearly four.' His heart was beating against his chest, the words clambering to his mouth—he just couldn't speak quickly enough right now. 'I haven't seen in her over two years. Her mother, Alison, disappeared with her. We had a...' he flung his hands in the air

'…sort of informal custody arrangement. Alison was a doctor as well, and we looked after Melody between us.'

Cassidy's face looked set in stone. 'She was your wife? Your girlfriend? The one you told me you didn't have?' Her tone said it all.

Brad spoke firmly. 'She wasn't my wife and she wasn't my girlfriend, well, not after a few months. We had a very short-lived fling that resulted in Melody. We'd broken up by the time Alison discovered she was pregnant, and neither of us were interested in getting back together.'

He leaned back in the chair, wishing he could tell the whole story in the blink of an eye. Everything about this was painful to him. Every time he spoke about things, he thought about the mistakes he had made and what he could have done differently.

Anything that could have affected the eventual outcome.

Cassidy hadn't moved. Her face was expressionless and her breakfast lay untouched in front of her.

'I don't really know what happened, Cass. I went to pick up Melody as arranged one day, and they were gone.' He flicked his hand in the air. 'Just like that. Vanished. I was frantic. I went to Alison's work and found out she'd resigned and no one knew where she'd gone. Some of her colleagues said she'd met a doctor from the US and been head over heels in love. They thought she might have gone to the US with him.' He shook his head as a wave of desperation swept over him. It was the same every time he spoke about this.

'I hired a lawyer and two private investigators and tried to track her down. I've been trying to track her down for the last two years—with no success. I haven't seen or heard from her in two years. Right now, I have no idea how my little girl is, where she is or if she even remembers me.' His eyes were fixed on the window, staring out into space.

Cassidy felt numb. 'You have a daughter,' she said.

He nodded, it appeared, almost unconsciously.

'You have a daughter you "forgot" to tell me about?' She couldn't help it—she raised her hands in the air and made the sign of quotation marks.

She could feel rage and anger bubbling beneath the surface, ready to erupt at any moment. She hadn't imagined anything the other night. It hadn't been all in her head. It had been right before her eyes—or it should have been.

Brad looked in pain. He may have been gazing outside, but the look in his eyes was haunted. A father who had lost his child. She couldn't begin to imagine the pain that would cause. But right now she couldn't contain her anger.

'Why didn't you mention this before?'

He sighed. A huge sigh, as if the weight of the world was on his shoulders. His gaze went to his hands that were clenched in his lap. 'I know, I know, I should have. But it just never felt like the right time.'

'How about as soon as you met me?'

His brow wrinkled. 'Oh, yeah. Right. Pleased to meet you, I'm Brad Donovan. I've got a missing daughter, Melody, that I've been searching for the last two years. And before you ask—no—I've no idea why her mother disappeared with her. No—I didn't do anything wrong or mistreat my child. Yes—I've spent an absolute fortune trying to find her and I've been on two wild-goose chases to the US.' He waved his hand in frustration. 'Is that how you wanted me to tell you?'

Cassidy took a deep breath. She wanted to yell. She

wanted to scream. She could see how damaged he was by all this. But she couldn't see past how hurt she felt. Hadn't he trusted her enough to tell her? He trusted her enough to sleep with her—but not to tell her about his daughter? It seemed unreal.

She looked around, her eyes scanning the walls. 'So where are they?'

His brow furrowed. 'Where are what?'

She threw her hands up in frustration. 'The photos of your daughter. I've never seen a single one. Where do you keep them?'

He grimaced and stood up. She could hear him walking through to the living room and opening a drawer. He walked through and sat a wooden framed photograph down on the table.

Cassidy felt her heart jump into her mouth as she stared at the image in front of her. The gorgeous toddler with blonde ringlets and Brad's eyes was as pretty as a picture. She felt her lip tremble and she lifted her eyes to meet his. 'You put these away when you knew I would be here?'

He nodded. 'I planned to tell you.' He hesitated, having the good grace to look shamefaced. 'I just hadn't got around to it.'

'Why didn't you tell me when I first asked you about your family? When I asked you if you had a wife or a girlfriend? When I told you about my ex-fiancé and his new Miss Spain wife? How about telling me then? Correct me if I'm wrong, but wasn't that your ideal opportunity?'

She folded her arms across her chest. It didn't matter that she'd tried to play down how hurt she'd been over her breakup with her fiancé. The fact was she'd *told* him about it—albeit in sparing detail. There was no way he was getting away with this. She didn't care about the wonderful night before. She didn't care how many times he'd taken her to heaven and back.

This was about trust. This was about honesty. This was about the things you *should* tell someone before you slept with them.

Brad shook his head. 'You make it all sound so simple, Cass.'

She cringed. The exact thought she'd had when he'd asked her about Bobby. 'It is.'

'No. It's not.' His voice was determined. 'Okay, so you may have asked me about a wife or girlfriend—and I didn't have either, so I didn't tell you any lies. And I'd only just met you then, Cass. I don't want everyone to know my business, and this isn't the easiest thing to talk about. People talk. People make judgements.' He pressed his fingers against his temples.

'When Alison and Melody vanished at first, people were suspicious about me in Australia. People, colleagues even, wondered if I'd done something to them. It was only after the Australian police confirmed they'd left on an international flight that people stopped assuming I'd done something awful.'

Cassidy felt her heart constrict. It was something she hadn't even considered. It hadn't even entered her mind that someone would think like that about Brad. How could friends or colleagues have done that?

Her head was instantly filled with stories in the media, and after only a few seconds she realised it was true. As soon as anyone went missing, suspicion was generally directed at those around them. What on earth would that feel like?

She could only imagine the worst. The frustration of

not knowing where your child was. Continually shouting but not being heard. It must have been excruciating.

He leaned his elbows on the table. His fingers moved in small circles at the side of his head. 'It didn't stop there either.' He lifted his head and stared at Cassidy. 'Once people realised I hadn't done something unmentionable to them, they started to say that Alison must have done a runner with Melody to get away from me. As if I'd done something to my child.'

The words hung in the air. Too hideous for thoughts even to form.

'Oh, Brad,' she breathed. Now she understood. Now she understood the pain in his eyes. 'That's awful.'

'You bet it is.'

A lump stuck in her throat. She was angry. She was hurt. And she had no idea what this could mean for them. But right now she had to show some compassion. She stood up, the chair scraping along the kitchen floor, and walked around to the other side of the table.

Brad looked as if he was in shock. As if he was wondering what she might do next.

She might never have had a child stolen from her, but she knew what it was like to be left.

Her parents had done it. Bobby had done it.

But she was calm and lifted his hands from the table, sitting down on his knee and wrapping her hands around his neck, hugging him closely. She could feel his tense muscles beneath her fingers, and she rubbed her hand across his back, waiting for a few moments until he relaxed and the pent-up strain had started to abate.

After a few minutes she leaned back, watching him carefully.

'I'm not happy, Brad. I can't believe you didn't tell me something as important as this.'

She felt him take a deep breath. Right now his blue eyes were almost a window into his soul. She could see his regret. She could see his pain. And although hers could only pale in comparison, she wondered if he could see hers.

'I didn't mean things to turn out like this. This wasn't in my plans.'

In an instant she could almost feel his withdrawal. The hackles rose at the back of her neck. 'What do you mean?'

His hands touched her waist. 'This. Us. I didn't realise things would get so serious.'

'What did you expect? You've practically spent the last five weeks by my side. Every time I turn around, you're right there next to me. If you didn't want us to be more than friends, you should have stayed away.' She hated how she sounded. She hated the tone of her voice, but she just couldn't help it.

The muscles on his shoulders tensed again and he blew some hair from his forehead, obviously in exasperation. What on earth was he thinking? She had a hollow feeling in her stomach. After the wonderful night before, did he want to walk away?

Everything about this was confusing. She didn't even know how she felt about the fact he had a daughter—she hadn't had time to process those thoughts. Why was she even considering any of this? Her head had always told her this relationship was a bad idea. She wanted someone who would stay in Scotland with her, and the sinking feeling in her stomach told her Brad could obviously never do that.

But her body and soul told her something else entirely. Brad was the first man in a long time that she'd been attracted to—that she'd even been interested in.

She loved spending time in his company. She loved his normally easygoing manner. She loved the fact she could depend on him at work—his clinical skills and judgement were excellent.

But most of all she loved the way she felt around him. Even yesterday, in her grandmother's house, doing a task that should have made her feel sad and depressed, there had been so much comfort from having Brad around.

And as for how her body reacted to him…that was something else entirely.

Brad reached up and touched her hair, winding his fingers through one of her curls. Her head tilted instantly—an automatic response—towards the palm of his hand. His eyes were closed. 'How could I stay away from this, Cass?'

He pulled her head down and touched a gentle kiss to her lips. 'You're like a drug to me, Cassidy Rae. Apart from Melody, you're the first thing I think about when I get up in the morning and the last thing I think about when I fall asleep at night.' His eyes opened and she could tell instantly he meant every word.

This was no gentle let-down. This was no attempt to look for an excuse to end their relationship. He was every bit as confused as she was.

She pulled back. This was too much. She was getting in too deep. She pushed herself upwards, her legs trembling as she walked around to the other side of the table and pushed her untouched plate of food away.

'I can't think when you do that. I can't think straight when you touch me. It's too distracting.'

Brad let out a short laugh, shaking his head.

'What? What is it?'

'That word, Cass—distraction. That's what I thought about you at first.'

Cassidy frowned. A distraction. Hardly a flattering description. But he reached across the table and touched her hand again.

'You have no idea how I was feeling when I got here. I'd just had the year from hell in Australia. I'd been to the US twice, chasing false leads trying to find Melody. None of them worked. I'd spent a fortune and still had no idea about my daughter. Last Christmas...' He raised his eyes to the ceiling.

'Let's just say it was the worst ever. Then a few of my friends sat me down and had a conversation with me that was hard for all us. They told me I should never give up looking for Melody, but I had to accept I had a life of my own to live. And they came prepared—they had an armful of job ads for all over the world. I'd let my career slide. I'd been consumed by doing everything I could to find my daughter. The job I'd always loved had become a noose around my neck. I didn't make any mistakes but I'd lost the enthusiasm and passion for the job.

'My friends knew the career paths I'd been interested in before, and they convinced me it was the right time for a break—a change of scenery and a time for new horizons.'

He gave her a rueful smile. 'I didn't come to Scotland with the intention of meeting anyone. I came to Scotland to experience the infamous Scottish winter and the ream of medical admissions that always follow. I planned to just immerse myself in work. To try and give myself a break from constantly checking my emails and phoning the private investigator in the US.'

Cassidy didn't know what to think. A distraction. That's what he'd just called her. She couldn't stop herself from fixating on it. And it gave her the strangest sensation—a feeling of panic.

Maybe this was it. Maybe she should grab her clothes—wherever they were—and get out of here. She needed time to think. She needed a chance to get her head around what he'd just told her. Right now she was suffering from information overload.

Her gaze drifted out the kitchen and onto the coffee table in the living room. She hated that word. It made her feel worthless. As if he didn't value her. The way Bobby had made her feel when he'd left. He'd never used that word, but that's the way she'd felt—as if he'd used her as a distraction, as if he hadn't valued her enough to stay. The same way her parents had made her feel. As if she wasn't worth coming home for.

The only person who hadn't made her feel like that had been Gran. Solid. Dependable. Warm and loving. But even that had changed now. Her gran was a mere shadow of her former self. And what about those letters? She really needed to sit down and decide what she wanted to do with them.

'Cass?'

She was startled. Brad's forehead was wrinkled. He'd still been talking to her, and she'd been lost in her own thoughts. 'What?' she answered quickly.

'You didn't hear me, did you?'

She shook her head. 'You've given me a lot to think about. Maybe I should leave? Maybe you don't need any more distractions.' Her mind could only focus on one thing and she stood up again, ready to leave.

But he was quicker than her, and it took him less than a second to have her in his arms. His face was just above hers. His stubbled jaw, tanned skin and blue eyes definitely distracted *her*.

'I said it was nice to meet someone who enjoyed Christmas so much. Last year is something I don't want to repeat. I was hoping you would help try to get me into the spirit.'

She blinked. He was using her weak spot. Her Christmas rush. And he was doing it with that lazy smile on his face and his fingers winding under her T-shirt.

She sighed. 'This isn't all just going to be okay. I'm going to need some time—to see how I feel.' Then the sticking point came to the forefront of her brain. 'And are you still just using me as a distraction?'

His head moved slowly from side to side. 'I'm not using you as anything. I just want to be around you, Cass. I have no idea where this is going to go. I have no idea what's going to happen between us. But I'd like to find out. What do you say?'

There it was. That feeling. For five weeks he'd made her feel special. Made her feel wanted and important— as if she were the centre of his life. She wanted to say a hundred things. She wanted to sit him down and ask more questions. But his fingers were trailing up her side…

'I need some time to think about all this, Brad. You certainly know how to spring something on a girl.'

He pulled back a little. 'I know, and I'm sorry. I should have told you about Melody.'

Right now she didn't know what to do. She'd learned more about Brad in the last fifteen minutes than she had in the last five weeks. He was hurt, he was damaged. She had seen that in his eyes. And for the last five weeks he'd come to work every day and been a conscientious and proficient doctor. Could she have done the same?

Who did he really have here as a friend? Who was there for him to talk to, to share with, apart from her?

More importantly, did she really want to walk away right now?

It would be the sensible thing to do. She was already feeling hurt, and walking away now could save her from any more heartache in the future. But she'd still need to work with him, she'd still see him at work every single day. How would she cope then? And how would she feel if she saw him with anyone else?

The thought sent a chill down her spine. She didn't want to see him with anyone else. In her head he was already *hers*. And even if this didn't go anywhere, why shouldn't she enjoy what they had right now? She certainly wouldn't mind a repeat of last night. The sooner, the better.

Her hands wound around his neck. 'How about we try to create some new Christmas memories—some nice ones—ones that you could only experience here with me in Scotland?'

He nodded his head slowly. 'That sounds like a plan. What do I have to do in return?'

A thousand suggestions sprang to mind—most of them X-rated. She couldn't stand the pain she'd seen in his eyes earlier. But this definitely wasn't what she'd signed up for. She had to think about herself. She didn't want to end up hurt and alone. She didn't want to end up without Brad.

'I'm sure I'll think of something,' she murmured as she took him by the hand and led him back to the bedroom.

CHAPTER SIX

15 November

CASSIDY hurried up the stairs. Her cardigan was useless this morning, and her new-style uniform wasn't keeping out the freezing temperatures. She touched one of the old-fashioned radiators positioned nearby the hallway. Barely lukewarm. That was the trouble in old stone buildings with antiquated heating systems; the temperature barely rose to anything resembling normal.

The true Scottish winter had hit with a blast over the last few days. This morning, on the way to work Cassidy had slipped and skidded twice on the glistening pavements. She dreaded to think what A and E had been like last night.

Brad had been on call, so she hadn't seen him. He'd phoned her once, around midnight, to say he was expecting a few admissions and to chat for a few minutes. But things had felt a little strained—just as they had for the last week. She still couldn't get her head around all this. Not least the part he hadn't told her he had a daughter.

But the thing she was struggling with most was how much she actually liked him. It didn't matter her head had told her he was ultimately unsuitable. For the last few weeks she'd spent every minute with him. And no matter how confused she was, one emotion topped the rest. She was happy.

Brad made her happy. Spending time with him made her happy. Talking to him every day made her happy. Working with him made her happy. Cuddling up on the sofa with him made her happy. Kissing made her *very* happy, and anything else…

Her heart sank as she saw the bright lights and bustling figures at the end of the corridor. It wasn't even seven o'clock in the morning and her normally darkened ward was going like a fair.

She strode into the ward, glancing at the board. Jackie, one of her nurses, came out of the treatment room, holding a medicine cup with pills and clutching an electronic chart.

'What's going on, Jackie?' She could see instantly that the normally cool and reliable member of staff looked frazzled. Jackie had worked nights here for over twenty years—it took a lot to frazzle her.

Jackie looked pale and tired, and she had two cardigans wrapped around her. 'What do you think?' She pointed at the board. 'I'll give you a full report in a few minutes, but we've had six admissions in the last few hours and we need to clear some beds—there are another four in A and E waiting to come up.'

Cassidy nodded quickly. 'What kind of admissions?'

Jackie pointed at the window to the still-dark view outside. 'All elderly, all undernourished, two with hypothermia and the other four all with ailments affected by the cold. Just what we always see this time of year.'

The stream of elderly, vulnerable patients reminded Cassidy of her gran.

'You rang?' Lucy appeared at Cassidy's side.

'I heard you needed to transfer four patients to my ward. Thought it would be easier if I just came along, got the report and then transferred them along myself.'

Cassidy nodded. 'Perfect.' She walked over to Jackie and took the medicine cup and electronic chart from her hands. 'Introduce me to this patient and I'll take over from you, then you can hand over to Lucy before we do the report this morning.'

Jackie nodded happily. 'That's great. If we get these patients transferred, I'll give you a proper handover before the beds get filled again.' She shrugged her shoulders. 'Brad's around here somewhere. I saw him a few moments ago. He hasn't stopped all night and…' she smiled '…our normally tanned doctor is looking distinctly pale this morning.' She winked at Cass. 'I hope he hasn't been having too many late nights.'

Cassidy froze. The words sank in quickly. She didn't think that anyone knew about Brad and herself. But she should have known better. Word always spread quickly in a hospital like this.

She tried to regain her composure and pretend she hadn't heard the comment—best not to make a big deal of these things and hope the gossip would disperse quickly.

Half an hour later, with the report given and Jackie quickly leaving to go home, Cassidy gave a sigh and went to make a cup of tea. The breakfast trolley had just rolled onto the ward. The auxiliary nurses and domestics were helping the patients, and her two staff nurses had started the morning drug round.

Lucy appeared at her side. 'Make one for me, too, please. I've just taken the last patient round to my ward.'

Cassidy nodded and put two tea bags into mugs. She could kill for a skinny caramel latte right now.

Lucy nudged her. 'So, spill. What's happening with you and Dr Wonderful? I haven't seen you for over a week.'

Cassidy bit the inside of her lip. There was no point beating around the bush. Lucy would only pester her until she told anyway. She poured the boiling water into the cups.

Lucy nudged her again. 'Come on. Is the prediction going to come true? Are you going to be a Christmas bride?'

Cassidy dropped her teaspoon into the sink. 'What? Are you mad?' She'd forgotten all about smelly-cat woman and her mad predictions.

'What's wrong? I thought things were going swimmingly between you and surf boy. Come on, you must have done the dirty deed by now—surely?'

Cassidy felt the instant flush as the heat spilled into her cheeks. It was just a pity her body didn't know how to tell lies.

'I knew it! Well—tell all. Is he wonderful?'

She took a deep breath. 'Do you want me to answer everything at once?'

'I just want you to say something. Anything. What's wrong, Cass?'

'Well, in that case…' She counted off on her fingers. 'No, I definitely won't be a Christmas bride—and I'd forgotten all about that rubbish. Yes, I've done the dirty deed. Yes, it was wonderful—or it was until the next day when he told me he had a daughter.'

'A daughter? Brad has a daughter?'

Cassidy nodded slowly.

'Why hasn't he ever mentioned her? What's the big secret?'

Cassidy picked up her tea and leaned back against

the sink. 'The big secret is he doesn't know where she is. Her mother vanished with her two years ago. Apparently she fell in love with some doctor from the US and didn't tell Brad anything about it. He thinks she didn't want to get into a custody battle with him, so basically she did a moonlight flit.'

Lucy looked stunned and shook her head slowly. 'Wow, he's a dark horse, isn't he? I would never have guessed.'

Cassidy sighed again. 'Neither would I.'

There was silence for a few seconds. Lucy touched her arm. 'Whoa, you've got it bad, girl, haven't you?'

Cassidy closed her eyes. 'You could say that.'

Lucy stepped in front of her, clutching her steaming cup of tea with one hand and wagging her finger with the other. 'What happened to Cassidy Rae and *"I'm never going to fall in love with another foreign doctor"*? Where did she go? And what's the big deal about Brad having a daughter? She's lost. The US is a big place, and chances are she might never be found.'

'Cassidy Rae met Brad Donovan. That's what happened. And as for his daughter, I've no idea what will happen. But one thing is for sure—ultimately he won't stay in Scotland with me.'

Lucy leaned forward and gave her a hug. 'Cassidy, you might be making a whole lot of something out of nothing.'

Cassidy stopped for a few moments. Maybe Lucy was right. He hadn't managed to find Melody so far—and that was with a private investigator working for him. Maybe he would never find her? Maybe she could just forget about Melody and start to focus on them again?

But she still had an uneasy feeling in her stomach.

Brad wouldn't stay in Scotland—whether he found his daughter or not. Why on earth was she pursuing a relationship with a man who wasn't right for her?

She shook her head. 'A daughter isn't nothing, Lucy. It's a whole big something. What happens if we get serious, and then he gets a call to say his daughter has been found? I'll be left high and dry while he jets off somewhere to find his lost child. It's hardly the ideal setup for a lasting relationship.'

Lucy took a sip of her tea, watching Cassidy carefully. 'That's the first time I've ever heard you say anything like that.'

'Like what?'

'The whole words—"lasting relationship". I never even heard you say that about Mr Spain. You must really like our Dr Donovan.'

'I guess I do.' There. She'd said the words out loud. And to someone other than herself. It almost felt like a confession.

A little smile appeared at the corner of Lucy's mouth. 'That's what Lynn and I were talking about at Belinda the fortune-teller's house. We'd already pegged Brad for you and thought you'd make a nice couple.'

Cassidy stared at her as memories of that night and their knowing nods sprang up in her brain. 'You've got to be joking.'

Lucy shook her head, looking quite pleased with herself. 'No. We thought you'd be a good fit together. And we were right.'

Cassidy put down her mug and started to fiddle with her hair clip. 'Well, you can't exactly say that now, can you?'

'Yes, I can. I still think you're a good fit.' She folded her arms across her chest. 'So what's been the outcome of Brad's big disclosure? Did you run screaming from the room? Have a tantrum? Go off in a huff?'

Cassidy lowered her head. 'That's just it. There's not really been an outcome. I'm still seeing him and we've talked about it a few times—but we've really only skirted around the edges.' She shrugged her shoulders. 'I've no idea what the big outcome will be.' She shook her head, 'I don't think he knows either.'

Lucy's brow puckered. She nipped Cassidy's arm. 'Who are you, and what have you done with the real Cassidy Rae? The one that always knows precisely what she, and everyone around about her, is doing?'

'Don't, Lucy. Don't remind me how much of an idiot I'm being.'

Lucy's face broke into a smile as she tipped the rest of her tea down the sink and rinsed her cup. 'I don't think you're being an idiot, Cass. For the first time in your life I think you are head over heels in love.' And with that comment she walked out the ward, leaving a shocked Cass still standing at the sink.

The rest of Cassidy's shift was bedlam. Every patient that was admitted was elderly and suffering from effects of the cold. It broke her heart.

'Is this the last one?' she asked as Brad appeared next to another patient being wheeled onto the ward.

He shook his head and ran his hand through his rumpled hair. 'Nope. I've just been paged by the doctor on-call service. They're sending another one in. Ten patients in the last twenty-four hours, all suffering from some effects of cold.' He shook his head in disbelief. 'You don't see this often in Australia. I think I've only ever looked after one case of hypothermia before. Today has been a huge learning curve.'

'Why so many?'

'The temperature apparently dropped to minus twenty last night. Some of these patients only get social-care services during the week—so some of them weren't discovered until this morning. The sad thing is, only two had heating systems that weren't working. The rest were just too scared to put them on because of the huge rise in their heating bills.'

Cassidy waited as they moved their patient over into the hospital bed. He was very frail, hardly any muscle tone at all, his skin hanging in folds around his thin frame. She bundled the covers around him. 'Go and see if you can find any spare duvets or blankets,' she asked one of the nursing auxiliaries.

Brad handed over his chart. 'Frank Johnson is eighty, lives alone and has a past history of COPD and heart disease. You can see he's underweight. He hasn't been eating, and when he was admitted his temperature was thirty-four degrees centigrade. He'd got so confused he'd actually started taking his clothes off, as he thought he was overheating. He was barely conscious when the social-care staff found him this morning.'

Cassidy nodded. It wasn't the first time she'd heard this. She looked at the IV fluids currently connected—often the patients admitted with hypothermia were also dehydrated. 'What's the plan for him?'

Brad pointed to the chart. 'He's been in A and E for a few hours, and his temperature is gradually climbing. It's thirty-six now, still below normal, but he's certainly less confused. Try and get some more fluids and some food into him. I want four-hourly obs and refer him to Social Services and Dietetics. We've got to try and get him some better assistance.' He waved his hand around the ward.

'In fact, those rules apply to just about everyone

that's been admitted in the last twenty-four hours.' He looked down at his own bare arms, where his hairs were practically standing on end. 'It doesn't help that this place is freezing, too. What's going on?'

Cassidy gave him a weary smile. 'Old hospital, old heating system. This place is always like this in winter.'

'Tomorrow I'm going to bring in a sleeping bag and walk about in it. Do you think they'll get the hint and try to sort this place out?'

She laughed. 'That would be a sight to see. But good luck. Look at all the staff on the ward—all wearing two cardigans over their uniforms. I hate long sleeves—it's an infection-control hazard. But the temperature in this place is ridiculous. I can hardly tell them to take them off.'

'If you come into my office, I can think of an alternative way to heat you up.'

Cassidy's cheeks instantly flushed and she looked around to check no one had heard his comment. 'Brad!'

He gave her a wicked smile. 'We both know cold temperatures can cause confusion, and it wouldn't do for the doctors and nurses to be confused. I'm just trying to keep us at the top of our game.'

She titled her head to one side. 'Dr Donovan, if the cold is getting to you, I'll even go so far as to make you a cup of coffee. That should heat you up.'

'And if I'd prefer something else?'

'Then you'll just have to wait.' She folded her arms across her chest. It was almost time for the shift change—time to go home. And Brad must be due to finish as he'd been on call the night before. He looked knackered. As if he could keel over at any moment. But he could still manage to give her that sexy smile and those come-to-bed eyes. And no matter how much she told herself she should walk away, she just couldn't.

'I have something for you.'

'What?'

He pulled something from the pocket of his pale blue scrubs. A pair of rumpled tickets. Cassidy recognised the insignia on them instantly. Her mouth fell open. 'The skating rink! You remembered.'

'Of course I remembered. You said you wanted to go skating the night the ice rink opened in George Square so I bought us some tickets.'

She stared at the tickets. There it was again. Just when everything in her head was giving her lots of reasons to end this relationship. Just when she hadn't been alone with him for a few days and felt as though she was starting to shake him out her system—he did something like this.

Something thoughtful. Something kind. Something that would matter only to her. He'd even managed to plan ahead—a trait distinctly lacking in most men she knew.

'So are we going to capture the spirit of Christmas?' he whispered in her ear.

One look from those big blue eyes and he was instantly back in her system. Like a double-shot espresso. 'You bet ya!' She smiled at him.

20 November

'I don't think we need an ice rink. These pavements are bad enough,' Brad grumbled as he grabbed hold of Cassidy's waist to stop her skidding one more time.

She slid her hand, encased in a red leather glove, into

his. 'Don't be such a grump. And look at this place, it's buzzing! Isn't it great?'

Brad looked around. He had to admit Glasgow did the whole Christmas-decoration thing well. There were gold and red Christmas lights strung along the length of Buchanan Street, twinkling against the dark night sky, trying to keep the late-night shoppers in the mood for Christmas. The street was thronged with hundreds of people, all wrapped against the bitter-cold weather, their warm breath visible in the cold night air.

But even though the lights were impressive, he couldn't take his eyes off Cassidy. She seemed to have a coat for every colour of the rainbow. And in the last few days he had seen them all.

But it was her grandmother's red wool coat that suited her most, even though it probably wouldn't withstand the freezing temperatures of tonight.

This evening Cassidy had layered up with two cardigans beneath the slim-fitting coat. She had accessorised with a black hat and scarf and red leather gloves, with a pair of thick black boots on her feet. But even in all those clothes it was her eyes that sparkled most.

As they turned the corner into George Square, the lights were even brighter.

An international Christmas market filled the edges of the square, immediately swamping them in a delicious array of smells. The ice rink took up the middle of the square, with a huge Christmas tree—still to be lit—at one end and an observation wheel at the other. Around the edges were an old-fashioned helter-skelter, a café/bar and a merry-go-round. Families were everywhere, children chattering with excitement about the lights being switched on.

For a second Brad felt something twisting around

his heart. He wished more than anything that Melody could be here with him now. He'd never experienced Christmas in a cold climate, and he'd love it if his daughter could see this with him. He'd even seen an ad posted on the hospital notice-board the other day about a Santa's grotto with real, live reindeer down on the Ayrshire coast. If only he could take Melody to see something like that. The thought instantly clouded his head with difficult memories and yearnings.

He watched as a father lifted his daughter up onto one of the huge white horses with red reins on the merry-go-round. As the music started and the ride slowly began to move, he could see the father standing next to the horse, holding his daughter safely in place as her face glowed with excitement.

'Brad?'

He turned abruptly. Cassidy was watching him with her all-seeing, all-knowing brown eyes. She gave his arm a little tug. 'Are you okay?'

She followed his eyes to the merry-go-round, the question hesitating on her lips.

This wasn't the time to be melancholy. This was the time to be positive and thankful that he could create new memories with someone who tugged at his heart-strings. He reached out and grabbed her leather-gloved hand. 'Have I told you how beautiful you look tonight in your grandmother's coat? That red suits you perfectly.'

He pulled her forward for a kiss, ducking underneath the black furred hat that was currently containing her wayward curls. 'Do you remember those little girls who used to be on top of the chocolate boxes at Christmas? That's just what you look like.'

'Welcome, everyone.' The compère's voice echoed around the square and they turned to face him.

'Who is he?' Brad whispered.

'Some reality TV star,' she whispered back, 'but I've no idea which one.'

The guy was swamped in the biggest coat Brad had even seen. He obviously wasn't from around these parts. 'We're here in Glasgow tonight to light up our Christmas tree.'

There was a cheer around about them.

'Can anyone guess what colour the tree lights will be this year?'

He waited as the crowd shouted out around him. 'Let's count down and see. Altogether now, ten, nine, eight...'

Cassidy started to join in, shouting down the numbers with rest of the crowd. 'Come on, you.' She nudged him.

Brad smiled and started chanting with people around them. 'Five, four, three, two, *one*!'

There was a gasp as the tree lit up instantly with a whole host of red lights, like winter berries on the tree. A few seconds later they were joined by some tiny silver twinkling stars. A round of applause went up then, and only a few seconds later, Brad noticed Cassidy blink as a cheer erupted all around them. People were holding their hands out and laughing as the first smattering of snow appeared in tiny flakes around them. It only took a few seconds for some to land in the curls of her hair and on her cheeks. She gave a big smile, looking up-wards to the dark sky. 'Nothing like a little dusting of snow for the occasion.'

Brad pulled his hand out of his thermal glove and held it out like the people around them. 'First time I've been snowed on,' he said, watching as the tiny flakes melted instantly as they touched his hand. 'This is fabulous.'

Cassidy sighed. 'Wait until the morning. If the snow lies on the roads and streets, it will be even more treacherous than before. In my experience snow generally means we'll be more busy at work.'

Brad grabbed her waist again. 'Work? Let's not talk about work. Let's go and have some fun.'

They walked around some of the nearby market stalls. Cassidy sampled some sautéed potatoes with onions and bacon then moved on to the next stall to try their vast array of chocolates. 'What's your favourite?' Brad asked. 'I'll buy you some.'

Cassidy's nose wrinkled and she glanced over her shoulder. 'Actually, I'm a tat collector. I'd prefer another ornament for my Christmas tree.'

He gave her a surprised look. 'A tree ornament instead of chocolate? I would never have guessed. Well, let's see what they've got.'

She was like a child in the proverbial sweetie shop as she oohed and aahed over tiny green sequin trees, little white angels and traditional wooden crafted Santa Claus ornaments. A few moments later Cassidy had selected a Russian doll for her tree with red and gold zigzags adorning its tiny wooden frame. 'This is perfect,' she said. 'I've never seen anything like this before.'

Brad smiled and handed over some money, but not before picking up a second one for Melody. She would have loved this stall, too.

They walked over to the nearby booth to collect their skates and spent a few minutes sitting at the side, lacing them up. Cassidy stood up, wobbling around as she tried to gain her balance. Brad appeared at her side, equally unsteady. 'Are we ready for this?' He held out his hand towards her.

They stepped onto the ice together. It was busy, families skating and wobbling with interlinked hands as they tried to find their way around the ice. Brad took a few moments to get his balance—he'd only ever skated a few times in his life but had always managed to stay upright. Cassidy, however, took him completely by surprise.

She let go of his hand and within seconds was gliding over the ice as if it was something she did every day. Her paces were long and even as she bobbed and weaved through the crowd of people on the ice. She spun round, her red coat swinging out around her. Brad held on to the side rail for a few more seconds.

'Come on, Dr Donovan, show us what you're made of!' she shouted from the middle of the rink.

She looked gorgeous. Her cheeks were flushed with colour, and the red coat with its nipped-in waist highlighted her figure perfectly. The perfect Christmas picture.

Her words were like a challenge. And no matter how unsteady he was on the ice, Brad wasn't one to ignore a challenge. He pushed himself off as best he could towards her, nearly taking out a few children in the process. He reached her in a few seconds with only a few unsteady steps and wrapped his arms around her in the middle of the rink. 'You're a scammer, Cassidy Rae. You didn't say you knew how to ice skate.'

'You didn't ask.' Her eyes were twinkling as she pushed off and spun around him again, skating backwards for a few seconds before ending in an Olympic-style twirl.

'Show-off,' he growled. 'Where on earth did you learn how to do that?'

She started skating backwards around him. 'In Australia you surf—in Scotland you skate!' She reversed into him, allowing him to collapse his arms around her waist. 'That's not strictly true,' she said. 'I skated for around five years but, to be honest, as a young girl I was a bit flighty. I tried ballet, majorettes, country dancing and horse riding before I started skating.'

His head rested on her shoulder, his nose touching her pink flushed cheek. 'I like the sound of a flighty Cassidy Rae. She sounds like fun.'

Cassidy pushed off and turned to face him again, tilting her head to one side. 'Are you trying to say I'm not fun now, Dr Donovan?'

'Oh, you're lots of fun, Ms Rae.' He tried to take a grab at her, but his unsteady gait sent him wobbling across the ice. 'Help!'

She skated alongside him and slotted her hand into his. 'Let's just take things easy. We'll just skate around in a simple circle like the rest of the people are doing.' She pointed at some kids teetering past them. 'See? Anyone can do it.'

Brad groaned and tried to push more firmly on the ice. It was easier while Cassidy was gripping his hand, and he gained confidence as they circled round and round the rink. By the time the old-fashioned klaxon sounded, signalling the end of their session, Brad felt as though he could finally stand upright with some confidence.

'Is that an hour already? I can't believe it. I was finally starting to get the hang of this.'

'We can come back again,' said Cassidy with a smile

as she skated around him again. The rink was starting to empty as people crowded toward the small exit. He watched for a few seconds as Cassidy took advantage of the now-empty ice and did a few twirls. A squeal stopped her in her tracks.

Brad pushed through the throng, reaching a little girl who was being pulled up by her father and clutching her hand to her chest. Her face was pale and Brad could see a few drips of crimson blood on the ice at her feet.

'Let me have a look at her,' he said, lifting her up in his strong arms. 'I'm a doctor.' He turned his head towards Cassidy, who had appeared at his back. 'Can you ask the booth if they have a first-aid kit?'

The crowd parted easily, concerned by the cries of a child, and he walked unsteadily to the adjacent wooden bench at the side of the rink. He positioned the child underneath the nearest light and held her hand tightly for a few seconds.

'What's your name?' he asked the pale-faced, trembling little girl.

'Victoria,' she whispered. Brad smiled. It was clear she was trying very hard not to cry. Her father had his arms wrapped around her shoulders.

'She just fell over as we were waiting to get off the ice. Someone must have caught her hand with their skate.'

Cassidy appeared with the first-aid kit and opened it quickly, pulling out some gloves, antiseptic wipes, sterile dressings and elastic bandages.

Brad got off the bench and lowered himself near the ground, his face parallel with Victoria's. 'I'm just going to have a little look at your hand—just for a second. Is that okay?'

She nodded but clutched her hand even closer to her chest.

He pulled off his gloves and held his hand at the side of her face. 'Can you feel how cold my fingers are?' He touched her cheek and she flinched a little, before smiling and nodding.

He picked up the gloves. 'I'm going to put these really funky blue gloves on before I have a little look. I might want to put a special bandage on your hand—is that okay?'

Victoria nodded, still looking tearful, but held her hand out tremulously to Brad.

Brad worked swiftly. He cleared her hand from her anorak sleeve and had a quick glance at the cut before stemming the flow of blood with a sterile pad. 'I'm going to give this a quick clean and bandage it up for you.' He nodded at Cassidy as she ripped open the antiseptic wipes for him.

'Ouch!' squealed Victoria, as the wipe lightly touched her skin.

'All done,' said Brad almost simultaneously. He took one more look now that the blood was clear, then applied another sterile non-adherent pad and elastic bandage to put a little pressure on the wound. He looked at Cassidy. 'Which hospital is nearest to here?'

'The Royal Infirmary,' she answered. 'Less than five minutes in a taxi.'

Brad gave the anxious father a smile. 'I'm afraid she's going to need some stitches and the wound cleaned properly. The pad shouldn't stick to her skin and the elastic bandage gives a little pressure to stem the flow of blood before you get to the hospital. But it's not a long-term solution. Are you able to take her up to the A and E unit?'

The father nodded. He pulled a phone from his pocket and started pressing buttons. 'I have a friend who's a taxi driver in the city centre. He'll come and get us.'

Brad leaned forward and whispered in Victoria's ear. 'You're a very brave girl. And do you know what brave girls get?' He reached into his pocket and pulled out his little Russian doll. It was almost identical to the one he'd just bought for Cassidy, but this one had silver and pink zigzags and a long silver string to hang it from the tree.

'This is a special Christmas-tree decoration—just for you.'

Victoria's eyes lit up, his distraction technique working like a charm. Cassidy's felt a lump at the back of her throat that she tried to swallow. He must have bought an extra ornament when he'd paid for hers earlier. And it didn't take much imagination to know who he'd bought it for.

There it was.

Right in front of her, glowing like a beacon. All the reasons why Brad shouldn't be without his daughter. She gathered up the remnants of the first-aid kit, stuffing them back inside, and disappeared back to the booth.

She couldn't watch that. She couldn't watch him interact with a child in such an easy and relaxed manner. It showed what she already knew deep down but hadn't wanted to admit.

Brad was good with kids. No, Brad was *great* with kids. He knew just when to act and what to say. He deserved to have kids. He deserved to be with his daughter. He deserved to know where she was and play a part in her life.

And even though he hadn't said much around her

over the last few days, it was clear that Melody was in the forefront of his mind.

She felt ashamed. Ashamed of the words she'd uttered and the thoughts she'd had while she'd been talking to Lucy. Thoughts that he might be willing to forget about his daughter and just have a life with her. What kind of person was she?

She'd seen the haunted look in his eyes earlier when he'd been watching the father and daughter on the merry-go-round. But she hadn't been able to say the words—to ask him if he was hurting and what she could do to help.

She looked over at him now, and he gave her a wave as he walked with Victoria and her father to a black cab parked at the side of the square. Her hand lifted automatically in response, but it was the expression on his face that was killing her.

She'd never seen Brad look so comfortable and so at ease.

She knew what he needed more than anything. He needed to find his daughter.

CHAPTER SEVEN

29 November

'Hi, Cassidy, nice to see you.'

'Hi, Grace, how's Gran today?'

The nurse walked around the desk and joined Cassidy. 'She's in here today,' she said as she walked into a large sitting room looking out over well-tended gardens. 'She's been really confused these last few days, but unusually quiet, too.'

'Is she eating okay?'

Grace nodded. 'She's eating well. She seems quite focused when she gets her meals. But as soon as she's finished, she's off wandering.' She walked over and touched Cassidy's gran on her shoulder. 'Tillie, your granddaughter is here to see you again.'

Cassidy's heart fell as her gran barely even looked up, her eyes still fixed on the garden. She gave Grace a half-hearted smile. 'Thank you, Grace.'

'No problem. Give me a shout if you need anything.'

Cassidy sat down in the chair opposite her gran. Her heart was fluttering in her chest. She was wearing her gran's red wool coat and she wondered if she would notice. She pulled off her leather gloves and reached over and took her gran's hand.

'Hi, Gran.' She brushed a kiss on her cheek.

Tillie looked at her only for a second, her confusion immediately evident. She didn't recognise Cassidy.

Cassidy took a deep breath. It had been like this for the last few months. The little spells of recognition and memory were becoming fewer and fewer. She'd had some episodes where she'd mistaken Cassidy for her mother, but it had been over a year since she'd recognised Cassidy for herself.

This was the part that broke her heart. Her gran had always been her confidante, her go-to person. The person who gave her the best advice in the world—something she badly needed right now.

She opened her bag and stared at the pile of envelopes inside. They'd revealed more than she wanted to know. But it was the photograph that haunted her most. Her gran had always been warm and caring towards her. But she couldn't remember ever seeing her gran like she was in that photograph—her eyes filled with adoration for the man standing by her side. Her whole face glowing with happiness. Had she really known her gran at all?

'I've been at the house, Gran. Everything's fine.' Her fingers caught the edge of the collar of her coat and she bit her lip nervously. 'I found this beautiful coat in the one of the cupboards. It was wrapped up with some letters.' She pulled the bundle from her bag, But Tillie's eyes were still fixed on the garden. Cassidy swallowed, trying to get rid of the lump in her throat.

The garden was covered in frost and a light dusting of snow, but the beds in front of the window brimmed with life. They were filled with evergreen bushes with red berries, coloured heather plants and deep pink pernettya plants. The planters around the edges had an eruption of coloured cyclamen and white heathers. It was beautiful.

Cassidy looked out over the horizon. Everything about this spelled Christmas to her. She wondered what plants they had in Australia at this time of year. Would there be anything as nice as this? How could anyone feel festive in a baking-hot climate?

She'd thought about that often over the last few days, the thoughts just drifting into her mind when she least expected them. She'd had numerous friends who'd emigrated and they all raved about it, saying it had been the best move of their lives. They sent her pictures of spending Christmas Day on the beach, cooking on the barbeque or having dinner in the sunshine next to the pool.

But Christmas always meant cold weather, frost and snow to Cassidy. She just couldn't imagine it any other way. Could she really feel festive in a bikini?

'Hello, dear. Who are you?'

Cassidy flinched and pushed the thoughts from her mind as her gran spoke to her, her eyes suddenly bright with life.

'I'm Cassidy, your granddaughter. I've come for a visit, Gran.'

'How lovely. Do you have any tea?'

Cassidy smiled. Her gran was a true tea genie and could drink twenty cups a day. She slid her hand into her gran's. 'I've come to tell you that I've met a nice man, Gran. One who's making me think about a lot of things.'

Tillie nodded but didn't say anything. Cassidy took a deep breath. 'When I found your coat, I also found a parcel of letters.' She hesitated for a second. 'I hope you don't mind, but I read them, Gran. The ones from Peter Johnson, your US Air Force friend.'

She paused, waiting to see if would get any reaction. She knew some people would think she was strange, trying to have a normal conversation with a confused old lady, but to Cassidy she couldn't communicate any other way. She loved and respected her gran, and she hoped beyond hope that some of what she said might get through. 'He looked lovely, Gran.'

She pulled out the black-and-white photograph. 'I found a picture of you—you look so happy.' She couldn't help the forlorn sound to her voice as she handed the photo to her gran.

Tillie took it in her frail fingers and touched the surface of the photograph. 'So pretty,' she murmured, before handing it back.

Cassidy sat backwards in her chair. 'He wrote you some lovely letters. You never told me about him—I wish you had.' She stared out the windows, lost in thought.

She'd read the letters the night before, tears rolling down her face. Peter Johnson had met her gran while he'd been stationed in Prestwick with the US Army Air Force. His letters were full of young love and hope for the future. Filled with promises of a life in the US. Most had come from Prestwick, with a few from Indiana at a later date.

Had he been her gran's first love? What had happened to him? Had he gone back to the US and forgotten about her? Her gran could have had the chance of another life, on another continent. Had she wanted to go to the US? What had stopped her? Had she suffered from any of the doubts and confusion that she herself was feeling right now?

She looked back at her gran, who was running her fingers over the sleeve of her coat. 'I wish you could tell me, Gran.' Tears were threatening to spill down her cheeks. 'I really need some advice. I need you to tell me what I should do.'

'What a lovely colour,' her gran said suddenly, before sitting back in her chair. 'Did you bring tea?' she asked.

Cassidy gave Tillie's hand a squeeze. 'I'll go and get you some tea, Gran,' she said, standing up and heading over to the kitchen. She'd been here often enough to know where everything was kept.

The girl in the kitchen gave her a nod and handed over a teapot and two cups. She glanced at her watch. 'I thought it was about that time for your gran. I was just about to bring this over.' She smiled as Cassidy lifted up the tray, before reaching over and touching the shoulder of her coat. 'What a beautiful coat, Cassidy. It's a really nice style. It suits you.'

Cassidy blushed. 'Thank you. I found it the other day.' She nodded over her shoulder. 'It was Gran's.'

'Really? I'm surprised. It looks brand new.' She raised her eyebrows. 'I bet she cut up a storm in that coat a few years ago.'

Cassidy's felt her shoulders sag. 'I don't know, Karen. Truth is, I never saw my gran wear this coat. But I found a picture of her in it and she looked amazing.'

'I bet she did.' Karen gave her a smile. 'You know, Cassidy, I know it's hard seeing your gran like this, but you've got to remember that she's happy here. Although she's frail, her physical health is good for someone her age and most days she seems really content.'

Cassidy nodded gratefully. 'I know, Karen.' She looked over to where her gran was sitting, staring out the window again. 'I just wish I could have the old her back sometimes—even for just a few minutes.'

Karen gave her arm a squeeze. 'I know, honey.'

Cassidy carried the tea tray over and waited a few minutes before pouring a cup for her gran. She was fussy about her tea—not too weak, not too strong, with just the right amount of milk.

Cassidy kept chatting as she sat next to her. It didn't matter to her that her gran didn't understand or acknowledge what she was saying. It felt better just telling her things. In the last year she'd found that just knowing she'd told her gran something could make her feel a million times better—sometimes even help her work things out in her head.

'I've met a nice Australian man. He's a doctor who's working with me right now.' Her gran nodded and smiled. Often it seemed as if she liked to hear the music and tone of Cassidy's voice. 'The only thing is, he has a little girl who is missing right now. He really wants to find her. And when he does…' she took a deep breath '…he'll go.'

The words sounded so painful when she said them out loud.

And for a second they stopped her in her tracks.

What would she do if Brad just upped and disappeared? How would she feel if she could never see him again?

It didn't take long for the little part of her she didn't like to creep into her brain again. Chances were Melody might never be found. Brad might decide to stay in Scotland for a while longer.

She felt a wave of heat wash over her like a comfort blanket. That would be perfect. Maybe she could consider a trip to Australia? That wouldn't be so hard. It was a beautiful country and it might even be interesting to see the differences in nursing in another country.

She looked outside at the frosty weather. Her gran

had started singing under her breath. A sweet lullaby that she used to sing to Cassidy as a child. Memories came flooding back, of dark nights in front of the fire cuddled up on Gran's couch.

Part of the issue for Cassidy was that she loved the Scottish winters and cold weather. As a pale-skinned Scot, she'd never been a fan of the blazing-hot sunshine. And even when she'd gone on holiday, she hadn't lain beside the pool for a fortnight; she'd needed to be up and about doing things.

Most people she knew would love the opportunity to live in a warmer climate but Cassidy had never even considered it. Not for a second.

Could she really start to consider something like that now?

Everything was making her head spin. Her relationship with Brad was becoming serious. She really needed to sit down and talk to him again.

She looked at her gran, who was sipping her tea delicately, trying to hear the words she thought her gran might say in her head.

She could imagine the elderly lady telling her not to be so pathetic. To make up her mind about what she wanted and to go get it. She could also sense the old-fashioned disapproval her gran might have about the fact Brad had a child with someone else. A child he wasn't being allowed to fulfil his parental duties towards. Her gran would certainly have had something to say about that.

But would she have been suspicious like some of Brad's colleagues in Australia? Or would she have been sympathetic towards him?

Cassidy just wasn't sure. And finding the letters and photographs made her even less sure. She'd thought she'd known everything about her gran. Turned out she hadn't. And now she'd no way of picking up those lost strands of her life.

She heaved a sigh and looked out over the garden again. She was going to have to sort this out for herself.

30 November

Brad came rushing into the restaurant ten minutes late, with his tie skewed to one side and his top button still undone. 'I'm so sorry,' he gasped as he sat down opposite her. 'There was a last-minute admission just before I left, and Luca was at a cardiac arrest so I couldn't leave.'

Cassidy gave him a smile and lifted her glass of wine towards him. 'No worries, Brad, I started without you.'

He reached over and pulled the bottle of wine from the cooler at the side of the table and filled his glass. She leaned across the table. 'Here, let me,' she said as her deft fingers did up his top button and straightened his tie.

She didn't care that he'd been late. His conscientiousness at work was one of the reasons she liked him so much.

He raised his glass to her. 'Cheers.' The glasses clinked together and Cassidy relaxed back into her chair.

Brad ducked under the table. 'Here, I bought you something.' He handed a plastic bag over to Cassidy.

She raised her eyebrows. 'Did you wrap it yourself?' she quipped.

'Ha, ha. Just look and see what it is.'

Cassidy peeked inside the plastic bag and gingerly put her hand inside—all she could see was a mixture of red and green felt. She pulled out her present and felt a mixture of surprise and a tiny bit of disappointment.

It was an advent calendar, the fabric kind with pockets for each of the twenty-four days. The kind she'd told Brad she didn't like.

She looked over at him and he gave her a beaming smile. 'I thought in the spirit of making some nice Christmas memories I would try and convert you.'

She wrinkled her nose. 'Convert me? Why?'

He shrugged. 'You like the paper-type advent calendar. I always had one of these in Australia that my mum made for me. She used to put something in the pockets for only a few days at a time because she knew I would have looked ahead otherwise.' He touched the first few pockets and she heard a rustling sound. 'And they're *not* all chocolates.'

She nodded and gave him a smile. 'So, you're trying to convert me, are you? Well, I'm willing to give it a go. But how do you plan on filling up the other pockets?'

There it was. That little twinkle in his eye as he took a sip of his wine. 'That's the thing. If you want your calendar filled, you'll have to keep letting me into your flat. In fact, I'll need unlimited access.'

She loved the way his smile stretched from ear to ear. The restaurant was dim, with subdued lighting and flickering candlelight. His eyes seemed even bluer than normal, their colour amplified as they reflected off his pale blue shirt.

'Did you plan this just so you could get into my flat?'

He shook his head, his face becoming a little more serious. 'I just think you've been a little quiet these past few days. As if something was on your mind.' His fingers reached across the table and intertwined with hers. 'I'm just trying to find a way to stay in your life.'

She felt shocked by the openness and honesty of his words. She kept her gaze stuck on the advent calendar as she tried to think of what to say. Things had been a little unsettled between them.

'I'm just a little unsure of what's happening between us,' she started slowly. She lifted her eyes. 'I like you, Brad.'

'And I like you, too, Cassidy. You know that.'

He wasn't making this any easier. It was hard enough, trying to get the words out. His fingers were tracing little circles on the palm of her hand. Just like he did after they'd made love together.

'I'm just worried that I'm getting in too deep and before we know it you'll be gone.'

His brow creased. 'Why would you think that?'

She pulled her hand away from his. It was too distracting. 'I don't know. I just think that I'm from Scotland, you're from Australia…' She threw her hands up in frustration, then levelled her gaze at him. 'I know you don't want to stay here and I don't want to move away. So where does that leave us?'

She could feel tears nestling behind her eyes. That was the last thing she wanted to happen. She didn't want to cry.

Her mind was flooded with thoughts of her gran. Truth was, she would never find out what happened between her gran and Peter Johnson. Maybe it had only been a wartime fling, with no substance behind it. Or maybe her gran had given up the chance of a lifetime to go and live abroad with the man who'd made her face sparkle.

What Cassidy would never know was whether her gran regretted her decisions. If she could go back, would she do something different?

Was *she* about to make the same mistake?

Brad reached back over and took her hand again.

'Cassidy, I have no idea what's going to happen. All I know is I love spending time with you and I don't want it to end. I've no idea what will happen in the next few years—I've been offered an extension to my job here for another six months, and I've decided to take it. You know I'm not going to stop looking for my daughter. Is that what this is all about? Melody?'

Cassidy shook her head. 'No, it's not about Melody.' Then she hesitated. 'But I don't know what to think about all that. At the end of the day, Brad, we could continue to have a relationship for the next few months and then you could get a call one day about Melody and just disappear. I don't think I could handle that.'

And there it was, staring him in the face. All the while he was practically telling her she was bullheaded and stubborn, her biggest vulnerability lay on the table between them. Abandonment.

He'd sensed it in her for a while. When she'd mentioned her ex-fiancé, her parents or her ill grandmother. That fear of being alone.

He shook his head, the expression on his face pained. 'Remember, Cassidy, I've been on the other side of this fence. I've had someone disappear out of my life with no warning. And I know how much it hurts. I would never do that to another human being.'

She could tell her words had stung, and she hadn't meant them to. It was just so difficult to describe the mishmash of emotions in her head. Even she couldn't understand them, so how could she expect Brad to?

The waiter appeared at their side with some menus, and Cassidy pulled her hand from Brad's to take one. Her eyes ran up and down the menu quickly before Brad lifted it from her hands.

'Don't tell me, you'll have the mushrooms and the chicken.'

Cassidy groaned. 'Don't tell me I'm that predictable.' She grabbed the menu back and ran her eyes along the text again with a sinking realisation that Brad was right. She *did* always have the mushrooms and the chicken. The only time she ever deviated was if neither was on the menu.

He leaned forward, giving her that smile again. 'Why don't you surprise us both and pick something totally different? In fact, close your eyes and just point at something and order that.'

Cassidy shivered. 'Yuck.' Even the thought of doing that was too much for her. Imagine if she ended up with something she didn't like—or never ate? That would be hideous. 'I can't do that, Brad, I might get seaweed or fillet steak.'

His eyes gleamed as he did a pretend shudder. 'Mmm, and that would be awful, wouldn't it? Take this as a test, Cassidy.'

'A test for what?'

He folded his napkin in his lap, as if he was choosing his words carefully. 'For a thoroughly modern woman, you can be pretty closed-minded about some things.'

An uncomfortable feeling crept down her spine. 'What do you mean?'

'You can have some pretty fixed ideas.'

Cassidy shook her head. 'I just know my own mind. There's nothing wrong with that.'

He paused. 'I didn't say there was. But sometimes you make your mind up about things without looking at the whole picture.'

Cassidy was feeling rattled now and a little irritated.

So much for a romantic dinner. 'What do you mean exactly?'

He licked his lips and she saw him take a deep breath. There was something different in his eyes. The normal laid-back look was gone. 'What I mean, Cassidy, is that you've written me—and others—off with no thought or regard for our feelings, just because we live in a different country. Now, if you'd been abroad and stayed there for a while and didn't enjoy it, it might seem a reasonable conclusion to have come to. But you haven't. You've never done it. You've never even tried. And what's more—you won't even consider it.'

He looked frustrated by her, angry even, and she felt a tight feeling spread across her chest. Not even Bobby, her Spanish fiancé, had called her like this. She'd just refused to go with him and that had been that. He hadn't questioned her reasoning behind her decision. He hadn't made *her* question her reasoning behind the decision.

But Brad hadn't finished. He was on a roll. 'It's the same with your menu choices and your Christmas traditions.' He leaned over and picked up the advent calendar. 'You say you only like the picture calendars but you've never even tried one of these, have you?' She saw his shoulders sag, tension easing out of them, and the tone of his voice altered.

'All I'm trying to do is get you to look outside your box. To look at the world that surrounds you and open your mind to other ideas, other experiences, other...' he paused before ending '...possibilities.'

He was holding his breath, waiting to see what she would say. She should stop, she should think and ponder what he was saying to her and why. But Cassidy went with her first instinct. She was mad.

She flung her napkin on the table. 'So why are you

bothering with me, Brad? You don't date someone with the idea of changing them. You date someone because you like them the way they are, not the way *you* want them to be.' She spat the words at him.

'I'm not trying to change you. I like you, everything about you. But if we have any hope of a future together, you're going to have to learn to bend a little.'

'Meaning what?'

'Meaning that I would love to promise to stay with you in Scotland for the next thirty years, but what if I do get that call about my daughter? What if I do need to go to the States? That's it for us? Just like that— because you won't even consider any other possibility?'

He made it all sound so unreasonable. So closed-minded. But inside she didn't feel like that.

'Or what if I get a great opportunity to work in another country? You won't even consider coming with me? Because you can't leave Scotland?'

'But my gran, I can't leave my gran.' It was the first thing that sprang to mind. The first brick in her feeble wall of defence.

Brad shook his head. 'I'm not asking you to leave your gran, Cassidy. Even though you know she's somewhere she's been taken care of. I'm just trying to see if you'll at least *consider* the possibility.'

Silence hung in the air between them. Her temper had dissipated as quickly as it had arisen.

He was making sense. Inside she knew he was making sense. But to admit it made her seem so petty.

The waiter appeared at their side again. 'Are you ready to order?'

Cassidy didn't even glance at the menu, she just thrust it back at the waiter. 'I'll have the chilli prawns and the Cajun salmon,' she said as she looked Brad square in the eye.

She could see the pulse at the side of his neck flickering furiously. How long had he been holding all this in? Chances were he'd been waiting to say this to her for the last few weeks. And he was right.

Although there was no way she was going to admit it right now.

Tiny little thoughts of Australia had started to penetrate her brain. Little sparks, curiosity and wonder had been creeping in over the last few weeks. Would she like it there? What would it be like to be in a different country for more than a two-week holiday?

It wasn't as if she'd never left the sunny shores of Scotland. She'd been all over the world—Spain, Italy, the US, even the Bahamas. But only for two weeks at a time. And by the time the plane had hit the tarmac back at Glasgow Airport, she'd always been glad to get back home.

But she had lots of friends who'd gone to other countries to work. The most popular place lately had been Dubai. Five of the nurses she'd worked with in Glasgow City Hospital had all upped sticks and gone to work there. All of them loved it and most had no intention of coming back to Glasgow. Two other members of staff had gone to work for aid organisations—one to Africa and one to Médecins Sans Frontières.

Why was she so different? Why had she never wanted to go and work somewhere else? Why did she feel as if her roots were firmly planted in Scottish soil?

Brad lifted the wine bottle and topped up her glass. She hadn't even heard what he'd ordered. She only hoped it was chicken so she could swap her salmon for it.

He lifted his glass to her. 'So, what do you say, Cassidy? Can we raise a toast to trying new things?'

She swallowed hard, her fingers brushing the tiny pockets of the advent calendar on the table in front of her. This couldn't be too hard. She could try this, couldn't she?

He was staring across the table at her, with those big blue eyes, tanned skin and perfect smile. Everything about him made her stomach still lurch. She'd never felt like this before. Could she honestly just walk away?

This had to be worth fighting for.

CHAPTER EIGHT

4 December

CASSIDY woke up with a smile on her face. She glanced at the calendar hanging on her wall. Maybe embracing new change wasn't such a bad thing.

Brad's gifts had proved personal and thoughtful. She'd found an orange Belgian chocolate in the first pocket—one that she'd remarked on that night at the George Square market. For once she hadn't been instantly offended by the thought of a chocolate-filled calendar.

Next had been a tiny green sequin Christmas tree complete with red string, and in the third pocket she'd found a sprig of mistletoe.

It only took her seconds to push her feet into her red slippers and wrap her dressing gown around her shoulders. Brad had been on call again last night, so she hadn't seen him.

Her brow wrinkled. Pocket number four looked distinctly flat—maybe he hadn't had time to put something in there yet? She flicked the switch on the kettle and pulled a cup from the cupboard, before finally touching the pocket. There was a faint rustling noise. She pulled a piece of paper from the pocket and unfolded it.

It said, *'Look under the tree—not everything can fit in these tiny pockets!'*

She left the kettle boiling and walked through to her living room. There, under the tree he'd helped her decorate a few days before, was a red, glistening parcel. She couldn't wipe the smile from her face as she unwrapped the paper. It was a book. But not just any book. It was the latest thriller from her favourite Glasgow author—one she'd been meaning to buy herself.

Cassidy sagged back against the cushions on her sofa. Yet another thoughtful gift. One that meant something to her. Picked up from a chance conversation they'd had in the middle of the night on one shift.

She looked out at the overcast sky. It was going to be another miserable day. Time to wrap up warmly and head up the frosty hill to the hospital. She heard a noise at her door—a key turning in the lock and a whoosh of cold air blasting across the room.

'Brad, what are you doing here?'

Brad was barely recognisable among the layers of clothing he was wearing. All she could really see clearly were his blue eyes peering out from the balaclava-type headwear he'd started wearing to protect himself from the cold. He was brandishing some cups. 'A skinny caramel latte for my favourite woman.'

She smiled. 'I'd hug you, but you're too cold.'

He sat down next to her, hands clenched around his cup. 'I'd take off my jacket but let me heat up first. It's Baltic out there.'

She laughed. 'So, you're finally connecting with our language. That's something I would normally say—not you.'

He nudged her. 'You must be rubbing off on me.' He

bent over, his cold nose brushing against her, and she let out a squeal.

'Get away, ice man!' He wrapped his arms around her, trapping her on the sofa.

'This is an emergency. I need some body heat. I can't take these cold winters!'

She pretended to squirm as he held her tight. 'Drink your coffee. That will heat you up.'

'I can think of a better way to heat up,' he whispered as he grabbed her hand and led her back through to her warm bed.

10 December

Today she had a magic wand. Pocket ten had held another little note that had led her to find it wrapped in silver paper, balanced on the branches of the tree.

He'd asked her favourite film character the other night and she'd declared she'd always wanted to be Glinda, the good witch of the north, from *The Wizard of Oz*. So he'd bought her a magic wand. And right now she really wanted to wave it above her medical receiving unit.

In the last twenty-four hours every single one of the thirty beds in the unit had been emptied and refilled. Patients were never supposed to stay in the medical receiving unit. Patients were supposed to be assessed and transferred to one of the other wards, but the current rate of transfer was ridiculous, for both the staff and the patients.

She replaced the phone receiver. Her staff was run ragged. The bed manager was getting snarky—she had patients in A and E waiting to be admitted. The normally pristine ward looked chaotic. There were a few random patient belonging bags sitting at the nurses' station, obviously misplaced or forgotten in the preceding few hours. And as for the ward clerk—she'd disappeared in tears five minutes ago.

Cassidy took a deep breath. This was the story of Scottish hospitals in the middle of an icy winter. It was only eight o'clock in the morning. She had to take control of this situation. Something was going to give. And she didn't want it to be her—or her staff.

She lifted her hands above her head. 'Everyone, stop!'

For a second there was silence. Cassidy never raised her voice on the ward and her staff looked startled. A few heads stuck out from doors down the corridor.

'Everyone...' she gestured her hands towards the desk '...come here. This will take five minutes.'

Her bewildered staff walked towards the nursing station. Some were carrying electronic nursing notes, some bed linen and towels.

Cassidy waited until they'd all assembled. One of the phlebotomists and ECG technicians appeared, too. She took another deep breath.

'Everyone, let's calm down. I want you all to take a deep breath and tell me calmly what help you need.' She laid one hand on the desk. 'I can tell you that right now, no matter what the bed manager says, we will not move another patient until after lunchtime today. We need time to assess these patients properly.'

She gestured to the bags on the floor. 'We need to make sure that patients' belongings don't go astray.' She lowered her voice. 'More importantly, I need my team to know that they do a good job.'

She could see the visible calm descending on the ward as the rumble of the meal trolley could be heard approaching. 'What about the patients in A and E?' asked one of the younger staff nurses.

Cassidy shook her head. 'A and E is full of competent nursing staff. They are more than capable of starting the assessments for their patients. I'm going to phone them now and tell them to arrange breakfast and lunch for those patients. They won't be moving any more up here until after lunchtime.'

A number of shoulders relaxed around her.

'What about the bed manager?'

Cassidy smiled. 'Let me deal with her. Now...' she looked over at the staff surrounding her '...Fiona and Claire, go for your tea break. Michael...' she nodded to the tall, dark-haired nurse beside her '...you start the drug round. Linda and Ann, you help Joanne, the domestic, with the breakfasts.' The two auxiliaries scurried off, glad to have a simple task to perform.

Cassidy noticed Janice, the ward clerk, sniffing at her side. 'What's wrong, Janice?'

'It's the off-duty. It was supposed to be in for yesterday. But there's still a few shifts that need to be covered.'

Cassidy's eyes swept over the blank spaces in the book. Her brain shifted into gear. One of her senior staff nurses had asked if she could start taking over the off-duty rota. And she'd made an absolute mess of it, something Cassidy would have to deal with at a later date.

Just what she would have expected. One short for the night shift on Christmas Eve. The same thing happened every year without fail.

Her mind drifted back to the night at smelly-cat-woman's house. She almost cringed as she remembered she'd offered to do the night shift if she was a Christmas bride.

She could almost laugh out loud. Although the thought didn't seem anything like as ridiculous as it had before.

Things between her and Brad were good—better than good. Her brain had started to rationalise things for her. Australia was one day away. All twenty-four hours of one day, but still only one day away from Scotland.

The more stories he told her about his life there, the more curious she became. But something else was becoming clearer to her. Just like it had when Brad had naturally came home to her flat the other day after his shift had finished.

She wanted to see him all the time. She wanted to be with him all the time. If he was on call and she didn't see him one day, she missed him. Something that had hit her like a bolt out of the blue.

Cassidy had spent the last two years living life on her own. Her gran's memory had deteriorated to the point she didn't recognise Cassidy, and it had left her feeling even more alone than before. She rarely heard from her parents. But all of sudden it felt as if she had family again.

And having Brad around just felt so *right*.

She didn't expect to be a Christmas bride, but she did expect to have Brad in her future.

She pointed. 'Swap these two around. Lorna prefers her night shifts together. And I'll cover the night shift on Christmas Eve. Okay?'

'Are you sure?' The clerk was looking at her through red-rimmed eyes.

She gave her shoulder a squeeze. 'Yes, I'm sure. Now, just send it in and go make yourself a cup of tea.'

She went through to her office and made an uncomfortable call to the bed manager then walked quickly through the ward, helping the auxiliaries sit some patients up in bed for breakfast and helping another few patients into chairs. Luca appeared at her side and started reviewing some of the patients who had been admitted overnight. He gave her a smile. 'I hear you're leading a revolt up here this morning.'

She nodded. 'Happy to join in?'

'Absolutely. I feel as if I hardly got to see some of these patients in A and E.'

'It was the same for my staff. We weren't getting the chance to assess the patients properly before we sent them on.' She looked up and down the length of the ward, which seemed much calmer. 'I'm not allowing that to happen. We have a duty of care to these patients and I won't compromise.'

'Tell that to the bed manager.'

'I just did.' She shrugged her shoulders. 'Although she hates me right now, first and foremost she is a nurse, so she does understand the issues.'

The phone started ringing again, and since she'd sent the ward clerk off for tea, Cassidy leaned forward and picked it up. 'Medical receiving unit, Sister Rae speaking. Can I help you?'

The words she heard chilled her to the bone, and she gestured frantically to Luca for a piece of paper and then started scribbling furiously.

'What's wrong?' he asked as she replaced the phone.

'It's my grandmother. She's had a fall at the nursing home—they think she might have broken her hip.' She started to look around about her, searching for her bag. 'I need to go. They've taken her to another hospital at the other side of the city.'

Luca stood up. 'What can I do?'

Cassidy started pulling on the cardigan that was

draped over her chair. She couldn't think straight. She couldn't think at all. The rational parts of her brain had stopped working. Gran was in her eighties and had chest problems. How often did an elderly person have problems with the anaesthetic? What if this was the last time she'd ever see her gran again?

She started to pace up the corridor. 'Michael, are you there?'

His head ducked out from behind a set of curtains.

'I'm really sorry but I need to go. It's an emergency— my gran. They think she might have broken her hip.'

'Of course, Cassidy. No problem.'

'You've got the keys to the drug trolley, haven't you? Here's the controlled-drug key.' She unpinned it from inside her uniform pocket. 'Can you let Lucy, Sister Burns from next door, know that I've had to leave?' She was babbling and she knew it.

'Cassidy, we'll be fine. I'll get some help from next door if we need it. And I won't start transferring any patients until after lunch.' He gave her a quick hug, then placed a hand firmly at her back. 'Now, go.'

His pager sounded again, and Brad growled and rolled over. 'I'm sleeping. I'm not on call any more. Leave me alone,' he groaned.

But the pager wasn't listening. It sounded again. And again. And again.

Brad was mad. Last night had been ridiculous. He hadn't stopped—not even for a minute. And on the way to work last night his Mini had made the strangest sound then phutted to a stop at the side of the road. And all he wanted to do this morning was lie in his bed and vegetate.

He flung back the covers, squinting at the light

coming through the blinds, and lifted the pager to his scrunched-up eyes.

'Call Joe immediately.'

All of a sudden he was wide awake, his heart thumping in his chest. Joe Scott was his very expensive, US private investigator. He emailed Brad every few weeks, telling him any leads he was following and how he was getting on.

They had an understanding. Joe knew that Brad was a doctor, frequently on call, and had agreed that Joe would only contact Brad via his pager if something significant turned up. It had seemed the easiest solution as messages to a busy hospital could be lost, and depending on his rota sometimes Brad could be away from his house and normal emails for a few days at a time.

He reached for his phone, pushing in the number that was ingrained there.

'Joe, it's Brad Donovan. What have you found?'

'Haven't you read the email I sent you? I sent you some photographs.'

It took a few seconds for Brad's ears to adjust to the American accent. Email. He hadn't looked at his emails for two days.

He moved automatically to his laptop, his bare feet padding across the floor. It took for ever to boot up.

'I'm just opening the email now, Joe,' he said. 'Give me a few minutes.' He wasn't sure what was waking him up more quickly—the shock phone call or the cold air.

The email took for ever to open. He could sense Joe waiting impatiently at the other end of the phone. He didn't even read the content, just clicked on one of the attached photographs.

There she was. Blonde ringlets framing her face,

dressed in a green puffy coat, throwing back her head and laughing. It was a beautiful sight.

'Is it her?' The US voice cut into his thoughts.

For a moment he couldn't speak. She'd grown so much. She looked like a proper little girl now—a little lady even, rather than a toddler. His eyes swept the surrounding area. Alison was standing in the background, holding a baby. She was laughing, too. Melody was positioned on the pebbled shoreline of a lake and was clutching stones in her hands.

He tried not to let the rage overwhelm him. He couldn't let that get in the way right now. This was the first time he'd laid eyes on his little girl in nearly two years.

'Brad? Are you there?' The voice was strained now, obviously worried by his lack of response.

'Yes,' he croaked. 'It's Melody.' There was an unfamiliar sensation overwhelming him right now. It was a mixture of relief, joy, bitterness and excitement.

'Great. I was sure I'd found them, but needed you to confirm it.'

Brad's mind started to race. His eyes couldn't move from the photograph. They looked to be out in the middle of nowhere.

'Where are they?'

'North Woods, Wisconsin. Lots of hills and dense woods, terrible phone and internet reception. Took the photo two days ago. You were right about Alison, she got married. Her name is now Alison Johnson. Married to Blane Johnson—a paediatrician in Wisconsin—and they have a baby daughter, Temperance.'

Brad could tell he was reading from the notes in front of him. But he didn't care. He still couldn't believe it. And the picture was crystal clear. Not some blurry snap, which he might have expected. He could almost reach out and touch her. Did she remember him? Did she remember she had a dad who loved her very much?

His fingers brushed the screen. She looked happy. She looked healthy. Part of him gave a little sigh of relief. His daughter was alive, happy and healthy. For any parent, that should be the most important thing.

He was trying so hard to keep a lid on his feelings. He'd spent the last two years thinking about what he'd do when he found her. Thoughts of taking his time and trying to contact Alison separately, engaging a lawyer, getting advice on his legal rights in another country, finding out about extradition from that particular state in the US. And now all those rational, sensible thoughts were flying out the window.

Something registered in his brain—geography had never been his strong point. 'Where is it? Where's North Woods, Wisconsin?'

He heard Joe let out a guffaw. 'I thought you might ask that. Not the most straightforward place to get to. For you, the nearest international airports are Minnesota or Chicago. I don't think you can get a flight from Glasgow to either of them direct. Probably best to fly from Glasgow via Amsterdam and then Chicago. I'll make arrangements for you from there. Just let me know if you're coming into O'Hare or Midway International.'

Brad nodded. Chicago—some place that he'd heard of. He'd be able to find a flight there. 'I'll get online now. I'll get the quickest flight out that I can. Give me a couple of hours and I'll email you back the details.'

'No problem, son. See you soon.'

Brad put down the phone. His hands were shaking. He clicked into the rest of the email. There were four photographs. Two pictures of Alison with her baby and two of Melody. She was still his little girl. She had his blond hair and blue eyes. She even had his smile. And if he played his cards right, he would get to see her again.

He quickly dialled another number he had in his phone. A US attorney he'd been put in touch with who specialised in family law. Best to get some advice before he set foot on US soil. The last thing he wanted to do was cause a scene and get deported.

His brain whirring, he opened a travel website to search for flights. Only one from Glasgow. Leaving in six hours. He didn't hesitate. A few clicks and he was booked. He'd already been to the US in the last two years and knew his machine-readable passport meant he didn't need a visa.

This was it—he was finally going to see his daughter again.

Then something else hit him. Cassidy. He had to tell Cassidy.

He looked at the clock. It wouldn't take him long to pack. He groaned as he remembered his Mini still abandoned at the side of the road. He could get a taxi to the airport. But he couldn't leave without speaking to Cassidy first. It took a few minutes to wrap up his call to the lawyer then he pulled on his jogging trousers and trainers. He could run up the hill to the hospital. Cassidy would be on the ward. He could speak to her there.

He remembered that look on her face in the restaurant. She'd worried about this moment. And to be honest, he'd reached the stage that he'd wondered if this would ever happen.

And now it had.

And he had to go.

But he wouldn't go without speaking to Cassidy.

Without reassuring her that he would come back for her. He loved his daughter with his whole heart. But he loved Cassidy, too, and he wanted her to be a part of his life. He looked over to the table where he had an array of little gifts organised for her—all to be placed in the pockets of the calendar. He would do that once he got back from the hospital.

First he had to reassure her. First, he had to tell her that he loved her.

'Where is she?'

'Where's who?' Michael was in the middle of drawing up some heparin. 'Who are you looking for?'

'Cassidy, of course!' Who did that big oaf think he would be looking for? He was out of breath, panting. He wasn't really dressed for the cold, with just a T-shirt and tracksuit top in place, and the run up the hill in the biting cold hadn't helped.

Michael's face paled a little. 'Oh, I take it you haven't heard?'

'Haven't heard what?' Brad's frustration was growing by the second.

'Cassidy had to leave. Her gran had a fall in the nursing home and they thought she might have broken her hip. They are taking her to the Wallace Hospital—on the other side of the city. Cassidy left about an hour ago.'

Brad felt the air whoosh out from him. He pulled out his phone and started dialling her number. But it connected directly to her voice mail.

'Not supposed to use that in here,' muttered Michael.

Brad grabbed his arm. 'How far away is the Wallace? How would I get there at this time of day?' This was the worst possible time for his car to die.

Michael frowned. 'You in a hurry?'

Brad nodded. 'I need to see Cassidy, speak to the boss and arrange a few days off, then get to the airport.'

'You are joking, aren't you?' Michael's eyebrows were raised.

'No. No, I'm not. Give me some directions.'

Michael shook his head. 'At this time of day it will be a bit of a nightmare. You'd need to take the clock-work orange...'

'The what?'

'The underground. That's what we call it around here. You'd need to take the clockwork orange to Cessnock and then get the bus to the hospital. It'll take you about an hour.' He looked at the clock on the wall opposite. 'What time do you need to get to the airport? Because you'll need to get a train to Paisley for that. Then a bus to the airport.'

Brad's head was currently mush. There was no way he was going to get across the city—find Cassidy in a strange hospital, get back, pack and get to the airport in time.

He threw up his hands in frustration and left the hospital, walking back down the hill towards his flat.

He tried her phone again three times and sent her two text messages—but it was obvious she had her phone switched off. What could he do?

He got back home and pulled the biggest suitcase he had from the wardrobe and started throwing things inside. Jeans, jumpers, boots, T-shirts—anything he could think of.

He sat down and tried her phone again. Straight to voice mail. 'Cassidy—it's Brad. I heard about your gran. I'm really sorry and I hope she's okay. I really, really need to speak to you and I don't want to do it over the phone. Please phone me back as soon as you get this message. Please…' He hesitated for a second. 'I love you, Cass.'

He put the phone down. A wave of regret was washing over him. The first time he told her he loved her should have been when he was staring into her big brown eyes—not leaving a message on a phone. But he needed to let her know how he felt. She had to know how much she meant to him.

He looked at the rest of the items on the table. Her flat was only five minutes away—he could go around now and put them in the calendar for her. He could also take some time to write her a letter and explain what had happened. That way, if he didn't get to speak to her, she'd know he'd never meant to leave like this.

He looked at the clock again. Did he really not have the time to get to the other side of the city and back? His heart fell. He knew he didn't. Latest check-in time at the airport was two hours before his flight left. He would never make it. This was the only flight to Chicago that left in the next three days. He had to be on it. The chance to see his daughter again was just too important. He'd waited too long for this moment. He couldn't put this off, no matter how much he wanted to see Cassidy.

He picked up the items from the table and grabbed his keys. He had to try and make this right.

Cassidy leaned back against the wall. The cool hospital concrete was freezing, cutting straight through her thin top, but she welcomed it as she felt completely frazzled. Six hours after she'd got here, her gran was finally being wheeled to Theatre. Her hip was definitely fractured and she was in pain. The orthopaedic surgeon had tried to put her off until the next day, but he hadn't met Cassidy Rae before.

She'd waited until she was sure her gran had disappeared along the corridor to Theatre before she started rummaging around her bag. She badly needed a coffee. Her mobile clattered to the floor as she tried to find her purse.

She picked it up and switched it back on. It had sounded earlier in the A and E department and one of the staff had told her to switch it off. The phone buzzed back into life and started to beep constantly.

Text message from Brad. *'Phone me.'*

Another text message from Brad. *'Phone me as soon as you get this.'*

Text message. *Two voice-mail messages.*

Cassidy felt her heart start to flutter in her chest. She hadn't managed to phone Brad since her gran's accident. Was he worried about her? Or was it something else?

She walked along the corridor and out of the main door, standing to one side and pressing the phone to her ear. She listened to the first message. What on earth was wrong? What didn't he want to say on the phone? Her brain started to panic so much she almost missed the end of the message. *'I love you.'*

Brad had just told her he loved her. On the phone. And while she wanted the warm feeling to spread throughout her body, she couldn't help feeling something was wrong. His voice—the tone of it.

Had something happened to him? She pressed for the next message.

'Cassidy, honey, I'm so sorry. I really wanted to speak to you. I've left you a letter at home—it explains everything. I will be back, I promise. And I'll phone you as soon as I get there. And I'll email you as soon as I get near a computer. I love you, Cassidy.'

Get back from where? Her fingers scrolled for his

name and pressed 'dial'. It rang and then diverted to voice mail. His phone must be switched off.

Where was he?

Her agitation was rising. She didn't need this right now. Her gran was in Theatre. She should be concentrating on that. And he should be here with her, helping her through this. Where was he?

She sent him a quick text. *'Still at hospital with Gran. What's going on? Won't be home for a few hours.'*

Maybe he'd been called into work again? Maybe that was it. But something inside her didn't agree.

She walked back inside. There was nothing she could do right now. She had to stay here and be with her gran. There was no telling how she'd be when she woke from her anaesthetic. Cassidy wanted to be close.

And no matter how much she wanted to know what was going on with Brad, he'd just have to wait.

CHAPTER NINE

20 December

THE alarm sounded and Cassidy groaned and thumped the reset button with her hand. Even stretching out from under the warm duvet for a second was too cold. She heard a little muffled sound and seconds later felt a little draught at the bottom of the duvet.

Bert. The alarm had woken him and he was cold, too, so he'd sneaked into the bottom of her bed just as he'd done for the last ten days.

Ten days. Two hundred and forty hours—no, it had actually been forty-seven hours since she'd last spoken to Brad.

Sometimes when she woke in the morning—just for a millisecond—she thought everything was all right again. But then she remembered he was gone, searching for his daughter in North-blooming-Woods, Wisconsin. She'd had to look the place up on the internet—she didn't even know where it was.

By the time she'd got back from the hospital that night, Brad's flight had been in the air for four hours. He was long gone.

And although it helped just a little that he'd tried to contact her and that he'd left her a letter, it didn't take away from the fact that he'd gone. Just like that. At the drop of a hat.

She knew she was being unreasonable. He'd waited nearly two years to find his daughter—of course he should go. But her heart wasn't as rational as her head tried to be.

Her heart was broken in two.

What if he never came back? What if the only way he could have contact with his daughter was to stay in Wisconsin? What if he fell back in love with Melody's mother?

Every irrational thought in the world had circulated in her mind constantly for the last ten days and nights. Even Bert wasn't helping.

He kept looking at the door and sniffing around Brad's shoes in the hope he would reappear again.

She had to be the unluckiest woman in the world. Twice Brad had phoned her mobile—and both times she had missed his call. Both times she'd been working and both times she'd been with a patient.

He'd phoned the ward one day but she hadn't been on duty. And when he'd phoned the flat she'd been visiting her gran, who was still in hospital.

Every time she tried to call him back she'd received an 'unobtainable' signal.

He'd warned her. He'd warned her that North Woods was aptly named, surrounded by thick woods and hills with poor reception for mobiles and internet connections.

He'd sent two emails letting her know that he'd contacted a family lawyer and made contact with Alison. After some fraught negotiations he'd been allowed supervised access to see Melody twice. They were currently stuck in the land of legal mumbo-jumbo, trying to figure out the parental rights of two Australians in the US. Alison was covered—she'd married an American. But Brad's position was more difficult, particularly when he was officially only on 'holiday'.

It didn't help that his lawyer was advising him to look at extradition since Melody had been removed from Australia without permission.

She really, really wanted to talk to him.

She wanted to hear his voice, feel his arms around her, feel his body pressed next to hers. Particularly now. A warm dog around her feet might be nice, but it just didn't cut it.

She didn't even feel festive any more. Her favourite time of year had been blighted by the fact the man she loved was on the other side of the Atlantic. The flight had taken fourteen hours to reach Chicago, and then another few for the air transfer to North Woods. It wasn't exactly the easiest place to get to. And it wouldn't be the easiest place to get home from either.

But as soon as he did, she knew what she was going to do. She knew what she was going to say. This forced separation had clarified everything for her. She'd made up her mind.

Now all she could do was wait.

Brad's heart was in his mouth. His little girl seemed completely unfazed by him. Alison was another matter entirely.

Ten days of trying to keep his temper in check. Ten days of biting back all the things he really, really wanted to say.

Once she'd got over the initial shock, Alison had been shamed into a visit at his lawyer's office. She'd brought her husband along, who seemed equally outraged that Brad had dared to appear into their lives in North Woods, Wisconsin.

It hadn't taken long for his lawyer to go through the legal aspects of removing a child from another country without parental consent. Alison's lawyer had been surprisingly quiet and encouraged his client to agree in principle to some short supervised access spells.

He'd been here ten days and had spent three hours with his daughter.

He'd also spent innumerable hours trying to contact Cassidy back home.

Home? Scotland?

In Brad's mind right now, home was wherever Cassidy was. Wherever they could be together. He wanted to spend hours on the phone to her, talking through things with her and telling her how he felt.

But North Woods didn't seem to be a place with normal communication methods in mind—and to be fair, Joe, his private detective, had warned him about this. In theory, he would have managed to co-ordinate time differences, shift patterns and visiting schedules. But reality was much harder. Right now it seemed as if an old-fashioned carrier pigeon would be more effective than modern-day technology.

He glanced at his watch. Time for another visit. Time to see his gorgeous blonde, curly-headed daughter, who could skim stones across the lake like a professional. Time to get the wheels in motion to learn about more permanent types of access. Time to set up an agreed method of communication between them all. One that meant he could talk to his beautiful daughter without having to face the minefield that was her mother.

Time to get his life in order.

22 December

A Christmas bride. That's what smelly-cat woman had told her. Was there any chance she could go and demand her twenty quid back?

Right now it felt as if she'd been conned. False pretences. That's what they called it. But she'd never heard of a fortune-teller being sued. Just as well she'd never believed any of it.

Cassidy tugged her thick black boots on, trying to ignore the trickle of water inside that instantly soaked through her sock. There was about three feet of snow outside. It had been the same last night when she'd come home from work.

If she'd been organised—or cared enough—she would have stuffed her already soaked boots with newspaper and stuck them under the radiator. Instead, she'd flung them across the room and fallen into bed instantly.

She couldn't even be bothered to prepare something to eat. Her cupboards were a disgrace. Oh, if she wanted chocolate or crisps or bakery items like chocolate éclairs or cupcakes, she was fine. If she wanted anything substantial to eat, she was well and truly snookered.

Cassidy pulled on a cardigan, her gran's red wool coat and a black furry hat. It shouldn't take too long to get up the hill to the hospital. Her only problem would be if the pavement hadn't been gritted. Yesterday she'd picked up three people who'd slipped, trying to climb the hill, and caught another as he'd almost slid past her.

Maybe a coffee would help? A skinny caramel latte would be perfect.

She gave Bert a pat on the way out—even he was too intelligent to want to go out in this weather.

The cold air instantly stung her cheeks. Snow was

starting to fall again already. Within a few hours there could easily be another few feet on the ground. Getting home again would be a nightmare.

The aroma caught her. The smell of a freshly prepared caramel latte. She closed her eyes. Heaven on earth.

'Cassidy?'

The voice stopped her in her tracks. It was quiet. Like a question. Unsure, uncertain.

'Brad!'

She didn't hesitate. She didn't care who was in the street around them. She didn't worry about the slippery pavement covered in snow beneath her feet. She launched herself at him.

'Oof…'

He fell backwards and the latte he'd been carrying toppled, leaving a trail of pale brown on the white snow.

'Why didn't you tell me you were coming home? When did you arrive? Do you know how many times I tried to phone you? What on earth is wrong with that place? Why can't you get a decent signal there? And how dare you tell me you love me in a message?' She finished by slapping her gloved hand on his chest. Her knees pinned him to the ground beneath her.

All he could see was her face. Her curls were escaping from the sides of the black furry hat and her cheeks were tinged with red. A face that he'd longed to see for the last twelve days. It looked perfect.

He lifted his head from the snow. 'Is this a happy-to-see-me greeting or a mad-as-hell greeting?'

She furrowed her brow for a second then she broke into a smile and bent towards him, kissing the tip of his nose. 'What do you think?'

His head sagged back against the snow. 'Thank goodness.' He moved underneath her. 'Can I get up now?'

Her grin spread from ear to ear as she turned her head sideways and noticed people staring at them lying on the pavement. 'I suppose so.'

He stood up and brushed the snow from his back. 'I've missed you,' he said as he wrapped his arm around her shoulders.

'Me, too.'

'Can we go inside?'

'Yes, I mean no. I want to do something first. I promised myself I would do something the next time I saw you. Come with me.' She grabbed his hand, waiting until he'd grabbed the handle of his wheeled suitcase and pulled him across the road.

'Sounds ominous. Where are we going?'

'You'll see.'

She walked quickly along the road, in her excitement almost forgetting he was pulling a heavy suitcase through snow. But in a few moments she stopped and smiled. 'In here,' she said.

He looked around him, puzzled by the surroundings. They'd moved away from the busy street to a small church with an even smaller cemetery, virtually hidden from the road. Its tiny spire was the only thing that made it noticeable among the surrounding buildings.

'I didn't even know this was here.'

'Lots of people don't. But two hundred years ago this was one of the main roads into Glasgow.'

He waited while she pushed open an iron gate and walked behind the railings. He followed her in, totally bemused.

'What on earth are we doing here? Is this the church

you normally go to? You've never mentioned it.' He looked around at the old worn gravestones. Some of the writing was barely visible now, washed away through time, wind, rain and grime. 'Looks like no one's been buried here in a very long time.'

Cassidy nodded and pulled him under one of the trees. All of a sudden her rose-tinged cheeks looked pale. He could feel the tremors in her skin under her coat. The snow was starting to coat the fur on her hat in a white haze.

Her voice was shaking as she started to speak. 'You told me you loved me.'

He clasped his hands around her. 'And I do, Cassidy. I didn't want to tell you like that, but things happened so quickly and I didn't want you to think I'd just walked away. I wanted you to know how I felt about you. I wanted you to know that I was definitely coming back.' His voice tailed off.

'I didn't want you to think I was abandoning you.' It was so important to him. To tell her that he wasn't like Bobby or her parents. To tell her that he would never abandon her. That he wanted to be with her for ever.

Her eyes were glazed with hidden tears, but she didn't look unhappy. Just very determined.

'What is it, Cassidy? What's wrong?'

'I was wrong. When I spoke to you about Christmas and its traditions and not leaving Scotland—I was wrong.'

The cold air was making her breath come out in a steam. Short blasts.

'You were right when you said it was about the people—or person—you spend it with.' Her eyes swept around them, taking in the ancient church and graveyard. 'I love Scotland. You know I love Scotland. But I love you more and I want to be wherever you are.'

Brad blinked, snowflakes getting in his eyes. A two-hour flight, followed by another fourteen-hour flight, all worrying about Cassidy. How she would be, whether she would forgive him for leaving without saying good-bye, whether she would be angry with him. 'You love me,' he said slowly, his sense of relief sending a flood of warm blood through his chilled skin.

She nodded, the smile on her face reaching right up into her brown eyes.

'You love me,' he said again.

'Yes, yes, I love you. Do you want me to shout it out loud?' Her voice rose, sending some birds fluttering from the tree above.

He bent his head and kissed her. Taking her sweet lips against his own, pulling her close to him, keeping out all the cold that surrounded them. He'd wanted to do nothing else for the last twelve days. Twelve days and twelve long nights without Cassidy in his arms had driven him crazy.

'How do you feel about fourteen-hour flights?' he whispered.

She pulled backwards a little, nodding slowly. 'To North Woods, Wisconsin?' She reached up, pulling her hand from her red leather glove and running her finger down the side of his cheek. 'I think that's something we can do together.'

He sucked in a breath. She was prepared to go with him to see his daughter. She was prepared to meet the challenge of their life together. She'd come full circle. Just like he had. Eighteen months ago he couldn't have been lower. Cassidy had lit up his world in every way possible. He couldn't imagine life without her.

A shiver stole down his spine. He nuzzled into her neck. 'You've still not told me, what are we doing here, Cass?'

He watched her take a deep breath. She looked at him steadily. 'I've decided I'm a modern woman and want to embrace life—in every way possible. I've always loved this place—especially in the winter.' She swept her arm across the scene. 'How do you feel about this as a wedding setting?'

Brad froze. She hadn't. She hadn't just said that, had she?

She looked terrified. Now that the words were out, she looked as if she could faint on the spot.

'Did you just propose?' He lifted his eyebrow at her in disbelief.

'I think so.' She trembled.

He picked her up and spun her around. 'Isn't this supposed to be my job? Aren't I supposed to go down on one knee and propose to you with a single red rose and a diamond ring?' He pressed his face next to hers, his lips connecting with hers again.

'You were taking too long,' she mumbled. 'It took you a full month to kiss me. What chance did I have?' She hesitated. 'So what do you think?' There was fear in her voice, still that little piece of uncertainty.

'I think you should look in pocket twenty-four of your calendar.'

'What?' She looked momentarily stunned. Not the answer she was expecting.

Cassidy's brain was desperately trying to click into gear. She'd just asked the biggest question in her life. What kind of an answer was that? She hadn't looked at the calendar since the night Brad had left—she'd just assumed he wouldn't have had a chance to fill it before he'd gone.

He set her feet down on the ground. The grin on his face spread from ear to ear, his head, shoulders and eyelashes covered in snowflakes. 'Well, I'm not entirely a modern man. This is my job.' He dropped to one knee on the snow-covered grass. 'So much for taking too long—let's just cut right to the chase. Cassidy Rae, will you do me the honour of being my wife? Will you promise to love, honour and keep me, in sickness and in health, for as long as we both shall live?'

She dropped to her knees beside him. 'That's not a proposal.' She looked stunned. 'That's a wedding vow.'

'That's okay,' he whispered, pulling her even closer. 'I've already got the wedding ring.'

Her eyes widened. 'Pocket twenty-four?'

He nodded. 'Pocket twenty-four. I didn't know there was a church around here. I was hoping that we could say our own vows.'

She giggled. 'Looks like I'm going to be a Christmas bride after all.'

He looked completely confused. 'What on earth are you talking about?'

She smiled. 'Well, one day I might tell you a little story…'

EPILOGUE

One year later

'YOU'VE got to pick the best stones, Cassidy. They need to be flat on both sides.' The blue eyes regarded her seriously before the little face broke into a broad smile. 'That's why I always win,' she whispered, giving a conspiratorial glance over her shoulder towards Brad, who was standing at the lakeside waiting for them both.

'What's going on with my girls?' he shouted.

Melody held her gloved hand out towards Cassidy as they walked back over to Brad.

Cassidy looked down at the blonde curls spilling out from the green woolly hat. She gave Brad a smile. This was their third visit to North Woods, Wisconsin, and Brad had finally been allowed some unsupervised access to his child. Melody was a loving, easy child who, luckily enough, seemed totally oblivious to the tensions between her natural parents.

She spoke to Brad online every week and had been happy to meet Cassidy, loving the fact that her dad had a Scottish wife. She'd even painted Cassidy a picture of them all living in a Scottish castle.

Cassidy winked at Brad. 'Melody and I needed some time to make our plan. We think we've found a sixer.'

'A sixer? What on earth is that?' He shook his head in amusement at them both.

Melody's voice piped up. 'You should know what a sixer is, Daddy.' The stone-skimming champion looked at him seriously, holding up the flat grey stone in her hand like an winning prize. 'This stone will skim across the water *six* times before it goes under.'

'Aha.' He knelt down beside her, touching the stone with his finger, 'A sixer? Really?' He shook his head and folded him arm across his chest. 'No way. Not that stone.'

'It really is, Daddy.'

Brad's face broke into a big smile as he straightened up and slung his arm around Cassidy's shoulder. 'Prove it.'

They watched as Melody took her position at the lakeside edge, narrowing her gaze and pulling her hand back to her shoulder. She let out a yell as she released the stone, sending it skimming over the flat water, bouncing across the lake.

Cassidy leaned against Brad's shoulder. 'One, two, three, four, five, six. Your daughter was absolutely right. It was a sixer. Now, where does she get that skill from, I wonder?'

He laughed. 'Her dad, definitely her dad. I could throw a mean ball as a kid.'

He picked up Melody, who was shrieking over her success. 'What a star!' he shouted as he threw her into the air, catching her in his arms and spinning her round.

Cassidy pulled her red wool coat further around her, trying to ward off the biting cold. North Woods was nearly as cold as Glasgow at this time of year.

Brad came over and whispered in her ear. 'Happy anniversary, Mrs Donovan.' His cold nose was pressed against her cheek as he wrapped his arms around her waist.

Cassidy felt herself relax against him. After all her worries, all her stresses, things had worked out just fine. They'd married two weeks after his proposal in the churchyard—as quickly as they legally could.

Her gran had recovered quickly from her broken hip and recuperated back in the nursing home with some expert care. She was on a new drug trial, and although her Alzheimer's hadn't improved, it certainly hadn't got any worse. The relief for Cassidy was that the episodes of aggression seemed to have abated. She still visited her gran as often as possible but she was confident in the care the nursing home provided.

That had given her the freedom she'd needed to join Brad on a two-month visit to Australia and on three trips to the States to see Melody.

After a few tense months, Alison's lawyer had finally talked some sense into his client and visiting rights had been sorted out. It meant that every few months they could have Melody for a week at a time to stay with them.

Brad had looked at a few jobs nearby and been interviewed for a position at the local hospital. Cassidy had just seen an ad for a specialist nurse to help set up an anticoagulant clinic and knew it was just what she was looking for. There was only one more thing that could make this perfect.

She turned round and put her arms around his neck. 'Happy anniversary, Dr Donovan.' She kissed him on his cold lips.

'So how do you feel about North Woods, Wisconsin?' he asked, his smile reaching from one ear to the other.

Cassidy looked over her shoulder at the lake with

ice around the edges and thick trees surrounding it. 'I think it has potential.' She smiled.

He raised his eyebrows. 'Potential? Potential for what?'

He was waiting. Waiting to see what she would say. He didn't know she'd just found an ad for her dream job. He didn't know that there had been a message from the hospital after he'd left to collect Melody, offering him the job he'd just been interviewed for. But all of that could wait. Right now she wanted the chance to still surprise her new husband.

She rose up on the tips of her toes and whispered in his ear, 'I think North Woods, Wisconsin might be a nice place to make a baby.'

His jaw dropped and his eyes twinkled as he picked her up and spun her round. 'You know, Mrs Donovan, I think you could be right.'

* * * * *

THE HOLIDAY GIFT

RAEANNE THAYNE

To Lisa Townsend, trainer extraordinaire, who is gorgeous inside and out. And to Jennie, Trudy, Karen, Becky, Jill and everyone else in our group for your example, your encouragement, your friendship, your laughter—and especially for making me look forward to workouts (except the burpees—I'll never look forward to those!).

Chapter One

Something was wrong, but Faith Dustin didn't have the first idea what.

She glanced at Chase Brannon again, behind the wheel of his pickup truck. Sunglasses shielded his eyes but his strong jaw was still flexed, his shoulders tense.

Since they had left the Idaho Falls livestock auction forty-five minutes earlier, heading back to Cold Creek Canyon, the big rancher hadn't smiled once and had answered most of her questions in monosyllables, his mind clearly a million miles away.

Faith frowned. He wasn't acting at all like himself. They were frequent travel companions, visiting various livestock auctions around the region at least once or twice a month for the last few years. They had even gone on a few buying trips to Denver together, an eight-hour drive from their little corner of eastern Idaho. He was her oldest friend—and had been since she and her sisters came to live with their aunt and uncle nearly two decades ago.

In many ways, she and Chase were really a team and comingled their ranch operations, since his ranch, Brannon Ridge, bordered the Star N on two sides.

Usually when they traveled, they never ran out of things to talk about. Her kids and their current dramas, real or imagined; his daughter, Addie, who lived with her mother in Boise; Faith's sisters and their growing families. Their ranches, the community, the price of beef, their future plans. It was all grist for their conversational mill. She valued his opinion—often she would run ideas past him—and she wanted to think he rated hers as highly.

The drive to Idaho Falls earlier that morning had seemed just like usual, filled with conversation and their usual banter. Everything had seemed normal during the auction. He had stayed right by her side, a quiet, steady support, while she engaged in—and eventually won—a fierce bidding war for a beautiful paint filly with excellent barrel racing bloodlines.

That horse, intended as a Christmas gift for her twelve-year-old daughter, Louisa, was the whole reason they had gone to the auction. Yes, she'd been a little carried away by winning the auction so that she'd hugged him hard and kissed him smack on the lips, but surely that wasn't what was bothering him. She'd kissed and hugged him tons of times.

Okay, maybe she had been careful not to be so casual

with her affection for him the last six or seven months, for reasons she didn't want to explore, but she couldn't imagine he would go all cold and cranky over something as simple as a little kiss.

No. His mood had shifted after that, but all her subtle efforts to wiggle out what was wrong had been for nothing.

His mood certainly matched the afternoon. Faith glanced out at the uniformly gray sky and the few random, hard-edged snowflakes clicking against the windshield. The weather wasn't pleasant but it wasn't horrible either. The snowflakes weren't sticking to the road yet, anyway, though she expected they would see at least a few inches on the ground by morning.

Even the familiar festive streets of Pine Gulch— wreaths hanging on the streetlamps and each downtown business decorated with lights and window dressings— didn't seem to lift his dark mood.

When he hit the edge of town and turned into Cold Creek Canyon toward home, she decided to try one last time to figure out what might be bothering him.

"Did something happen at the auction?"

He glanced away from the road briefly, the expression in his silver-blue eyes shielded by the amber lenses of his sunglasses. "Why would you think that?"

She studied his dearly familiar profile, struck by his full mouth and his tanned, chiseled features—covered now with just a hint of dark afternoon shadow. Funny, how she saw him just about every single day but was sometimes taken by surprise all over again by how great-looking he was.

With his dark, wavy hair covered by the black Stetson he wore, that slow, sexy smile, and his broad shoulders and slim hips, he looked rugged and dangerous and completely male. It was no wonder the waitresses at the café next to the auction house always fought each other to serve their table.

She shifted her attention away from such ridiculous things and back to the conversation. "I don't know. Maybe because that's the longest sentence you've given me since we left Idaho Falls. You've replied to everything else with either a grunt or a monosyllable."

Beneath that afternoon shadow, a muscle clenched in his jaw. "That doesn't mean anything happened. Maybe I'm just not in a chatty mood."

She certainly had days like that. Heaven knew she'd had her share of blue days over the last two and a half years. Through every one of them, Chase had been her rock.

"Nothing wrong with that, I guess. Are you sure that's all? Was it something Beckett McKinley said? I saw him corner you at lunch."

He glanced over at her briefly and again she wished she could see the expression behind his sunglasses. "He wanted to know how I like the new baler I bought this year and he also wanted my opinion on a…personal matter. I told him I liked the baler fine but told him the other thing wasn't any of my damn business."

She blinked at both his clipped tone and the language. Chase didn't swear very often. When he did, there was usually a good reason.

"Now you've got my curiosity going. What kind of

personal matter would Beck want your opinion about? The only thing I can think the man needs is a nanny for those hellion boys of his."

He didn't say anything for a long moment, just watched the road and those snowflakes spitting against windshield. When he finally spoke, his voice was clipped. "It was about you."

She stared. "Me?"

Chase's hands tightened on the steering wheel. "He wants to ask you out, specifically to go as his date to the stockgrowers association's Christmas party on Friday."

If he had just told her Beck wanted her to dress up like a Christmas angel and jump from his barn roof, she wouldn't have been more surprised—and likely would have been far less panicky.

"I... He...what?"

"Beck wants to take you to the Christmas party this weekend. I understand there's going to be dancing and a full dinner this year."

Beck McKinley. The idea of dating the man took her by complete surprise. Yes, he was a great guy, with a prosperous ranch on the other side of Pine Gulch. She considered him a good friend but she had never *once* thought of him in romantic terms.

The unexpected paradigm shift wasn't the only thing bothering her about what Chase had just said.

"Hold on. If he wanted to take me to the party, why wouldn't Beck just ask me himself instead of feeling like he has to go through you first?"

That muscle flexed in his jaw again. "You'll have to ask him that."

The things he wasn't saying in this conversation would fill a radio broadcast. She frowned as Chase pulled into the drive leading to his ranch. "You told him I'm already going with you, didn't you?"

He didn't answer for a long moment. "No," he finally said. "I didn't."

Unease twanged through her, the same vague sense that had haunted her at stray moments for several months. Something was off between her and Chase and, for the life of her, she couldn't put a finger on it.

"Oh. Did you already make plans?" She forced a cheerful smile. "We've gone together the last few years so I just sort of assumed we would go together again this year but I guess we should have talked about it. If you already have something going, don't worry about me. Seriously. I don't mind going by myself. I'll have plenty of other friends there I can sit with. Or I could always skip it and stay home with the kids. Jenna McRaven does a fantastic job with the food and I always enjoy the company of other grown-ups, but if you've got a hot date lined up, I'm perfectly fine."

As she said the words, she tasted the lie in them. Was this weird ache in her stomach because she had been looking forward to the evening out—or because she didn't like the idea of him with a hot date?

"I don't have a date, hot or otherwise," he growled as he pulled the pickup and trailer to a stop next to a small paddock near the barn of the Brannon Ridge Ranch.

She eased back in the bench seat, a curious relief seeping through her. "Good. That's that. We can go together, just like always. It will be a fun night out for us."

Though she knew him well enough to know something was still on his mind, he said nothing as he pulled off his sunglasses and hooked them on the rearview mirror. What did his silence mean? Didn't he *want* to go with her?

"Faith," he began, but suddenly she didn't want to hear what he had to say.

"We'd better get the beautiful girl in your trailer unloaded before the kids get home."

She opened her door and jumped out before he could answer her. Yes, sometimes she was like her son, Barrett, who would rather hide out in his room all day and miss dinner than be scolded for something he'd done. She didn't like to face bad things. It was a normal reaction, she told herself. Hadn't she already had to face enough bad things in her life?

After a moment, Chase climbed out after her and came around to unhook the back of the trailer. The striking black-and-white paint yearling whinnied as he led her out into the patchy snow.

"She's a beauty, isn't she?" Faith said, struck all over again by the horse's elegant lines.

"Yeah," Chase said. Again with the monosyllables. She sighed.

"Thanks for letting me keep her here for a couple of weeks. Louisa will be so shocked on Christmas morning."

"Shouldn't be a problem."

He guided the horse into the pasture, where his own favorite horse, Tor, immediately trotted over as Faith closed the gate behind them. As soon as Chase unhooked the young horse from her lead line, she raced to the other side of the pasture, mane and tail flying out behind her.

She was fast. That was the truth. Grateful for her own cowboy hat that shielded her face from the worst of the frost-tipped snowflakes, Faith watched the horse race to the other corner of the pasture and back, obviously overflowing with energy after the stress of a day at the auction and then a trailer ride with strangers.

"Do you think she's too much horse for Lou?" she asked while Chase patted Tor beside her.

He looked at the paint and then down at Faith. "She comes from prime barrel racing stock. That's what Lou wants to do. For twelve, she's a strong rider. Yeah, the horse is only green broke but Seth Dalton can train a horse to do just about anything but recite its ABCs."

"I guess that's true. It was nice of him to agree to take her, with his crazy training schedule."

"He's a good friend."

"He is," she agreed. "Though I know he only agreed to do it as a favor to you."

"Maybe it was a favor to you," he commented as he pulled a bale of hay over and opened it inside the pasture for the horses.

"Maybe," she answered. All three Dalton brothers had been wonderful neighbors and good friends to her. They and others in the close-knit ranching community in Cold Creek Canyon and around Pine Gulch had stepped up in a hundred different ways over the last two and a half years since Travis died.

She would have been lost without any of them, but especially without Chase.

That vague unease slithered through her again. What was wrong between them? And how could she fix it?

She didn't have the first clue.

What was a guy supposed to do?

Ever since Beck McKinley cornered him at the diner to talk about taking Faith to the stockgrowers' holiday party, Chase hadn't been able to think straight. He felt like the other guy had grabbed his face and dunked it in an ice-cold water trough, then kicked him in the gut for good measure.

For a full ten seconds, he had stared at Beck as a host of emotions galloped through him faster than a pack of wild horses spooked by a thunderstorm.

Beckett McKinley wanted to date Faith. *Chase's* Faith.

"She's great. That's all," Beck had said into the suddenly tense silence. "It's been more than two years since Travis died, right? I just thought maybe she'd be ready to start getting out there."

Chase had thought for a minute his whole face had turned numb, especially his tongue. It made it tough for him to get any words out at all—or maybe that was the ice-cold coating around his brain.

"Why are you asking me?" he had finally managed to say.

If possible, Beck had looked even more uncomfortable. "The two of you are always together. Here at the auction, at the feed store, at the diner in town. I know you're neighbors and you've been friends for a long time. But if there's something more than that, I don't want to be an ass and step on toes. You don't have to tell me what happens to bulls who wander into somebody else's pen."

It was all he could do not to haul off and deck the guy for the implied comparison that Faith was just some lonely heifer, waiting for some smooth-talking bull to wander by.

Instead, he had managed to grip his hands into fists, all while one thought kept echoing through his head.

Not again.

He thought he was giving her time to grieve, to make room in her heart for someone else besides Travis Dustin, the man she had loved since she was a traumatized girl trying to carve out a new home for her and her sisters.

Chase had been too slow once before. He had been a steady friend and confidant from the beginning. He figured he had all the time in the world as he waited for her to heal and to settle into life in Pine Gulch. She had been so young, barely sixteen. He wasn't much older, not yet nineteen, and had been busy with his own struggles. Even then, he had been running his family's ranch on his own while his father lay dying.

For six months, he offered friendship to Faith, fully expecting that one day when both of them were in a better place, he could start moving things to a different level.

And then Travis Dustin came home for the summer

to help out Claude and Mary, the distant relatives who had raised him his last few years of high school.

Chase's father was in his last few agonizing weeks of life from lung cancer that summer. While he was busy coping with that and accepting his new responsibilities on the ranch, Travis had wasted no time sweeping in and stealing Faith's heart. By the time Chase woke up and realized what was happening, it was too late. His two closest friends were in love with each other and he couldn't do a damn thing about it.

He could have fought for her, he supposed, but it was clear from the beginning that Travis made her happy. After everything she and her sisters had been through, she deserved to find a little peace.

Instead, he had managed to put his feelings away and maintain his friendship with both of them. He had even tried to move on himself and date other women, with disastrous consequences.

Beck McKinley was a good guy. A solid rancher, a devoted father, a pillar of the community. Any woman would probably be very lucky to have him, as long as she could get past those hellion boys of his.

Maybe McKinley was exactly the kind of guy she wanted. The thought gnawed at him, but he took some small solace in remembering that she hadn't seemed all that enthusiastic at the idea of going out with him.

Didn't matter. He knew damn well it was only a matter of time before she found someone she *did* want to go out with. If not Beck, some other smooth-talking cowboy would sweep in.

He hadn't fought for her last time. Instead, he had

stood by like a damn statue and watched her fall in love with his best friend.

He wouldn't go through that again. It was time he made a move—but what if he made the wrong one and ruined everything between them?

He felt like a man given a choice between a hangman's noose and a firing squad. He was damned either way.

He was still trying to figure out what to do when she shifted from watching the young horse dance around the pasture in the cold December air. Faith gazed up at the overcast sky, still dribbling out the occasional stray snowflake.

"I probably should get back. The kids will be out of school soon and I'm sure you have plenty of things of your own to do. You don't have to walk me back," she said when he started to head in that direction behind her. "Stay and unhitch the horse trailer if you need to."

"It can keep. I'll walk you back up to your truck. I've got to plug in my phone anyway."

A couple of his ranch dogs came out from the barn to say hello as they walked the short distance to his house. He reached down and petted them both, in total sympathy. He felt like a ranch dog to her: a constant, steady companion with a few useful skills that came in handy once in a while.

Would she ever be able to see him as anything more?

"Thanks again, Chase," Faith said when they reached her own pickup truck—the one she had insisted on driving over that morning, even though he told her he could easily pick her up and drop her back off at the Star N.

"You're welcome," he said.

"Seriously, I was out of my depth. Horses aren't exactly my area of expertise. Who knows, I might have brought home a nag. As always, I don't know what I would do without you."

He could feel tension clutch at his shoulders again. "Not true," he said, his voice more abrupt than he intended. "You didn't need me. Not really. You'd already done your research and knew what you wanted in a barrel racer. You just needed somebody to back you up."

She smiled as they reached her pickup truck and a pale shaft of sunlight somehow managed to pierce the cloud cover and land right on her delicate features, so soft and lovely it made his heart hurt.

"I'm so lucky that somebody is always you," she said.

He let out a breath, fighting the urge to pull her into his arms. He didn't have that right—nor could he let things go on as they were.

"About the stockgrowers' party," he began.

If he hadn't been looking, he might have missed the leap of something that looked suspiciously like fear in her green eyes before she shifted her gaze away from him.

"Really, it doesn't bother me to skip it this year if you want to make other plans."

"I don't want to skip it," he growled. "I want to go. With you. On a date."

He intended to stress the last word, to make it plain this wouldn't be two buddies just hanging out together, like they always did. As a result, the word took on unnatural proportions and he nearly snapped it out until it arced between them like an arrow twanged from a crossbow.

Eyes wide, she gazed at him for a long moment, clearly startled by his vehemence. After a moment, she nodded. "Okay. That's settled, then. We can figure out the details later."

Nothing was settled. He needed to tell her *date* was the operative word here, that he didn't want to take her to the party as her neighbor and friend who gave her random advice on a barrel racing horse for her daughter or helped her with the hay season.

He wanted the right to hold her—to dance with her and flirt and whisper soft, sexy words in her ear.

How the hell could he tell her that, after all this time, when he had so carefully cultivated a safe, casual relationship that was the exact opposite of what he really wanted? Before he could figure that out, an SUV he didn't recognize drove up the lane toward his house.

"Were you expecting company?" she asked.

"Don't think so." He frowned as the car pulled up beside them—and his frown intensified when the passenger door opened and a girl jumped out, then raced toward him. "Daddy!"

Chapter Two

He stared at his eleven-year-old daughter, dressed to the nines in an outfit more suited to a photo shoot for a children's clothing store than for a working cattle ranch.

"Adaline! What are you doing here? I didn't expect to see you until next weekend."

"I know, Dad! Isn't it great? We get extra time together—maybe even two whole weeks! Mom pulled me out of school until after Christmas. Isn't that awesome? My teachers are going to email me all my homework so I don't miss too much—not that they ever do anything the last few weeks before Christmas vacation anyway but waste time showing movies and doing busywork and stuff."

That sounded like a direct quote from her mother, who had little respect for the educational system, even the expensive private school she insisted on sending their daughter to.

As if on cue, his ex-wife climbed out of the driver's side of what must be a new vehicle, judging by the temporary license plates in the window.

She looked uncharacteristically disordered, with her sweater askew and her hair a little messy in back where she must have been leaning against the headrest as she drove.

"I'm so glad you're home," she said. "We took a chance. I've been trying to call you all afternoon. Why didn't you answer?"

"My phone ran out of juice and I forgot to take the charger to the auction with us. What's going on?"

He knew it had to be something dramatic for her to bring Addie all this way on an unscheduled midweek visit.

Cindy frowned. "My mother had a stroke early this morning and she's in the hospital in Idaho Falls."

"Oh, no! I hadn't heard. I'm so sorry."

He had tried very hard to earn the approval of his in-laws but the president of the Pine Gulch bank and his wife had been very slow to warm up to him. He didn't know if they had disliked him because Cindy had been pregnant when they married or because they didn't think a cattle rancher with cow manure on his boots was good enough for their precious only child.

They had reached a peace accord of sorts after Addie came along. Still, he almost thought his and Cindy's divorce had been a relief to them—and he had no doubt they had been thrilled at her second marriage to an eminently successful oral surgeon in Boise.

"The doctors say it appears to be a mini stroke. They suspect it's not the first one so they want to keep her for observation for a few days. My dad said I didn't have to come down but it seemed like the right thing to do," Cindy said. "Considering I was coming this way anyway, I didn't think you would mind having extra visitation with Addie, especially since she won't be here over the holidays."

He was aware of a familiar pang in his chest, probably no different from what most part-time divorced fathers felt at not being able to live with their children all the time. Holidays were the worst.

"Sure. Extra time is always great."

Cindy turned to Faith with that hard look she always wore when she saw the two of them together. His ex-wife had never said anything but he suspected she had long guessed the feelings he had tried to bury after Faith and Travis got married.

"We're interrupting," she said. "I'm sorry."

"Not at all," Faith assured her. "Please don't be sorry. I'm the one who's sorry about your mother."

"Thanks," Cindy said, her voice cool. "We spent an hour at the hospital before we came out here and she seems in good spirits. Doctors just want to keep her for observation to see if they can figure out what's going on. Dad is kind of a mess right now, which is why I thought it would be a good idea for me to stay with him, at least for the first few days."

"That sounds like a good idea."

"Thanks for taking Addie. Sorry to drop her off without calling first. I did try."

"It's no problem at all. I'm thrilled to have her."

The sad truth was, they got along and seemed to parent together better now that they were divorced than during the difficult five years of their marriage, though things still weren't perfect.

"I packed enough for a week. To be honest, I don't know what I grabbed, since I was kind of a mess this morning. Keith was worried about me driving alone but he had three surgeries scheduled today and couldn't come with me. His patients needed him."

"He's a busy man," Chase said. What else *could* he say? It would have been terribly hypocritical to lambast another man in the husband department when Chase had been so very lousy at it.

"I should get back to the hospital. Thanks, Chase. You're a lifesaver."

"No problem."

"I'm so sorry about your mother," Faith said.

"Thank you. I appreciate that."

Cindy opened the hatchback of the SUV and pulled out Addie's familiar pink suitcase. He hated the tangible reminder that his daughter had to live out of a suitcase half her life.

After setting the suitcase on the sidewalk, Cindy went through her usual drawn-out farewell routine with Addie that ended in a big hug and a sloppy kiss, then climbed into her SUV and drove away.

"My feet are cold," Addie announced calmly, apparently not fazed at all to watch her mother leave, despite the requisite drama. "I'm going to take my suitcase to my room and change my clothes."

She headed to the house without waiting for him to answer, leaving him alone with Faith.

"That was a curveball I wasn't expecting this afternoon,"

"Strokes can be scary," Faith said. "It sounds like Carol's was a mild one, though, which I'm sure is a relief to everyone. At least you'll get to spend a little extra time with Addie."

"True. Always a bonus."

He had plenty of regrets about his life but his wise, funny, kind daughter was the one amazing thing his lousy marriage had produced.

"I know this was a busy week for you," Faith said. "If you need help with her, she's welcome to spend time at the Star N. Louisa would be completely thrilled."

He had appointments all week with suppliers, the vet and his accountant, but he could take her with him. She was a remarkably adaptable child.

"The only time I might need help is Friday night. Think Aunt Mary would mind if she stayed at your place with Lou and Barrett while we're at the party?"

Her forehead briefly furrowed in confusion. "Oh. I almost forgot about that. Look, the situation has changed. If you'd rather stay home with Addie, I completely understand. I can tag along with Wade and Caroline Dalton or Justin and Ashley Hartford. Or, again, I can always just skip it."

Was she looking for excuses not to go with him? He didn't want to believe that. "I asked you out. I want to go, as long as Mary doesn't mind one more at your place."

"Addie's never any trouble. I'm sure Mary will be fine with it. I'll talk to her," she promised. "If she can't do it, I'm sure all the kids could hang out with Hope or Celeste for the evening."

Her sisters and their husbands lived close to the Star N and often helped with Barrett and Louisa, just as Faith helped out with their respective children.

"I'll be in touch later in the week to work out the details."

"Sounds good." She glanced at her watch. "I really do need to go. Thanks again for your help with the horse."

"You're welcome."

As she climbed into the Star N king-cab pickup, he was struck by how small and delicate she looked compared to the big truck.

Physically, she might be slight—barely five-four and slender—but she was tough as nails. Over the last two and a half years, she had worked tirelessly to drag the ranch from the brink. He had tried to take some of the burden from her but there was only so much she would let him do.

He stepped forward so she couldn't close the door yet.

"One last thing."

"What's that?"

Heart pounding, he leaned in to face her. He wanted her to see his expression. He wanted no ambiguity about his intentions.

"You need to be clear on one thing before Friday. I said it earlier but in all the confusion with Addie showing up, I'm not sure it registered completely. As far as I'm concerned, this is a date."

"Sure. We're going together. What else would it be?"

"I mean a date-date. I want to go out with you where we're not only good friends hanging out on a Friday night or two neighboring ranchers carpooling to the same event. I want you to be my date, with everything that goes along with that."

There. She couldn't mistake *that*.

He saw a host of emotions quickly cross her features—shock, uncertainty and a wild flare of panic. "Chase, I—"

He could see she wasn't even going to give him a chance. She was ready to throw up barriers to the idea before he even had a chance. Frustration coiled through him, sharp as barbed wire fencing.

"It's been two and a half years since Travis died."

Her hands clamped tight onto the steering wheel as if it were a bull rider's strap and she had to hang on or she would fall off and be trampled. "Yes. I believe I'm fully aware of that."

"You're going to have to enter the dating scene at some point. You've already got cowboys clamoring to ask you out. McKinley is just the first one to step up, but he won't be the last. Why not ease into it by going out with somebody you already know?"

"You."

"Why not?"

Instead of answering, she turned the tables on him.

"You and Cindy have been divorced for years. Why are you suddenly interested in dating again?"

"Maybe I'm tired of being alone." That, at least, was the truth, just not the whole truth.

"So this would be like a…trial run for both of us? A way to dip our toes into the water without jumping in headfirst?"

No. He had jumped in a long, long time ago and had just been treading water, waiting for her.

He couldn't tell her that. Not yet.

"Sure, if you want to look at it that way," he said instead.

He knew her well enough that he could almost watch her brain whir as she tried to think through all the ram-ifications. She overthought everything. It was by turns endearing and endlessly frustrating.

Finally she seemed to have sifted through the possi-bilities and come up with a scenario she could live with. "You're such a good friend, Chase. You've always got my back. You want to help make this easier for me, just like you helped me buy the horse for Louisa. Thank you."

He opened his mouth to say that wasn't at all his in-tention but he could see by the stubborn set of her jaw that she wasn't ready to hear that yet.

"I'll talk to Aunt Mary about keeping an eye on the kids on Friday. We can work out the details later. I re-ally do have to go. Thanks again."

Her tone was clearly dismissive. Left with no real choice, he stepped back so she could close the vehicle door.

She was deliberately misunderstanding him and he

didn't know how to argue with her. After all these years of being her friend and so carefully hiding his feelings, how did he convince her he wanted to be more than that?

He had no idea. He only knew he had to try.

Faith refused to let herself panic.

I want you to be my date, with everything that goes along with that.

Despite her best efforts, fear seemed to curl around her insides, coating everything with a thin layer of ice.

She couldn't let things change. End of story. Chase had been her rock for two years, her best friend, the one constant in her crazy, tumultuous life. He had been the first one she had called when she had gone looking for Travis after he didn't answer his cell and found him unconscious and near death, with severe internal injuries and a shattered spine, next to his overturned ATV.

Chase had been there within five minutes and had taken charge of the scene, had called the medics and the helicopter, had been there at the hospital and had held her after the doctors came out with their solemn faces and their sad eyes.

While she had been numb and broken, Chase had stepped in, organizing all the neighbors to bring in the fall harvest. He had helped her clean up and streamline the Star N operation and sell off all the unnecessary stock to keep their head above water those first few months.

Now the ranch was in the black again—thanks in large part to the crash course in smart ranch practices

Chase had given her. She knew perfectly well that without him, there wouldn't *be* a Star N right now or The Christmas Ranch. She and her sisters would have had to sell off the land, the cattle, *everything* to pay their debts.

Travis hadn't been a very good businessman. At his death, she'd found the ranch was seriously overextended with creditors and had been operating under a system of gross inefficiencies for years.

She winced with the guilt the disloyal thought always stirred in her, but it was nothing less than the truth. If her husband hadn't died and things had continued on the same course, the ranch would have gone bankrupt within a few years. Through Chase's extensive help, she had been able to turn things around.

The ranch was doing so much better. The Christmas Ranch—the seasonal attraction started by her uncle and aunt after she and her sisters came to live with them— was finally in the black, too. Hope and her husband, Rafe, had done an amazing job revitalizing it and making it a powerful draw. That success had only been augmented by the wild viral popularity of the charming children's book Celeste had written and Hope had illustrated featuring the ranch's starring attraction, Sparkle the Reindeer.

She couldn't be more proud of her sisters—though she did find it funny that, of the three of them, *Faith* seemed the one most excited that Celeste and Hope had signed an agreement to allow a production company to make an animated movie out of the first Sparkle book.

Despite a few preproduction problems, the process

was currently under way, though the animated movie wouldn't come out for another year. The buzz around it only heightened interest in The Christmas Ranch and led to increased revenue.

The book had helped push The Christmas Ranch to self-sufficiency. Without that steady drain on the Star N side of the family operation, Faith had been able to plow profits back into the cattle ranch operation.

As she drove past the Saint Nicholas Lodge on the way to the ranch house, she spotted both of her sisters' vehicles in the parking lot.

After taking up most of the day at the auction, she had a hundred things to do. As she had told Chase, Barrett and Louisa would be home from school soon. When she could swing it, she liked being there to greet them, to ask about their day and help manage their homework and chore responsibilities.

On a whim, though, she pulled into the parking lot and hurriedly texted both of her children as well as Aunt Mary to tell them she was stopping at the lodge for a moment and would be home soon.

The urge to talk to her sisters was suddenly overwhelming. Hope and Celeste weren't just her sisters, they were her best friends.

She had to park three rows back, which she considered a great sign for a Tuesday afternoon in mid-December.

Tourists from as far away as Boise and Salt Lake City were making the trek here to visit their quaint little Christmas attraction, with its sleigh rides, the reindeer herd, the village—and especially because this was the home of Sparkle.

As far as she was concerned, this was just home.

The familiar scents inside the lodge encircled her the moment she walked inside—cinnamon and vanilla and pine, mixed with old logs and the musty smell of a building that stood empty most of the year.

She heard her younger sisters bickering in the office before she saw them.

"Cry your sad song to someone else," Celeste was saying. "I told you I wasn't going to do it again this year and I won't let you guilt me into it."

"But you did such a great job last year," Hope protested.

"Yes I did," their youngest sister said. "And I swore I wouldn't ever do it again."

Faith poked her head into the office in time to see Hope pout. She was nearly three months pregnant and only just beginning to show.

"It didn't turn out so badly," Hope pointed out. "You ended up with a fabulous husband and a new stepdaughter out of the deal, didn't you?"

"Seriously? You're giving the children's show credit for my marriage to Flynn?"

"Think about it. Would you be married to your hunky contractor right now and deliriously happy if you hadn't directed the show for me last year—and if his daughter hadn't begged to participate?"

It was an excellent point, Faith thought with inward amusement that Celeste didn't appear to share.

"Why can't you do it?" Celeste demanded.

"We are booked solid with tour groups at the ranch until Christmas Eve. I won't have a minute to breathe from now until the New Year—and that's with Rafe making me cut down my hours."

"You knew you were going to be slammed," Celeste said, not at all persuaded. "Talk about procrastination. I can't believe you didn't find somebody to organize the variety show weeks ago!"

"I *had* somebody. Linda Keller told me clear back in September she would do it. I thought we were set, but she fell this morning and broke her arm, which leaves me back at square one. The kids are going to be coming to practice a week from today and I've got absolutely no one to lead them."

Hope shifted her attention to Faith with a considering look that struck fear in her heart.

"Oh, no," she exclaimed. "You can forget that idea right now."

"Why?" Hope pouted. "You love kids and senior citizens both, plus you sing like a dream. You even used to direct the choir at church, which I say makes you the perfect one to run the Christmas show."

She rolled her eyes. Hope knew better than to seriously consider that idea. "Right. Because you know I've got absolutely nothing else going on right now."

"Everyone is busy. That's the problem. Whose idea was it to put on a show at Christmas, the busiest time of the year?"

"Yours." Faith and Celeste answered simultaneously.

Hope sighed. "I know. It just seemed natural for The Christmas Ranch to throw a holiday celebration for the senior citizens. Maybe next year we'll do a Christmas in July kind of thing."

"Except you'll be having a baby in July," Faith pointed out. "And I'll be even more busy during the summer."

"You're right." She looked glum. "Do you have any suggestions for someone else who might be interested in directing it? I would hate to see the pageant fade out, especially after last year was such a smash success, thanks to CeCe. You wouldn't believe how many people have stopped me in town during the past year to tell me how much they enjoyed it and hoped we were doing another one."

"I believe it," Celeste said. "I've had my share of people telling me the same thing. That still doesn't mean I want to run it again."

"I wasn't even involved with the show and I still have people stop me in town to tell me they hope we're doing it again," Faith offered.

"That's because you're a Nichols," Hope said.

"Right. Which to some people automatically means I burp tinsel and have eggnog running through my veins."

Celeste laughed. "You don't?"

"Nope. Hope inherited all the Christmas spirit from Uncle Claude and Aunt Mary."

The sister in question made a face. "That may be true, but it still doesn't give me someone to run the show this year. But never fear. I've got a few ideas up my sleeves."

"I can help," Celeste said. "I just don't want to be the one in charge."

Faith couldn't let her younger sister be the only generous one in the family. She sighed. "Okay. I'll help again, too. But only behind the scenes—and only because you're pregnant and I don't want you to overdo."

Hope's eyes glittered and her smile wobbled. "Oh. You're both going to make me cry and Rafe tells me I've already hit my tear quota for the day. Quick, talk about something else. How did the auction go today?"

At the question, all her angst about Chase flooded back.

She suddenly desperately wanted to confide in her sisters. That was the whole reason she'd stopped at the lodge, she realized, because she yearned to share this startling development with them and obtain their advice.

I want you to be my date, with everything that goes along with that.

What was she going to do?

She wanted to ask them but they both adored Chase and it suddenly seemed wrong to talk about him with Hope and Celeste. If she had to guess, she expected they would probably take his side. They wouldn't understand how he had just upended everything safe and secure she had come to depend upon.

When she didn't answer right away, both of her sisters looked at her with concern. "Did something go wrong with the horse you wanted to buy?" Celeste asked. "You weren't outbid, were you? If you were, I'm sure you'll be able to find another one."

She shook her head. "No. We bought the horse for about five percent under what I was expecting to pay and she's beautiful. Mostly white with black spots and lovely black boot markings on her legs. I can't wait for Louisa to see her."

"I want to see her!" Hope said. "You took her to Chase's pasture?"

"Yes, and a few moments after we unloaded her, Cindy pulled up with Addie. Apparently Carol Johnson had a small stroke this morning and she's in the hospital in Idaho Falls so Cindy came home to be with her and help her father."

At the mention of Chase's ex-wife, both of her sisters' mouths tightened in almost exactly the same way. There had been no love lost between any of them, especially after Cindy's affair with the oral surgeon who eventually became her husband.

"So Cindy just dropped off Addie like UPS delivering a surprise package?" Hope asked, disgust clear in her voice.

"What about school?" ever-practical Celeste asked. "Surely she's not out for Christmas break yet."

"No. She's going to do her homework from here." She paused, remembering the one other complication. "I haven't asked Mary yet if she's available but in case she's not, would either of you like a couple of extra kids on Friday night? Three, actually—my two and Addie. Chase and I have a…a thing and it might run late."

"Oh, I wish I could," Hope exclaimed. "Rafe and I promised Joey we would take him to Boise to see his mom. We're staying overnight and doing some shopping while we're there."

"How is Cami doing?" Faith asked. "She's been out of prison, what, three months now?"

"Ten weeks. She's doing so well. Much better than Rafe expected, really. The court-ordered drug rehab she had in prison worked in her case and the halfway house is really helping her get back on her feet. Another six months and she's hoping she can have her own place and be ready to take Joey back. Maybe even by the time the baby comes."

Hope tried to smile but it didn't quite reach her eyes and Faith couldn't resist giving her sister's hand a squeeze. Celeste did the same to the other hand. Hope and her husband had cared for Rafe's nephew Joey since before their marriage after his sister's conviction on drug and robbery charges. They loved him and would both be sad to see him go.

Joey seemed like a different kid than he'd been when he first showed up at The Christmas Ranch with Rafe, two years earlier, sullen and confused and angry…

"We're trying to convince her to come back to Pine Gulch," Hope said, trying to smile. "It might help her stay out of trouble, and that way we can remain part of Joey's life. So far it's an uphill battle, as she feels like this is where all her troubles started."

Her sister's turmoil was a sharp reminder to Faith. Hope might be losing the boy she considered a son, and Celeste's stepdaughter, Olivia, still struggled to recover from both physical injuries and the emotional trauma of witnessing her mother's murder at the hands of her mentally ill and suicidal boyfriend.

In contrast, the problem of trying to figure out what to do with Chase seemed much more manageable.

"Anyway," Hope said, "that's why I won't be around Friday to help you with the kids. Sorry again."

"Don't give it another thought. That's exactly where you need to be."

"The kids are more than welcome at our place," Celeste said. "Flynn and Olivia are having a movie marathon and watching *Miracle on 34th Street* and *White Christmas*. I'll be writing during most of it, but hope to sneak in and watch the dancing in *White Christmas*."

She used to love those movies, Faith remembered. When she was young, her parents had a handful of very old, very worn VCR tapes of several holiday classics and would drag them from place to place, sometimes even showing them at social events for people in whatever small village they had set their latest medical clinic in at the time.

She probably had been just as baffled as the villagers at the world shown in the movies, which seemed so completely foreign to her own life experience, with the handsomely dressed people and the luxurious train rides and the children surrounded by toys she could only imagine.

"That sounds like the perfect evening," she said now. "Maybe I'll join the movie night instead of going to a boring Christmas party with Chase. I can bring the popcorn."

"You can't skip the stockgrowers' party," Celeste said. "It's the big social event of the year, isn't it? Jenna McRaven always caters that gala so you know the food will be fantastic, plus you'll be going with Chase. How can any party be boring with him around?"

Again, she wanted to blurt out to her sisters how strangely he was acting. She even opened her mouth to do it but before she could force the words out, she heard familiar young voices outside in the hallway just an instant before Barrett and Louisa poked their heads in, followed in short order by Celeste's stepdaughter, Olivia, and Joey. Liv went straight to Celeste while Joey practically jumped into Hope's outstretched arms.

It warmed her heart so much to see her sisters being such loving mother figures to children who needed them desperately.

"Joey and Olivia were coming to the house to hang out when I got your text," Louisa said. "We saw all your cars so decided to stop here to say hi before we walk up to the house from the bus stop."

"I'm so glad you did," Faith said.

She hugged them both, her heart aching with love. "Good day?" she asked.

Louisa nodded. "Pretty good. I had a substitute for science and she was way nicer than Mr. Lewis."

"Guess who got a hundred-ten percent on his math test?" Barrett said with a huge grin "Go on. Guess."

She made a big show of looking confused and glancing in the other boy's direction. "You did, Joey? Good job, kid!"

Rafe's nephew giggled. "I only got a hundred percent. I missed the extra credit but Barrett didn't."

Her son preened. "I was the only one in the class who got it right."

"I'm proud of both of you. What a smart family we have!"

Except for her, the one who couldn't figure out how to protect the friendship that meant the world to her.

Chapter Three

As he drove up to the Star N ranch house four days after the auction, Chase couldn't remember the last time he'd been so on edge. He wasn't nervous—or at least he would never admit to it. He was just unsettled.

So many things seemed to hinge on this night. How was he supposed to make Faith ever view him as more than just her neighbor and best friend? She had to see him for himself, a man who had spent nearly half his life waiting for her.

He didn't like the way that made him sound weak, like some kind of mongrel hanging on the fringes of her life, content for whatever scraps she threw out the kitchen door at him. It hadn't been like that. He had genuinely tried to put his unrequited feelings behind him after she and Travis got married. For the most part, he had succeeded.

He had dated a great deal and had genuinely liked several of the women he dated. In the beginning, he had liked Cindy, too. She had been funny and smart and beautiful. He was a man and had been flattered— and susceptible—when she aggressively pursued him.

When she told him she was pregnant, he decided marrying her and making a home for their child was the right thing to do. He really had tried to make their marriage work but he and Cindy were a horrible mismatch from the beginning. He could see now that they would never have suited each other, even if that little dusty corner of his heart hadn't belonged to the wife of another man.

"This is going to be so fun," Addie declared beside him. She was just about dancing out of her seat belt with excitement. "Seems like it's been forever since I've had a chance to hang out with Louisa and Olivia. It's going to be awesome."

The plan for the evening had changed at the last minute, Faith had told him in a quick, rather awkward conversation earlier that day. Celeste and Flynn decided to move their movie party to the Star N ranch house and the three girls were going to stay overnight after the movie.

If Lou and Olivia were as excited as Addie, Celeste and Mary were in for a night full of giggling girls.

His daughter let out a little shriek when he pulled up and turned off the engine.

"This is going to be *so fun*!" she repeated.

He had to smile as he climbed out and walked around to open the door. He never got tired of seeing the joy his daughter found in the simple things in life.

"Hand me your suitcase."

"Here. You don't have to carry everything, though. I can take the rest."

After pulling her suitcase from behind the seat, she hopped out with her pillow and sleeping bag.

"Careful. It's icy," he said as they headed up the sidewalk to the sprawling ranch house.

She sent him an appraising look as they reached the front door. "You look really good, Dad," she declared. "Like, Nick Jonas good."

"That's quite a compliment." Or it would be if he had more than the vaguest idea who Nick Jonas was.

"It's true. I bet you'll be the hottest guy at the party, especially since everyone else will be a bunch of married old dudes, right?"

He wasn't sure about that. Justin Hartford was a famous—though retired—movie star and Seth Dalton had once been quite a lady's man in these parts.

"You're sweet, kiddo," he said, kissing the top of her head that smelled like grape-scented shampoo.

Man, he loved this kid and missed her like crazy when she was staying with her mother.

"Doesn't their house look pretty?" she said cheerfully as she rang the doorbell.

The Star N ranch house was ablaze with multicolored Christmas lights around the windows and along the roofline, and their Christmas tree glowed merrily in the front bay window.

It was warm and welcoming against the cold, starry night.

The first year after Travis died, Faith had refused to hang any outside Christmas lights on the house and had only had a Christmas tree because Chase had decorated her Christmas tree with the kids and Aunt Mary. Faith hadn't been up to it and had claimed ranch business elsewhere while they did it.

Last year, he and Rafe had hung the outside Christmas lights.

This year, Faith herself had hung the lights, with Barrett and Lou helping her.

He wanted to think there was some symbolism in that, one more example that she was moving forward with her life.

Addie was about to ring the doorbell again when it suddenly opened. Faith's aunt stood on the other side and at the sight of him, Mary gave a low, appreciative whistle that made him feel extremely self-conscious.

"I should yell at you for ringing the doorbell when I've told you a hundred times you're family, but you look so good, I was about to ask Miss Addie what handsome stranger brought her to our door."

His daughter giggled and kissed the wrinkled cheek Mary offered. "Hi, Aunt Mary. It's just my dad. But I told him on the way that he looked super hot. For an old guy, anyway."

He *felt* hot in his suit and tie, but probably not the way she meant. Mary grinned. "You're absolutely right," she said. "Nice to see you dressed up for once."

"Thanks," he answered.

Before he could say more, Louisa burst into the room and started dancing around Addie. "You're here! You're here! I've been dying to see you and do more than just talk on the phone and text and stuff. It feels like *forever* since you've been here."

The girls hugged as if they had been separated for months.

"Need me to carry your stuff to your room?" he asked.

"It's just a suitcase and sleeping bag, Dad. I think we can handle it."

"Let's hurry, before Barrett finds out you're here and starts bugging us," Louisa said.

Poor Barrett, who until recently had been completely outnumbered by all the women in his life. At least now he had a couple of uncles and an honorary cousin in Rafe's nephew, Joey.

"Faith only came in from the barn about half an hour ago so she's still getting ready," Mary said, her plump features tight with disapproval for a moment before she wiped the expression away and gave him a smile instead. "I heard the shower turn off a few minutes ago so it shouldn't be long now."

He tried not to picture Faith climbing out of the shower, all creamy skin with her tight, slender body covered in water droplets. Once the image bloomed there, it was tough to get it out of his head again to focus on anything else.

"It's fine," he answered. "We've got plenty of time."

"You're too patient," Mary said. Her voice had an unusually barbed tone to it that made him think she wasn't necessarily talking about him waiting for Faith to get dressed for their night out.

"Maybe I just don't want to make anybody feel rushed," he answered carefully—also talking about more than just that evening.

Mary sniffed. "That's all well and good, but sometimes time can be your worst enemy, son. People get set in their ways and can't see the world is still brimming over with possibilities. Sometimes they need a sharp boot in the keister to point them in the right direction."

Well, that was clear enough. Mary *definitely* wasn't talking about the time Faith was taking to get ready. He gave her a searching look. Maybe he hadn't been as careful as he thought about not wearing his heart on his sleeve.

He loved Faith's aunt, who had opened her home and her heart to Faith and her sisters after the horrible events before they came to Pine Gulch. She and Claude had offered a safe haven for three grieving girls but they had provided much more than that. Through steady love and care, the couple had helped the girls begin to heal.

Mary had truly been a lifesaver after Travis's death, as well. She had moved back into the ranch house and stepped up to help with the children while Faith struggled to juggle widowhood and single motherhood while suddenly saddled with the responsibilities of running a big cattle ranch on her own.

"I'm just saying," Mary went on, "maybe it's time to get off your duff and make a move."

He could feel tension spread out from his head to

his shoulders. "That's the plan. What do you think to-night is about?"

"I was hoping."

She frowned, blue eyes troubled. "Just between me and you and that Christmas tree, I've got a feeling that might be the reason why a certain person just came in from the barn only a half hour ago, even though she knew all day you were on the way and exactly what time she would need to start getting ready."

Did that mean Mary thought Faith was avoiding the idea of going on a real date with him? He couldn't tell and before he had the chance to ask for clarification, Flynn Delaney came into the living room.

The other man did a double take when he spotted Chase talking to Mary. "Wow. A tie and everything."

Chase shrugged, though he could feel his skin prickle. "A Christmas party for the local stockgrowers association might not be a red-carpet Hollywood affair, but it's still a pretty big deal around here."

"Take it from me—it will be much more enjoyable for everyone involved."

He wasn't so sure about that, especially if Faith was showing reluctance about the evening.

"Sometime this week, Rafe and I are planning to spruce up the set we used last year for the Christmas show. If you want to lend a hand, we'll pay you in beer."

He had come to truly enjoy the company of both of Faith's brothers-in-law. They were both decent men who, as far as he was concerned, were almost good enough for her sisters.

"Addie's in town right now and I feel bad enough

about leaving her tonight when our time together is limited. I'll have to see what she wants to do but I'm sure she wouldn't mind coming out again and riding horses with Lou."

"I get it. Believe me."

Flynn had been a divorced father, too. He and his famous actress wife had been divorced several years before she was eventually killed so tragically.

The other man looked down the hallway, apparently to make sure none of the kids were in earshot. "I hear a certain *H-O-R-S-E* is safely ensconced at your place now."

"Lou is twelve years old and can spell, you know," Mary said with a snort.

Flynn grinned at the older woman. "Yeah. But will she slow down long enough to bother taking time to do it? That's the question."

Chase had to laugh. The horse and Louisa would be perfect for each other. "Yeah. She's a beauty. Louisa is going to be thrilled, I think. You all are in for a fun Christmas morning."

"You'll come over for breakfast like you usually do, won't you?" Mary asked.

He wasn't so sure about that. Maybe he would have to see how that evening went first. He hoped like hell that he wasn't about to ruin all his most important relationships with Faith's family by muddying the water with her.

"I hope so," he started to say, but the words died when he heard a commotion on the stairs and a moment later, Faith hurried down them wearing a silver-and-blue dress that made her look like a snow princess.

"Sorry. I'm so sorry I'm late," Faith exclaimed as she fastened a dangly silver earring.

He couldn't have responded, since his brain seemed to have shut down.

She looked absolutely stunning, with her hair piled on top of her head in a messy, sexy bun, strands artfully escaping in delectable ways. She wore a rosy lipstick and more eye makeup than usual, with mascara and eyeliner that made her eyes look huge and exotically slanted.

The dress hugged her shape, with a neckline that revealed just a hint of cleavage. She wore strappy sandals that made him wonder if he was going to have to scoop her up and carry her through the snow.

He was so used to seeing her in jeans and a T-shirt and boots, wearing a ponytail and little makeup except lip balm.

She was beautiful either way.

He swallowed, realizing he had to say something and not just stand there like an idiot.

"You're worth the wait," he said.

His voice came out rough and she flashed him a startled look before he saw color climb her cheeks.

"I don't know about that. It's been a crazy day and I feel like I've been running since five a.m. I'll probably fall asleep the moment I get into your truck."

He would love to have her curl up beside him and sleep. It certainly wouldn't be the first time.

"I'll have to see what I can do to keep you awake," he murmured.

"Driving with the windows down and the music cranked always helps me," Flynn offered.

"I spent too long fixing that hair for you to mess it up with a wind tunnel," Celeste Nichols Delaney said as she followed her sister down the stairs.

Her words brought Chase to his senses and he realized he had been standing in the entryway, gaping at her like he'd never seen a beautiful woman before.

He cleared his throat and forced himself to smile at Celeste. "We can't have that. You did a great job."

"I did, especially with Faith trying to send three emails, put on her makeup and help Barrett with his English homework at the same time."

"I appreciate your hard work," Faith said. "I think I'm finally ready. I just need my coat."

She made it the rest of the way down the stairs on the high heels and reached inside the closet in the entryway, but before she could pull off the serviceable ranch coat she always wore, Celeste slapped her hand away. "Oh, no you don't."

Faith frowned at her sister. "Why not? This is a stockgrowers' dinner. You think they've never seen a ranch coat before?"

"Not with that dress, they haven't. That's why I brought over this."

She pulled a soft fawn coat reverently from the arm of the sofa. "I bought this last month in New York when Hope and I were there meeting with our publisher."

"I don't want to wear your fancy coat."

"Too bad. You're going to."

Celeste could be as stubborn as the other sisters. "Fine," Faith finally sighed, reaching for the coat that looked cashmere and expensive. With a subtle wink, Celeste ignored her sister's outstretched hand and gave it to Chase instead. It was soft as a newborn kitten. He felt inordinately breathless as he moved behind Faith and helped her into it.

She smelled…different. Usually she smelled of vanilla and oranges from her favorite soap but this was a little more intense, with a low, flowery note that made him want to bury his face in her neck and inhale.

"There you go," he said gruffly.

"Thanks." It was obvious she wasn't comfortable dressing up, perhaps because so much of her childhood was spent with parents who gave away most of their material possessions to the people they worked with in impoverished countries.

"Are you happy now?" Faith said to her sister.

"Yes. You're beautiful." Celeste's eyes were soft and a little teary. "Sometimes you look so much like Mom."

"She must have been stunning," Flynn said, kissing his sister-in-law on the cheek.

Chase cleared away the little catch in his throat. "Breathtaking," he agreed.

Her cheeks turned pink at the attention. "I still think we'd have much more fun staying home and watching Christmas movies with the kids," she said. She smiled at the three of them but he was almost certain he saw a flicker of nervousness in her eyes again.

"Now, there's absolutely no reason for the two of

you to rush back," Celeste assured them. "The three of us have got this covered. The kids will all be fine. Go and have a great time."

"That's right," Mary said. She gave Chase a pointed look, as if to remind him of their conversation earlier. "You ask me, these parties end way too soon. I suppose that's what you get when you hang out with people who have to wake up early to feed their livestock. So don't feel like you have to come straight home when it's over. You could even go catch a movie in town if you wanted or grab drinks at that fancy new bar that opened up on the outskirts of town."

"The only trouble is we both *also* have to wake up early to take care of our livestock," Faith said with a laugh that sounded slightly strained.

"Louisa. Barrett," she called. "I'm leaving. Come give me a hug."

All the children, not only her two, hurried down the stairs to join them.

"You look beautiful, Faith," Addie exclaimed. "What a cute couple you guys are. Wait. Let me get a picture so I can show my friends."

She pulled out the smartphone he didn't think she needed yet and snapped a picture.

"Oh! What a good idea," Celeste said. "I want a picture, too."

"We're just going to a Christmas party. It's not the prom," Faith said. Her color ratcheted up a notch, especially when Aunt Mary pulled out her phone as well and started clicking away taking pictures.

"I'm posting this one," her aunt declared. "You both

look so good. In fact, you better watch it, Chase, or you'll have about a hundred marriage proposals before the night is over. My friends on social media can be a wild bunch."

Faith's cheeks by now were as red as the ornaments on the tree. This was distressing her, and though he didn't quite understand why, it didn't matter. His job was to protect her—even from loving relatives with cell phone cameras.

"Okay, that's enough paparazzi for tonight. We'll really be late if this keeps up."

"You don't want that. You'll miss all of Jenna McRaven's good food," Mary said.

"Exactly." He hugged his daughter. "Be good, Ads. I imagine you'll still be up when I bring Faith back but if you're not, I'll see you in the morning."

"Bye, Dad. Have fun."

He waited for Faith to hug and kiss her kids and admonish them to behave for Aunt Mary and the Delaneys, then he held the door open for her and they headed out into the cold air that felt refreshing on his overheated skin.

Neither of them said anything as he led her to his pickup and helped her inside. He wished he had some kind of luxury sedan to take her to the party but that kind of vehicle wasn't very practical on an eastern Idaho ranch. At least he'd taken the truck for a wash and had vacuumed up any dried mud and straw bits out of the inside.

It took a little effort to tuck the soft length of her coat inside. "Better make sure I don't shut the door on

Celeste's coat," he joked. "She would probably never forgive me."

He went around and climbed inside, then turned his pickup truck around and started heading toward the canyon road that would take them to Pine Gulch and the party.

"My family. Ugh. You'd think I never went to a Christmas party before, the way they carry on." Faith didn't look at him as she fiddled with the air vent. "I don't know what's gotten into them all. I mean, we went together last year to the exact same party and nobody gave it a second thought."

A wise man would probably keep his mouth shut, just go with the flow.

Maybe he was tired of keeping his mouth shut.

"If I had to guess," he said, after giving her a long look, "they're making a fuss because they know this is different, that we're finally going out on a real date."

Chapter Four

At his words, tension seemed to clamp around her spine with icy fingers.

We're finally going out on a real date.

She had really been hoping he had forgotten all that nonsense by now and they could go to the party as they always had done things, as dear friends.

She didn't know what to say. She couldn't stop thinking about that moment when she had started down the stairs and had seen him standing there, looking tall and rugged and gorgeous, freshly shaved and wearing a dark Western-cut suit and tie.

He had looked like he should be going to a country music awards show with a beautiful starlet on his arm or something, not the silly local stockgrowers association party with *her*.

She had barely been able to think straight and literally had felt so weak-kneed she considered it a minor miracle that she hadn't stumbled down the stairs right at his feet.

Then he had spotted her and the heat in his eyes had sent an entire flock of butterflies swarming through her insides.

"Every time I bring up that this is a date, you go silent as dirt," he murmured. "Why is that?"

She drew in a breath. "I don't know what to say."

He shot her a quick look across the bench seat of his truck. "Is the idea of dating me so incomprehensible?"

"Not incomprehensible. Just…disconcerting," she answered honestly.

"Why?" he pressed.

How was she supposed to answer that? He was her best friend and knew all her weaknesses and faults. Surely he knew she was a giant coward at heart, that she didn't *want* these new and terrifying feelings.

She had no idea how to answer him so she opted to change the subject. "I haven't had a chance to ask you. How's Louisa's new horse?"

He shifted his gaze from the road, this time to give her a long look. She thought for a moment he would call her on it and press for an answer. To her relief, he turned back to the road and, after a long pause, finally answered her.

"Settling in, I guess. She seems to have really taken to Tor—and vice versa."

"I hope they won't be too upset at being separated

when we send the new horse to Seth Dalton's after Christmas."

"I'm sure they'll survive. If not, we can always arrange visitation."

That word inevitably reminded her of his ex-wife.

"How is Cindy's mother doing?" she asked.

He shrugged. "Fine, from what I hear. She's probably going to be in the hospital another week."

"Does that mean the cruise is off?"

"Cindy insists they don't want to cancel the cruise unless it's absolutely necessary. I'm still planning my Christmas celebration with Addie on December 20."

"It's just another day on the calendar," she said.

"Don't let Hope hear you say that or she might ban you from The Christmas Ranch," he joked.

They spoke of the upcoming children's Christmas show and the crowds at the ranch and the progress of her sisters' movie for the remainder of the short drive to the reception hall where the annual dinner and party was always held.

He found a parking space not far from the building and climbed out to walk around the vehicle to her side. While she waited for him to open her door, Faith took a deep breath.

She could do this. Tonight was no different from dozens of other social events they had attended together. Weddings, birthday parties, Fourth of July barbecues. Things had never been awkward between them until now.

We're finally going out on a real date.

When she thought of those words, little starbursts of panic flared inside her.

She couldn't give in. Chase was her dear friend and she cared about him deeply. As long as she kept that in mind, everything would be just fine.

She wasn't certain she completely believed that but she refused to consider the alternative right now.

The party was in full swing when they arrived. The reception hall had been decorated with an abundance of twinkling fairy lights strung end to end and Christmas trees stood in each corner. Delectable smells wafted out of the kitchen and her stomach growled, almost in time to the band playing a bluegrass version of "Good King Wenceslas." A few couples were even dancing and she watched them with no small amount of envy. She missed dancing.

"You'd better give me Celeste's New York City coat so I can hang it up," Chase said from beside her.

She gave him a rueful smile. "I'm a little afraid to let it out of my sight but I guess I can't wear it all night."

"No, you can't. Go on inside. I'll hang this and be there in a moment."

She nodded and stepped into the reception room. Her good friend Jennie Dalton—Seth Dalton's wife and principal of the elementary school—stood just inside. Jennie was talking with Ashley Hartford, who taught kindergarten at the elementary school.

While their husbands were lost in conversation, the two women were speaking with a young, lovely woman she didn't recognize—which was odd, since she knew just about everyone who came to these events.

Jennie held out a hand when she spotted her. "Hello, my dear. You look gorgeous, as always."

Faith made a face, wishing she didn't feel like a frazzled, overburdened rancher and single mother.

She held a hand out to the woman she didn't know. "Hi. I'm Faith Dustin."

The woman had pretty features and a sweet smile. "Hello. I'm Ella Baker. You may know my father, Curt."

"Yes, of course. Hello. Lovely to meet you."

Curt Baker had a ranch on the other side of town. She didn't know him well but she had heard he had a daughter he didn't know well who had spent most of her life living with her mother back East somewhere. From what she understood, his daughter had returned to help him through a health scare.

"Your dad is looking well."

Ella glanced at her father with a troubled look, then forced a smile. "He's doing better, I suppose."

"Ella is a music therapist and she just agreed to take the job of music teacher at the school for the rest of the school year," Jennie said, looking thrilled at the prospect.

"That's a long time coming."

"Right. We've had the funding for it but haven't been able to find someone suitable since Linda Keller retired two years ago. We've been relying on parent volunteers, who have been wonderful, but can only take the program so far. I'm a firm believer that children learn better when we can incorporate the arts in the classroom."

"I completely agree," Faith said, then was suddenly struck by a small moment of brilliance. "Hey, I've got a terrific way for you to get to know some of the young people in the community."

"Oh?"

"My family runs The Christmas Ranch. You may have seen signs for it around town."

"Absolutely. I haven't had time to stop yet but it looks utterly delightful."

"It is." She didn't bother telling the woman she had very little to do with the actual operations of The Christmas Ranch. It was always too complicated explaining that she ran the cattle side of things—hence her presence at this particular holiday party.

"Last year we started a new tradition of offering a children's Christmas variety show and dinner for the senior citizens in town. It's nothing grand, more for fun than anything else. The children only practice for the week leading up to the show, since everyone is so busy this time of year. Linda Keller, the woman who retired a few years ago from the school district, had offered to help us this year but apparently she just broke her arm."

"That's as good an excuse as any," Ashley said.

"I suppose. The point is my sisters are desperate for someone to help them organize the show. I don't suppose there's any chance you might be interested."

It seemed a nervy thing to ask a woman she had only met five minutes earlier. To Faith's relief, Ella Baker didn't seem offended.

"That sounds like a blast," Ella exclaimed. "I've been looking for something to keep me busy until the New Year when I start at the school part-time."

Hope was going to owe her *big-time*—so much that Faith might even claim naming rights over the new baby.

"Great! You'll have fun, I promise. The kids are so cute and we've got some real talent."

"This is true," Ashley said. "Especially Faith's niece, Olivia. She sings like an angel. Last year the show was so wonderful."

"The senior citizens in the area really ate it up," Jennie affirmed. "My dad couldn't stop talking about it. The Nichols family has started a wonderful thing for the community."

"This sounds like a great thing. I'm excited you asked me."

"If you give me your contact info, I can forward it to my sister Hope. She's really the one in charge."

"Your name is Faith and you have a sister named Hope. Let me guess, do you have another one named Charity?"

"That would be logical, wouldn't it? But my parents never did what was expected. They named our youngest sister Celeste."

"Celeste is the children's librarian in town and she's also an author," Ashley said. "And Hope is an illustrator."

"Oh! Of course! Celeste and Hope Nichols. They wrote 'Sparkle and the Magic Snowball'! The kids at the developmental skills center where I used to work loved that story. They even wrote a song about Sparkle."

Faith smiled. "You'll have to share it with Celeste and Hope. They'll be thrilled."

She and Ella were sending contact information to each other's phones when she felt a subtle ripple in the air and a moment later Chase joined them.

Speaking with the women had begun to push out some of the butterflies inside her but they suddenly returned in full force.

"Sorry I was gone so long. I got cornered by Pete Jeppeson at the coatrack and just barely managed to get away."

"No worries. I've been meeting someone who is about to make my sisters very, very happy. Chase Brannon, this is Ella Baker. She's Curt's daughter and she's a music therapist who has just agreed to help out with the second annual Christmas Ranch holiday show."

Chase gave Ella a warm smile. "That's very kind of you—not to mention extremely brave."

The woman returned his smile and Faith didn't miss the sudden appreciative light in her eyes, along with a slightly regretful look, the sort a woman might wear while shopping when someone else in line at the checkout just ahead of her picks out the exact one-of-a-kind piece of jewelry she would have chosen for herself.

"Brave or crazy," Ella said. "I'm not sure which yet."

"You said it. I didn't," Chase said.

Both of them laughed and as she saw them together, a strange thought lodged in her brain.

The two of them could be perfect for each other.

She didn't want to admit it but Ella Baker seemed on the surface just the sort of woman Chase needed. She had only just met the woman but she trusted her instincts. Ella seemed smart and pretty, funny and kind.

Exactly the sort of woman Chase deserved.

He said he was ready to date again and here was a perfect candidate. Wouldn't a truehearted friend do everything in her power to push the two of them together—at least give Chase the chance to get to know the other woman?

She hated the very idea of it, but she wanted Chase to be happy. "Will you both excuse me for a moment? I just spotted Jenna McRaven and remembered I need to talk to her about a slight change in the menu for the dinner next week."

She aimed a bright smile at them. "You two should dance or something. Go ahead! I won't be long."

She caught a glimpse of Ella's startled features and the beginnings of a thundercloud forming on Chase's but she hurried away before he could respond.

He would thank her later, she told herself, especially if Ella turned out to be absolutely perfect for him.

He only needed to spend a little time with her to realize the lovely young woman who had put her life on hold to help her ailing father was a much better option than a prickly widow who didn't have anything left in her heart to give him.

She found Jenna in the kitchen, up to her eyeballs in appetizers.

This was the absolute worst time to bug her about a catering job, when she was busy at a different one. Faith couldn't bother her with a small change in salad dressing—especially when she was only using this as an excuse to leave Chase alone with Ella Baker. She would call Jenna later and tell her about the change at a better time.

"Hi, Faith! Don't you look beautiful tonight!"

She almost gave an inelegant snort. Jenna's blond curls were piled on her head in an adorable messy bun and her cheeks looked rosy from the heat of the kitchen and probably from the exertion of preparing a meal for so many people, while Faith had split ends and hands desperately in need of a manicure.

"I was just going to say the same to you," she said. "Seriously, you're the only person I know who can be neck-deep in making canapés and still manage to look like a model."

Jenna rolled her eyes as she continued setting out appetizers on the tray. "You're sweet but delusional. Did you need something?"

Faith glanced through the open doorway, where she could see Chase bending down to listen more closely to something Ella was saying. The sight made her stomach hurt—but maybe that was just hunger.

"Not at all. I was just wondering if you need any help back here."

Jenna looked startled at her question but not ungrateful. "That's very sweet but I'm being paid to hang out here in the kitchen. You're not. You should be out there enjoying the party."

"I can hear the music from here, plus helping you out in the kitchen would give me the chance to talk to a dear friend I don't see often enough. Need me to carry out a tray or two?"

Jenna blew out a breath. "I should say no. You're a

guest at the party. I hate to admit it, but I could really use some help for a minute. It's a two-person job but my assistant has the flu so I'm a little frantic here. Carson will be here to help me as soon as he can, but his flight from San Francisco was delayed because of weather so he's running about an hour behind."

Faith found it unbearably sweet that Jenna's billionaire husband—who commuted back and forth between Silicon Valley and Pine Gulch—was ready to help the wife he adored with a catering job. "I can help you until he gets here. No problem."

Jenna lifted her head from her task long enough to frown. "Didn't I see you come in with Chase when I was out replenishing the Parmesan smashed potatoes? I can't let you just ditch him."

She glanced at the door where he was now smiling at something Ella said.

"We drove here together, yes," she answered. "But I'm hoping he'll be dancing with Curt Baker's daughter in a moment."

"Oh. Ella. Jolie just started taking piano lessons from her. She's a delight."

"I think she would be great for Chase so I'm trying to give them a chance to get to know each other. Let nature take its course and all."

Jenna's busy hands paused in her work and she gave Faith a careful look. "You might want to ask Chase his opinion on that idea," she said mildly.

"I don't need to ask him. He's my best friend. I know what he needs probably better than he knows himself."

Jenna opened her mouth to answer, then appeared to think better of it.

She was right, Faith told herself. Chase would thank her later; she was almost certain of it.

Chapter Five

Faith was trying to ditch him.

He knew exactly what she was doing as she moved in and out of the kitchen carrying trays of food for Jenna McRaven's catering company. It wasn't completely unusual for her to help out behind the scenes, but he knew in this case she was just looking for an excuse to avoid him.

He curled his hands into fists, trying to decide if he was more annoyed or hurt. Either way, he still wanted to punch something.

The woman beside him hummed along with the bluegrass version of "Silver Bells." Ella Baker had a pretty voice and kind eyes. He felt like a jerk for ignoring her while he glowered after Faith, even though Ella wasn't the date he had walked in with.

"What were you doing before you came back to Pine Gulch to stay with your father?" he asked.

"I was the music instructor at a residential school for developmentally delayed children in Upstate New York, the same town where you can find the boarding school I attended myself from the age of eight, actually."

Boarding school? What was the story there? He wouldn't have taken Curt Baker as the sort of guy to send his kid to boarding school to be raised by someone else most of the year. He couldn't imagine it—it was hard enough packing Addie off to live with her mother half the time.

"Sounds like you were doing good work."

"I found it very rewarding. Some of my students have made remarkable progress. Music can be a comfort and a joy, as well as open doors to language and auditory processing skills I wouldn't have imagined before I started in this field."

"That sounds interesting."

She made a face. "To me, anyway. Sorry. I tend to get a little passionate when I talk about my job."

"I admire that in a person."

"It's not all I do, I promise. I did play piano and I sing in a jazz trio on the weekends."

"That's great! Maybe you ought to perform at the holiday show yourself."

She made a face. "I probably would be a little out of place, since it sounds like this is mostly a show featuring children. I'm happy enough behind the scenes."

The band changed to a slower song, a wistful holiday tune about regret and lost loves.

"Oh, I love this song," she exclaimed, swaying a little in time to the music.

What was the etiquette here? He had come to the party with a woman who was doing her best to stay away from him. Meanwhile another one was making it clear she wanted to dance.

He didn't know the social conventions but he figured simple politeness trumped the rules anyway.

"Would you like to dance?" he finally asked. If Faith would rather hide out in the kitchen than spend time in conversation with him, he probably wasn't committing some grave faux pas by asking another woman for a simple dance.

Ella's smile was soft with delight. "I would, actually. Thanks."

How weird was this night turning out? Chase wondered as he led the woman out to the dance floor with about a dozen other couples. He had come to the party hoping to end up with Faith in his arms. Instead, she was currently busy carrying out a pot of soup while he was dancing with a woman he had only just met.

Ella was a good conversationalist. She asked him about his ranch and Pine Gulch and the surroundings. He told her about Addie and the cruise she was going on with her mother and stepfather over the holidays and his plans to have their own Christmas celebration a few days before the twenty-fifth.

He actually enjoyed himself more than he might have expected, though beneath the enjoyment he was aware of a simmering frustration at Faith.

When the song ended, he spotted Ella's father on

the edge of the dance floor speaking with a ranching couple he knew who lived up near Driggs. He led her there, visited with the group for a moment, then made his excuses and headed straight for the kitchen.

He found Faith plating pieces of apple pie. She was talking to Jenna McRaven but her words seemed to stall when she spotted him.

"Are you going to hide out in here all night?"

Her gaze shifted away from his but not before he saw the shadow of nervousness there. "I'm not hiding out," she protested. "I was just giving Jen a hand for a minute. Anyway, you've been busy dancing with Ella Baker."

Only because his real date was as slippery as a newborn calf.

"You've done more than enough," Jenna assured her. "I'm grateful for your help but I'm finally caught up in here. Carson's plane just landed and he's on his way here to help me with the rest of the night. You really need to go out and enjoy the party."

Faith opened her mouth to protest but Jenna gave her a stern look. "I'm serious, sweetie. Go out and enjoy all this delicious food I've been slaving over for a week. Now hand over the apron and back away slowly and nobody will get hurt."

"Fine. If you insist." Faith huffed out a little breath but untied her apron and set it on an empty space on the counter. Chase wasn't about to let her wriggle away again. He hooked his hand in the crook of her elbow and steered her out into the reception hall and over to the buffet line.

They grabbed their food, which all appeared delicious, then Faith scanned the room. "I see a couple of chairs over by Em and Ashley. Why don't we go sit with them?"

He enjoyed hanging out with their neighbors but right now he would rather find a secluded corner and have this out. Barring that, he would rather just go home and get the hell out of this suit and tie.

Nothing was working out as he planned and he felt stupid and shortsighted for thinking it might.

"Sure. Sounds good," he lied.

She led the way and as soon as they were seated, she immediately launched into a long conversation with the other couples.

By the time dinner was over, he was more than ready to throw up his hands and declare the evening a disaster, convinced she was too stubborn to ever consider they could be anything but friends.

Sitting at this table with their neighbors and friends filled him with a deep-seated envy that left him feeling small. They were all long-married yet still obviously enamored with each other, with casual little touches and private smiles that left him feeling more lonely than ever.

The band had begun to move away from strictly playing holiday songs and began a cover of a popular upbeat pop song, adding a bluegrass flair, of course. Ashley Hartford lit up. "Oh! I love this song. Come dance with me, darling."

Though they had four children and had been married for years, Justin gave her the sort of smoldering look Chase guessed women enjoyed, since the man had made millions on the big screen, before he walked away from it all to come to Pine Gulch.

"Let's do it," he said.

"We can't let them show us up," Emery declared to her husband. "I know you hate to dance but will you, just this once?"

Nate Cavazos, former army Special Forces and tough as nails, sighed but obediently rose to follow his petite wife out to the dance floor. Their departure left him alone at the table with Faith, along with an awkward silence.

He gestured to the floor. "Do you want to dance?"

Panic flickered in her eyes and his gut ached. She had been his friend for nearly two decades. They had laughed together, cried together, confided secrets to each other.

Why the hell couldn't she see they were perfect for each other?

"Forget it," he said. "You're not enjoying this. Why don't I just go get Celeste's fabulous coat and we can take off?"

Her lush mouth twisted into a frown. "That's not fair to you."

She looked at the dance floor for a moment, then back at him. "Actually, let's go dance. I would like it very much."

He wanted to call her out for the lie but it seemed stupid to argue. Instead, Chase scraped his chair back, then reached a hand out. She placed her slim, cool, working-rancher hand in his and he led her out to the dance floor.

Just as they reached it, the music shifted to a song

he didn't know, something slow and dreamy, jazzy and soft. He pulled her into his arms—finally!—and they began to move in time to the music.

"This is nice," she murmured, and he took that as encouragement to pull her a little closer. She smelled delicious, that subtle scent he had picked up earlier, and he closed his eyes and tried to burn the moment into his memory.

She stumbled a little and when he glanced down, she was blushing. "Sorry. I'm not very good at this. I never learned to dance, unless you count some of the native dances we did in South America and Papua New Guinea."

"I'd like to see some of those."

She laughed. "I doubt I could remember a single one. Hope probably can. She was always more into them than I was. You're a very good dancer. Why didn't I know that?"

"I guess we haven't had much call to dance together."

His mother had taught him, he remembered, when he was about fourteen or fifteen, before his father's diagnosis and his family fell apart.

His mother had told him he needed to learn so he wouldn't be embarrassed at school dances. Turns out, he hadn't needed the lessons. His father's cancer and the toll the treatment had taken on him had left Chase little time for frivolous things like proms. It was all he could do to keep the ranch running while his mother ran his dad back and forth to the cancer center in Salt Lake City.

Despite the long, difficult fight, his father had lost

the battle. After he died, things had been worse. His mother had completely fallen apart that first year and had slipped into a deep, soul-crushing depression that lasted for a tough four years, until she finally went to visit a sister in Seattle, fell in love with a restaurant owner she met there and moved there permanently.

Sometimes he wondered what might have happened if his father hadn't died, if Chase hadn't been forced to put his own plans for college on the back burner.

If he had been in a better place to pursue Faith first.

If.

It was a word he really hated.

A few more turns around the dance floor and she appeared to relax and seemed to be enjoying the music and the moment. He even made her laugh a few times. The music shifted into another slow dance and she didn't seem in a hurry to stop dancing so he decided to just go with it.

If he had his choice, he would have frozen that moment forever in time, just savoring the scent of her hair and the way her curves brushed against him and the way she fit so perfectly in his arms.

Too quickly, the music ended and she pulled away.

"That was nice," she said. "Thanks."

Dancing with him had been a big step for her, he knew.

"They're about to serve dessert," he said on impulse. "What do you say we grab a couple slices of that apple pie in a couple of to-go boxes and take off somewhere to enjoy it where we can look at Christmas lights?"

"We don't have to leave if you're enjoying yourself."

"I just want to be with you. I really don't care where."

He probably shouldn't have been that blunt. She nibbled on her lip, clearly mulling her options, then smiled. "Let's go."

She hated being a coward.

Her sister Hope plowed through life, exploring the world as their parents had, experiencing life and collecting friends everywhere she went. Celeste, the youngest, was shy and timid and could be socially awkward. That seemed to have changed significantly since her marriage to Flynn and since her literary career took off, requiring more public appearances and radio interviews. Celeste seemed to be far more comfortable in her own skin these days.

Now Faith was the timid one.

Losing her husband and becoming a widow at thirty-two had changed her in substantial ways. Sometimes she wasn't even sure who she was anymore.

She had never considered herself particularly brave, though she had tried to put on a strong front for Hope and Celeste after their parents died. They had needed her and while she wanted to curl up into herself, she had tried to set an example of courage for her sisters.

After Travis died, she had wanted to do the same. That time, her children had needed her. She had to show them that even in the midst of overwhelming grief they could survive and even thrive.

Right now, that facade of strength seemed about to crumble to dust. In her heart, she was terrified and it seemed to be growing worse. She was so afraid of shaking up the status quo, setting herself up for more pain.

More than that, she was afraid of hurting Chase.

She wouldn't worry about that now. Once they were alone, just the two of them, they could forget all this date nonsense and just be Chase and Faith again, like always.

Jenna McRaven didn't ask questions when they asked if she had any to-go boxes. She pulled out a cardboard container that she loaded with two pieces of caramel-topped apple pie.

A moment later, without giving explanations to anyone, they grabbed Celeste's luxurious coat and hurried outside into the December night.

Her breath puffed out as they made their way to his pickup but she wasn't cold. She wanted to give credit to the fine cashmere wool but in truth she was still overheated from the warm dance floor and her own ridiculous nerves.

"Where should we go for dessert?" he asked. "What do you think about Orchard Park? It offers a nice view of town."

She would rather go back to the Star N and change into jeans and a T-shirt. Barring that, Orchard Park would have to do. "Sounds good," she answered.

He turned on a Christmas station and soft, jazzy music filled the interior of his pickup truck as he drove the short distance from the reception hall to an area of new development in Pine Gulch.

A small subdivision of single-family homes was being built here on land that had once been filled with fruit trees. The streets had names like Apple Blossom Drive, Jubilee Lane and McIntosh Court and only about half the lots had new houses.

Chase pulled above the last row of houses to a clearing at the end of the road, probably where the developer planned to add more houses eventually.

He put the vehicle in Park but left the engine running. Warm air poured out of the vents from the heater, wrapping them in a cozy embrace.

"I'm sorry I didn't think to get a bottle of wine but I should have some water in my emergency stash."

He climbed out and rummaged in a cargo box in the backseat before emerging with a couple of water bottles.

Given the harsh winters in the region, most people she knew kept kits in their vehicles with water bottles, granola bars and foil emergency blankets in case they were stranded in a blizzard.

"Don't forget to replenish your supply," she said when he slid back in the front seat.

"I won't. Nothing worse than being stuck in four-foot-high drifts somewhere with nothing to drink but melted snow."

That had never happened to her, thankfully. She unscrewed the cap and took a drink of the water, which was remarkably cold and refreshing, then handed him the to-go carton of pie Jenna had given them along with the fork her friend had provided.

"I guess it's fitting we should eat an apple pie here," she said.

His teeth gleamed in the darkness as he smiled. "Anything else wouldn't seem as appropriate, would it?"

With the glittery stars above them and the color-ful lights of town below, she took a bite of her pie and nearly swooned from the sheer sensory overload.

"Wow. That's fantastic," she breathed. It was flaky and crusty and buttery, with just the right hint of cara-mel. "Jenna is a master of the simple apple pie. I've got her recipe but I can never make it just like this. I don't know what she does differently from me or Aunt Mary or my sisters but it's so fantastic."

"Even without ice cream."

She laughed. "I was thinking that but didn't want to say it."

It seemed a perfect moment, so much better away from the public social pressure of the party. She took a deep breath and realized she hadn't fully filled her lungs all evening. Stupid nerves.

"I love the view from this area," she said. "Pine Gulch seems so peaceful and quiet."

"I suppose it looks so peaceful because you can't see from up here how old Doris Packer is such a bitter old hag or how Ben Tillman has a habit of shortchang-ing his customers at the tavern or how Wilma Rivera is probably talking trash about her sister-in-law."

He was so right. "It's easy to simply look at the sur-face and think you know a place, isn't it?"

"Right." He sent her a sidelong look. "People are much the same. You have to dig beneath the nice clothes and the polite polish to find the essence of a person."

She knew the essence of Chase Brannon. He was a kind, decent, *good* man who so deserved to be happy.

She sighed and could feel the heat of his gaze.

"That sounded heavy. What's on your mind?"

She had a million things racing through her thoughts and didn't know how to talk to him about any of it. She couldn't tell him that she felt like she stood on the edge of a precipice, toes tingling from the vast, unknown chasm below her, and she just didn't know how much courage she had left inside her to jump.

"I'm feeling bad about taking you away from the party," she lied.

"You didn't take me away. Leaving was my idea, remember?"

He reached up to loosen his tie. Funny how that simple act seemed to help her remember this was Chase, her best friend. She wanted him to be happy, no matter what.

"It was a good idea. Still, if we had stayed, maybe you could have danced with Ella Baker again."

He said nothing but annoyance suddenly seemed to radiate out of him in pointed rays.

"She seems very nice," Faith pressed.

"Yes."

"And she's musical, too."

"Yes."

"Not to mention beautiful, don't you think?"

"She's lovely."

"You should ask her out, since you suddenly want to start dating again."

He made a low sound in the back of his throat, the kind of noise he made when his tractor broke down or one of his ranch hands called in sick too many times.

"Who said I wanted to start dating again?" he said, his voice clipped.

"You did. You're the one who insisted this was a *date-date*. You made a big deal that it wasn't just two friends carpooling to the stockgrowers' party together, remember?"

"That doesn't mean I'm ready to start dating again, at least not in general terms. It only means I'm ready to start dating *you*."

There it was.

Out in the open.

The reality she had been trying so desperately to avoid. He wanted more from her than friendship and she was scared out of her ever-loving mind at the possibility.

The air in the vehicle suddenly seemed charged, crackling with tension. She had to say something but had no idea what.

"I… Chase—"

"Don't. Don't say it."

His voice was low, intense, with an edge to it she rarely heard. She had so hoped they could return to the easy friendship they had always known. Was that gone forever, replaced by this jagged uneasiness?

"Say…what?"

"Whatever the hell you were gearing up for in that tone of voice like you were knocking on the door to tell me you just ran over my favorite dog."

"What do you want me to say?" she whispered.

"I sure as hell don't want you trying to set me up with another woman when you're the only one I want."

She stared at him, the heat in his voice rippling down

her spine. She swallowed hard, not knowing what to say as awareness seemed to spread out to her fingertips, her shoulder blades, the muscles of her thighs.

He was so gorgeous and she couldn't help wondering what it would be like to taste that mouth that was only a few feet away.

He gazed down at her for a long, charged moment, then with a muffled curse, he leaned forward on the bench seat and lowered his mouth to hers.

Given the heat of his voice and the hunger she thought she glimpsed in his eyes, she might have expected the kiss to be intense, fierce.

She might have been able to resist that.

Instead, it was much, much worse.

It was soft and unbearably sweet, with a tenderness that completely overwhelmed her. His mouth tasted of caramel and apples and the wine he'd had at dinner—delectable and enticing—and she was astonished by the urge she had to throw her arms around him and never let go.

Chapter Six

For nearly fifteen years, he had been trying *not* to imagine this moment.

When she was married to one of his closest friends, he had no idea she tasted of apples and cinnamon, that she smelled like oranges and vanilla sprinkled across a meadow of wildflowers.

He hadn't wanted to know she made tiny little sounds of arousal, little breathy sighs he wanted to capture inside his mouth and hold there forever.

It was easier *not* knowing those things. He could see that now.

He had hugged her many times and already knew how perfectly she fit against him. Sometimes when they would come back from traveling out of town together— Idaho Falls for the livestock auction or points farther away to pick up ranch equipment or parts—she would fall asleep, lulled by the motion of the vehicle and the rare chance to sit in one place for longer than five minutes.

He loved those times. Invariably, she would end up curled against him, her head on his shoulder. It would always take every ounce of strength he possessed not to pull her close, tuck her against him and drive off into the sunset.

He had always tried to remember his place as her friend, her support system.

Aching and wistful, he would spend those drives wishing he could keep driving a little extra or that when they arrived at their destination, he could gently turn her face to his and wake her with a kiss.

It was a damn good thing he hadn't ever risked something so stupid. If he had, he would never have been able to let her go.

He had her now, though, and he wasn't about to let this moment go to waste. She needed to see that she was still a lovely, sensual woman who couldn't spend the rest of her life hidden away at the Star N, afraid to let anybody else inside.

If he couldn't talk her into giving him a chance, perhaps he could seduce her into it.

It wasn't the most honorable thought he'd ever had, but right now, with her mouth warm and open against his and her silky hair under his fingertips, he didn't care.

He deepened the kiss and she froze for a second, and then her lips parted and she welcomed him inside, her tongue tangling with his and her hands clutching his shirt.

She might never be able to love him as he wanted but at least she should know she was a beautiful, desirable woman who had an entire life ahead of her.

He wasn't sure how long they spent wrapped around each other. What guy could possibly pay attention to insignificant little details like that when the woman he loved was kissing him with abandon?

He only knew he had never been so grateful for his decision to get a bench seat in his pickup instead of two buckets. Without a console in the way, she was nearly in his lap, exactly where he wanted her...

This was the dumbest thing he had ever done.

Even as he tried to lose himself in the kiss, the thought seemed to slither across his mind like a rattlesnake across his boot.

He was only setting himself up for more heartache. He should have thought this through, looked ahead past the moment and what he wanted right now.

How could he ever go back to being friends with her, trying like hell to be respectful of the subtle distance she so carefully maintained between them? He couldn't scrub these moments from his mind. Every time he looked at her now, he would remember this cold, star-filled night with the glittering holiday lights of Pine Gulch spread out below them and her warm, delicious mouth tangling with his.

Some small but powerful instinct for self-preservation clamored at him that maybe he better stop this while he still could, before all these years of pent-up desire burst through his control like irrigation water through a busted wheel line. He couldn't completely lose his head here.

He drew in a sharp breath and eased away from her. Her features were a pale blur in the moonlight but her lips were swollen from his kiss, her eyes half-closed. Her hair was tousled from his hands and she looked completely luscious.

He nearly groaned aloud at the effort it took to slide away from her when his entire body was yelling at him to pull her closer.

She opened her eyes and gazed at him, pupils dilated and her ragged breathing just about the most erotic sound he'd ever heard.

He saw the instant awareness returned to her eyes. They widened with shock and something else, then color soaked her cheeks.

She untangled her hands from around his neck and eased away from him.

"It's been a long time since I made out with a pretty girl in a pickup truck," he said into the suddenly heavy silence. "I forgot how awkward it could be."

She swallowed hard. "Right," she said slowly. "It's the pickup truck making things awkward."

They both knew it was much more than that. It was the years of history between them and the weight of a friendship that was important to both of them.

"I so wish you hadn't done that," she said in a small voice.

Her words carved out another little slice of his heart.

"Which? Kissed you? Or stopped?"

She shifted farther away from him and turned her face to look out at the town below them.

Instead of answering him directly, she offered up what seemed to him like a completely random change of topic.

"Do you remember the first time we met?"

Of course he remembered. Most guys remembered the days that left them feeling as if they had been run over by a tractor.

"Yes. You and your sisters had only been here with Mary and Claude a day or two."

"It was February 18, a week after our mother's funeral. We had been in Idaho exactly forty-eight hours."

She remembered it so exactly? He wasn't sure what to think about that. He only remembered that he had been sent by his mother to drop off a meal for "Mary's poor nieces."

The whole community knew what had happened to her and her sisters—that their parents had been providing medical care in a poor jungle town in Colombia when the entire family had been kidnapped by rebels looking for a healthy ransom.

After all these years, he still didn't know everything that had happened to her in that rebel camp. She didn't talk about it and he didn't ask. He did know her father had been shot and killed by rebels during a daring rescue mission orchestrated by US Navy SEALs, including a very young Rafe Santiago, now Hope's husband.

He didn't know much more now than he had that first time he met her. When the news broke a few months earlier and her family returned to the US, it had been big news in town. How could it be otherwise, given that her father had grown up in Pine Gulch and everyone knew the family's connection to Claude and Mary?

Unfortunately, the family's tragedy hadn't ended with her father's death. After their rescue, her mother had been diagnosed with an aggressive cancer that might have been treatable if she hadn't been living in primitive conditions for years—and if she hadn't spent the last month as a hostage in a rebel camp.

That had been Chase's mother's opinion, anyway. She had been on her way out of town to his own father's cancer treatment but had told him to drop off a chicken rice casserole and a plate of brownies to the Nichols family.

He remembered being frustrated at the order. Why couldn't she have dropped it off on her way out of town? Didn't he have enough to do on the ranch, since he was basically running things single-handedly?

Claude had answered the door, with the phone held to his ear, and told him Mary was in the kitchen and to go on back. He had complied, not knowing the next few moments would change his life.

He vividly remembered that moment when he had seen Faith standing at the sink with Mary, peeling potatoes.

She had been slim and pretty and fragile, with huge green eyes, that sweet, soft mouth and short, choppy blond hair—which she later told him she had cut herself with a butter knife sharpened on a brick, because of lice in the rebel camp.

He also suspected it had been an effort to avoid unwanted attention from the rebels, though she had never told him that. He couldn't imagine they couldn't see past her choppy hair to the rare beauty beneath.

Yeah, a guy tended to remember the moment he lost his heart.

"I gave you a ride into town," he said now. "Mary needed a gallon of milk or something."

"That's what she said, anyway," Faith said, her mouth tilted up a little. "I think she only wanted me to get out of the house and have a look at our new community and also give me a chance to talk to someone around my own age."

Not *that* close in age. He had been eighteen and had felt a million years older.

She had been so serious, he remembered, her eyes solemn and watchful and filled with a pain that had touched his heart.

"Whatever the reason, I was happy to help out."

"Everyone else treated us like we were going to crack apart at any moment. You were simply kind. You weren't overly solicitous and you didn't treat me like I had some kind of contagious disease."

She turned to face him, still smiling softly at the memories. "That was the best afternoon I'd had in *forever*. You told me jokes and you showed me the bus stop and the high school and the places where the kids in Pine Gulch liked to hang out. At the grocery store, you introduced me to everyone we met and made sure cranky Mr. Gibbons didn't cheat me, since I didn't have a lot of experience with American money."

She had been an instant object of attention everywhere they went, partly because she was new to town and partly because she looked so exotic, with a half-dozen woven bracelets on each wrist, the choppy hair, her wide, interested eyes.

"A few days later, you came back and said you were heading into town and asked if Aunt Mary needed you to come with me to pick anything else up."

That had basically been a transparent ploy to spend more time with her, which everyone else had figured out but Faith.

"That meant so much to me," she said. "Your own father was dying but that didn't stop you from reaching out and trying to help me acclimatize. I've never forgotten how kind you were to me."

Was it truly kindness, when he was the one who had benefited most? "It couldn't have been easy to find yourself settled in a small Idaho town, after spending most of your childhood wandering around the world."

"It was easier for me than it was for Hope and Celeste, I think. All I ever wanted was to stay in one place for a while, to have the chance to make friends finally. Friends like you."

She gave him a long, steady look. "You are my oldest and dearest friend, Chase. Our friendship is one of the most important things in my life."

He wanted to squeeze her hand, to tell her he agreed with her sentiments completely, but he didn't dare touch her again right now.

"Ditto," he said gruffly.

She drew in a breath that seemed to hitch a little. She looked out the windshield, where a few clouds had begun to gather, spitting out stray snowflakes that spiraled down and caught the light of the stars.

"That's why I have to ask you not to kiss me again."

Chapter Seven

Though she didn't raise her voice, her hard-edged words seemed to echo through his pickup truck.

I have to ask you not to kiss me again.

She meant what she said. He knew that tone of voice. It was the same one she used with the kids when meting out punishment for behavioral infractions or with cattle buyers when they tried to negotiate and offered a price below market value.

Her mind was made up and she wouldn't be swayed by anything he had to say.

Tension gripped his shoulders and he didn't know what the hell to say.

"That's blunt enough, I guess," he finally answered. "Funny, but you seemed to be into it at the moment. I guess I misread the signs."

Her mouth tightened. "It's a strange night. Neither of us is acting like ourselves. Can we just…leave it at that?"

That was the last thing he wanted to do. He wanted to kiss her again until she couldn't think straight.

He hadn't misread *any* signs and they both knew it. After that first moment of shock, she returned the kiss with an enthusiasm and eagerness that had left him stunned and hungry.

"Can you just take me home?" she asked in a low voice.

"If that's what you want," he said.

"It is," she answered tersely.

A few moments ago she had wanted *him*.

She was attracted to him. Lately he had been almost sure of it but some part of him had worried his own feelings for her were clouding his judgment. That kiss and her response told him the sexual spark hadn't been one-sided.

Nice to know he was right about that, at least.

She was attracted to him but she didn't want to be. How did a guy work past that conundrum?

The task suddenly seemed insurmountable.

He put the pickup in gear and focused on driving instead of on the growing realization that she might never be willing to accept him as anything more than her oldest and dearest friend.

Maybe, just maybe, it was time he accepted that and moved on with his life.

Though his features remained set and hard as he drove her back to the Star N, Chase carried on a casual conversation with her about the new horse, about a bit of gossip he heard about cattle futures at the stockgrowers' party, about Addie's Christmas presents that still needed to be wrapped.

Under other circumstances, she might have been quite proud of her halfway intelligent responses—especially when she really wanted to collapse into a boneless, quivering heap on the truck seat.

She couldn't stop remembering that kiss—the heat and the magic and the wild intensity of it.

Her heartbeat still seemed unnaturally loud in her ears and she hadn't quite managed to catch her breath, though she could almost manage to string two thoughts together now.

She felt very much like a tiny island in the middle of a vast arctic river just beginning the spring thaw, with chunks of ice and fast-flowing water buffeting against it in equal parts, bringing life back to the frozen landscape.

She didn't *want* to come to life again. She wanted that river of need to stay submerged under a hard layer of impenetrable ice forever.

Knowing that hollow ache was still there, that her sexuality hadn't shriveled up and died with Travis, completely terrified her.

She was a little angry about it, too, if she were honest. Why couldn't she just resume the state of affairs of the last thirty months, that sense of suspended animation?

This was *Chase*. Her best friend. The man she relied on for a hundred different things. How could she possibly laugh and joke with him like always when she would now be remembering just how his mouth had slid across hers, the glide of his tongue, the heat of his muscles against her chest.

She didn't want that river of need to come to churning, seething life again.

Yes, her world had been cold and sterile since Travis died, but it was *safe*.

She felt like she was suffocating suddenly, as if that wild flare of heat between them had consumed all the oxygen.

She rolled her window down a crack and closed her eyes at the welcome blast of cold air.

"Too warm?" he asked.

Oh, yes. He didn't know the half of it. "A little," she answered in a grave understatement.

He turned the fan down on the heating system just as her phone buzzed. She pulled it from the small beaded handbag Celeste had offered for the occasion.

It was a text from her sister: Girls are asleep. Don't rush home. Have fun.

She glanced at the message, then slid her phone back into the totally impractical bag.

"Problem?" he asked.

"Not really. I think Celeste was just checking in. She said the girls are asleep."

"I hope Addie was good."

"She's never any trouble. Really, we love having her around. She always seems to set a good example for my kids."

"Even Barrett?"

She relaxed a little. Talking about their children was much easier than discussing everything else.

"He can be such a rascal when Addie's there. I don't get it. He teases both of them mercilessly. I try to tell him to cut it out but the truth is I think he has a little crush on her."

"Older women. They're nothing but trouble. I had the worst crush on Maggie Cruz but she never paid me the slightest bit of attention. Why would she? I was in fifth grade and she was in eighth and we were on totally different planets."

The only crush she could remember having was the son of the butcher in the last village where they'd lived in Colombia. He had dark, soulful eyes and curly dark hair and always gave her all the best cuts when she went to the market for her family.

That seemed another lifetime ago. She couldn't even remember being that girl who once smiled at a cute boy.

By the time Chase pulled up to the Star N a few moments later, her hormones had almost stopped zinging around.

He put the truck in Park and opened his door.

"Since Addie's asleep, you don't have to come in," she said quickly, before he could climb out. "You don't really have to walk me to the door like this was a real date."

Why did she have to say that? The words seemed to slip out from nowhere and she wanted to wince. She didn't need to remind him of the awkwardness of the evening.

He said nothing, though she didn't miss the way his

mouth tightened and his eyes cooled a fraction before he completely ignored what she said and climbed out anyway.

Everything between them had changed and it made her chest ache with regret.

"Thanks, Chase," she said as they walked side by side through the cold night. "I had a really great time."

"You don't have to lie. It was a disaster from start to finish."

The grim note in his voice made her sad all over again. She sighed. "None of that was your fault. Only mine."

"The old, *it's not you, it's me* line?" he asked as they reached the door. "Really, Faith? You can't be more original than that?"

"It *is* me," she whispered, knowing he deserved the truth no matter how painful. "I'm such a coward and I always have been."

He made a low sound of disbelief. "A coward. You."

"I am!"

"This is the same woman who woke up the day after her husband's funeral, put on her boots and went to work—and who hasn't stopped since?"

"What choice did I have? The ranch was our livelihood. Someone had to run it."

"Right. Just like somebody jumped into a river to save a villager in Guatemala while everybody else was standing on the shore wringing their hands."

She stared at him. "How did you... Where did you hear that?"

"Hope told me once. I think it was after Travis died.

She also told me how you took more than one beating while you were all being held hostage because you stepped up to take responsibility for something she or Celeste had done."

She was the oldest. It had been her job to protect her sisters. What else could she do especially since it was her fault they had all been taken hostage to begin with?

She had told that cute boy she had a crush on the day they were supposed to go to Bogota so her mother could see a doctor and that they would probably be leaving for good in a few weeks.

She had hoped maybe he might want to write to her. Instead, he must have told the psychotic rebel leader their plans. The next time she saw that boy, he had been proudly wearing ragged army fatigues and carrying a Russian-made submachine gun.

"You're not a coward, Faith," Chase said now. "No matter how much you might try to convince yourself of that."

A stray snowflake landed on her cheek and she brushed it away. "You are my best friend, Chase. I'm so afraid of destroying that friendship, like I've screwed up everything else."

He gave her a careful look that made her wish she hadn't said anything, had just told him good-night and slipped into the house.

"Can we... More than anything, I would like to go back to the way things were a few weeks ago. Without all this...awkwardness. When we were just Faith and Chase."

He raised an eyebrow. "You really think we can do that, after that kiss?"

She shivered a little, from more than simply the cold night. "I would like to try. Please, Chase."

"How do two people take a step backward? Something is always lost."

"Can't we at least give it a shot? At least until after the holidays?"

She hoped he couldn't hear the begging tone of her voice that seemed so loud to her.

"I won't wait forever, Faith."

"I know," she whispered.

"Fine. We can talk again after the New Year."

Her relief was so fierce that she wanted to weep. At least she would have his friendship through the holidays. Maybe in a few more weeks, she would be able to find the courage to face a future without his constant presence.

"Thank you. That's the best gift anyone could give me this year."

She reached up to give him a casual kiss on the cheek, the kind she had given him dozens of times before. At the last minute, he turned his head, surprise in his eyes, and her kiss landed on the corner of his mouth.

Instantly, the mood shifted between them and once more she was aware of the heat of him and the coiled muscles and the ache deep within her for him and only him.

He kissed her fully, his mouth a warm, delicious refuge against the cold night. His scent surrounded her—leather and pine and sexy, masculine cowboy—and she desperately wanted to lean into his strength and surrender to the delicious heat that stirred instantly to life again.

Too soon, he stepped away.

"Good night," he said, his eyes dark in the glow from the porch light. He opened the door for her and waited until she managed to force her wobbly knees to carry her inside, then he turned around and walked to his pickup truck.

She really wanted nothing more than to shrug out of Celeste's luxurious coat, kick off her high heels, slip away to her room and climb into bed for the next week or two.

Unfortunately, a welcoming party waited for her inside. Celeste, Flynn and Aunt Mary were at the table with mugs of hot chocolate steaming into the air and what looked like a fierce game of Scrabble scattered around the table—which hardly seemed a fair battle since Celeste was a librarian and an author with a freaky-vast vocabulary.

All three looked up when she walked into the kitchen.

"Chase didn't come in?" Mary asked, clear disappointment on her wrinkled face.

Sometimes Faith thought her great-aunt had a little crush on Chase herself. What other reason did she have for always inviting him over?

"No," she said abruptly.

How on earth was she going to face him, again, now that they had kissed twice?

"How was your date?" Celeste asked. Though the question was casual enough, her sister gave her a searching look and she suddenly wanted desperately to confide in her.

She couldn't do it, at least not with Flynn and Mary listening in. "Fine," she answered.

"Only fine?" Mary asked, clearly surprised.

"Fun," she amended quickly. "Dinner was delicious, of course, and we danced a bit."

"Chase is a great dancer," Mary said, her eyes lighting up. "I could have danced with him all night at Celeste's wedding, except Agatha Lindley kept trying to cut in. I don't think he wanted to dance with her at all but he was just too nice."

"She was there tonight, though she didn't cut in. Unless she tried it when he was busy dancing with Ella Baker."

"Ella Baker?" Celeste frowned. "I don't think I know her."

"She's Curt Baker's daughter. She's moved to Pine Gulch to look after her father."

"The girls at the salon were talking about her when I went for my color this week," Mary said. "She teaches music or something, doesn't she?"

With a jolt, Faith suddenly remembered her conversation with the woman at the beginning of the party, which seemed like a dozen lifetimes ago. "Oh! I have news. Big news! I can't believe I almost forgot."

"You probably had other things on your mind," Flynn murmured, his voice so dry that she shot him a quick look.

Did her lips look as swollen as they felt, tight and achy and full? She really hoped not.

"You owe me so big," she said. "I begged Ella Baker to help out with the Christmas program. I told her my sisters were desperate and she totally agreed to do it!"

Celeste's eyes widened. "Are you kidding? What's wrong with the woman?"

"Nothing. She was very gracious about it and even said it sounded like fun."

"Right. Fun," Celeste said with a shake of her head.

"You had fun, don't deny it," Mary said. "Look how it ended up for you. Married to a hot contractor, tool belt and all."

"Thanks, my dear." Flynn gave a slow grin and picked up Mary's hand and kissed the back of it in a totally un-Flynn-like gesture that made Celeste laugh and Mary blush and pull her hand away.

"That was a definite side benefit," Celeste murmured, and Flynn gave her a private smile that made the temperature in the room shoot up a dozen degrees or so.

"Well, I'm afraid we don't exactly have more hot contractors to go around for Ella Baker," Faith said. "Though I do think she would be absolutely perfect for Chase. I told him so, but for some reason, he didn't seem to want to hear it."

All three of them stared at Faith as if she had just unleashed a rabid squirrel in the kitchen.

"You told Chase you think this Ella Baker would be perfect for him," Celeste repeated, with such disbelief in her voice that Faith squirmed.

"Yes. She seems like a lovely person," she said, more than a little defensive.

"I'm sure she is," Celeste said. "That doesn't mean

you should have tried to set Chase up with her while the two of you were out together on a date. I'll admit I didn't have a lot of experience before I met Flynn but even I know most guys in general probably wouldn't appreciate that kind of thing. Chase in particular probably didn't want to hear you suggest other women you think he ought to date."

Why Chase in particular? She frowned, though she was aware she had botched the entire evening from the get-go. How was she possibly going to fix things between them?

"We're friends," she retorted. "That's the kind of things friends do for each other, pick out potential dating prospects."

None of them seemed particularly convinced and she was too exhausted to press the point. It was none of their business anyway.

She pulled off Celeste's coat and hung it over one of the empty chairs and also pulled all her personal things out of the little evening bag.

"Thanks for letting me use your coat and bag."

"You're welcome. Anytime."

Right. She wasn't going to another stockgrowers' party. *Ever.*

"I'm going to go change into something comfortable."

"I'll come help you with the zipper. That one sticks, if I remember correctly."

"I don't need help," she said.

"That, my dear, is a matter of opinion."

Celeste rose and followed her up the stairs. As she

helped Faith out of the dress, her sister talked of the children and what they had done that evening and about the latest controversy at the library.

Beneath the light conversation, she sensed Celeste had something more to say. She wasn't sure she wanted to hear it but she couldn't stand the charged subtext either.

After she changed into her favorite comfy pajamas, she sat on the edge of her bed and finally braced herself. "Okay. Out with it."

Celeste deliberately avoided her gaze, confirming Faith's suspicions. "Out with what?" she asked, her tone vague.

"Whatever is lurking there on your tongue, dying to spill out. I can tell you have something to say. You might as well get it over with, for both our sakes. What did I do wrong?"

After a pause, Celeste sat down next to her on the bed.

"I'm trying to figure out if you're being deliberately obtuse or if you honestly don't know—all while I'm debating whether it's any of my business anyway."

"Remember what mom used to say? Better to keep your nose in a book than in someone else's business. Most of your life, you've had a pretty good track record in that department. Don't ruin it now."

Celeste sighed. "Fine. Deliberately obtuse it is, then."

She pulled her favorite sweatshirt over her head. This was more like it, in her favorite soft pajama bottoms and a comfortable hoodie. She felt much more at ease dressed like this than she ever would in the fancy clothes she had been wearing all evening.

"I don't know about *deliberate* but I'll admit I must be obtuse, since I have no idea what you're trying to dance around here."

"Really? No idea?"

The skepticism in her sister's voice burned. "None. What did I do wrong? I was careful with your coat, I promise."

"For heaven's sake, this isn't about the stupid coat."

"I'm not in the mood to play twenty questions with you. If you don't want to tell me, don't."

Celeste's mouth tightened. "Fine. I'll come out and say it, then. Can you honestly tell me you have no idea Chase is in love with you?"

At her sister's blunt words, all the blood seemed to rush away from her brain and she was very glad she was sitting down. Her skin felt hot for an instant and then icy, icy cold.

"Shut up. He is not."

Celeste made a disgusted sound. "Of course he is, Faith! Open your eyes! He's been in love with you *forever*. You had to have known!"

Whatever might be left of the apple pie and the small amount she had eaten at dinner seemed to congeal into a hard, greasy lump in her stomach.

She didn't know whether to laugh at the ridiculous joke that wasn't really funny at all or to tell her sister she was absolutely insane to make such an outrageous accusation. Underneath both those reactions was a tangled surge of emotion and the sudden burn of tears.

"He's not. He *can't* be," she whispered.

It couldn't be true. Could it?

Celeste squeezed her fingers gently, looking as if she regretted saying anything. "Use your head, honey. He's a good neighbor, yes, and a true friend. But can you really not see that his concern for you goes way beyond simple friendship?"

Chase was always there, a true and loyal friend. The one constant, unshakable force in her world.

"I don't want him to be." Her chest felt tight now and she could feel one of those tears slip free. "What am I going to do?"

Celeste squeezed her fingers. "You could try being honest with yourself and admit that you have feelings for him, too."

"As a friend. That's all," she insisted.

Celeste's eyes were full of compassion and exasperation in equal measures. "I love you dearly, Faith. You know I do. You've been my second mother since the day I was born, and from the time I was twelve years old you helped Aunt Mary and Uncle Claude raise me. You're kind and loving, a fantastic mom to Barrett and Lou, a ferociously hard worker. You've taught me so much about what it is to be a good person."

She tugged her hand away, sensing her sister had plenty more to say, and steeled herself to hear the rest.

"But?"

Celeste huffed out a breath. "But when it comes to Chase Brannon, you are being completely stupid and, as much as I hate to say it, more than a little cruel."

"That's a harsh word."

"The man is in love with you and when you sit there pretending you didn't know, you are lying to me, yourself and especially to Chase."

"He has never *once* said anything." She still couldn't make herself believe it.

"The last two years, he has shown you in a thousand different ways. You think he comes over three or four times a week to help Barrett with his homework because he loves fourth grade arithmetic? Can anyone really be naive enough to think he adores cleaning out the rain gutters in the spring and autumn because it's his favorite outdoor activity? Does he check the knock in your pickup's engine or help you figure out the ranch accounts or take a look at any sick cattle you might have because he wants to? No! He does all of those things because of *you*."

Faith could come up with a hundred other things he did for her or for the kids or Aunt Mary. That didn't necessary mean he was in *love* with her, only that he was a good, caring man trying to step up and help them after Travis's death.

The nausea inside her now had an element of panic. Had she been ignoring the truth all this time because she simply hadn't wanted to see it? What kind of horrible person was she? It made her feel like the worst kind of user.

"He's my best friend," she whispered. "What would I do without him?"

"I'm afraid you might have to figure that out sooner than you'd like, especially if you can't admit that you might have feelings for him, too."

With that, her sister rose, gave her a quick hug. "We all loved Travis. He was like the big brother I never had. He was a great guy and a good father. But he's gone, honey. You're not. I'll give you the benefit of the doubt and accept that maybe you didn't want to see that Chase is in love with you so you have avoided facing the truth. But now that you know, what are you going to do about it?"

Her sister slipped from the room before she could come up with a response—which was probably a good thing since Faith had no idea how to answer her.

Chapter Eight

"Why couldn't Lou come with us to take me home?" Addie asked Faith as they pulled out of the Star N driveway to head toward Chase's place.

Faith tried to smile but it ended in a yawn. She was completely wrung out after a fragmented, tortured night spent mostly staring up at her ceiling, reliving the evening—those kisses!—and her conversation with Celeste and wondering what she should do.

She must have slept for a few hours, on and off. When she awoke at her five-thirty alarm, all she wanted to do was pull the covers over her head, curl up and block out the world for a week or two.

Faith blinked away the yawn and tried to smile at Chase's daughter again. "She had a few chores to do this morning and I decided it was better for her to finish them as soon as she could. Sorry about that."

Addie gave her a sudden grin. "Oh. I thought it was maybe because you didn't want her to see her Christmas present in the pasture."

She winced. She should have known Addie would figure it out. The girl was too smart for her own britches. She only hoped she could also keep a secret. "How did you know about that?"

"My dad didn't tell me, in case you're wondering. It wasn't that hard to figure it out, though, especially since Lou hasn't stopped talking about the new barrel racing horse she wants. It seemed like too much of a coincidence when I saw a new horse suddenly had shown up in my dad's pasture."

Faith didn't see any point in dissembling. Christmas was only a few weeks away and the secret would be out anyway. "It wasn't a coincidence," she confirmed. "Your dad helped me pick her out and offered to keep her at Brannon Ridge until after Christmas, when we take her to the Dalton ranch to be trained."

"Louisa is going to be so excited!"

"I think so." Her daughter was a smart, kind, *good* girl. Louisa worked hard in school, did her chores when asked and was generally kind to her brother. She had channeled her grief over losing her father at such a young age into a passion for horse riding and Faith wanted to encourage that.

"I won't tell. I promise," Addie said.

"Thank you, honey."

Addie was a good girl, as well. Some children of divorce became troubled and angry—sometimes even manipulative and sly, pitting one parent against the other for their own gain as they tried to navigate the difficult waters of living in two separate households. Addie was the sweetest girl—which seemed a minor miracle, considering her situation.

"Maybe once she's trained, Lou might let me ride her once in a while," the girl said.

Faith didn't miss the wistful note in Addie's voice. "You know, if you want a horse of your own, you could probably talk your dad into it."

Quite frankly, Faith was surprised Chase hadn't already bought a horse for his daughter.

"I know. Dad has offered to get me one since I was like five. It would be nice, but it doesn't seem very fair to have a horse of my own when I could only see it and ride it once or twice a month. My dad would have to take care of it the rest of the time without me."

"I'm sure he wouldn't mind. He already has Tor. It wouldn't be any trouble at all for him to take care of two horses instead of only one."

"Maybe if I lived here all the time," Addie said in a matter-of-fact tone. "It's hard enough, only seeing my dad a few times a month. I hate when I have to go back to Boise. It would be even harder if I had to leave a horse I loved, too."

Faith swallowed around the sudden lump in her throat. The girl's sad wisdom just about broke her heart. "I can understand that. But you do usually spend summers on the ranch," she pointed out. "That's the best time for riding horses anyway."

"I guess." Addie didn't seem convinced. "I just wish I could stay here longer. Maybe come for the whole school year sometime, even if I wouldn't be in the same grade with Louisa."

"Do you think you might come here to go to school at some point?"

"I wish," she said with a sigh. "My mom always says she would miss me too much. I guess she thinks it's okay for Dad to miss me the rest of the time, when I'm with her."

If she hadn't been driving, Faith would have hugged her hard at the forlorn note in her voice. Poor girl, torn between two parents who loved and wanted her. It was an impossible situation for all of them.

She and Addie talked about the girl's upcoming cruise over the holidays with her mother until they arrived at Chase's ranch. When she pulled up to the ranch, she spotted him throwing a bale of hay into the back of his pickup truck like it weighed no more than a basketball.

She shivered, remembering the heat of his mouth on hers, the solid strength of those muscles against her.

On the heels of that thought came the far more disconcerting one born out of her conversation with Celeste.

The man is in love with you and when you sit there pretending you didn't know, you are lying to me, yourself and especially to Chase.

Butterflies jumped around in her stomach and she realized her fingers on the steering wheel were trembling.

Oh. This would never do. This was *Chase*, her best

friend. She *couldn't* let things get funky between them. That was exactly what she worried about most.

Celeste had to be wrong. Faith couldn't accept any other possibility.

The moment she turned off the vehicle, Addie opened the door and raced to hug her dad.

Could she just take off now? Faith wondered. She was half-serious, until she remembered Addie's things were still in the back of the pickup truck.

In an effort to push away all the weirdness, she drew in a couple of cleansing breaths. It didn't work as well as she hoped but the extra oxygen made her realize she had probably been taking nervous, shallow breaths all morning, knowing she was going to have to face him again.

She pulled Addie's sleeping bag out from behind the seat and pasted on a casual smile, knowing even as she did it that he would be able to spot it instantly as fake.

When she turned around, she found him and Addie just a few feet away from her. His eyes were shaded by his black Stetson and she couldn't read the expression there but his features were still, his mouth unsmiling.

"Looks like we caught you going somewhere," she said.

"Just down to the horse pasture to check on, uh, things there."

If she hadn't been fighting against the weight of this terrible awkwardness, she might have managed a genuine smile at his attempt be vague.

"You don't need to use code. Your daughter is too smart for either of us."

"You don't have to tell me that." He smiled down at

Addie and something seemed to unfurl inside Faith's chest. He was an excellent father—and not only to his daughter.

Since Travis died, he had become the de facto father figure for Louisa and Barrett. Oh, Rafe and Flynn did an admirable job as uncles and showed her children how good, decent men took care of their families. But Louisa and Barrett turned to Chase for guidance most. They saw him nearly every day. He was the one Louisa had invited when her class at school had a father-daughter dance and that Barrett had taken along to the Doughnuts with Dad reading hour at school.

They loved him—and he loved them in return. That had nothing to do with any of the nonsense Celeste had talked about the night before.

"Did you have fun last night?" Chase asked Addie now.

"Tons," she declared. "We popped popcorn and watched movies and played games. I beat everybody at UNO like three times in a row and Barrett said I was cheating only I wasn't. And then we all opened our sleeping bags under the Christmas tree and put on another movie and I fell asleep. This morning we had hot chocolate with marshmallows and pancakes shaped like snowmen. It was awesome."

"I'm so glad. Here, I can take that stuff."

He reached to grab the sleeping bag and backpack from Faith. As he did, his hand brushed her chest. It was a touch that barely connected through the multiple layers she wore—coat, a fleece pullover and her

silk long underwear—but she could hardly hold back
a shiver anyway.

"I'll just take it all into the house now," Addie said.
"Thanks for the ride, Faith."

"You're very welcome," she said.

After she strapped the bag over her shoulder and
Chase handed her the sleeping bag, she waved at Faith
and skipped into the house, humming a Christmas carol.

What a sweet girl, Faith thought again. She didn't let
her somewhat chaotic circumstances impact her enjoyment of the world around her. Faith could learn a great
deal from the girl's example.

"I'll add my thanks to you for bringing her home,"
Chase said. "I appreciate it, though I could have driven
over to get her."

"I really didn't mind. I've got to run into Pine Gulch
for a few things anyway. Can I bring you back anything
from the grocery store?"

They did this sort of thing all the time. He would call
her on his way to the feed store and ask if she needed
anything. She would bring back a part from the imple-
ment store in Idaho Falls if she had to go for any reason.

She really hoped the easy, casual give-and-take
didn't change now that everything seemed so different.

"We could use paper towels, I guess," he said, after
a pause. "Oh, and dishwasher detergent and dish soap."

"Sure. I can drop it off on my way home."

"No rush. I'll pick it up next time I come over."

"Sounds good," she answered. At his words, her
smile turned more genuine. This seemed much like their
normal interactions—and if he was talking about com-

ing to the ranch again, at least he wasn't so upset at her that he was going to penalize the kids by staying away.

"Did you hear Jim Laird messed up his knee?" he asked. "Apparently he slipped on ice and wrenched things and Doc Dalton sent him over to Idaho Falls for surgery yesterday. I wondered why he wasn't at the party last night. I was hoping Mary Beth wasn't in the middle of a relapse or something."

She didn't like hearing when bad things happened to their neighbors. Jim was a sweet older man in his seventies whose wife had multiple sclerosis. They ran a small herd of about fifty head and he often bought alfalfa from her.

"As if he didn't have enough on his plate! What is Mary Beth going to do? She can't possibly do the feedings in the winter by herself."

"Wade Dalton, Justin Hartford and I are going to split the load for a few weeks, until he can get around again."

He was always doing things like that for others in the community.

"I want into the rotation. I can take a turn."

"Not necessary. The three of us have it covered."

She narrowed her gaze. "For six months after Travis died, ranchers up and down the Cold Creek stepped up to help us at the Star N. I'm in a good place now, finally, and want to give back when I can."

The ranch wouldn't have survived without help from her neighbors and friends—especially Chase. She had been completely clueless about running a cattle ranch and would have been lost.

Now that she had stronger footing under her, she wanted to start doing her best to pay it forward.

Chase looked as if he wanted to argue but he must have seen the determination in her expression. After a moment, he gave an exasperated sigh.

"Fine. I'll have Wade give you a call to work out the details."

She smiled. "Thanks. I don't mind the early-morning feedings either."

"I'll let Wade know."

There. That was much more like normal. Celeste had to be wrong. Yes, Chase loved her—just as she loved him. They were dear friends. That was all.

"I better run to the store before the shelves are empty. You know how Saturdays get in town."

"I do."

"So paper towels, dish soap and dish detergent. You can pick up everything tomorrow when you come for dinner," she said.

"That would work."

She felt a little more of the tension trickle away. At least he was still planning to come for dinner.

She loved their Sunday night tradition, when she and her sisters and Aunt Mary always fixed a big family meal and invited any neighbors or friends who would care to join them. Chase invariably made it, unless he was driving Addie back to Boise after a weekend visitation.

"Great. I'll see you tomorrow."

He looked as if he wanted to say something more but she didn't give him the chance. Instead, she jumped into her pickup and pulled away, trying her best not to look at him in the rearview mirror, standing lean-hipped and gorgeous and watching after her.

They had survived their first encounter post-kiss. Yes, it had been tense, but not unbearably so. After this, things between them would become more comfortable each time until they were back to the easy friendship they had always enjoyed.

She cared about him far too much to accept any other alternative.

He stood and watched her drive away, fighting the urge to rub the ache in his chest.

The entire time they talked about groceries and hot chocolate and Jim Laird's bum knee, his damn imagination had been back in a starlit wintry night, steaming up the windows of his pickup truck.

That kiss seemed to be all he could think about. No matter what else he might be trying to focus on, his brain kept going back to those moments when he had held her and she had kissed him back with an enthusiasm he had only dreamed about.

Hot on the heels of those delicious memories, though, came the cold, hard slap of reality.

I have to ask you not to kiss me again.

She was so stubborn, fighting her feelings with every bit of her. How was he supposed to win against that?

He pondered his dwindling options as he headed inside to find Addie so she could put on her winter clothes and help him feed the horses.

He found her just finishing a call on her cell phone with a look of resignation.

"Who was that?" he asked, though he was fairly sure he knew the answer. He and Cindy were just about the only ones Addie ever talked to on the phone.

"Mom," she said, confirming his suspicion. "She said Grandma is doing better and Grandpa says he doesn't really need her help anymore. She decided to take me back tomorrow so I can finish the last week of school."

Why didn't she call him first to work out the details?

He was surrounded by frustrating women.

"That's too bad. I know you were looking forward to practicing for the show with Louisa."

Her face fell further. "I forgot about that!" she wailed. "If I don't go to practice, I don't know if I can be in the show."

"I'm sure we can talk to Celeste and Hope and get special permission for you to practice at home. You'll be here next weekend and the first part of next week so you'll be able to be at the last few practices."

"I hope they'll let me. I really, really, *really* wanted to be in the Christmas show."

"We'll work something out," he assured her, hoping he wasn't giving her unrealistic expectations. "Meanwhile, why don't you grab your coat and boots. Since you're so smart and already figured out the new horse is for Lou, do you want to meet her for real so you can tell me what you think?"

"Yes!" she exclaimed.

"You'll have to work hard to keep it a secret."

"I know. I would never ruin the surprise."

With that promise, his daughter raced for the mud-room and her winter gear and Chase leaned a hip against the kitchen island to wait for her and tried not to let his mind wander back to those moments in his pickup that were now permanently imprinted on his brain.

Chase headed up the porch steps of the Star N ranch house with a bag of chips in one hand and a bottle of his own homemade salsa in the other, the same thing he brought along to dinner nearly every Sunday.

The lights of the house were blazing a warm wel-come against the cold and snowy Sunday evening but his instincts were still urging him to forget the whole thing and head back home, where he could glower and stomp around in private.

He was in a sour mood and had been since Cindy showed up three hours earlier than planned to pick up Addie, right as they were on their way out the door to go to their favorite lunch place.

It was always tough saying goodbye to his daugh-ter. This parting seemed especially poignant, probably because Addie so clearly hadn't wanted to go. She had dragged her feet about packing up her things, had asked if they could wait to leave until after she and Chase had lunch, had begged to say goodbye to the horses.

Cindy, annoyed at the delays, had turned sharp-tongued and hard, which in turn made Addie more pouty than normal. Addie had finally gone out to her mother's new SUV with tears in her eyes that broke his heart.

Being a divorced father seriously sucked sometimes.

In his crazier moments, he thought about selling the ranch and moving to Boise to be closer to her, though he didn't know what the hell he would do for a living. Ranching was all he knew, all he had ever known. But he would do whatever it took—work in a shoe factory if he had to—if his daughter needed him.

He wasn't sure that was the answer, though. She loved her time here and seemed to relish ranch life, in a way Cindy never had.

With a sigh, he rang the doorbell, grimly aware that much of his sour mood had roots that had nothing to do with Cindy or Addie.

He had been restless and edgy since the last time he rang this doorbell, when he had shown up at this same ranch to pick up Faith for that disaster of a date two nights earlier.

How many mistakes could one man make in a single evening? Part of him wished he could go back and start the whole stupid week over again and just let his relationship with Faith naturally evolve from friendship to something more.

How long would that take, though? He had a feeling he could have given her five years—ten—and she would still have the same arguments.

Despite all his mistakes, he had to hope he hadn't completely screwed up their friendship for good, that things weren't completely wrecked between them now.

As she had a few nights earlier, Aunt Mary was the one who finally answered the doorbell.

"It's about time," she said, planting hands on her hips. "Faith needs a man in the worst way."

He blinked at that, his imagination suddenly on fire. "O-kay."

Mary looked amused and he guessed she could tell immediately what detour his brain had taken.

"She needs your grilling skills," she informed him.

He told himself that wasn't disappointment coursing through him. "Grilling skills. Ah. You're grilling tonight."

"We *would* be, but Faith is having trouble again with that stupid gas grill. I swear that thing has it out for us."

He gestured behind him to the elements just beyond the porch. "You do know it's starting to snow, right?"

Aunt Mary shrugged. "You hardly notice out there, with the patio heater and that cover Flynn built us for the deck. Steaks sounded like a great idea at the time, better than roast or chicken tonight, but now the grill is being troublesome. Rafe and Hope aren't back yet from visiting Joey's mom, and Flynn had to fly out to California to finish a project there. That leaves Celeste, Faith and me. We could really use somebody with a little more testosterone to figure out what we're doing wrong."

"I'm not an expert on gas grills but I'll see what I can do."

"Thanks, honey."

He followed Mary inside, where they were greeted by delectable smells of roasting potatoes and yeasty rolls. No place on earth smelled better than this old ranch house on Sunday evenings.

"I've got to finish the salad. Go on ahead," Mary said.

He walked through the kitchen to the door that led to the covered deck. Faith didn't see him at first; she was too busy swearing and fiddling with the controls of the huge, fancy silver grill Travis had splurged on a few months before his death.

She was dressed in a fleece jacket, jeans and boots, with her hair loose and curling around her shoulders. His chest ached at the sight of her, like it always did. He wished, more than anything, that he had the right to go up behind her, brush her hair out of the way and kiss the back of that slender neck.

Little multicolored twinkly Christmas lights covered all the shrubs around the deck and had been draped around the edges of the roof. He didn't remember seeing Christmas lights back here and wondered if Hope had done it to make the rear of the house look more festive. It did look over The Christmas Ranch, after all.

Faith wasn't the biggest fan of Christmas, which he found quite ironic, considering she was part owner of the largest seasonal attraction in these parts.

She fiddled with the knobs again, then smacked the front of the grill. "Why won't you light, you stupid thing?"

"Yelling at it probably won't help much."

She whirled around at his comment and he watched as delectable color soaked her cheeks. "Chase! Oh, I'm so glad to see you!"

He was aware of a fierce, deep-seated need to have her say those words because she wanted to see *him*, not because she had a problem for him to solve.

"Mary said you're having grill trouble."

"The darn thing won't ignite, no matter what I do. It's not getting propane, for some reason. I've been out here for ten minutes trying to figure it out. It's a brand-new tank that Flynn got for us a few weeks ago and we haven't used it since. I checked the propane tank. I tried dropping a match in case it was the ignition. I tried all the knobs about a thousand times. I just think this grill hates me."

He found it more than a little amusing that she had learned to drive every piece of complicated farm machinery on the place over the last two years and could round up a hundred head of cattle on her own, with only the dogs for help, but she was intimidated by a barbecue grill.

"This one can be finicky, that's for sure."

She frowned at the thing. "Travis had to buy the biggest, most expensive grill he could order—forget that the controls on it are more confusing than the space shuttle."

She didn't say disparaging things about her late husband very often. In this case, he had to agree with her. He had loved the guy, but she was absolutely right. Travis Dustin always had to have the best, even when they couldn't afford it. His poor management and expensive tastes in equipment—and his gross negligence in not leaving her with proper life insurance—had all contributed to the big financial hole he had left his family when he died.

"I'll take a look," he said.

She stepped aside and he knelt down to peer at the connection. It only took him a moment to figure out why the grill wouldn't work.

"Here's your trouble. Looks like the gas hose isn't connected tightly. It's come loose from the tank."

He made the necessary adjustment, then stood, turned on the propane and hit the ignition. The grill ignited with a whoosh of instant heat.

She made a face. "Now I feel like an idiot. I swear I checked that already."

"It's easy to overlook."

"I guess my mind must have been on something else."

He had to wonder what. Was she remembering that kiss, too? He cast her a sidelong look and found a pink tinge on her cheeks again that might have been a blush—or just as easily might have been from the cold.

"Thank you for figuring it out," she said.

"No problem. You'll need to let the grill heat up for about ten minutes, then I can come back and take care of the steaks."

"Thank you. No matter how well I think I know my way around all the appliances in my kitchen, apparently this finicky grill remains my bugaboo. Or maybe it's outdoor cookery in general."

"I can't agree with that. I seem to remember some mean Dutch oven meals where you acted as camp cook when Trav and I would combine forces for roundup in the fall."

"That seems like a long time ago."

"Not that long. I still dream about your peach cobbler." Usually his dreams involved her kissing him between thick, gooey spoonfuls, but he decided it would probably be wise not to add that part.

Still, something of his thoughts must have appeared on his face because she seemed to catch her breath and gazed wide-eyed at him in the multicolored glow from the Christmas lights.

"I didn't know you liked it that much," she said after a moment, her voice a little husky. "Dutch oven cooking is easy compared to working this complicated grill. I'll be happy to make you a peach cobbler this summer, when the fruit is in season."

"Sounds delicious," he answered, his own voice a little more gruff than usual, which he told himself was because of the cold—though right now he was much warmer than he might have expected.

She swallowed hard and he was almost positive her gaze drifted to his mouth and then quickly away again. He *was* sure the color on her cheeks intensified, which had to be from more than the cold.

Was she remembering that kiss, too? He wanted to ask her—or better yet, to step forward and steal another one, but the door from the house opened and Louisa popped her head out.

"Hey, Chase! Where's Addie? Didn't she come with you?"

He took a subtle step back. "No. She went back to Boise with her mom this afternoon. Didn't she tell you?"

Her face fell. "Oh, no! Does that mean she won't be able to do the show with us? She thought she could! She and I and Olivia were going to sing a song together!"

"She still wants to. She'll have to miss the first few rehearsals, but she should be here next week for the actual show. We'll do our best to get her back here for rehearsal by Thursday. I might have to run into Boise to make it happen."

"Isn't that your day to help out at Jim Laird's place?"

Rats. He had forgotten all about that. "Yes. I'll figure out a way to swing it."

"I'll help," she said promptly. "I can either run to Boise for you or take your day at Jim's house. Either way, we will get Addie here."

His heart twisted a little that with everything she had to do here at the Star N, she would even consider driving six hours round-trip to pick up his daughter.

"Thank you, but I think I can manage both. If I take off as soon as I finish feeding my stock and his, I should be able to have Addie back in time for practice. It's important to her so I'll figure out a way to make it happen."

Both Faith and her daughter gave him matching warm looks that made him forget all about the snow just beyond their little covered patio.

"Thanks, Chase. You're the *best*," Lou said. Despite the cold, she padded out to the deck in her stocking feet and threw her arms around his waist. He smiled a little and hugged her back, thinking how much he loved both Louisa and her brother. They were great kids, always thinking of others. They were like their mother in that respect.

"Better head back inside. It's cold out here and you don't have shoes or a coat."

"I do have to go back in. I have to finish dessert. I made it myself. Aunt Mary hardly helped at all."

"I can't wait," he assured her.

She grinned and skipped back into the house, leaving him alone again with Faith. When he turned away from the doorway, he found her watching him with an expression he couldn't read.

"What did I say?" he asked.

"I… Nothing," she mumbled. "I'll go get the steaks."

She hurried past him before he could press her, leaving him standing alone in the cold.

Chapter Nine

Faith couldn't leave the intimacy of the covered deck quickly enough.

She felt rattled and unsettled and she hated it. With a deep sense of longing, she remembered dinner just the previous Sunday, when they had laughed and joked and teased like always. He had stayed to watch a movie and she had thrown popcorn into his mouth and teased him about not shaving for a few days.

There had been none of this tension, this awareness that seemed to hiss and flare between them like that stupid grill coming to life.

She had wanted him to kiss her. It was all she could seem to think about, that wondrous feeling of being alive, desired.

Another few moments and she would have been the one to kiss him.

She forced herself to move away from the door and into the kitchen, where Aunt Mary looked up from the rolls she was pulling apart.

"Tell me Chase saved the day again."

"We're in business. It was all about the gas connection. I feel stupid I didn't look there first."

"Sometimes it takes an outside set of eyes to identify the problem and find the solution."

Could someone outside her particular situation help her figure out how to go back in time and fix what felt so very wrong between her and Chase?

"Where are the steaks?" she asked her aunt.

"Over there, by the microwave."

"Whoa," she exclaimed when she spotted them. "That's a lot of steak for just us."

"I took out a few extras in case we had company or so we could use the leftovers for fajitas one day this week. Good thing, because Rafe and Hope said they're only about fifteen minutes out. I'm sure glad they'll beat the worst of the snow. I feel a big storm coming on."

"The weather forecast said most of the storm will clip us."

"Weather forecasts can be wrong. Don't be surprised if we get hit with heavy winds, too."

She had learned not to doubt her great-aunt's intuition when it came to winter storms. After a lifetime of living in this particular corner of Idaho, Mary could read the weather like some people read stock reports.

Sure enough, the wind had already picked up a little

when she carried the tray of steaks out to the covered deck. Chase stood near the propane heater, frowning as he checked something on his phone.

"Trouble?" she asked, nodding at the phone.

"Just Cindy," he answered, his voice terse.

"I'm sorry."

He made a face as he took the tray from her and used the tongs to transfer the steaks onto the grill.

"Nothing new," he said as the air filled with sizzle and scent. "Apparently Addie sulked all the way to Boise about having to go back when she was expecting to stay through the week with me and practice for the show with Olivia and Lou. Of course Cindy blames me. I shouldn't have gotten her hopes up, etc. etc.—even though *she* was the one who changed her mind from her original plan."

Faith wanted to smack the woman. Why did she have to be so difficult?

"Maybe you should petition again for primary custody."

He sighed. "She would never agree. I don't know if that would be the best thing for Addie anyway. Her mom and stepfather have given her a good life in Boise. I just wish she could be closer."

She decided not to tell him about her conversation with Addie the previous morning. What a difficult situation for everyone involved. Her heart ached and she wished, more than anything, that she could give him more time with his daughter for Christmas.

He was such a good man, kind and generous. He

deserved to be happy—which was yet another reason she needed to help him find someone like Ella Baker.

That was what a true friend would do, help him find someone whose heart was whole and undamaged, who could cherish all the wonderful things about him.

Some of her emotions must have appeared on her features because he gave her an apologetic look. "Sorry. I didn't mean to bring you down."

She mustered a smile. "You didn't. What are friends for, if you can't complain about your ex once in a while?"

"I shouldn't complain about her at all. She's my child's mother and overall she takes excellent care of her. She loves her, too. I have to keep reminding myself of that." He shrugged. "I'm not going to worry about it more tonight. For now, let's just enjoy dinner. And speaking of which, I can handle the steaks from here, if you want to go back inside. That wind is really picking up."

"I was planning on grilling," she protested. "You should be the one to go inside. I can take over, as long as you've got the grill working."

"I don't mind."

"If you go inside now, I bet you could nab a hot roll from Aunt Mary."

"Tempting. But no." He wiggled the utensil in his hand. "I've got the tongs, which gives me all the power."

She gave him a mock glare. "Hand them over."

"Come get them, if you think you're worthy."

He held them over his head, which was way over *her* head.

Despite the cold wind, relief wrapped around her like a warm blanket. He was teasing her, just like normal and for a ridiculous moment, she wanted to weep.

Perhaps they *could* find an even footing, return to their easy, dependable friendship.

"Come on. Give," she demanded. She stretched on tiptoe but the tongs were still completely out of reach.

He grinned. "Is that the best you can do?"

Never one to back down from a challenge, she hopped up and her fingers managed to brush the tongs. So close! She tried again but she forgot the wooden planks of the deck were a bit slippery with cold and condensation. This time when she came down, one boot slid and she stumbled a little.

She might have fallen but before she could, his arms instantly came around her, tongs and all.

They froze that way, with his arms around her and her curves pressed against his hard chest. Their smiles both seemed to freeze and crack apart. Her gaze met his and all the heat and tension she had been carefully shoving down seemed to burst to the surface all over again. His mouth was *right there*. She only had to stand on tiptoe again and press her lips to his.

Yearning, wild and sweet, gushed through her and she was aware of the thick churn of her blood, a low flutter in her stomach.

She hitched in a breath and coiled her muscles to do just that when she heard the creak of the door hinges.

She froze for half a second, then quickly stepped away an instant before Rafe tromped out to the deck.

Her brother-in-law paused and gave them a long, con-sidering look, eyebrows raised nearly to his hairline. He hesitated briefly before he moved farther onto the deck.

"You people are crazy. Don't you know December in Idaho isn't the time to be firing up the grill?"

Something was definitely fired up out here. The grill was only part of it. Her face felt hot, her skin itchy, and she could only hope she had moved away before Rafe saw anything—*not* that there had been anything to see.

"Steaks just don't taste the same when you try to cook them under the broiler," Chase said. "Though the purist in me would prefer to be cooking them over hot coals instead of a gas flame."

"You ever tried any of that specialty charcoal?" Rafe asked. "When I was stationed out of Hawaii, I tried the Ono coals they use for luaus. Man, that's some good stuff. Burns hot and gives a nice crisp crust."

"I'll have to try it," Chase said.

"I came to see if you needed help but it looks like you don't need me. You two appear to have things well in hand," he said.

Was his phrasing deliberate? Faith wondered, feel-ing her face heat even more.

"Doing our best," Chase replied blandly.

She decided it would be wise to take the chance to leave while she could. "Thanks for offering, Rafe. I actually have a few things I just remembered I have to do before dinner. It would great if you two could fin-ish up out here."

She rushed into the house and tried to tell herself she was grateful for the narrow escape.

* * *

Chase took another taste of Aunt Mary's delicious mashed potatoes dripping with creamy, rich gravy, and listened to the conversation ebb and flow around him.

He loved listening to the interactions of Faith and her family. With no siblings of his own, he had always envied the close relationships among them all. They never seemed to run out of things to talk about, from current events to Celeste's recent visit to New York to the progress of Hope's pregnancy.

The conversation was lively, at times intense and heated, and never boring. The sisters might disagree with each other or Mary about a particular topic but they always did so with respect and affection.

It was obvious this was a family that loved each other. The girls' itinerant childhood—and especially the tragedy that had followed—seemed to have forged deep, lasting bonds between Faith and her sisters.

Sometimes they opened their circle to include others. Rafe and his nephew Joey. Flynn and Olivia. Chase.

He could lose this.

If this gamble he was taking—trying to force Faith to let things move to the next level between them—didn't pay off, he highly doubted whether Mary would continue to welcome him to these Sunday dinners he treasured.

Things very well might become irreparably broken between them. His jaw tightened. Some part of him wondered if he might be better off backing down and keeping the status quo, this friendship he treasured.

But then he would see Rafe touch Hope's hand as he

made a point or watch Celeste's features soften when she talked about Flynn and he knew he couldn't let it ride. He wanted to have that with Faith. It was possible; he knew it was. That evening on the deck had only re-inforced that she was attracted to him but was fighting it with everything she had.

They could be as happy as Rafe and Hope, Celeste and Flynn. Couldn't she see that?

He had told her he would give her time but even though it had only been a few days, he could feel his patience trickling away. He had waited so long already.

"Who's ready for dessert?" Louisa asked eagerly, as the meal was drawing to a close.

Barrett rolled his eyes. "I haven't even finished my steak. You're just in a hurry because you made it."

"So? I never made a whole cheesecake by myself be-fore. Mom or Aunt Mary always helped me, but I made this one all by myself. I even made the crust."

"I saw it in the kitchen and it looks delicious," Chase assured her. "I can't wait to dig in."

She beamed at him and his heart gave a sharp little ache. This was another reason he didn't want to remain on the edge of Faith's life forever. Louisa and Barrett were amazing kids, despite everything they had been through. He wanted so much to be able to help Faith raise them into the good, kind people they were be-coming.

He had no idea what he would do next if she was so afraid to take a chance on a relationship with him that she ended up pushing him out of all of their lives.

He would be lost without them.

He set his fork down, the last piece of delicious steak he had been chewing suddenly losing all its flavor.

He had to keep trying to make her see how good they could all be together, even when the risks of this all-or-nothing roll of the dice scared the hell out of him.

"Okay, do you want chocolate sauce or raspberry?" Lou asked.

He managed a smile. "How about a little of both?"

"Great idea," Mary said. "Think I'll have both, too."

Louisa went around the table taking orders like a server in a fancy restaurant, then she and Olivia headed for the kitchen. When Faith rose to go with them to help, Louisa made her sit back down.

"We can do it," she insisted.

The girls left just as another gust of wind rattled the windows and howled beneath the eaves of the old house. The electricity flickered but didn't go out and he couldn't help thinking how cozy it was in here.

They talked about the record-breaking crowd at The Christmas Ranch that weekend until the girls came back with a tray loaded with slices of cheesecake. They were cut a little crooked and the presentation was a bit messy but nobody seemed to mind.

"This is delicious. The best cheesecake I think I've ever had," Chase said after his first bite, which earned him a huge grin from Louisa.

"It is really excellent," Celeste said. "And I've had cheesecake in New York City, where they know cheese-cake."

Louisa couldn't have looked happier. "Thanks. I'm going to try an apple pie next week."

He couldn't resist darting a glance at Faith and wondered if he would ever be able to eat apple pie again without remembering the cinnamon-sugar taste of her mouth.

She licked her lips, then caught his eyes and her cheeks turned an instant pink that made him suddenly certain she was thinking about the kiss, too.

"That wind is sure blowing up a storm," Rafe commented.

"The last update I heard on the weather said we're supposed to have another half foot of snow before morning," Hope said.

"Yay!" all of the children exclaimed together.

"Maybe we won't have school," Joey said with an unmistakably hopeful note in his voice.

"Yeah!" Barrett exclaimed. "That would be awesome!"

"I wouldn't plan on it," Mary said. "I hate to be a downer but I've lived here most of my life and can tell you they hardly ever close school on account of snow. As long as the buses can run, you'll have school."

"It really depends on the timing of the storm and the kind of snowdrifts it leaves behind," Chase said, not wanting the kids to completely give up hope. "If it's early in the morning before the plows can make it around, you might be in luck."

"We should probably head home before the worst of it hits," Rafe said.

"Same here," Celeste said. "I'm so glad Flynn put new storm windows in that old house this summer."

Flynn had spent six months renovating and adding

on to his late grandmother's old house down the road, a project which had been done just days before their wedding in August.

Chase remembered that lovely ceremony on the banks of the Cold Creek, when the two of them—so very perfect for each other—had both glowed with happiness.

Watching them together had only reinforced his determination to forge his own happy ending with Faith, no matter what it took. He had spent the past few months touching her more in their regular interactions, teasing her, trying anything he could think of to convince her to think of him as more than just her friend and confidant.

Right now he felt further from that goal than ever.

Sometimes their Sunday evening dinners would stretch long into the night when they would watch a movie or play games at the kitchen table, but with the storm, everyone seemed in a hurry to leave. They stayed only long enough to clean up the kitchen and then only he, Mary, Faith and her children were left.

"How's the homework situation?" Faith asked from her spot at the kitchen sink drying dishes, a general question aimed at both of her children.

"I had a math work sheet but I finished it on the bus on the way home from school Friday," Louisa said. Chase wasn't really surprised. She was a conscientious student who rarely left schoolwork until Sunday evening.

"How about you, Barrett?"

"I'm almost done. I just had a few problems in math

and they're *hard*. I can ask my teacher tomorrow. We might not even have school anyway so maybe I won't have to turn them in until Tuesday."

"Let's take a look at them," Chase said.

Barrett groaned a little but went to his room for his backpack.

"You don't have to do that," Faith said.

"I don't mind," he assured her.

They sat together at the desk in the great room while the Christmas lights glowed on the tree and a fire flickered in the fireplace. It wasn't a bad way to spend a Sunday night.

After only three or four problems, a lightbulb seemed to switch on in the boy's head—as it usually did.

"Oh! I get it now. That's easy."

"I told you it was."

"It wasn't easy the way my teacher explained it. Why can't you be my teacher?"

He tried not to shudder at the suggestion. "I'm afraid I've already got a job."

"And you're good at it," Mary offered from the chair where she sat knitting.

"Thanks, Mary. I do my best," he answered humbly. He loved being a rancher and wanted to think he was a responsible one.

Now that the boy seemed to be in the groove with his homework, Chase lifted his head from the book and suddenly spotted Faith in the mudroom, putting on her winter gear. He had been so busy helping Barrett, he hadn't noticed.

"Where are you off to? Not out into that wind, I hope."

"I just need to make sure the tarp over the outside haystack is secure. Oh, and check on Rosie," she said, referring to one of her border collies. "She was acting strangely this morning, which makes me think she might be close to having her puppies. I've been trying to keep her in the barn but she wanders off. Before the storm front moves in, I want to be sure she's warm and safe."

Chase scraped his chair back. "I'll come with you."

"You don't need to. You just spent a half hour working on Barrett's homework. I'm sure you've got things to worry about at your place."

He couldn't think of anything. He generally tried to keep things in good order, addressing problems when they came up. He always figured he couldn't go wrong following his father's favorite adage: an ounce of prevention was worth a pound of cure. Better to stop trouble before it could start.

"I'll help," he said. "I'll check the hay cover while you focus on Rosie."

Her mouth tightened for an instant but she finally nodded and waited while he threw his coat on, then together they walked out into the storm.

Darkness came early this time of year near the winter solstice but a few high-wattage electric lights on poles lit their way. The wind howled viciously already and puffed out random snowflakes at them, hard as sharp pebbles.

Below the ranch house, he could see that the parking lot of The Christmas Ranch—which had been full when he pulled up—was mostly cleared out now, with a horse-drawn sleigh on what was probably its last go-round of the evening making its way back to the barn near the lodge.

He would really like to find time before Christmas to take Addie on a ride, along with Faith and her children.

The Saint Nicholas Lodge glowed cheerily against the cold night. Beyond it, the cluster of small structures that made up the life-size Christmas village—complete with indoor animatronic scenes of elves hammering and Santa eating from a plate of cookies—looked like something from a Christmas card.

Her family had created a celebration of the holidays here, unlike anything else in the region. People came from miles around, eager to enhance their holiday spirit.

"It's nice that Hope has hired enough staff now that she doesn't have to do everything on her own," he said.

"With the baby coming, Rafe insisted she cut back her hours. No more fourteen-hour days, seven days a week from Thanksgiving to New Year's."

Those hours were probably not unlike what Faith did year-round on the Star N—at least during calving and haying season and roundup. In other words, most of the year.

She worked so hard and never complained about the burden that had fallen onto her shoulders after Travis died.

When they reached the haystack, tucked beneath a huge open-sided structure with a metal roof, he heard the problem before he saw it, the thwack of a loose tarp cover flapping in the wind. Each time the wind dug underneath the tarp, it pulled it loose a little further. If they didn't tie it down, it would eventually pull the whole thing loose and she would not only lose an expensive tarp but potentially the whole haystack to the storm.

"That's gotten a lot worse, just in the last few hours," she said, pitching her voice louder to be heard over the wind. "I should have taken time to fix it earlier when I first spotted the problem, but I was doing about a hundred other things at the time. I was going to fix it in the morning, but I didn't take into account the storm."

"It's fine," he said. "We'll have it safe and secure in no time. It might take both of us, though—one to hold the flap down and hold the flashlight while the other ties it."

They went to work together, as they had done a hundred times before. He wrestled the tarp down, which wasn't easy amid the increasing wind, then held it while she tied multiple knots to keep it in place.

"That should do it," she said.

"While we're out here, let's tighten the other corners," he suggested.

When he was satisfied the tarp was secure—and when the bite of the wind was close to becoming uncomfortable—he tightened the last knot.

"Thanks, Chase," she said.

"No problem. Let's go see if Rosie is smart enough to stay in from the cold."

She clutched at her hat to keep the wind from tugging it away and they made their way into the relative warmth and safety of her large, clean barn.

The wind still howled outside but it was muted, more like a low, angry buzz, making the barn feel like a refuge.

"That wind has to be thirty or forty miles an hour," she said, shaking her head as she turned on the lights inside the barn.

"At least this storm isn't supposed to bring bitter cold along with it," he said. "Where's Rosie?"

"I set her up in the back stall but who knows if she decided to stay put? I really hope she's not out in that wind somewhere."

Apparently the dog knew this cozy spot was best for her and her pups. They found her lying on her side on an old horse blanket with five brand-new white-and-black puppies nuzzling at her.

"Oh. Will you look at that?" Faith breathed. Her eyes looked bright and happy in the fluorescent barn lights. "Hi there, Rosie. Look at you! What a good girl. Five babies. Good job, little mama!"

She leaned on the top railing of the stall and he joined her. "The kids will be excited," he observed.

"Are you kidding? *Excited* is an understatement. Puppies for Christmas. They'll be thrilled. If I let her, Louisa probably would be down here in a minute and want to spend the night right there in the straw with Rosie."

The dog flapped her tail at the sound of her name and they watched for a moment before he noticed her water bowl was getting low. He slipped inside the stall and picked up the food and the water bowls and filled them each before returning them to the cozy little pen.

For his trouble, he earned another tail wag from Rosie and a smile from Faith.

"Thank you. Do you think they'll be warm enough out here? I can take them into the house."

"They should be okay. She might not appreciate being moved now. They're warm enough in here and they're out of the wind. If you're really worried about it, I can bring over a warming lamp."

"That's a good idea, at least for the first few days. I've got one here. I should have thought of that."

She headed to another corner of the barn and returned a moment later with the large lamp and they spent a few moments hanging it from the top beam of the stall.

"Perfect. That should do the trick."

While the wind howled outside, they stood for a while watching the dog and her pups beneath the glow of the heat lamp. He wasn't in a big hurry to leave this quiet little scene and he sensed Faith wasn't either.

"Seems like just a minute ago that she was a pup herself," she said in a soft voice. "I guess it's been a while, though. Three years. She was in the last litter we had out of Lillybelle, so she would have been born just a few months before Travis…"

Her voice broke off and she gazed down at the puppies with her mouth trembling a little.

"Life rolls on," he said quietly.

"Like it or not, I guess," she answered after a moment. "Thanks for your help tonight, first with Barrett's homework and then with storm preparation. You're too good to us."

"You know I'm always happy to help."

"You shouldn't be," she whispered.

He frowned. "Shouldn't be what?"

She kept her attention fixed on the wriggling puppies. "Celeste gave me a lecture the other night. She told me I'm not being fair to you. She said I take you for granted."

"We're friends. Friends help each other. You feed me every Sunday and usually more often than that. Addie practically lives over here when I have visitation and also ranch work I can't avoid. And you bought my groceries the other day, right?"

"Don't forget to take them home when you go." She released a heavy sigh. "We both know the ledger will never be balanced, no matter how many groceries I buy for you. The Star N wouldn't have survived without you. I don't know why you are so generous with your time and energy on our behalf but I hope you know how very grateful we are. How very grateful *I* am. Thank you. And I hope you know how…how much we all love you."

He looked down at her, wondering at the murky subtext he couldn't quite read here.

"I'm happy to help out," he answered again.

She swallowed hard, avoiding his gaze. "I guess what I wanted to tell you is that things are better now. The Star N is back in the black, thanks in large part to you and to The Christmas Ranch finally being self-sustaining. I'll never been an expert at ranching but I kind of feel like

I know a little more what I'm doing now. If you…want to ease away a bit so you can focus more on your own ranch, I would completely understand. Don't worry. We'll be fine."

It took about two seconds for him to go from confusion to being seriously annoyed.

"So you're basically telling me you don't want me hanging around anymore."

She looked instantly horrified. "No! That's not what I'm saying at all. I just…don't want you to feel obligated to do as much as you have for us. For me. I needed help and would have been lost without you the last two years but you can't prop us up forever. At some point, I have to stand on my own."

"Would you be saying this if I hadn't kissed you the other night?"

Her eyes widened and she looked startled that he had brought the kiss up when they both had been so carefully avoiding the subject.

Finally she sighed. "I don't know," she said, her voice low again and her gaze fixed on the five little border collie puppies. "It feels like everything has changed."

She sounded so miserable, he wanted to pull her into his arms and tell her he was sorry, that he would do his best to make sure things returned to the way they were a week ago.

"Life has a way of doing that, whether we always like it or not," he said, knowing full well he wouldn't go back, even if he could. "Nobody escapes it. The trick is figuring out how to roll with the changes."

She was silent for a long time and he would have given anything to know what she was thinking.

When she spoke, her voice was low. "I can't stop thinking about that kiss."

Chapter Ten

At first he wasn't sure he heard her correctly or if his own subconscious had conjured the words out of nowhere.

But then he looked at her and her eyes were solemn, intense and more than a little nervous.

He swallowed hard. "Same here. It's all I could think about during dinner. I would like, more than anything, to kiss you again."

She opened her mouth as if she wanted to object. He waited for it, bracing himself for yet one more disappointment. To his utter shock, she took a step forward instead, placed her hands against his chest and lifted her face in clear invitation.

He didn't hesitate for an instant. How could he? He wasn't a stupid man. He framed her face with his hands, then lowered his mouth, brushing against hers once, twice. Her mouth was cool, her lips trembling, and she tasted of raspberry and chocolate from Louisa's cheese-cake—rich, heady. Irresistible.

At first she seemed nervous, unsure, but after only a moment, her hands slid around his neck and she pressed against him, surrendering to the heat swirling between them.

He was awash in tenderness, completely enamored with the courageous woman in his arms.

Optimism bubbled up inside him, a tiny trickle at first, then growing stronger as she sighed against his mouth and returned his kiss with a renewed enthusi-asm that took his breath away. For the first time in days, he began to think that maybe, just maybe, she was beginning to see that this was real, that they were perfect together.

They kissed for several delicious moments, until his breathing was ragged and he wanted nothing more than to find a soft pile of straw somewhere, lower her down and show her exactly how amazing things could be be-tween them.

A particularly fierce gust of wind rattled the win-dows of the barn, distracting him enough to realize a cold, drafty barn that smelled of animals and hay might not be the most romantic of spots.

With supreme effort, he forced his mouth to slide away from hers, pressing his forehead to hers and giv-ing them both a chance to collect their breath and their thoughts.

Her eyes were dazed, aroused. "I feel like I've been

asleep for nearly three years and now…I'm not," she admitted.

He pressed a soft kiss on her mouth again. "Welcome back."

She smiled a little but it slid away too soon, replaced by an anxious expression, and she took another step away. He wanted to tug her back into his arms but he knew he couldn't kiss her into accepting the possibilities between them, as tempting as he found that idea.

"I'm afraid," she admitted.

His growing optimism cooled like the air that rushed between them. "Of what? I hope you know I would rather stab myself in the foot with a pitchfork than ever hurt you."

"Maybe I don't want to hurt *you*," she whispered, her features distressed. "You're the best man I know, Chase. When I think about…about not having you in my life, I feel like I'm going to throw up. But I'm not sure I'm ready for this again—or that I ever will be."

Well. That was honest enough. He had to respect it, even if he didn't like it. It took him a moment to grab his scrambled thoughts and formulate them into something he hoped came out coherently.

"That's a decision you'll have to make," he said, choosing his words with care. "But think about those puppies. We can keep them here under that heat lamp forever where it's safe and warm and dry. That's the best place for them right now, I agree, while they're tiny and vulnerable. But they won't always be the way they are right now, and what kind of existence would those puppies have if they could never really have the chance to experience the world? They're meant to run across fields and chase birds and lie stretched out in the summer sunshine. To live."

She let out a breath. "You're comparing me to those puppies."

"I'm only saying I understand you've suffered a terrible loss. I know how hard you've fought to work through the grief. It's only natural to want to protect yourself, to be afraid of moving out of the safe place you've created for yourself out of that grief."

"Terrified," she admitted.

His heart ached for her and the struggle he had forced on her. He wanted to reach for her hands but didn't trust himself to touch her right now. "I can tell you this, Faith. You have too much love inside you to spend the rest of your life hiding inside that safe haven while the world moves on without you."

Her gaze narrowed. "That's easy for you to say. You never lost someone you loved with all your heart."

He wanted to tell her he *had*, only in a different way. He had lost her over and over again—though could a guy really lose what he'd never had?

"You're right. I can only imagine," he lied.

As tempting as it was to tell her everything in his heart—that he had loved her since that afternoon he took her shopping for Aunt Mary—he didn't dare. Not yet. Something told him that would send her running away even faster.

She would have to be the one to make the decision about whether she was ready to open her heart again.

The storm rattled the window again, fierce and demanding, and she shivered suddenly, though he couldn't tell if it was from the cold or from the emotional winds battering them. Either way, he didn't want her to suffer.

"Let's get you back to the house. Mary will be wondering where we are."

She nodded. After one more check of the puppies, she tugged her gloves back on and headed out into the night.

Faith was fiercely aware of him as they walked from the barn to the ranch house with the wind and snow howling around them.

She felt as if all the progress she had made toward rebuilding her world had been tossed out into this storm. She had been so proud of herself these last few months. The kids were doing well, the ranch was prospering, she had finally developed a new routine and had begun to be more confident in what she was doing.

While she wouldn't say she had been particularly happy, at least she had found some kind of acceptance with her new role as a widow. She was more comfortable in her own skin.

Now she felt as if everything had changed again. Once more she was confused, off balance, not sure how to put one more step in front of the other and forge a new path.

She didn't like it.

Even in the midst of her turmoil, she couldn't miss the way he placed his body in the path of the wind to protect her from the worst of it. That was so much like

Chase, always looking out for her. It warmed her heart, even as it made her ache.

"You still need your groceries," she said when they reached the house. "Come in and I'll grab them."

He looked as if he had something more to say but he finally nodded and followed her inside.

Though she could hear the television playing down the hall in the den, the kitchen was dark and empty. A clean, vacant kitchen on Sunday night after the big family party always left her feeling a little bereft, for some strange reason.

She flipped on the light and discovered a brown paper bag on the counter with his name on it. She couldn't resist peeking inside and discovered it contained a half dozen of the dinner rolls. Knowing Aunt Mary and her habits, she pulled open the refrigerator and found another bag with his name on it.

"It looks like Mary saved some leftovers for you."

"Excellent. It will be nice not having to worry about dinner tomorrow."

She knew he rarely cooked when Addie was with her mother, subsisting on frozen meals, sandwiches and the occasional steaks he grilled in a batch. Mary knew it, too, which might be another reason she invited him over so often.

Faith headed to the walk-in pantry where she had left the things she bought at the store for him.

"Here you go. Dishwashing detergent, dish soap and paper towels."

"That should do it. Thanks for picking them up for me."

"It was no trouble at all."

"I'll check in with you first thing in the morning to see if you had any storm damage."

If she were stronger, she would tell him thank you but it wasn't necessary. At some point in a woman's life, she had to figure out how to clean up her own messes. Instead, she did her best to muster a smile. "Be careful driving home."

He nodded. Still looking as if he had something more to say, he headed for the door. He put a hand on the knob but before he could turn it, he whirled back around, stalked over to her and kissed her hard with a ferocity and intensity that made her knees so weak she had to clutch at his coat to keep from falling.

She could only be grateful none of her family members came into the kitchen just then and stumbled over them.

When he pulled away, a muscle in his jaw worked but he only looked at her out of solemn, intense eyes.

"Good night," he said.

She didn't have the breath to speak, even if she trusted herself to say anything, so she only nodded.

The moment he left, she pulled her ranch coat off with slow, painstaking effort, hung it in the mudroom, then sank down into a kitchen chair, fighting the urge to bury her face in her hands and weep.

She felt like the world's biggest idiot.

She knew she relied on him, that he had become her rock and the core of her support system since Travis died. He made her laugh and think, he challenged her, he praised her when things went well and held her when they didn't.

All this time, when she considered him her dearest friend, some part of her already knew the feelings she had for him ran deeper than that.

She felt so stupid that it had taken her this long to figure it out. She had always known she loved him, just as she had told him earlier.

She had just never realized she was also *in love* with him.

How had it happened? How could she have *let* it happen?

She should have known something had shifted over the last few months when she started anticipating the times she knew she would see him with a new sort of intensity, when she became more aware of the way other women looked at him when they were together, as she started noticing a ripple of muscle, the solid strength of him as he did some ordinary task in the barn.

She should have realized, but it all just seemed so… natural.

She was still sitting there trying to come to terms with the shock when Mary came into the kitchen wearing her favorite flannel nightgown over long underwear and thick socks.

"Did Chase take off? I had leftovers for him."

She summoned a smile that felt a little wobbly at the edges. "He took them. Don't worry."

"Oh, you know me. Worrying is what I do best." Mary looked out the window where the snow lashed in hard pellets. "I'll tell you, I don't like him driving into the teeth of that nasty wind. All it would take would be one tree limb to fall on his pickup truck."

Her heart clutched at the unbearable thought.

This. This was why she couldn't let herself love him. She would not survive losing a man she loved a second time.

She pushed the grim fear away, choosing instead to focus on something positive.

"Rosie had her puppies. Five of them."

"Is that right?" Mary looked pleased.

"They're adorable. I'm sure the kids will want to see them first thing."

"I made them take their showers for the night. Barrett isn't very happy with me right now but I'm sure he'll get over it. They're both in their rooms, reading."

She would go read to them in a moment. It was her favorite part of the day, those quiet moments when she could cuddle her children and explore literary worlds with them. "Thank you," she said to her aunt. "I don't tell you enough how much I appreciate your help."

Mary sat down across from her at the table. "Are you okay? You seem upset."

For a moment, she desperately wanted to confide in her beloved great-aunt, who was just about the wisest person she knew. The words wouldn't come, though. Mary wouldn't be an unbiased observer in this particular case as Mary adored Chase and always had.

"I'm just feeling a little down tonight."

Mary took Faith's hands in her own wrinkled, age-spotted ones. "I get that way sometimes. The holidays sure make me feel alone."

A hard nugget of guilt lodged in her chest. She wasn't the only one in the world who had ever suffered heartache. Uncle Claude had died five years earlier and they all still missed him desperately.

"You're not alone," she told her aunt. "You've got us, as long as you want us."

"I know that, my dear, and I can't tell you how grateful I am for that." Mary squeezed her fingers. "It's not quite the same. I miss my Claude."

She thought of her big, burly, white-haired greatuncle, who had adored Christmas so much that he had started The Christmas Ranch with one small herd of reindeer to share his love of the holiday with the community.

"I'm thinking about dating again," Mary announced. "What do you think?"

She blinked at that completely unexpected piece of information. "Really?"

"Why not? Your uncle's been gone for years and I'm not getting any younger."

"I… No. You're not. I think it's great. Really great."

Her aunt made a face. "I don't know about *great*. More like a necessary evil. I'd like to get married again, have a companion in my old age, and unfortunately you usually have to go through the motions and go on a few dates first in order to get there."

Her seventy-year-old great-aunt was braver than she was. It was another humbling realization. "Do you have someone in mind?"

Her aunt shrugged. "A couple of widowers at the senior citizens center have asked me out. They're nice enough, but I was thinking about asking Pat Walters out to dinner."

She tried not to visibly react to yet another stunner. For years, Pat had been one of the men who played Santa Claus at The Christmas Ranch. His wife had died just a few months after Uncle Claude.

She digested the information and the odd *rightness* of the idea.

"You absolutely should," she finally said. "He's a great guy."

"He is. Truth is, we went out a few times three years ago when I was living in town and we had a lot of fun together. I didn't tell you girls because it was early days yet and there was nothing much to tell."

She shrugged her ample shoulders. "But then Travis died and I moved back in here to help you with the kids. I just didn't feel like the time was right to complicate things so Pat and I put things on the back burner for a while."

Oh, the guilt. The nugget turned into a full-on boulder. Had she really been so wrapped up in her own pain that she hadn't noticed a romance simmering right under her nose?

What else had she missed?

"I wish you had told me," she said. "I hate that you put your life on hold for me. I would have been okay. Celeste was here to help me out in the evenings and I could have hired someone to help me with Lou and Barrett when I was busy on the ranch and couldn't take them with me."

Mary frowned. "I didn't tell you about Pat to make you feel guilty. You didn't force me to move in after

Travis died. You didn't even *ask* me. I did it because I needed to, because that's what family does for each other."

Mary and Claude had been helping her and her sisters for eighteen years, since they had been three traumatized, frightened, grieving girls.

Her aunt, with her quiet strength, support and wisdom, had been a lifesaver to her after her parents died and even more of one after Travis died.

"I can never repay you for everything you've done," she said, her throat tight and the hot burn of tears behind her eyes.

Mary sat back in her chair and skewered her with a stern look. "Is that what you think I want? For you to repay me?"

"Of course! I wish I could."

"Well, you're right. I do."

She blinked. "Okay."

"You can do that by showing me I taught you a thing or two over the years about surviving and thriving, even when the going is tough."

She stared at her aunt, wondering where this was coming from. "I… What do you mean?"

"Life isn't meant to be lived in fear, honey," Mary said.

It was so similar to her recent conversation with Chase that she had to swallow. "I know."

"Do you?" Mary pressed. "I'm just saying. Chase won't wait around for you forever, you know."

Faith pulled her hands from her aunt's and curled

them into fists on her lap. "I don't know what you mean."

Mary snorted. "Of the three of you, you were always the worst liar. You know exactly what I mean. That boy is in love with you and has been forever."

She felt hot and then ice-cold. First Celeste, now Aunt Mary. What had they seen that she had missed all this time?

She wanted to protest but even in her head, any counterargument she tried to formulate sounded stupid and trite. Was it true? Had he been in love with her and had she been so preoccupied with life that she hadn't realized?

Or worse, much worse, had she realized it on some subconscious level and simply taken it for granted all this time?

"Chase is my best friend, Mary. He's been like a father to the kids since Travis died. And you and I both know we would have had to sell the ranch if he hadn't helped me pull it back from the brink."

Her aunt gave her a hard look. "Seems to me there are worse things to base a relationship on. Not to mention, he's one good-looking son of a gun."

She couldn't deny that. And he kissed like a dream.

"I'm so scared," she whispered.

Mary made that snorting noise again. "Who isn't, honey? If you're not scared sometimes, you're just plain stupid. The trick is to decide how much of your life you're willing to sacrifice for those fears."

Before she could come up with an answer, her aunt

rose. "I'm going to turn in and you've got kids waiting for you to read to them."

She rose, as well. "Thank you, Mary."

She didn't know if she was thanking her for the advice or the last eighteen years of wisdom. She supposed it didn't really matter.

Her aunt hugged her. "Don't worry. You'll figure it out. Good night, honey. Sleep well."

She would have laughed if she thought she could pull it off without sounding hysterical.

Something told her more than the wind would be keeping her up that night.

She didn't see Chase at all the next week. Maybe he was only giving her space, as she had asked, or maybe he was as busy at his place as she was at the Star N, trying to finish up random jobs before the holidays.

Or maybe he was finally fed up with her cowardice and indecision.

Though she didn't see him, she did talk to him on the phone twice.

He called her once on Monday morning, the day after the storm and that stunning kiss in the barn, to make sure her ranch hadn't sustained significant damage from the winds and snows.

On Thursday afternoon, he called to tell her he was driving to Boise to pick up Addie a day earlier than planned and asked if she needed him to bring anything back from Boise for the kids' stockings.

He had sounded distant and frazzled. She knew how tough it was for him to be separated from Addie over the holidays, which made his thoughtfulness in worrying about Louisa and Barrett even more touching.

Again, she wanted to smack Cindy for her selfishness in booking a cruise over the holidays without consulting him.

He could have withheld permission and the court would have sided with him. After Cindy sprang the news on him, though, he had told Faith he hadn't wanted to drag Addie into a war between her parents.

As a result, he was planning their own Christmas celebration a few days before the actual holiday, complete with Christmas Eve dinner, presents and all.

"I think we're covered," she told him, her heart aching. "Be careful driving back. Oh, and let Addie know she's still on to sing with Louisa and Olivia. Ella is planning on it."

"I'll tell her. She'll be thrilled. Thanks."

She wanted to tell him so many other things. That she hadn't stopped thinking about him. That their kisses seemed to play through her head on an endless loop. That she just needed a little more time. She couldn't find the courage to say any of it so he ended up telling her goodbye rather abruptly and severing the connection.

There had been times when they stayed on the phone the entire time he drove to Boise to pick up his daughter, never running out of things to talk about.

Were those days gone forever?

She sighed now and headed toward Saint Nicholas Lodge with a couple of letters that had been delivered to the main house by accident, probably because the post office had temporary help handling the holiday mail volume.

Though she waved at the longtime clerk at the gift store, she didn't stop to chat, heading straight for the office instead, where she found Hope sitting behind her desk.

"Mail delivery," Faith announced, setting the letters on the desk. "It looks like a bill for reindeer food and one for candy canes. I might have a tough time convincing my accountant those are legitimate expenses for a cattle ranch."

When Hope didn't reply, Faith's gaze sharpened on her sister. Fear suddenly clutched her when she registered her sister's pale features, her pinched mouth, the haunted eyes. "What is it, honey? What's wrong?"

"Oh, Faith. I... I was just about to call you."

Her sister's last word ended in a sob that she tried to hide but Faith wasn't fooled. She also suddenly realized her sister's arms were crossed protectively across her abdomen.

"What's wrong? Is it the baby?"

Hope nodded, tears dripping down the corners of her eyes. "I've been having crampy aches all day and I... I just don't feel good. I was just in the bathroom and...had some spotting. Oh, Faith. I'm afraid I'm losing the baby."

She burst into tears and Faith instantly went to her side and wrapped her arms around her. Her younger sister was normally so controlled in any crisis. Even when they had been kidnapped, Hope had been calm and cool.

Seeing her lose it like this broke Faith's heart in two.

"What do you need me to do? I can call Rafe. I can run you into the doctor's. Whatever you need."

"I just called Rafe." Hope wiped at her eyes, though she continued to weep. "He's on his way and we're running into Jake Dalton's office. It might be nothing. I might be overreacting. I hope so."

"I do, too." She whispered a prayer that her sister could endure whatever outcome.

She wouldn't let herself focus on the worst, thinking instead about what a wonderful mother Hope would be. She was made for it. She loved children and had spent much of her adult life following their parents' examples and trying to help those in need around the world in her own way.

Really, coming home and running The Christmas Ranch had been one more way Hope wanted to help people, by giving them a little bit of holiday spirit in a frazzled word.

"It's the worst possible time," Hope said, her eyes distressed. "Within the hour, I've got forty kids showing up to practice for the play."

"That is absolutely the least of your concerns," Faith said, going into big sister mode. "I forbid you to worry about a single thing at The Christmas Ranch. You've got an excellent staff, not to mention a family ready to step in and cover whatever else you might need. Focus on yourself and on the baby. That's an order."

Hope managed a wobbly smile that did nothing to conceal the fear beneath it. "You're always so bossy."

"That's right." She squeezed her sister's fingers.

"And right now I'm ordering you to lie down and wait for your husband, this instant."

Hope went to the low sofa in the office and complied. While she rested, Faith found her sister's coat and her voluminous tote bag and carried them both to her, then sat holding her hand for a few more moments, until Rafe arrived.

He looked as pale as his wife and hugged her tightly, green eyes murky with worry. "Whatever happens, we'll be okay," he assured her.

It took all her strength not to sob at the gentleness of the big, tough former navy SEAL as he all but carried Hope out to his SUV and settled her into the passenger side. Faith handed her the tote bag she had carried along.

"Call me the minute you know anything," she ordered.

"I will. I promise. Faith, can you stay during rehearsals to make sure Ella has everything she needs?"

"Of course."

"Don't tell Barrett and Lou yet. I don't want them to worry."

"Nothing to tell," she said. "Because you and that baby are going to be absolutely fine."

If she kept saying that, perhaps she could make it true.

She watched them drive away, shivering a little until she realized she had left her own coat in Hope's office. Before she could go inside for it, she spotted Chase's familiar pickup truck.

How did he always know when she needed him? she

wondered, then realized he must be dropping Addie off for rehearsal.

She didn't care why he had come. Only that he was there.

She moved across the parking lot without even thinking it through. Desperate for the strength and comfort of his embrace, she barely gave him time to climb out of his vehicle before she was at his side, wrapping her arms tightly around him.

She saw shock and concern flash in his eyes for just an instant before he held her tight against him. "What's going on? What's wrong?" he asked, his voice urgent.

Addie was with him, Faith realized with some dismay. She couldn't burst into tears, not without the girl wondering about it and then telling Lou and Barrett, contrary to Hope's wishes.

"It's Hope," she whispered in his ear. "She's threatening a miscarriage."

He growled a curse that made Addie blink.

"It's too early to know for sure yet," Faith said quietly. "Rafe just took her to the doctor."

"What can I do?"

It was so like him to want to fix everything. The thought would have made her smile if she weren't so very worried. "I don't think we can do anything yet. Just hope and pray she and the baby will both be okay."

"Will she need extra help here at The Christmas Ranch? I can cover you at the Star N if you need to step in here until the New Year."

Oh, the dear man. He was already doing extra work

for their neighbor and now he wanted to add Faith's workload to his pile, as well.

"I hope I don't have to take you up on that but it's too early to say right now."

"Keep me posted."

"I will. I… Thank you, Chase."

"You're welcome."

She would have said more but other children started to arrive and the moment was gone.

Chapter Eleven

Chase ended up staying to watch the rehearsal, figuring he could help corral kids if need be.

He had plenty of other things he should be doing but nothing else seemed as important as being here if Faith or her family needed him.

A few minutes after the rehearsal started, Celeste showed up. She went immediately to the office, where Faith was staring into space. The two of them embraced, both wiping tears. Not long after, Mary showed up, too, and the three of them sat together, not saying much.

He wanted to go in there but didn't quite feel it was his place so he stayed where he was and watched the children sing about Silver Bells and Holly Jolly Christmases and Silent Nights.

About an hour into rehearsal—when he felt more

antsy than he ever remembered—Faith took a call on her cell phone. The anxiety and fear on her features cut through him and he couldn't resist rising to his feet and going to the doorway.

"Are they sure? Yes. Yes. I understand." Her features softened and she gave a tremulous smile. "That's the best news, Rafe. The absolute best. Thank you for calling. I'll tell them. Yes. Give her all our love and tell her to take care of herself and not to worry about a thing. That's an order. Same goes for you. We love you, too, you know."

She hung up, her smile incandescent, then she gave a little cry that ended on a sob. "Dr. Dalton says for now everything seems okay with the baby. The heartbeat is strong and all indications are good for a healthy pregnancy."

"Oh, thank the Lord," Mary exclaimed.

She nodded and they all spent a silent moment doing just that.

"Jake wants to put her on strict bed rest for the next few weeks to be safe," Faith said after a moment. "That means the rest of us will have to step up here."

"I'm available for whatever you need," Chase offered once more.

She gave him a distracted smile. "I know but, again, you have plenty to do at your own place. We can handle it."

"I want to help." He tried to tamp down his annoyance that she was immediately pushing aside his help.

"We actually could use him tomorrow," Celeste said thoughtfully.

Faith didn't look convinced. "We'll just have to cancel that part of the party, under the circumstances. The kids will have to understand."

"They're kids," her sister pointed out. "They won't understand anything but disappointment."

"I'll just do it, then," Faith said.

"How, when you're supposed to be helping me with everything else?"

He looked from one to the other without the first idea what they were talking about. "What do you need me to do?"

"I've been running a holiday reading contest at the library for the last two months and the children who have read enough pages earned a special party tomorrow at the ranch," Celeste said. "Sparkle is supposed to make an appearance and we also promised the children wagon rides around the ranch. Our regular driver will be busy taking the regular customers to see the lights so Rafe has been practicing with our backup team so he could help out at the party. Obviously, he needs to be with Hope now. Flynn is coming back tomorrow but he won't be here in time to help, even if he learns overnight how to drive a team of draft horses."

Why hadn't they just asked him in the first place? Was it because things with him and Faith had become so damn complicated?

"I can do it, no problem—as long as you don't mind if Addie comes along."

Celeste gave him a grateful smile. "Oh, thank you! And Addie would be more than welcome. She's such a reader she probably would have earned the party anyway. Olivia, Lou and Faith are my volunteer helpers and I'm sure they would love Addie's help."

"Great. I'll plan on it, then. Just let me know what time."

They worked out a few more details, all while he was aware of Faith's stiff expression.

At least he would get to see her the next day, even if she clearly didn't want him there.

She lived in the most beautiful place on earth.

Faith lifted her face to the sky, pale lavender with the deepening twilight. As she drove the backup team of draft horses around the Star N barn so she could take them down to the lodge late Sunday afternoon, the moon was a slender crescent above the jagged Teton mountain range to the east and the entire landscape looked still and peaceful.

Sometimes she had to pinch herself to believe she really lived here.

When she was a girl, she had desperately wanted a place to call her own.

She had spent her entire childhood moving around the world while her parents tried to make a difference. She had loved and respected her parents and understood, even then, that they genuinely wanted to help people as they moved around to impoverished villages setting up medical clinics and providing the training to run them after they left.

She wasn't sure *they* understood the toll their self-ordained missionary efforts were taking on their daughters, even before the terrifying events shortly before their deaths.

Faith hadn't known anything other than their transitory lifestyle. She hadn't blinked an eye at the primitive conditions, the language barriers, making friends only to have to tearfully leave them a few months later.

Still, some part of her had yearned for *this*, though she never had a specific spot in mind. All she had really wanted was a place to call her own, anywhere. A loft in the city, a split-level house in the suburbs, a double-wide mobile home somewhere. She hadn't cared what. She just wanted roots somewhere.

For nearly sixteen years, that had been her secret dream, the one she hadn't dared share with her parents. That dream had become reality only after a series of traumas and tragedies. The kidnapping. The unspeakable ordeal of their month spent in the rebel camp. Her father's shocking death during the rescue attempt, then her mother's cancer diagnosis immediately afterward.

She had been shell-shocked, grieving, frightened out of her mind but trying to put on a brave front for her younger sisters as they traveled to their new home in Idaho to live with relatives they barely knew.

When Claude picked them up at the airport in Boise and drove them here, everything had seemed so strange and new, like they had been thrust into an alien landscape.

Until they drove onto the Star N, anyway.

Faith still remembered the moment they arrived at the ranch and the instant, fierce sense of belonging she had felt.

In the years since, it had never left her. She felt the same way every time she returned to the ranch after spending any amount of time away from it. This was home, each beautiful inch of it. She loved ranching more than she could have dreamed. Whoever would have guessed that she would one day become so comfortable at this life that she could not only hitch up a team of draft horses but drive them, too?

The bells on the horses jingled a festive song as she guided the team toward the shortcut to the Saint Nicholas Lodge. Before she could go twenty feet, she spotted a big, gorgeous man in a black Stetson blocking their way.

"I thought I was the hired driver for the night," Chase called out.

She pulled the horses to a stop and fought down the butterflies suddenly swarming through her on fragile wings.

"I figured I could get them down there for you. Anyway, we just bought new sleigh bells for the backup sleigh and I wanted to try them out."

"They sound good to me."

"I think they'll do. Where's Addie?"

"Down at the lodge, helping Olivia and Lou set things up for the party. We stopped there first and Celeste sent me up here to see if you needed help with the team."

Faith fought a frown. She had a feeling her sister sent him out here as yet another matchmaking ploy. Her family was going to drive her crazy. "I've got things under control," she lied. She was only recently coming to see it wasn't true, in any aspect of her life.

"That's good," he said as he greeted the horses, who were old friends of his. "How's Hope?"

"I checked on her a few hours ago and she is feeling fine. She had a good night and has had no further symptoms today. Looks like the crisis has passed."

In the fading light, she saw stark relief on his chiseled features. "I'm so glad. I've been worried all day. And how is your other little mama?"

It took her a moment to realize he meant Rosie. "All the pups are great. They opened their eyes yesterday. The kids have had so much fun watching them. You'll have to bring Addie over."

"I'll try to do that before she leaves on Wednesday but our schedule's pretty packed between now and then. I don't think we'll even have time for Sunday dinner tomorrow."

"Oh. That's too bad," she said, as he moved away from the horses toward the driver's seat of the sleigh. "The family will miss you."

"What about you?" he asked, his voice low and his expression intense.

She swallowed, not knowing what to say. "Yes," she finally said. "Good thing we're not having steak or we wouldn't know how to light the grill."

"Good thing." He tipped his hat back. "Is there room for me up there or are you going to make me walk back to the lodge?"

She slid over and he jumped up and took the reins she handed him.

Though there was plenty of space on the bench, she immediately felt crowded, fiercely aware of the heat of him beside her.

Maybe *she* ought to walk back to the lodge.

The thought hardly had time to register before he whistled to the horses and they obediently took off down the drive toward the lodge, bells jingling.

After a moment, she forced herself to relax and enjoy the evening. She could think of worse ways to spend an evening than driving across her beautiful land in the company of her best friend, who just happened to be a gorgeous cowboy.

"Wow, what a beautiful night," he said after a few moments. "Hard to believe that less than a week ago we were gearing up for that nasty storm."

"We're not supposed to have any more snow until Christmas Eve."

"With what we already have on the ground, I don't think there's any question that we'll have a white Christmas."

"Who knows? It's Idaho. We could have a heat wave between now and then."

"Don't break out your swimming suit yet," he advised. "Unless you want to take a dip in Carson and Jenna McRaven's pool at their annual party this week."

"Not me. I'm content watching the kids have fun in the pool."

The McRavens' holiday party, which would be the night *after* the show for the senior citizens, had become legendary around these parts, yet another tradition she cherished.

"I don't think I'll be able to make it to that one this year," he said. "It's my last day with Addie."

"You're still doing Christmas Eve the night of the show?"

"That's the plan."

It made her heart ache to think of him getting everything ready for his daughter on his own, hanging out stockings and scattering her presents under the tree.

"You're a wonderful father, Chase," she said softly.

He frowned as the sleigh's movement jostled her against him. "Not really. If I were, I might have tried harder to stay married to her mother. Instead, I've given my daughter a childhood where she feels constantly torn between the both of us."

"You did your best to make things work."

"Did I?"

"It looked that way from the outside."

"I should never have married her. If she hadn't been pregnant with Addie, I wouldn't have."

He was so rarely open about his marriage and divorce that she was momentarily shocked. The cheery jingle bells seemed discordant and wrong, given his serious tone.

"It was a mistake," he went on. "We both knew it. I just hate that Addie is the one who has suffered the most."

"She has a mother and stepfather who love her and a father who adores her. She's a sweet, kind, good-hearted girl. You're doing okay. Better than okay. You're a wonderful father and I won't let you beat yourself up."

He looked touched and amused at the same time as

he pulled the sleigh to a stop in front of the lodge. "I've been warned, I guess."

"You have," she said firmly. "Addie is lucky to have you for a father. Any child would be."

His expression warmed and he gazed down at her long enough that she started wondering if he might kiss her again. Instead, he climbed down from the sleigh, then held a hand up to help her out.

She hesitated, thinking she would probably be wise to make her way down by herself on the complete opposite side of the sleigh from him. But for the last ten minutes, they had been interacting with none of the recent awkwardness and she didn't want to destroy this fragile peace.

She took his hand and stepped gingerly over the side of the sleigh.

"Careful. It's icy right there," he said.

The words were no sooner out of his mouth when her boot slipped out from under her. She reached for the closest handhold, which just happened to be the shearling coat covering the muscled chest of a six-foot-two-inch male. At the same moment, he reacted instinctively, grabbing her close to keep her on her feet.

She froze, aware of his mouth just inches from hers. It would be easy, so easy, to step on tiptoe for more of those delicious kisses.

His gaze locked with hers and she saw a raw hunger there that stirred answering heat inside her.

The moment stretched between them, thick and rich like Aunt Mary's hot cocoa and just as sweet.

Why was she fighting this, again? In this moment,

as desire fluttered through her, she couldn't have given a single reason.

She was in love with him and according to two of her relatives, he might feel the same. It seemed stupid to deny both of them what they ached to find together.

"Chase," she murmured.

He inched closer, his breath warm on her skin. Just before she gathered her muscles to stand on tiptoe and meet him, one of the horses stamped in the cold, sending a cascade of jingles through the air.

Oh. What was she doing? This wasn't the time or the place to indulge herself, when a lodge full of young readers would descend on them at any moment.

With great effort, she stepped away. "Hang out here and I'll go check with Celeste to see when she'll be ready for the kids to go on the sleigh."

He tipped his hat back but not before she saw frustration on his features that completely matched her own.

Chapter Twelve

"Wow," Chase said as his daughter rushed down the stairs so they could leave for the Saint Nicholas Lodge. "Who is this strange young lady in my house who suddenly looks all grown-up?"

Addie grinned and swirled around in the fancy red-and-gold velvet dress she was wearing to perform her musical selection with Olivia and Louisa. "Thanks, Dad," she said. "I love this dress *so much*! I wish I could keep it but I have to give it back after the show tonight so maybe someone else can wear it for next year's Christmas show."

"Those are the breaks in show business, I guess," he said. "You've got clothes to change into, right?"

She held up a bag.

"Good. Are you're sure you don't need me to braid your hair or something?"

He was awful with hair but had forced himself to learn how to braid, since it was the easiest way to tame Addie's curls.

"No. Faith said she would help me fix it like Louisa and Olivia have theirs. That's why I have to hurry."

"Yes, my lady. Your carriage awaits." He gave an exaggerated bow and held out her coat, which earned him some of Addie's giggles.

"You're so weird," she said, with nothing but affection in her voice.

"That's what I hear. Merry Christmas, by the way."

She beamed. "I'm so glad we're having our pretend Christmas Eve on the same night as the show. It's perfect."

He buttoned up her coat, humbled by the way she always tried to find a silver lining. "Even though we can't spend the whole evening playing games and opening presents, like we usually do?"

"You only let me open one present on Christmas Eve," she reminded him. "We can still do that after the show, and then tomorrow we'll open the rest of them on our fake Christmas morning."

"True enough."

"Presents are fun and everything. I love them. Who doesn't?"

"I can't think of anyone," he replied, amused by her serious expression.

"But that's not what Christmas is really about. Christmas is about making other people happy—and our show will make a lot of lonely older people very happy. That's what Faith said, anyway."

His heart gave a sharp little jolt at her name, as it always did. "Faith is right," he answered.

About the show, anyway. She wasn't right about him, about them, about the fear that was holding her back from giving him a chance. He couldn't share that with his child so he merely smiled and held open the door for her.

"Let's go make some people happy," he said.

Her smile made her look wiser than her eleven years, then she hurried out into the December evening.

Three hours later, he stood and clapped with the delighted audience as the children walked out onto the small stage at the Saint Nicholas Lodge to take their final bow.

"That was amazing, wasn't it?" Next to him, Flynn beamed at his own daughter, Olivia, whose red-and-gold dress was a perfect match to those worn by Louisa and Addie.

"Even better than last year, which I didn't think was possible," Chase said.

"Those kids have truly outdone themselves this year," Flynn said, gazing out at the smiles on all the wrinkled and weathered faces in the audience as they applauded energetically. "Like it or not, I have a feeling this show for the senior citizens of Pine Gulch has now officially entered into the realm of annual traditions."

Chase had to agree. He had suspected as much after seeing the show the previous year. Though far from an elaborate production—the cast only started rehearsing the week before, after all—the performance was sweet and heartfelt, the music and dancing and dramatic performances a perfect mix of traditional and new favorites.

Of course the community would love it. How could they do otherwise?

"I'm a little biased, but our girls were the best," Flynn said.

Again, Chase couldn't disagree. Olivia had a pure, beautiful voice that never failed to give him chills, while Lou and Addie had done a more than adequate job of backing her up on a stirring rendition of "Angels We Have Heard on High" that had brought the audience to its feet.

"I overheard more than one person saying that was the highlight of the show," Chase said.

He knew Flynn had become more used to his daughter onstage over the last year as she came out of her shell a little more after witnessing the tragedy of her mother's death. While Flynn would probably never love it, he appeared to be resigned to the fact that Olivia, like her mother and grandmother before her, loved performing and making people happy.

Almost without conscious intention, his gaze strayed to Faith, who was hugging the children as they came offstage. She wore a silky red blouse that caught the light and she had her hair up again in a soft, romantic style that made him want to pull out every single pin.

She must have felt his attention. She looked up from laughing at something cute little Jolie Wheeler said and her gaze connected with his. Heat instantly sparked between them and he watched her smile slip away and her color rise.

They gazed at each other for a long moment. Neither of them seemed in a hurry to look away.

He missed her.

He hadn't really spoken with her since that sleigh ride the other night. She had seemed to avoid him for the rest of that evening, and he and Addie hadn't made it to Sunday dinner that week.

When he dropped Addie off earlier in the evening, he had greeted Faith, of course, but she had seemed frazzled and distracted as she hurried around helping the children with hair and makeup.

He hadn't had time to linger then anyway, as Rafe had sent him out to pick up some of the senior citizen guests who didn't feel comfortable driving at night amid icy conditions.

Now Jolie asked her a question and Faith was forced to look down to answer the girl, severing the connection between them and leaving him with the hollow ache that had become entirely too familiar over the last few weeks.

More than anything, he wished he knew what was in her head.

Addie came offstage and waved at him with an energy and enthusiasm that made Flynn laugh.

"I think someone is trying to get your attention," his friend said to Chase in a broad understatement.

"You think?" With a smile, Chase headed toward his daughter.

"Did you see me, Dad?" she exclaimed.

"It was my very favorite part of the show," he told her honestly.

"Lots of other people have told us that, too. We *were* good, but everyone else was, too. I'm so glad I got to do it, even though I missed the first rehearsals."

"So am I."

She hugged him and he felt a rush of love for his sweet-natured daughter.

"What now?" he asked.

"I need to change out of the dress and give it back, I guess," she said, her voice forlorn.

"You sound so sad about that," Faith said from behind him.

He hadn't seen her approach and the sound of her voice so near rippled down his spine as if she had kissed the back of his neck.

Addie sighed. "I just love this dress. I wish I could keep it. But I understand. They need to keep it nice for someone else to wear next year."

Faith hugged her. "Sorry, honey. I took a thousand pictures of you three girls, though. You did such a great job."

Addie grinned. "Thanks, Faith. I *love* my hair. Thank you for doing it. I wish it could be like this every day."

"You are so welcome, my dear," she said with a smile that sent a lump rising in his throat. These were the two females he loved most in the world, with Louisa, Mary and Faith's sisters filling in the other slots, and he loved seeing them interact.

"I guess I should be wishing you a Merry Christmas Eve," Faith said.

"It's the best Christmas Eve on December 20 I ever had," Addie said with a grin, which made Faith laugh.

The sound tightened the vise around his chest. She hadn't laughed nearly enough over the last three years.

What would everyone in the Saint Nicholas Lodge do if he suddenly tugged her to him and kissed her firmly on the mouth for all to see?

"What's for Christmas Eve dinner?" Faith asked him before he could think about acting on the impulse.

He managed to wrench his mind away from impossible fantasies. "You know what a genius I am in the kitchen. I bought a couple of takeout dinners from the café in town. We *are* having a big breakfast tomorrow, though. I can handle waffles and bacon."

"Why don't you eat your Christmas Eve dinner here? We have so much food left over. I think Jenna always overestimates the crowd. Once the crowd clears, we're going to pull some of it out. Everyone is starving, since we were all too busy for dinner before the show to take time for food. You're more than welcome to stay—though I completely understand if you have plans at home for your Christmas Eve celebration."

"Can we, Dad?" Addie begged. "I won't see my friends for three weeks after this."

She wouldn't see *him* for that amount of time either—a miserable thought.

He shrugged, already missing her. "We don't have any plans that are set in stone. I think the only other thing we talked about, besides the show, was playing a couple of games."

"And reading the Christmas story," she pointed out.

"Right. We can't forget that," he answered. "I don't mind if we stay, as long as you promise to go straight to bed when we're done. Santa can't come if you're not asleep."

She rolled her eyes but grinned at the same time. At eleven, she was too old for Santa but that didn't stop either of them from carrying on the pretense a little longer.

"I'm going to go change and tell Lou and Livvie that we're having dinner here," she announced.

She hurried away, leaving him alone with Faith—or as alone as they could be in a vast holiday-themed lodge still filled with about twenty other people.

"It really was a wonderful show," he said.

"I can't take any of the credit."

He had to smile, remembering how busy she had been before and during the show. The previous year had been the same. She claimed she wanted nothing to do with the holiday show, then pitched in and did whatever was necessary to pull it off.

His smile slid away when he realized she was gazing at his mouth again.

Yeah. He decided he didn't much care what people would think if he kissed her again right now.

She swallowed and looked away. "I need to, um, probably take Sparkle back to the barn for the night."

Besides the musical number with Addie and her friends, the other highlight of the show had been when

Celeste, under duress, read from her famous story "Sparkle and the Magic Snowball" to the captivated audience while the *real* Sparkle stood next to her, looking for all the world as if he were reading the story over her shoulder.

"I'll help," he offered.

Both of them knew she didn't need his help but after a moment, she shrugged and headed toward the front door and the enclosure where Sparkle hung out when he made appearances at the lodge.

Faith paused long enough to grab her coat off the rack by the door and toss his to him, then the two of them walked outside into the night.

The reindeer wandered over to greet them like old friends, the bells on his harness jingling merrily.

"Hey, Sparkle. How are you, pal?"

The reindeer lipped at his outstretched hand, making Chase wish he'd brought along an apple or something.

"I really don't need your help," Faith said. "He's so easygoing this is a one-person job—if that. I could probably tell him to go to bed and he would wander over to the barn, flip the latch and head straight for his stall. He might even turn off the lights on his way."

He had to smile at the whimsical image. "I'm here. Let's do this so we can eat, too."

With a sigh, she reached to unlatch the gate. Before she could, Ella Baker came out of the lodge, bundled against the cold and carrying an armload of sheet music.

"You're not staying for dinner?" Faith asked after they exchanged greetings.

"I can't. My dad is having a rough time right now so

I need to take off. But thank you again for asking me to do this. I had so much fun. If you do it again next year and I'm still in town, I would love to help out."

"That's terrific!" Faith exclaimed. "I'll let Hope know. I can guarantee she'll be thrilled to hear this. Thank you!"

"I'm so sorry your sister couldn't be here to see it," Ella said. "I hope the live video worked so she could watch it at home."

Hope was still taking it easy, Chase knew, though she'd had no other problems since that frightening day the week before.

"She saw it," Faith assured her. "I talked to her right afterward and she absolutely loved it, just like everyone else did."

"Oh, I'm so glad." Ella smiled, then turned to him. "Chase, it's really good to see you again. I didn't have the chance to tell you this the other night but I had such a great time dancing with you. I'd love to do it again sometime."

It was clearly an invitation and for a moment, he didn't know what to say. Any other single guy in Pine Gulch would probably think he'd just won the lottery. Ella was lovely and seemed very nice. A relationship with her would probably be easy and uncomplicated— unlike certain other women he could mention.

The only trouble was, that particular woman in question had him so wrapped up in knots, he couldn't untangle even a tiny thread of interest in Ella.

"I'm afraid opportunities to dance are few and far

between around here," he said, in what he hoped was a polite but clear message.

"You two could always go to the Renegade," Faith suggested blithely. "They have a live band with dancing just about every Saturday night."

For a moment, he could only stare at her. Seriously? She was pimping him out to take another woman dancing?

"That would be fun," Ella said, obviously taking Faith's suggestion as encouragement. "Maybe we could go after the holidays."

Chase didn't want to hurt her but he was not about to take her up on the invitation to go out dancing while he was standing in front of the woman he loved.

Even if it had been Faith's suggestion in the first place.

"I don't know," he said, in what he hoped was a noncommittal but clear voice. "I have my daughter a couple weekends a month and it's tough for me to get away."

Understanding flashed in her eyes along with a shadow of pained rejection. He hated that he had planted it there—and hated more that Faith had put him in the position in the first place.

"No problem," she said, some of the animation leaving her features. "Let me know if you have a free night. I've got to run. Good night. And Merry Christmas in advance."

She gave a smile that was only a degree or two shy of genuine and headed out into the parking lot toward her car.

He wasn't sure how, exactly, but Chase managed to

hold on to the slippery, fraying ends of his temper as they led the reindeer the short distance across the snowy landscape to The Christmas Ranch barn.

It coiled through him as they worked together to take off Sparkle's harness and bells, gave him a good brushing, then made sure he had food and water.

He should just let it go, he told himself after they stepped out of the stall and closed the gate.

The evening had been wonderful and he didn't want to ruin it by fighting with her.

He almost had himself convinced of that but somehow as he looked at her, his anger slipped free and the words rolled out anyway.

"Why the hell would you do that?"

Chapter Thirteen

Faith stared at him, stunned by the anger that seemed to seethe around them like storm-tossed sea waves.

"Do…what?"

"You know. You just tried to set me up with Ella Baker again."

Her face flamed even as she shivered at his hard tone. Oh. That.

"All I did was mention that the Renegade has dancing on Saturday nights. I only thought it would be fun for the two of you."

His jaw worked as he continued to stare down at her. "Is that right?"

"Ella is really great," she said. She might as well double down on her own stupidity. "I've seen her with the kids this week and she's amazing—so patient and kind and talented. You heard her sing. Any single guy would have to be crazy not to want to go out with her."

"Really, Faith. *Really?*" The words came at her like a whip snapping through the cold air.

He was furious, she realized. More angry than she had ever seen him. She could see it in every rigid line of his body, from his flexed jaw to his clenched fists.

"After everything that's happened between us these last few weeks, you seriously want to stand there and pretend you think I might have the slightest interest in someone else?"

She let out a breath, ashamed of herself for dragging an innocent—and very nice—woman into this. She didn't even know why she had. The words had just sort of come out. She certainly didn't *want* Chase dating Ella Baker but maybe on some level she was still hanging on to the hope that they could somehow return to the easy friendship of a few weeks ago and forget the rest of this.

"I can't help it if I want you to be happy," she said, her voice low. "You're my dearest friend."

"I don't want to be your friend." He growled an oath that had her blinking. "After everything, can you really not understand that? Fine. You want me to be clear, I'll be clear. I don't want to be your buddy and I don't want to date Ella Baker. She is very nice but I don't have the slightest flicker of interest in her."

"Okay," she whispered. She shouldn't be relieved about that but she couldn't seem to help it.

He gazed down at her, features hard and implacable. "There is only one woman I want in my life and it's you,

Faith. You have to know that. I'm in love with you. It's you. It has *always* been you."

She caught her breath at his words as joy burst through her like someone had switched on a thousand Christmas trees. She wanted to savor it, to simply close her eyes and soak it in.

I love you, too. So, so much.

The words crowded in her throat, jostling with each other to get out.

Over the last few weeks, she had come to accept that unalterable truth. She was in love with him and had been for a long time.

Perhaps some little part of her had loved him since that day he drove her into town when she was a frightened girl of fifteen.

What might have happened between them if his father hadn't been dying, if Travis hadn't come back to the Star N and she hadn't been overwhelmed by the sweet, kind safety he offered, the anchor she had so desperately needed?

She didn't know. She only knew that Chase had always been so very important in her world—more than she could ever have imagined after Travis died so suddenly.

The reminder slammed into her and she reached out for the rough planks of Sparkle's enclosure for support.

Travis.

The images of that awful moment when she had found him lying under his overturned ATV—covered in blood, so terribly still—seemed to flash through her mind in a grim, horrible slide show. She hadn't been able to save him, no matter how desperately she had tried as she begged him not to leave her like her father, her mother.

She had barely survived losing Travis. How could she find the strength to let herself be vulnerable to that sort of raw, all-consuming, soul-destroying pain again?

She couldn't. She had been a coward so many years ago as a helpless girl caught up in events beyond her control and she was still a coward.

Faith opened her mouth to speak but the words wouldn't come.

The silence dragged between them. She was afraid to meet his gaze but when she forced herself to do it, she found his eyes murky with sadness and what she thought might be disappointment.

"You don't have to say anything." All the anger seemed to have seeped out of him, leaving his features as bleak as the snow-covered mountains above the tree line. "I get it."

How could he, when *she* didn't understand? She had the chance for indescribable happiness here with the man she loved. Why couldn't she just take that step, find enough strength inside herself to try again?

"It doesn't matter how much time I give you. You've made up your mind not to let yourself see me as anything more than your *dearest friend* and nothing I do can change that."

She wanted to tell him that wasn't true. She saw him for exactly what he was. The strong, decent, wonderful man she loved with all her heart.

Fear held both her heart and her words in a tight, icy grip. "Chase, I—" she managed, but he shook his head.

"Don't," he said. "I pushed you too hard. I thought you might be ready to move forward but I can see now I only complicated things between us and wasted both of our time. It was a mistake and I'm sorry."

"I'm the one who's sorry," she said softly, but he had turned around and headed for the door and she wasn't sure he heard her.

The moment he left, she pressed a hand to her chest and the sharp, cold ache there, as if someone had pierced her skin with an icicle.

She wanted so badly to go after him but told herself maybe it was better this way.

Wasn't it better to lose a friendship than to risk having her heart cut out of her body?

Chase didn't know how he made it through the next few days.

The hardest thing had been walking back inside the Saint Nicholas Lodge and trying to pretend everything was fine, with his emotions a raw, tangled mess.

He was pretty sure he fooled nobody. Celeste and Mary seemed especially watchful and alert as he and Addie dined with the family. As for Faith, she had come in about fifteen minutes after he did with her eyes red and her features subdued. She sat on the exact opposite side of the room from him and picked at her food, her features tight and set.

He was aware of a small, selfish hope that perhaps

she was suffering a tiny portion of the vast pain that seemed to have taken over every thought.

She had left early, ostensibly with the excuse of taking some of the leftovers to Rafe and Hope, though he was fairly certain it was another effort to avoid him.

He did his best to put his pain on the back burner, focusing instead on making his remaining few hours with his daughter until after the New Year memorable for her.

Their premature Christmas Eve went off without a hitch. When they returned home, she changed into her pajamas and they played games and watched a favorite holiday movie, then she opened the one early present he allowed her—a carved ornament he had made from a pretty aspen burl on a downed tree he found in the mountains. In the morning she opened the rest of her presents from him and he fixed her breakfast, then she helped him take care of a few chores.

Too soon, her mother showed up after visiting her parents at the care center where Cindy's mother was still recovering from her stroke.

Chase tried to put on a smile for Cindy, sorry all over again for the mess he had made of his marriage.

He had tried so hard to love her. Those early days had been happy, getting ready for the baby and then their early days with Addie, but their shared love of their daughter hadn't provided strong enough glue to keep them together.

It hadn't been Cindy's fault that his heart hadn't been completely free. Despite his best efforts, she somehow had sensed it all along and he regretted that now.

He understood why disappointment and hurt turned her bitter and cold toward him and he resolved to do his best to be kinder.

Addie had decided to leave some of the gifts he had given her at the ranch so she could enjoy them during her time with him there, but she still had several she wanted to take home. After he loaded them into her mom's SUV, he hugged his daughter and kissed the top of her head. "Have a fun cruise, Addie-bug, and at Disney World. I want to hear every detail when you get back."

"Okay," she said, her arms tight around his neck. "You won't be by yourself on Christmas, will you, Dad? You'll go open presents at the Star N with Louisa and Barrett, right?"

His heart seemed to give a sharp little spasm. That's what he had done for several years, even before Travis died, but that was looking unlikely this year.

"I'm not sure," he lied. "I'll be fine, whatever I do. Merry Christmas, kiddo."

As they drove away, he caught sight of the lights of the Star N and The Christmas Ranch below the Brannon Ridge.

How was he going to make it through the remainder of his life without her—and without Lou and Barrett and the rest of her family he loved so much?

He didn't have the first idea.

"Why isn't Chase coming for dinner tonight?" Louisa asked as she and Barrett decorated Christmas cookie angels on the kitchen island.

"Yeah. He always comes over on Christmas Eve," Barrett said.

"And on Christmas morning when we open presents," Louisa added.

Faith had no idea how to answer her children. It made her chest ache all over again, just thinking about it.

That morning she had gathered her nerve and called to invite him for dinner and to make arrangements for transferring Louisa's Christmas present from Brannon Ridge to the Star N. She had been so anxious about talking to him again after four days of deafening silence, but the call went straight to voice mail.

He was avoiding her.

That was fairly obvious, especially when he texted just moments later declining her invitation but telling her that he already had a plan to take care of the other matter and she didn't need to worry about it.

The terse note after days of no contact hurt more than she could have imagined, even though she knew it was her own fault. She wanted so much to jump in her truck and drive to his ranch, to tell him she was sorry for all the pain she had put them both through.

"I guess he must have made other plans this year," she said now in answer to her daughter.

Mary made a harrumphing sort of noise from her side of the island but said nothing else in front of the children, much to Faith's relief.

Though her aunt didn't know what had transpired between Faith and Chase, Mary knew *something* had. She blamed Faith for it and had made no secret that she wasn't happy about it.

"Addie texted me a while ago. She's worried he'll be all by himself for the holidays," Louisa said. Her daughter made it sound like that was the worst possible fate anyone could endure and the guilty knot under Faith's rib cage seemed to expand.

Her children loved Chase—and vice versa. She hated being the cause of a rift between them.

"We should take him some of our cookies," Barrett suggested.

"That's a great idea," Mary said, with a pointed look at her. "Faith, why don't you take him some cookies? You could be there and back before everybody shows up for dinner."

He didn't want cookies from her. He didn't want *anything*—except the one thing she wasn't sure she had the strength to give.

"Maybe we can all take them over later," she said.

The three looked as if they wanted to argue but she made an impromptu excuse, desperate to escape the guilt and uncertainty. "I need to go. I've got a few things I need to do out in the barn before tonight."

"Now?" Mary asked doubtfully.

"If I finish the chores now, I won't have to go out to take care of them in the middle of our Christmas Eve party with Hope and Celeste," she said.

It was a flimsy excuse but not unreasonable. She did have chores—and she had plans to hang a big red ribbon she had already hidden away in the barn across the stall where she planned to put Lou's new horse. She could do that now, since Louisa had no reason to go out to the barn between now and Christmas morning.

She grabbed her coat and hurried out before any of them could argue with her.

Outside, a cold wind blew down off Brannon Ridge and she shivered at the same time she yawned.

She hadn't been sleeping much the last few weeks, which was probably why her head ached and her eyes felt as if they were coated with gritty sandpaper.

Maybe she could just go to bed and wake up when Christmas was over.

She sighed. However tempting, that was completely impossible. She had hours to go before she could sleep. It was not yet sunset on Christmas Eve—she still had to make it through dinner with her sisters and their families. Both of them were coming, since Hope had been cleared to return to her normal activities.

They would want to know where Chase was and she didn't know how to answer them.

Not only that but her kids would likely be awake for hours yet, jacked up on excitement and anticipation—not to mention copious amounts of sugar from the treats they had been making and sampling all day.

She should take sugar cookies to Chase. He loved them and probably hadn't made any for himself.

How could she possibly face him after their last encounter?

Tears burned behind her eyes. She wanted to tell herself it was from the wind and the lack of sleep but she knew better. This was the season of hope, joy, yet she felt as if all the color and light had been sucked away, leaving only uniform, lifeless gray.

She was in love with him and she didn't know what to do about it.

The worst part was knowing that even if she could find the strength and courage to admit she loved him, she was afraid it was too late.

He had looked so bleak the last time she saw him, so distant. Remembering the finality in that scene, the tears she had been fighting for days slipped past her defenses.

She looked out at the beautiful landscape—the snow-covered mountains and the orange and yellows of the sunset—and gave in to the torment of her emotions here, where no one could see her.

After a few moments, she forced herself to stop, wiping at the tears with her leather gloves. None of this maudlin stuff was helping her take care of her chores and now she would have to finish quickly so she could hurry back to the house to fix her makeup before her sisters saw evidence of her tears and pressed her about what was wrong.

How could she tell them what a mess she had made of things?

With another sigh, she forced herself to focus on the job at hand. She walked through the snow to the barn and pushed the door open but only made it a few steps before she faltered, her gaze searching the interior.

Something was wrong.

Over the past two and a half years, she had come to know the inside of this barn as well as she did her own bedroom. She knew it in all seasons, all weather, all moods.

She knew the scents and the sounds and the shifting light—and right now she could tell something was different.

Someone was here.

She moved quietly into the barn, reaching for the pitchfork that was usually there. It was missing but she found a shovel instead and decided that would have to do.

No one else should be here.

She had two part-time ranch hands but neither was scheduled to be here on Christmas Eve. She had given both time off for the holidays and didn't expect to see them until the twenty-seventh. Anyway, if it had been Bill or Jose, wouldn't she have seen their vehicles parked out front?

With the shovel in hand, she headed farther into the interior of the big barn, eyes scanning the dim interior. Seconds later she spotted it—a beautiful paint mare in one of the stalls near the far end of the barn.

At almost that exact moment, she heard a noise coming from above her. She whirled toward the hayloft that took up one half of the barn and spotted him there, his back to her, along with the missing pitchfork.

"Chase!" she exclaimed. "What are you doing here?"

He swiveled around, and for an arrested moment, he looked at her with so much love and longing, she almost wept again.

Too quickly, he veiled his features. "Feeding Lou's new horse. While I was at it, I figured I could take care of the rest of your stock in the barn so you wouldn't have to worry about it tonight. I was hoping to get out of here before you came down from the house but obviously I'm not fast enough."

He had done that for her, even though he was furious with her. She wanted to cry all over again.

Happiness seemed to bloom through her like springtime and the old barn had never looked so beautiful.

She swallowed, focusing on the least important thought running through her head. "How did you get the new horse down here? I never saw your trailer."

"I didn't want Lou to see it and wonder what was going on so I came in the back way, down the hill. I rode Tor and tied the mare's lead line to his saddle."

"You came down through all that snow?" she exclaimed. "How on earth did you manage that?" There were drifts at least four feet deep in places on that ridgeline.

"It was slow going but Tor is tough and so's the new little mare. She's going to be a great horse for Lou."

She felt completely overwhelmed suddenly, humbled and astonished that he would go to such lengths for her daughter.

And for her, she realized.

This was only one of a million other acts over the last few years that provided all the evidence anyone could need that he loved her.

"I can't believe you would do that."

"Don't make a big deal out of it," he said, his tone distant.

"It is a big deal to me. It's huge. Oh, Chase."

The tears from earlier broke free again and a small

sob escaped before she could cover her mouth with her fingers.

"Cut it out. Right now."

She almost laughed at the alarm in his voice, despite the tears that continued to trickle down her cheeks.

"I can't. I'm sorry. When the man I love shows me all over again how wonderful he is, I tend to get emotional. You're just going to have to deal with that."

Her words seemed to hang in the air of the barn like dust motes floating in the last pale shafts of Christmas Eve sunlight. He stared at her for a second, then lurched toward the ladder. Before he reached it, his boot heel caught on something. He staggered for just a moment and tried to regain his balance but he didn't have anything to hold on to.

He fell in what felt like slow motion, landing with a hard thud that sounded almost as loud as her instinctive scream.

He couldn't breathe—and not because her words had stunned him. No. He literally couldn't breathe.

For a good five seconds, his lungs were frozen, the wind knocked hard out of him. He was aware on some level of her running toward him to kneel next to him, of her panicked, tearstained features and her hands on his face and her cries of "breathe, breathe, *breathe*."

He wasn't sure if the advice was for him or herself but then, just as abruptly, the spasm in his diaphragm eased and he could inhale again, a small breath and then increasingly deeper until he dared talk again.

"I'm…okay."

She was reaching for her phone when he spoke. At his voice, she gasped, dropping it to the concrete floor of the barn and throwing herself across him with an impact that made him grunt.

She immediately eased away. "Where does it hurt? I need to call an ambulance. It will probably take them a while to get here so it might be faster for me to just drive you."

The panic in her voice seeped through his discomfort and he reached out a hand to cover hers.

"I don't…need an ambulance. The breath…was knocked out of me…but I'm okay."

The alfalfa he had been forking down for the animals had cushioned most of the impact and he knew there was no serious damage, even though everything still ached. He might have a broken rib in there, but he wasn't about to tell her that.

"Are you sure? That was a hard fall."

"I'm sure."

Her hand fluttered in his and he suddenly remembered what she had said and his complete shock that had made him lose his footing.

He sat up and wiped at her tears.

"Faith. What were you saying just before I fell?"

She looked down, her cheeks turning pink. "I… Nothing."

It was the exact antithesis of *nothing*. "You said you loved me," he murmured.

She rubbed her cheek on her shoulder as if trying to hide evidence of the tears trickling down. "That was a pretty hard fall," she said again. "Are you sure you didn't bump your head, too?"

"Positive. I know what I heard. Why do you think I fell? You shocked me so much I forgot I was ten feet up in the air. Say it again."

Her hand fluttered in his again but he held it tight. He wasn't going to let her wriggle away this time. After a moment, she stopped and everything about her seemed to sigh.

"I love you," she whispered. "I've known it for a while now. I just... I've been so afraid."

"I know. I'm sorry."

He hadn't wanted to make her suffer more than she already had. But maybe they both had to pass through this tough time to know they could make it through to the other side.

He pulled her toward him and his breath seemed to catch all over again—and not at all from the pain—when she wrapped her arms around his waist and rested her cheek against his chest.

Joy began to stir inside him, tentative at first and then stronger.

She belonged exactly here. Surely she had to know that by now.

"After Travis died, I never wanted to fall in love again. Ever," she said, her voice low. "I guess it's a good thing I didn't."

He frowned in confusion, nearly groaning at the possibility of more mixed signals from her.

And then she kissed him. Just like that. She lifted her head, found his mouth and kissed him with a fierce emotion that sent joy rushing through him like the Cold Creek swollen with runoff.

"I didn't need to fall in love," she said, her beautiful eyes bright with more tears and a tenderness that made *him* want to weep. "I was already there, in love with my best friend. That love surrounded me every moment of every day. I just had to find the strength to open my heart to it."

"And have you?"

She kissed him again in answer and he decided he wanted to spend every Christmas Eve right here with her in her barn, surrounded by animals and hay and possibilities.

He had no idea how all his Christmas wishes had come true but he wasn't about to question it.

"I love you, Chase Brannon," she murmured against his mouth.

He didn't want to ask but he had to know. "What changed?"

"Why am I not afraid to admit I love you?" She smiled a little. "Who said I'm not? But I have been thinking about something my dad told us over and over when we were held prisoner in Colombia. *Remember, girls*, he would say in that firm voice. *Faith is always stronger than fear*. He was talking about faith in the abstract, not me in particular, but I have decided to listen to his words and apply them to me. I can't let my fear control me. I *am* stronger than this—and during the times when I'm not, I've got your strength to lean on."

He kissed her, humbled and overwhelmed and incredibly grateful for this amazing woman in his arms, who had been through incredible pain but came through with grace, dignity and a beautiful courage.

He wiped a tear away with his thumb, grateful beyond words that such a woman was willing to face her completely justifiable fears for *him*.

"I thought I was going to have a heart attack just now when you fell. For an instant, it was like Travis all over again—but it also confirmed something I had already been thinking."

"Oh?"

She pressed her cheek against his hand. "I've been worried that I'm not strong enough to open my heart to you. The real question is whether I'm strong enough to live without you. When I saw you fall, in those horrible few seconds when you weren't breathing, I realized the answer to that is an unequivocal, emphatic no. I can't bear the idea of not being with you."

He couldn't promise nothing would ever happen to him—but he could promise he would love her fiercely every single day of his life.

"I love you, Chase. I love you, my kids love you, my entire family loves you. I need you. You are my oldest and dearest friend—and my oldest and dearest love."

He framed her face in his hands and kissed her with all the pent-up need from all these years of standing on the sidelines, waiting for their moment to be right. He almost couldn't believe this was real. Maybe he was simply hallucinating after having the wind knocked out of him. But his senses seemed even more acute than usual, alive and invigorated, and the joy expanding in his chest was too bright and wild and beautiful to be imaginary.

People said Christmas was a time for miracles.

He would never doubt that again.

Epilogue

Christmas Eve, one year later

"Okay, help me out, Mary. Where do you keep the salad tongs since you and Pat have renovated the kitchen?"

With whitewashed cabinets and new stainless steel appliances, the new Star N kitchen was beautiful, Faith had to admit—almost as pretty as the renovated kitchen at the Brannon Ridge that had been her wedding present from Chase. But after two months, she still couldn't seem to figure out how to find things here now.

Mary headed to a large drawer on the island. "It made more sense to keep all the utensils in the biggest drawer here where they can all fit instead of scattered throughout the kitchen. I don't know why it took me fifty years to figure that out. Is this what you're looking for?"

"Yes! Thank you."

She added the dressing to the rest of the ingredients in her favorite walnut cranberry salad and tossed it with the tongs. "There. That should do it. Everything looks great, Mary."

"Thanks." Her aunt beamed and Faith thought, not for the first time, that Mary seemed years younger since her marriage to Pat.

"Thank you for hosting the party here at the Star N."

"Christmas is about home and this old house is home to you girls," Mary said simply. "It seemed right, even though all of you have bigger places now. Your kitchen up at Brannon Ridge is twice the size as this one."

As they were discussing how they would merge their lives after they were married, she and Chase had looked at both houses and decided to run both ranches from Brannon Ridge. The house was bigger for all three of their kids and assorted horses, dogs and barn cats.

It had been a good decision, confirmed just a few months after Faith and Chase's wedding, when Mary announced she and her beau were getting married and wanted to renovate the Star N—a process now in the final phases.

"Anything else I can carry out to the dining room?" she asked.

"I made a fruit salad, too. It's in the refrigerator," Mary said.

Faith grabbed it and, with one bowl under each arm,

headed for the two long tables that had been set up in the great room to hold the growing family.

She was arranging the bowls when Hope wandered over. "Hey, do you have any idea where I can find tape? I've still got one present to wrap."

"Let me get this straight. You run the most famous Christmas attraction in the Intermountain West *and* you've illustrated a holiday book that was turned into a movie currently ranked number one at the box office for the fourth consecutive week. Yet here it is five p.m. on Christmas Eve and you're still not finished wrapping your presents?"

"Oh, give me a break. I've had a little bit on my plate. You would not *believe* how much of my day this little creature takes up."

Faith smiled. "I think I would. I've had two of my own, remember? Here. Give."

Her sister held up the wriggling adorableness that was her six-month-old son, Samuel, born healthy and full-term, with no complications whatsoever from that early scare more than a year ago.

"You can have him if you tell me where I can find tape."

"The desk drawer in the office." She grinned and admitted the truth. "That's where I put it a half hour ago, anyway, when I finished wrapping my last present."

Hope snorted but fulfilled her part of the deal by handing over the boy.

After she left, Faith nuzzled his neck. Oh, he smelled delicious. Her heart seemed to burst with happiness. "Hey, Sammy. How's my favorite guy?"

"Wow. I guess that puts us in our place, right, Barrett?"

She looked up to find Chase and her son in the doorway, stomping snow off their boots after coming in from shoveling the driveway.

He was smiling but she didn't miss the light in his gaze as he watched her cuddle Hope's cute little boy.

How was it possible that, even after a year, she loved Chase more every single time she saw him?

"My favorite *little* guy," she amended. "You two are my favorite bigger guys. How's the snow out there?"

"Still coming down," Chase said. "Mary said she thinks we'll get another six or seven inches out of the storm. Perfect for cuddling in by the fire and hanging out with the family on Christmas morning."

"I hope Celeste and Flynn make it."

"They pulled in right as we were finishing the driveway," he assured her.

"That's good," Mary said from the kitchen. "Everything's ready and I'm *starving*."

"Sorry we're late," Celeste said as she, Flynn and Olivia came in with their arms loaded down with gifts.

"We still had to wrap a couple of presents," Olivia explained.

Hope paused in the act of setting her hastily wrapped final present under the big tree in the window. "Seriously, CeCe? On Christmas Eve? Maybe next year you should plan ahead a little better," she said virtuously.

Faith had to laugh, which ended up startling Sammy. "Sorry, kiddo."

"Here, I'll take him back."

She didn't want to surrender the soft little bundle

but Mary came in just then. "Great. Everybody's here. Find your places."

After handing Sammy back to his mother, she found a place beside Chase. Addie and Louisa sat at her other side while Barrett sat on Chase's other side.

When they were all settled, Celeste looked around at their family.

"I have an announcement to make. *We* do, actually."

Olivia, Faith noticed, was just about jumping out of her chair in excitement.

"Is this about *Sparkle and the Magic Snowball* being number one again at the box office?" Addie asked.

"Everybody knows that already," Olivia said.

"Is it about the new Sparkle book that's coming out next summer or the movie sequel they're already making?" Louisa asked.

"No," Flynn said. "Though that's all very exciting."

He reached for Celeste's hand and Faith held her breath, sensing what was coming next before her sister even said it.

"We're having a baby."

The table erupted into squeals of excitement and hearty congratulations.

"Another baby. What wonderful news—and the perfect time to find out, on Christmas Eve," Mary exclaimed, her features soft with delight. "When are you due?"

"June. Right around the book launch, which isn't the greatest of timing, I know."

"We'll figure it out," Hope said. "This is so great!

Maybe you'll have a boy, too, and he and Sammy can be best friends!"

Faith felt a big, strong hand reach out and grip hers. She glanced at her husband and saw a secret little smile there, the same one exploding in her heart. The two new cousins would soon become three, but she and Chase were the only ones at the table who knew that, for now.

They wouldn't share their news yet. Faith was only eight weeks along and they had decided to wait until after the New Year to tell anyone. Even Barrett, Lou and Addie didn't know yet.

It was tough to keep the news under wraps but there would be time enough to let the family know even more joy would soon be on the way.

For now, she would celebrate her sister's happiness.

Her heart seemed filled to overflowing and tears welled up as she looked around the table at her family, these people she loved so much.

Pregnancy hormones were making her *crazy*. She cried at everything these days. This, the chance to spend Christmas Eve with all the people she loved most in the world, was worth a few tears, she decided.

Chase's strong, callused fingers threaded through hers and more tears leaked out. He nudged her shoulder with his, and then her oldest and dearest friend— and the man she loved with all her heart—handed her his napkin so she could dry her tears.

"What's wrong? Why are you crying, Mom?" Louisa asked, concern in her eyes that could look so fierce and determined when she and the horse she adored galloped through a barrel course.

Faith sniffled a little more. "I'm happy. That's all."

"Cut it out or you'll set me off," Celeste said.

"And me," Hope said. "Since I had Sammy, I cry if the wind blows at me from the wrong direction."

Faith gave her sisters a watery smile. Their father's words certainly held true for his daughters. Each of them had proved that faith *was* stronger than fear, that they could move past the tough experiences in their past and let love help them heal.

She tightened her fingers around Chase's, the joy in her heart blazing as brightly as the lights on Aunt Mary's big Christmas tree that sent out warmth and color and hope across the snowy night.

* * * * *

CHRISTMASTIME COURTSHIP

MARIE FERRARELLA

To
Melany,
The Best Daughter-in-Law
Anyone Could Ask For.
Welcome To The Family.

Prologue

"Is it true?"

Theresa Manetti looked up from the menu she was putting the final touches on to see who had just walked into her inner office. Most clients who wanted to avail themselves of her catering services either called or were brought in by one of her staff and announced.

As it turned out, this time Theresa found herself looking up at Jeannine Steele, an old friend she hadn't seen in at least six months. Not since she'd catered Jeannine's husband's funeral reception.

"Well, that's a new kind of greeting," Theresa commented, amused. "Most people usually say hello. Is *what* true?" she asked, nodding toward the chair on the other side of her desk, indicating that her friend should sit down.

Looking uncomfortable and nervous, Jeannine

lowered herself onto the chair, perching on its edge. "There's a rumor going around that in addition to your catering business, you're running some sort of a dating service on the side."

Theresa had known Jeannine since her own two children had been in elementary school with Jeannine's daughter, and in all that time, she couldn't recall the stately woman appearing anything but completely in control.

Always.

But not this time.

"Well, that's not exactly an accurate description," Theresa replied. "It's not really a 'dating service,' so much as a matchmaking service."

Confusion furrowed Jeannie's otherwise smooth, alabaster brow. "There's a difference?"

From her vantage point, Theresa could see the other woman twisting her long, slender fingers together. Theresa was experienced enough to know where this was heading, and did what she could to set her friend at ease.

"A big difference," she answered, pushing back her chair and rising to her feet. "Would you like something to drink, Jeannine?" she asked kindly. "I have everything from tea to soft drinks to something a little more 'bracing' if you'd rather have that."

Jeannine drew in a deep breath before answering. "I'll take tea," she replied. "Strong tea."

Theresa smiled as she went to the counter against the back wall, where she had a pot of hot water steaming. She had a preference for tea herself.

"So, it's been a while, Jeannine," she said in her customary easygoing manner. "How are you?"

"Concerned, frankly," the other woman admitted.

Recrossing the room, Theresa held out the cup of tea. "You're worried about Miranda, aren't you?"

Her friend nearly dropped the cup Theresa had handed her. Some hot liquid sloshed over the side. "How did you know?" she asked, surprised.

"To begin with, you asked me about my so-called 'sideline,'" Theresa answered, employing a whimsical term for the labor that had become near and dear not just to her heart, but to Maizie's and Celia's hearts, as well.

Theresa and the two women she had been best friends with since the third grade had weathered all of life's highs and lows together. The highs included marriage, children and the successful businesses all three had started in the second half of their lives and were currently running.

The lows included all three becoming widows. But she, Maizie and Celia had learned to push on past the pain. After all, they each had children to provide for. They were determined to lead productive, fulfilling lives. And above all else, they were always, always there for one another.

Their matchmaking had begun slowly, by finding matches for their own children. That was to be the end of it, but matching up the right two people brought such satisfaction with it, they'd decided to try their hand at it again.

And again.

With each successful match, their secondary vocation just seemed to take wings. They loved the businesses they had begun and nurtured individually, but there was something exceedingly fulfilling about bringing together two people who otherwise might never have found one another.

Two people who clearly belonged together.

It looked as if the adventure was about to begin again, Theresa thought.

"Tell me about Miranda," she coaxed, taking her seat once more. "How is she? Is she still as wonderfully generous and big-hearted as ever?"

Jeannine thought of her only daughter—her only living child—whose career path had been chosen at the age of ten. "Yes—and that's the problem. She's so busy giving of herself, working at the children's hospital, the women's shelter *and* the city's animal shelter, that she doesn't have any time to focus on herself. Don't get me wrong, Theresa. I'm prouder of Miranda than I can possibly say, but, well, I'm really afraid that if she keeps going like this, she's eventually going to wind up alone." Jeannine sighed. "I know that sounds like I'm being small-minded and meddling, but—"

Theresa cut her short. "Trust me, I know the feeling," she assured her. "We're mothers, Jeannine. It comes with the territory." With her business going full steam ahead the way it was these days, she could use a little diversion. "Tell me, do you have any idea what Miranda's dating life is like?"

"I have a very clear idea," Jeannine replied. "It's nonexistent these days."

"Really?"

"Really," she confirmed sadly. "The problem is that no man can compete with her full-time job, as well as all her volunteer work. Besides, what man wants to come in fourth?"

"Definitely not the kind of man we would want for your daughter," Theresa said with conviction.

Jeannine looked confused. "What are you saying?"

Theresa smiled as she began making plans. "I'm saying we need to change Miranda's focus a little."

"So you do think there's hope?" A glimmer of optimism entered the other woman's hazel eyes.

Theresa leaned over and patted her friend's hand. "Jeannine," she said confidently, "there is *always* hope."

Chapter One

"Ladies, we have work to do," Theresa announced the moment she entered Maizie Sommer's house.

She strode into Maizie's family room with the vigor of a woman half her age. Matchmaking projects always got her adrenaline going, creating a level of enthusiasm within her even greater than her usual line of work did—and it went without saying that she dearly loved her catering business.

"We certainly do," Cecilia Parnell agreed.

Already seated at the card table—their usual gathering place whenever they were discussing their newest undertaking in the matchmaking arena—Celia turned to look at her. "This one is going to be a real challenge for us."

"Oh, I don't know," Theresa protested, gracefully slipping into the chair that was set up between Celia and Maizie. "I don't think it'll be *that* hard finding someone suitable."

Taken aback, Celia looked quizzically at her old friend, who hadn't called ahead with any details about the person she felt should be their latest project. "Wait, how would you know?"

"How would I know?" Theresa repeated incredulously. "Because I've known Miranda Steele ever since she was a little girl. She has this incredibly huge heart and she's always trying to help everyone. Fix everyone," Theresa emphasized, which was why she had come to think of the young woman as "the fixer" in recent years.

"Miranda?" Celia echoed, decidedly more confused than she'd initially been. "Maizie and I were talking about Colin when you walked in."

It was Theresa's turn to be confused. "Who's Colin?" she asked, looking from Maizie to Celia.

"Police Officer Colin Kirby," Celia clarified, adding, "our latest matchmaking project. His aunt Lily is a friend of mine and she came to talk to me on the outside chance that maybe I—actually *we*—could find someone for him."

Without pausing, Celia launched into a brief version of the police officer's backstory. "Lily took him in when her sister, Vanessa, a single mother, died in a car accident. Colin was fourteen at the time. She said that he's a decent, hardworking young man who just shut down when he lost his mother. He enlisted in the Marines straight out of high school. When his tour of duty overseas ended, he was honorably discharged and immediately joined the police force in Los Angeles."

Maizie appeared a little dubious. "Los Angeles is a little out of our usual territory," she commented. "But I guess—"

"Oh no." Celia quickly cut in. "He's not in Los Angeles anymore, he's in Bedford now. Lily talked him into moving back down here. Her health isn't what it used to be and he's her only living relative, so he made the move for her, which, in my book, shows you what sort of a person he is.

"The problem is," Celia continued, "Lily says he's really closed off, especially after what he saw during his tour overseas and as a police officer in one of the roughest areas in Los Angeles. To put it in Lily's own words," she concluded, "Colin needs someone to 'fix him.'"

Smiling, Maizie shifted her gaze from Celia to Theresa. It was obvious that, in her estimation, they needed to look no further in either case. "You just said you have someone who likes to 'fix' people."

But Celia was more skeptical than her friend. She needed more to work with. "Fix how?"

Theresa gave them Miranda's background in a nutshell. "According to her mother, Miranda's a pediatric nurse at Bedford Children's Hospital who volunteers at a women's shelter in her free time. She also volunteers at the city's animal shelter and occasionally takes in strays until they can be placed in a permanent home."

Maizie's smile widened. "Ladies, maybe I'm getting ahead of myself, but this sounds to me like a match made in heaven. I'm assuming you both have a few more pertinent details that we can work with—like what these two look like and how old they are, for openers," said the woman whose decision to find her daughter a suitable match had initially gotten what turned out to be their "side business" rolling eight years ago.

"Miranda's thirty," Theresa told them, producing a photograph on her smartphone that Jeannie had sent her, and holding it up for the others to see.

"Colin's thirty-three," Celia said. "And I'll ask Lily to send me a picture."

So saying, she texted a message to the woman. In less than a minute, her cell phone buzzed, announcing that her request had been received and answered.

"Here we go," Celia declared. "Oh my," she murmured as she looked at the image that had materialized on her smartphone. Colin's aunt had sent her a photo of her nephew in his police uniform.

Maizie took Celia's hand and turned the phone around so she could look at it.

"Definitely 'oh my,'" she agreed wholeheartedly. Pushing the deck of cards aside, she gave up all pretense that they were going to engage in a game of poker this evening, even a single hand. Her gaze took in her two lifelong friends. "Ladies, let's get down to work. These two selfless servants of society need us. And from what I've heard, they also need each other," the successful Realtor added knowingly. "We'll require more information to bring about the perfect subtle 'meet' to get this particular ball rolling."

Filled with anticipation, the three old friends got busy.

Every year, the holiday season seemed to begin earlier and earlier, Miranda Steele thought.

Not that she was complaining. Christmas had always been her very favorite time of year. While others grumbled that the stores were putting up Christmas decorations way too soon, motivated by a desire to increase their already obscene profits, Miranda saw it as a way to stretch the spirit of Christmas a little further, thereby making the true meaning of the season last a little longer.

But sometimes, like now, the pace became a little too hectic even for her. She had just put in a ten-hour day at the hospital, coming in way before her shift actually began in order to help decorate the oncology ward, where she worked. She felt particularly driven because she knew that for some of the children there it would be their last Christmas.

As harsh and sad as that thought was to deal with, she chose to focus on the bright side: bringing the best possible Christmas she could to the children and their families.

At times, she felt like a lone cheerleader, tirelessly attempting to drum up enthusiasm and support from the other nurses, doctors and orderlies on the floor until she had everyone finally pitching in, even if they weren't all cheerful about it.

She didn't care if the rest of the staff was cheerful or not, as long as they helped out. And as was her habit, she worked harder than anyone to make sure that things were ultimately "just right."

If she were a normal person, about now she would be on her way home, having earned some serious bubble bath time.

But soaking in a hot tub was not on this afternoon's

agenda. She didn't have time for a bubble bath, as much as she longed for one. She had to get Lily's birthday party ready.

Lily Hayden was eight today. The little girl was one of the many children currently living with their moms at the Bedford Women's Home, a shelter where Miranda volunteered four days a week after work.

The other two or three days she spent at the city's no-kill animal shelter, where she worked with dogs and cats—and the occasional rabbit—that were rescued from a possible bleak demise on the street. Miranda had an affinity for all things homeless, be they four-footed or two-footed. In her opinion there never seemed to be enough hours in the day for her to help all these deserving creatures.

She had been working in all three areas for years now and felt she had barely been able to scratch the surface.

Agitated, Miranda looked at the clock on her dashboard. The minutes were flying by.

She was running the risk of being late.

"And if you don't get there with this cake, Lily is going to think you've forgotten all about her, just like her mom did," Miranda muttered to herself.

Lily's mother had left the little girl at the shelter when she'd gone to look for work. That was two days ago. No one had heard from the woman since. Miranda was beginning to worry that Gina Hayden, overwhelmed with her circumstances, had bailed out, using the excuse that the little girl was better off at the shelter, without her.

Stepping on the gas, Miranda made a sharp right

turn at the next corner, reaching out to hold the cake box on the passenger seat in place.

Focused on getting to the homeless shelter on time, Miranda wasn't aware of the dancing red and blue lights behind her until she heard the siren, high-pitched, demanding and shrill, slicing through the air. The sound drew her attention to the lights, simultaneously making her stomach drop with a jarring thud.

Oh damn, why today of all days? Miranda silently demanded as, resigned to her fate, she pulled her car over to the right. Even as she did so, something inside her wanted to push her foot down on the accelerator and just take off.

But considering that her newfound nemesis was riding a motorcycle and her car was a fifteen-year-old asthmatic vehicle way past its glory days, a clean getaway was simply not in the cards.

So she pulled over and waited for her inevitable ticket, fervently hoping the whole process was not going to take too long. She was already behind schedule. Miranda didn't want to disappoint Lily, who had already been disappointed far too often in her short life.

This wasn't his usual route. For some unknown reason, the desk sergeant had decided that today, he and Kaminski were going to trade routes.

Sergeant Bailey had made the switch, saying something about "mixing things up and keeping them fresh"—whatever that was supposed to mean, Colin thought, grumbling under his breath.

As far as he was concerned, one route was as good as

another. At least here in Bedford the only thing people shot at him were dirty looks, instead of bullets from the muzzles of illegally gotten handguns. He had to admit that patrolling the streets of Bedford was a far cry from patrolling the barrio in Los Angeles, or driving on the roads in Afghanistan. In those situations, a man had to develop eyes in the back of his head to stay alive.

Here in Bedford, those same eyes were in danger of shutting, but from boredom, not a fatal shot.

He supposed, after everything he had been through in the last ten years, a little boredom was welcome—at least for a while.

But he didn't exactly like the idea of hiding on the far side of the underpass, waiting to issue a ticket to some unsuspecting Bedford resident.

Yet those were the rules of the game here, and for now, he wasn't about to rock the boat.

First and foremost, he was here because of Aunt Lily. Because he owed her big-time. She had taken him in when no one else would, and to his discredit, he had repaid her by shutting her out and being surly. It wasn't her fault he had behaved that way; the blame was his.

In his defense—if he could call it that—he hadn't wanted to risk forming another attachment, only to have to endure the pain that came if and when he lost her. Lost her the way he'd lost everyone else in his life that ever mattered. His mother. Some of the men in his platoon. And Owens, his last partner in LA.

Colin's method of preventing that sort of pain was to cut himself off from everyone. That way, the pain had no chance of ever taking root, no chance of slicing him off at the knees.

At least that was what he told himself.

Still, he reasoned, playing his own devil's advocate, if there wasn't some part of him that cared, that was still capable of forming some sort of an attachment, however minor, would he have uprooted himself the way he had in order to be here because Aunt Lily had asked him to?

He didn't know.

Or maybe he did, and just didn't want to admit it to himself.

Either way, it wasn't something that was going to be resolved today. Today he needed to focus on the small stuff.

Right now he had a speeder to stop, he told himself, coming to life and increasing his own speed.

Because the woman in the old sedan was obviously not looking into her rearview mirror, Colin turned on his siren.

There, that got her attention. At least she wasn't one of those foolhardy birdbrains who thought they could outrace his motorcycle, Colin observed, as the car began to decrease its speed.

Watching the vehicle slow down and then come to a stop, Colin braced himself for what he knew was about to come. Either the driver was going to turn on the waterworks, attempting to cry her way out of a ticket by appealing to what she hoped was his chivalrous nature, or she was going to be belligerent, demanding to know if he had nothing better to do than to harass otherwise law-abiding citizens by issuing speeding tickets for offenses that were hardly noteworthy, instead of pursuing real criminals.

After parking his motorcycle behind her vehicle, he got off, then took his time walking up to the offending driver. Because the street was a busy one, with three lanes going in each direction, Colin made his way to the passenger side, to avoid getting hit by any passing motorist.

As he approached, he motioned for the driver to roll down her window.

She looked nervous. Well, the woman should have thought about this before she'd started speeding.

"Do you know why I pulled you over?" he asked gruffly.

Miranda took a breath before answering. "Because I was speeding."

A little surprised at the simplicity of her reply, Colin waited for more.

It didn't come.

The woman wasn't trying to talk her way out of the ticket she obviously knew was coming. He found that rather unusual. In his experience, people he pulled over in Bedford weren't normally this calm, or this seemingly polite.

Colin remained on his guard, anticipating a sudden turn on the driver's part.

"Right," he said, picking up on her answer. "You were speeding. Any particular reason why?"

He was aware that he was giving her the perfect opportunity to attempt to play on his sympathies, with some sort of a sob story. Such as she'd just gotten a call from the hospital saying her mother or father or some other important person in her life had just had a heart attack, and she was rushing to their side before they died.

He'd heard it all before. The excuses got pretty creative sometimes.

He had to admit that, for some reason, he was mildly curious to hear what this driver had to offer as *her* excuse.

"There's this little girl at the homeless shelter. It's her birthday today and I'm bringing the cake. The party starts in ten minutes and I got off my shift at the hospital later than I anticipated. I work at Children's Hospital and we had an emergency," she explained, inserting a sidebar.

"Where at Children's Hospital?" Colin asked, wondering just how far the woman was going to take this tale she was spinning.

"The oncology ward," she answered.

He should have seen that one coming. "Really?" he challenged.

Was he asking her for proof? That was simple enough, she thought. Because she'd been in such a rush, she was still wearing her uniform, and she had her hospital badge around her neck.

Holding up her ID, she showed it to him. "Yes, really, Officer," she answered politely. "Now if you'll please write out the ticket and give it to me so I can be on my way, I can still make the party on time. I don't want Lily to think I forgot about her, today of all days."

About to begin doing so, Colin looked up sharply. "Lily?" he questioned.

"That's her name," Miranda answered. "Lily."

Colin stared at the woman, a stoic expression on his face as he tried to make up his mind if she was actually serious, or trying to con him.

She couldn't possibly know about his aunt, he decided.

"My aunt's name is Lily," he told her, watching her face for some telltale sign that she was making all this up.

"It's a nice name," Miranda responded, waiting for him to begin writing.

Colin paused for a long moment, weighing the situation.

And then he did something he didn't ordinarily do. Actually, it was something he'd *never* done before. He closed his ticket book.

"All right, I'm letting you off with a warning," he told her. Then added an ominous "Watch yourself," before he turned on his heel and walked back to his motorcycle.

Chapter Two

Miranda's first impulse was to take off before the officer decided to change his mind about writing her that ticket. But as she thought about the fact that she had just dodged a bullet, an idea came to her. Rather than start her car and drive away under the police officer's watchful eye, Miranda opened her door and got out of her beloved vehicle.

"Officer?" she called, raising her voice.

Colin had already gotten on his motorcycle. Surprised, he looked in her direction. After a beat, he sighed and then slowly dismounted.

Now what? he silently demanded.

"Something on your mind, miss?" he asked, his voice low and far from friendly.

The officer sounded as if she was annoying him. But Miranda hadn't gotten where she was by giving in to the nervous quiver that occasionally popped up in her stomach—as it did now.

Raising her head so that her eyes met his—or where she assumed his eyes were, because he'd lowered the visor on his helmet, she stated, "I wanted to say thank you."

Colin grunted in response, because in his opinion, this wasn't the sort of situation where "you're welcome" suited the occasion. As far as he was concerned, she wasn't welcome. He'd just given in to an impulse that had come out of nowhere, and if he thought about it now, he was rather bewildered by his own actions.

"Do you have a card?" she asked him.

"A card?" Colin repeated, clearly perplexed by her question.

Miranda didn't think she was asking for anything out of the ordinary. "Yes, like a business card. The police department issues those to you, right?"

Instead of answering her question, or giving her one of the cards he carried in his pocket, Colin asked, "Why do you want it? You don't have anything to report me for," he pointed out gruffly.

It took Miranda a second to absorb what he was saying. Talk about being defensive. But then, maybe he had a reason. Some people were belligerent when dealing with the police.

"I don't want to report you," she assured him with feeling. "I just want to be able to call you."

So that was it, Colin thought. The woman was a groupie. He knew that there were people—mostly women—who were attracted to the uniform, some to the point of obsession. He had no patience when it came to groupies.

Colin got back on his motorcycle, ready to take off. "That's not a good idea," he told her in a voice that left no room for argument.

Or at least he thought it didn't.

"But the kids at the hospital would get such a big kick out of meeting a real live motorcycle cop," she said, hoping to change his mind.

She caught him completely off guard. He definitely hadn't been expecting that.

Now that he had transferred to Bedford, he didn't find himself interacting with any children. The ones back in the LA neighborhood he used to patrol saw police officers as the enemy, and either scattered whenever they saw him coming, or would throw things at him and *then* run.

"Look, I don't think—" Colin got no further than that.

Determined to convince him, Miranda attempted to submerge the police officer in a tidal wave of rhetoric. "A lot of the kids in that ward haven't been out of the hospital in months. I think meeting you would go a long way in cheering them up."

There had to be some sort of an ulterior motive at work here, Colin thought, and he wasn't about to fall for whatever trap she was trying to set for him.

"I really doubt that," he told her as he revved his motorcycle.

"I don't," Miranda countered cheerfully, refusing to be put off. "Why don't you come by the hospital and

we'll see which one of us is right?" Mindful of procedure, she told him, "I'd have to clear it with my super-
visor, but I don't see why she would say no."

"She might not, but I will." Then, just in case the
woman still had any doubt about what he was telling
her, Colin said, "No."

"But, Officer…" Rebounding quickly, Miranda tried
again. "…it's Christmas."

Colin's eyes narrowed. "It's November," he corrected.

"*Almost* Christmas," she amended.

The woman just wouldn't give up, he thought, his
irritation growing to astounding levels.

"Look, why don't you get back into your car and
drive off before I decide to change my mind about issuing you that ticket?" Colin suggested tersely. "You
said something about a birthday party for a little girl
named Lily," he reminded her.

"Oh my goodness! Lily!" Miranda cried, genuinely
upset. She'd gotten so caught up with her idea about
having the police officer visit the children in the oncology ward that she'd forgotten the mission she was on
right now. "The poor thing's going to really be upset if
I don't turn up on time."

Whirling around, Miranda hurried back to her car
and got in. She was starting the vehicle before she even
closed the door.

Raising his voice, Colin called after her, "Remember the speed limit!"

There was next to no traffic at the moment.

Reining herself in, knowing that the officer would be

watching her pull away from the curb, Miranda gripped the steering wheel and drove off at a respectable speed, all the while wishing herself already at her destination.

Despite her hurry to get to the women's shelter, she made a mental note to track down the officer and get his name and number from his precinct the first chance she got. This wasn't over yet, she promised herself.

Miranda managed to catch all the lights and breeze through them, arriving at the women's shelter fifteen minutes later.

Rather than wasting time driving around and looking for a parking spot near the gray, two-story building's front door, she pulled into the first space she came to.

Grabbing the cake, she hurried into the building— and nearly collided with the blonde little girl who was anxiously waiting for her at the door.

"You came!" Lily cried happily, her furrowed brow smoothing out the second she saw Miranda.

"Of course I came," she said, pausing to kiss the top of Lily's head as she balanced the large cake box in her arms. "I told you I would. It's your birthday and I wouldn't miss that for the world."

Lily was all but dancing on her toes, eagerly looking at the rectangular box in Miranda's arms. "Is that a cake?"

"Aw, you guessed," Miranda said, pretending to be disappointed that her secret had been uncovered. "What gave it away?"

"The box," Lily answered solemnly, as if she'd been asked a legitimate question. And then she giggled as she added, "And I can smell cake."

"Well, since you guessed what it is, I guess you get to keep it," Miranda told her.

Lily was all but bursting with excitement. "Can I carry it to the dining room?" she asked.

That wouldn't be a good idea, Miranda thought. The box was large and would prove to be rather unwieldy for a little girl to carry.

"Well, it's kind of heavy," she told her. "So why don't I carry it there for you and you can open the box once I put it on the table?"

"Okay," Lily responded, obviously ready to agree to anything her idol suggested.

The little girl literally skipped to the dining area at Miranda's side. And she never took her eyes off the box, as if afraid it would suddenly disappear if she did.

"What kind of cake is it?" she asked.

"A birthday cake," Miranda replied solemnly.

Lily giggled and waved her hand at her friend. "I know that, silly," she told her. "I mean what kind of birthday cake?"

"A good one," Miranda said, still pretending that she didn't understand what Lily was asking her.

"Besides that," Lily pressed, giggling again.

"It's a lemon cake with vanilla frosting," Miranda told the bubbly little girl beside her as they reached the dining area.

Lily's eyes grew huge with obvious delight. "Lemon cake's my very favorite in the whole world."

"Well, how about that." Miranda pretended to marvel. "I didn't know that."

"Yes, you did," Lily said, a surprisingly knowing look on her small, thin face.

And then Miranda smiled affectionately at the girl. "I guess I did at that. Guess what else I've got," she said.

"Candles?" Lily asked in a hopeful whisper.

Miranda nodded. "Eight big ones. And one extra one for luck."

Instead of saying anything in response to the information, Lily threaded her small arm through one of her friend's and hugged it hard, her excitement all but palpable.

Miranda could feel her heart practically squeezing within her chest. This moment she was sharing with Lily was both humbling and sad. Other children her age would have asked for toys or expensive video games, and not shown half the excitement when they received them that Lily displayed over the fact that she was getting a birthday cake—with candles.

Drawn by the sound of Lily's squeals, Amelia Sellers, the tall, angular-looking woman who ran the shelter, made her way over to them. Her smile was warm and genuine—and perhaps slightly relieved, as well.

Amelia'd probably thought she wasn't going to make it. Most likely because she had a habit of being early, not running late like this.

"Lily's been looking forward to this all day," Amelia told her the moment she reached them.

"So have I," Miranda assured both the director and the little girl, who was looking up at her with nothing short of adoration in her eyes.

"I put out the plates," Amelia announced, gesturing at one of the dining tables. "So let's get started."

Miranda smiled down at Lily, who was obviously waiting for her to make the first move. She had to be the most well-mannered eager little girl she'd ever met.

"Let's," Miranda agreed.

Carefully taking the half sheet cake out of the box, Miranda moved the rectangular container aside and out of the way. She then put the candles on the cake, making sure she spaced them close enough together that Lily would be able to blow them all out at once when she made her wish.

The moment the birthday cake was placed on the table, children began coming over, clustering around the table, all hoping to get a piece.

Taking out the book of matches she had picked up when she'd purchased the candles, Miranda struck one and then carefully lit the eight plus one wicks.

Blowing out the match, she looked at all the eager faces around the table. "All right," she told the small gathering. "Everybody sing!"

And she led the pint-size group, along with the smattering of adults also gathered around the table, in a loud, if slightly off-key chorus of "Happy Birthday." All the while she kept one eye on Lily, who looked positively radiant.

When the children stopped singing, Miranda told the little girl, "Okay, Lily, make a wish and blow out the candles."

Nodding, Lily pressed her lips together, clearly giving her wish a great deal of thought. Then she looked up at Miranda and smiled.

Taking in a deep breath, Lily leaned over the cake and blew as hard as she could. The candles flickered and went out.

"You got them all," Miranda declared, applauding the little girl's accomplishment.

The children and adults around the table joined in, some loudly cheering, as well.

Miranda felt someone tugging on the bottom of her tunic. Glancing down, she found herself looking into the upturned face of an animated little boy named Paul.

"Now can we have some cake?" he asked.

"Absolutely," she replied. "Right after Lily gets the first piece."

Removing all nine candles, she set them on a napkin. Miranda proceeded to cut a piece of cake for Lily, making sure it was an extra-large one.

Out of the corner of her eye she saw Lily folding the napkin over the candles she'd just removed. The little girl covertly slipped the napkin into the pocket of her jeans, a souvenir of her special day.

"There you go," Miranda told her, sliding the plate to her.

"Thank you," Lily said.

To Miranda's surprise, rather than devour the cake as she expected, the little girl ate the slice slowly, as if savoring every morsel.

"This is the best cake I ever had," Lily declared when she finally finished it.

The other children had made short work of the cake

that was left, but Miranda had anticipated that. "You can have another piece," she told Lily. Not waiting for a response, she pushed her own plate in front of the little girl.

Lily looked tempted, but left the slice untouched.

"What's wrong?" Miranda asked.

"I can't eat that. That's your piece," she protested.

Miranda smiled at the girl. *One in a million*, she thought.

Out loud she stated, "And I saved it for you. I wanted you to have an extra piece and knew that the rest of the cake would probably be gobbled up fast. So don't argue with me, young lady. Take this piece. It's yours," she coaxed.

Lily still looked uncertain. "Really?"

"Really," Miranda assured her. "I'm the grown-up here. You have to listen."

Lily's face was all smiles as she happily dug into the second piece.

When she finished, Miranda cleared away the plates, stacking them on the side.

"That was the best cake ever!" Lily told her with enthusiasm, and then hugged her again.

"Glad to hear that," Miranda said, when the little girl loosened her hold. "By the way, I have something for you."

"For me?" Lily cried, clearly amazed. It was obvious that she felt the cake was her big prize. Anything else was above and beyond all expectation. "What is it?"

Miranda reached into the oversize purse she'd left

on the floor and pulled out the gift she had wrapped for Lily early this morning, before she'd left for the hospital.

Handing it over, she said, "Why don't you open it and see?"

Lily held the gift as if she couldn't decide whether to unwrap it or just gaze at it adoringly for a while. Her curiosity finally won out and she started peeling away the wrapping paper.

The moment she'd done so, her mouth dropped open. "You got me a puppy!" she cried.

"Well," Miranda amended, "I can't get you a *real* puppy because the shelter won't allow it, so for now, I want you to have this stuffed one. But someday, when you're in a home again, I'll come and bring you a real one," she promised.

Heaven knew she had access to enough homeless dogs at the animal shelter to pick just the right one for the little girl.

Lily threw her arms around her a third time and hugged her as hard as she could. "I wish you were my mom," she said breathlessly.

Touched though she was, Miranda knew she couldn't have the girl feeling like that. "Don't say that, honey. Your real mom's out there and she's probably trying to get back here to you right now."

But Lily shook her head. "I still wish you were my mom," she insisted, burying her face against Miranda as she clutched the stuffed dog. "Thank you for my cake and my candles and my puppy. Thank you for everything," she cried.

Miranda hugged the little girl, moved almost to tears

and wishing there was something she could do for her beyond giving her a gift and a cake.

And then it came to her. She knew what she had to do.

She needed to track down the police officer on the motorcycle. Not to bring to the hospital with her—that would come later—but to help her find out what had happened to Lily's mother. The man had resources at his disposal that she certainly didn't have.

All she needed to do, once she located him, Miranda thought, was to appeal to his sense of justice or humanity, or whatever it took to get him to agree to look for Lily's mother.

Smiling, she hugged Lily a little harder.

Chapter Three

Because she didn't want to risk possibly getting the motorcycle officer in any sort of trouble by going to the precinct and asking about him, Miranda spent the rest of that evening and part of the night reviewing her viable options.

By the next morning, Miranda decided that her best course of action was to literally track down the officer. That meant driving by the overpass where he'd been yesterday. She could only hope that he'd be there, waiting to ticket someone going over the speed limit.

But when she swung by the area that afternoon, after her shift was over, the police officer wasn't there.

Disappointed, Miranda had to concede that not finding him there stood to reason. If an officer frequented the same spot day after day, word would quickly spread and drivers would either avoid the area altogether or at the very least be extra cautious about observing the speed limit.

Still, as she drove slowly by the overpass, Miranda wondered how far away the police officer could be. Unless he had been relocated, there must be a certain radius he had to adhere to, so as not to cross into another cop's territory, right?

Giving herself a fifteen-minute time limit to find him, Miranda drove up one street and down another. She knew she was attempting to second-guess a man she knew absolutely nothing about, but at the moment she couldn't think of an alternative.

Fifteen minutes later Miranda sighed. The time was up and she still hadn't found the officer. She didn't want to be too late getting to the women's shelter. She knew that Lily's mother still hadn't shown up—she'd called Amelia to check—and the little girl would be devastated if she didn't come to see her as she'd promised.

She had to go, Miranda thought. Maybe she'd come across the traffic cop tomorrow.

Slowing down, Miranda did a three-point turn in order to head toward the street that would ultimately take her to the shelter.

As she approached the red light at an intersection, a fleeting glint from the left caught her attention. The setting sun was reflecting off some sort of metal.

Miranda turned her head in that direction, and found the sun was hitting the handlebars of a motorcycle.

A police motorcycle.

His motorcycle.

Although the officer was wearing a helmet, and virtually *all* police motorcycles in Bedford looked alike, something told her that this particular officer was the one who had pulled her over yesterday. Pulled her over and didn't give her a ticket. Miranda could feel it in her gut.

When the light turned green, instead of driving straight ahead, she deliberately eased her car to the left, into the next lane. Far enough to allow her to make a left-hand turn.

As she did so, she rolled down her window and honked her horn twice. Getting the officer's attention, she waved her hand at the man, indicating that she wanted him to make a U-turn and follow her. She then mentally crossed her fingers that she hadn't accidentally made a mistake, and that this *was* the same officer she'd interacted with yesterday.

Always alert when he was on the job, Colin tensed when he heard the driver honking. Seeing an arm come out of the driver's window, waving to get his attention, he bit off a curse. Was the woman taunting him? Or did she actually *want* to get a ticket?

And then, as he looked closer, he realized that it was the same car he'd pulled over yesterday. The one driven by that petite blonde with the really deep blue eyes.

The one who had that birthday cake on the passenger seat.

What was she doing here? Was she deliberately trying to press her luck? Because if she was, she was in for a surprise.

Her luck had just run out, he thought.

Biting off a few choice words under his breath, Colin made a U-turn and took off after her.

Less than thirty seconds later, he realized that she wasn't going anywhere. The woman with the soulful doe eyes had pulled over to the curb.

Something was definitely off, Colin thought as he brought his motorcycle to a halt behind her vehicle.

Training from his days on the force in Los Angeles had Colin approaching the car with caution. Every police officer knew that the first thirty seconds after a vehicle was pulled over were the most dangerous ones. If something bad was going to happen, it usually took place within that space of time.

Ninety-nine times out of a hundred, the pulled-over driver was harmless. It was that one other time that turned out to be fatal.

Although he had volunteered for this detail, choosing to patrol the city streets on a motorcycle over riding around in a squad car with a partner, he was not unaware of the risk that came with the job. A risk that always had his adrenaline flowing and his breath backing up in his lungs for that short time that it took for him to dismount and approach the offending driver's vehicle.

If he had a partner, there would be someone close by who had his back. However, Owens, his last partner, had been killed on the job, and although Colin never said anything to anyone about it, that had weighed really heavily on him, and still did. After that tragic incident, he operated alone. Patrolling alone meant he had to watch out only for himself. He liked it that way.

The second he peered into the passenger window

and saw the driver, he knew that he was facing another kind of danger entirely.

No one was going to die today, but it was still a risk.

Miranda rolled down the passenger window and leaned toward him. "Hi. I wasn't speeding this time," she said, greeting him with a cheerful smile and a chipper demeanor he found almost annoyingly suspicious.

He scowled at her. "No, you were just executing a very strange turn."

"I had to," Miranda explained. "If I went straight and turned at the next light, by the time I came back, I was afraid that you'd be gone."

Only if I'd been lucky, Colin thought.

Just what was this woman's game? "And that would have been a problem because…?"

She never missed a beat. "Because I had to talk to you."

The idea of just turning away and getting back on his motorcycle was exceedingly tempting, but for some reason he couldn't quite put his finger on, Colin decided to hear this overly upbeat woman out.

"You are persistent, aren't you?" he retorted.

"You say that like it's a bad thing." Miranda did her best to try to get the officer to lighten up a little and smile.

His stoic expression never changed. "It is from where I'm standing." He'd glimpsed her driver's license yesterday and tried to recall the name he'd seen on it. Maybe if he made this personal, he'd succeed in scaring her off. "What do you want, Miriam?"

"Miranda," she corrected, still sounding annoyingly

cheerful. "That's okay, a lot of people get my name wrong at first. It takes getting used to."

"I have no intention of getting used to it," he informed her. *Or you.*

As far as he was concerned, the woman was really pushing her luck.

"Look, I let you off with a warning yesterday," he reminded her. "Would you like me to rescind that warning and give you a ticket?"

Colin was fairly confident that the threat of a ticket would be enough to make her back off.

"No. That was very nice of you yesterday. That's the reason I came looking for you today."

She wasn't making any sense. And then he remembered what she'd said yesterday about asking him to pay a visit to some ward at the hospital.

That's what this was about, he decided. Something about sick children. Well, he was not about to get roped into anything. Who knew what this woman's ultimate game really was?

"Look, I already told you," he retorted. "I'm not the type to come see kids in a hospital. I don't like hospitals."

Rather than look disappointed as he'd expected her to, the woman nodded. "A lot of people don't," she agreed.

Okay, she was obviously stalking him, and this was over. "Well then, have a nice day," Colin told her curtly, and then turned to walk back to his motorcycle.

"I'm not here about the hospital," Miranda called

after him. "Although I'd like to revisit that subject at a later time."

Colin stopped walking. The woman had to be one of the pushiest people he'd ever encountered, not to mention she had a hell of a lot of nerve.

Against his better judgment, he found himself turning around again to face her. "And just what are you 'here' about?" he asked.

There was absolutely nothing friendly in his voice that invited her to talk. But she did anyway.

"That little girl I told you about?" Miranda began, feeling as if she was picking her way through a minefield that could blow up on her at any moment. "The one with your aunt's name," she reminded him, hoping that would get the officer to listen, and buy her a little more time.

"Lily," he repeated, all but growling the name. "What about her?" he asked grudgingly.

He wasn't a curious man by any stretch of the imagination, but there was something about this overly eager woman that had him wondering just where she was taking this.

"Lily's mother is missing," she told him, never taking her eyes off his face.

Rather than show some sort of reaction to what she'd just said, his expression never changed. He looked, Miranda thought, as if she'd just given him a bland weather report.

She began to wonder what had damaged the man to this extent.

"So go to the precinct and report it," Colin told her. "That's the standard procedure."

"The director at the shelter already did that," Miranda answered.

"All right, then it's taken care of." What more did she expect him to do? Colin wondered irritably as he began to walk away again.

"No, it isn't," Miranda insisted, stepping out of her car and moving quickly between him and his motorcycle. "The officer who took down the information said that maybe Lily's mother took off. He said a lot of women in her situation feel overwhelmed and just leave. He said that maybe she'd come to her senses in a few days and return for her daughter."

"Okay, you have your answer," Colin said, moving around this human roadblock.

Again Miranda shifted quickly so he couldn't get to his motorcycle. She ignored the dark look he gave her. She wasn't about to give up. This was important. Lily was depending on her to do everything she could to find her mother.

"But what if she doesn't?" Miranda asked. "What if she didn't take off? What if something's happened to Lily's mother and that's why she never came back to the shelter?"

He felt as if this doe-eyed blonde was boxing him in. "That's life," he said, exasperated.

"There's a little eight-year-old girl at the shelter waiting for her mommy to come back," Miranda told him with feeling. "I can't just tell her 'that's life.'"

Taking hold of Miranda's shoulders, he moved her

firmly out of his way and finally reached his motorcycle. "Tell her whatever you like."

Miranda raised her voice so that he could hear her above the sound of the cars going by. "I'd like to tell her that this nice police officer is trying to find her mommy."

Colin turned sharply on his heel and glared at this woman who refused to take a hint. "Look, lady—"

"Miranda," she prompted.

"Miranda," Colin echoed between gritted teeth. "You are a royal pain, you know that?"

Miranda had always tried to glean something positive out of every situation, no matter how bleak it might appear. "Does that mean you'll look for her?" she asked hopefully.

Colin blew out an angry breath. "That means you're a royal pain," he repeated.

With nothing to lose, Miranda climbed out on a limb. "Please? I can give you a description of Lily's mother." And then she thought of something even better. "And if you come with me, I can get you a picture of her that'll be useful."

He had a feeling that this woman wasn't going to give up unless he agreed to help her. Although it irritated him beyond description, there was a very small part of him that had to admit he admired her tenacity.

Still, he gave getting her to back off one more try. "What will be useful is if you get out of my way and let me do my job."

Miranda didn't budge. "Isn't part of your job finding people who have gone missing?"

"She's not missing if she left of her own accord and just decided to keep on going," he told the blonde, enunciating every word.

"But we don't know that she decided to keep on going. She did leave the shelter to go look for work," Miranda told him.

"That's what the woman said," Colin countered impatiently.

"No, that's what she *did*," Miranda stressed. "Gina Hayden has an eight-year-old daughter. She wouldn't just leave her like that."

"How do you *know* that?" Colin challenged. The woman lived in a cotton candy world. Didn't she realize that the real world wasn't like that? "Lots of people say one thing and do another. And lots of people with families just walk out on them and never come back."

Miranda watched him for a long moment. So long that he thought she'd finally given up trying to wear him down. And then she spoke and blew that theory to pieces.

"Who left you?" she asked quietly.

"You, I hope," he snapped, turning back to face his motorcycle.

He sighed as she sashayed in front of him yet again. This was beginning to feel like some never-ending dance.

"No, you're not talking about me," Miranda told him. "You're talking about someone else. I can see it in your eyes. Someone walked out on you, probably when you were a kid. So you know what that feels like," she stressed.

He needed this like he needed a hole in the head. "Look, lady—"

"Miranda," she corrected again.

He ignored that. "You can take your amateur psycho-babble, get back in your car and drive away before I haul you in for harassing a police officer."

Was that what he thought this was?

She had to get through to him. Something in her heart told her that he'd find Gina, She just needed him to take this seriously.

"I'm not harassing you—"

He almost laughed out loud. "You want to bet?"

Miranda pushed on. "I'm just asking you to go out of your way a little and maybe make a little girl very happy. If her mother doesn't turn up, Lily's going to be sent to social services and placed in a foster home. The only reason she hasn't been taken there already is that the director of the shelter agreed with me about wait-ing for her mom to come back. The director bought us a little time." And that time was running out, Miranda added silently.

"The kid can still be taken away," Colin pointed out. "Her mother abandoned her."

Why couldn't she get through to this officer? "Not if something happened to her and she's unable to get back."

Colin sighed. He knew he should just get on his mo-torcycle and ride away from this woman. For the life of him, he didn't know why he was allowing himself to get involved in this.

"Did you call all the hospitals?"

She nodded. "All of them. There's no record of any-one fitting Gina's description coming in on her own or being brought in."

So what more did this woman want him to do? "Well then—"

"But there could be other reasons she hasn't come back," she insisted. "Gina could have been abducted, or worse." Miranda looked at him with eyes that were pleading with him to do something.

Colin shook his head. "I should have given you that ticket yesterday," he told her gruffly.

He was weakening; she could just feel it. "But you didn't because you're a good man."

"No, because I should have had my head examined," he grumbled. "All right," he relented, taking out his ticket book and flipping to an empty page.

Miranda's eyes widened. "You're writing me a ticket?" she asked.

"No, I'm taking down this woman's description. You said you'd give it to me. Now, what is it?" Colin de-manded.

"What did you say your name was?" she asked.

"I didn't." He could feel her looking at him. Swal-lowing a couple choice words, he said, "Officer Colin Kirby."

"Thank you, Officer Colin Kirby."

Maybe he was losing his mind, but he could swear he could *feel* her smile.

"The description?" he demanded.

Miranda lost no time in giving it to him.

Chapter Four

"Okay," Colin said, closing his ticket book and putting it away. "I'll check with the other officer your director talked to. What's his name or badge number?" he asked.

Miranda shook her head. She hadn't thought to ask for that information when the director had given her an update. "I'm afraid Amelia didn't mention either one."

Colin looked at her. The name meant nothing to him. "Amelia?"

"Amelia Sellers," Miranda specified. "That's the shelter's director. She didn't give me the officer's name, but seemed pretty upset that he wasn't taking the situation seriously."

Colin read between the lines. He assumed that the officer the shelter director had talked to hadn't told her that he would get back to her. Not that he blamed the man.

"I take it this Amelia isn't as pushy as you," he commented.

Miranda wasn't exactly happy with his description, but the situation was far too important for her to get sidelined by something so petty.

"Actually, she can be very forceful. But the officer taking down the information really didn't seem to think that Gina was missing," Miranda said.

She was looking at him with the kind of hopeful eyes that made men seriously consider leaping tall buildings in a single bound and bending steel with their bare hands in an attempt to impress her.

If he was going to interact with this woman for any length of time, he was going to have to remember to avoid looking into her eyes, Colin told himself. They were far too distracting.

"I bet you were prom queen, weren't you?" he asked.

The question came out of the blue and caught her completely off guard. It took Miranda a moment to collect herself and answer, "Actually, I didn't go to the prom."

"No one asked you?" He found that rather hard to believe. She struck him as the epitome of a cheerleader. Was she pulling his leg?

Miranda didn't answer his question directly. She actually had been asked, just hadn't said yes.

"I had a scheduling problem," she said vaguely. "The prom interfered with my volunteer work."

"In high school?" Colin asked incredulously.

"You look surprised," she noted, then told him, "People in high school volunteer for things." At least, the people she'd kept company with had.

Shrugging, he said, "If you say so." He'd never concerned himself with social activities, even back then, nor did he involve himself with any kind of volunteer work. Most of his life he'd been a loner.

Securing the ticket book in his back pocket, he told her, "I'll see what I can find out."

"Don't you want the phone number at the shelter?"

He caught himself thinking fleetingly that he'd rather have her number. The next second he deliberately pushed the thought away. If he had her number, that might very well lead to complications, which was the very *last* thing he wanted. He supposed that obtaining the shelter's number was innocuous enough. Most likely if he used it he'd wind up speaking to the director.

"Right," Colin answered, doing his best to exercise patience. "So what is it?"

Miranda gave him the number to the shelter's landline, then waited for him to take out the ticket book again so he could jot it down.

Sensing what she wanted, he did just that. As he put the book away a second time he heard her asking, "Aren't you going to follow me to the shelter?"

It just didn't end with her, did it? he thought, exasperated. "Why would I want to do that?"

"To see Gina's picture," she reminded him. "I told you that there's one at the shelter. Lily has it."

He looked at her blankly for a split second until the information clicked into place. "Lily. Right, the little girl."

For a moment, he thought about telling her—again—that this wasn't something he did. His main sphere of expertise was keeping the flow of traffic going at a reasonable rate.

There were patrol officers who took this kind of information down, as well as detectives back at the precinct who specialized in missing persons. But he had no desire to get into all that with her. It would just lead to another prolonged debate.

Besides, it wasn't as if leaving the area was tantamount to abandoning a hub of vehicular infractions and crimes. And how long would following her to the shelter and getting that photograph of the runaway mother take, anyway?

Making no effort to suppress the sigh that escaped his lips, he said, "Okay, lead the way."

The officer's answer surprised her. She'd expected more resistance from him. Finally!

Her mouth curved. "So then, you are going to follow me?"

The woman had a magnetic, not to mention hypnotic, smile. He forced himself to look away.

"That's what 'lead the way' usually means," he answered shortly.

"I know that," she acknowledged. "It's just that I realize I'm asking you to go above and beyond the call of duty."

And yet here you are, asking me, he thought, irritated. Colin was beginning to think that the woman could just go on talking indefinitely. He, on the other hand, wanted to get this over with as soon as possible.

"Just get in your car and drive, Miranda," he instructed gruffly.

Her mouth quirked in another smile that made him think of the first ray of sunshine coming out after a storm. "You remembered."

"Yeah," Colin said shortly. He wasn't about to tell her that, like it or not—and he didn't—this fleeting contact with her had already left a definite imprint on his brain. "Well?" he prodded, when she continued standing there. "I don't have all day."

"Right."

The next moment she was hurrying back to her vehicle. Getting in, she started up the engine mindful of the fact that she had to be careful to observe *all* the rules. She had no doubt that if she exceeded the speed limit—and there seemed to be a different one posted on each long block—the officer behind her wouldn't hesitate to give her a ticket this time.

He'd probably see it as a reward for humoring her, Miranda thought.

But it didn't matter. She'd gotten him to agree, however grudgingly, to try to find Lily's mother, and that was all that *did* matter.

The shelter wasn't far away. Parking near the entrance, she got out of her car and stood beside it, waiting for the officer to pull into the parking lot.

When he did, he found a spot several rows away from her.

She watched him stride toward her. The dark-haired officer was at least six-one, maybe a little taller, and moved like one of those strong, silent heroes straight out of the Old West. She sincerely hoped that he would turn out to be Lily's hero.

"You've got ten minutes," Colin told her the moment he reached her.

He expected her to protest being issued a time limit. But she surprised him by saying, "Then I'd better make the most of it. Lily will probably be in the common area," she added. "That's where she watches for me to arrive."

"You come every day?" he questioned. Didn't this woman have a social life? He would have expected someone who looked the way she did to have a very busy one.

"I come here four, sometimes five days a week," she told him matter-of-factly. "Other days I work at the animal shelter, exercising the dogs."

Nobody did that much volunteering, he thought, opening the door and holding it for her. She had to be putting him on.

"What do you do when you're not earning your merit badges?" he asked sarcastically.

"Sleep," she answered, without missing a beat.

She sounded serious, but he still wasn't sure if he was buying this saint act. He was about to ask the woman if her halo was on too tight, cutting off the circulation to her brain, but he never got the chance. She'd turned away from him, her attention shifting to the little blonde girl who was charging toward her.

"There she is," Miranda declared, opening her arms just in time.

The next second she was closing them around the

pint-size dynamo, who appeared to be hugging her for all she was worth.

"Did you find her?" the little girl cried eagerly, her high-pitched voice partially muffled against Miranda's hip. "Did you find my mommy?"

"Not yet, darling," Miranda answered.

Slowly, she moved the little girl back just far enough to be able to see the man she'd brought with her. "But this nice officer—" she nodded toward Colin "—is going to help us find her."

Colin noted that the firebrand who had dragged him here hadn't used the word *try*. She'd gone straight to the word *help*, making it sound as if it would be just a matter of time before he located this missing mother who might or might not have taken off for parts unknown of her own free will.

He didn't like being tied to promises he had absolutely no control over, nor did he like deceiving people into thinking he could deliver on goods that he had no way of knowing he could even locate.

But when he began to say as much to the little girl, he found himself looking down into incredible blue eyes that were brimming with more hope than he recalled seeing in a long, long time.

How could this kid exist in a place like this and still have hope? he wondered.

"Are you going to find her?" Lily asked, all four feet of her practically vibrating with excitement and anticipation. "Are you going to find my mommy?"

"I'm—" He started to tell her that he would do what he could, because he wasn't in the habit of lying, not to anyone. Not even to children, who usually fell beneath his radar.

"Officer Kirby is going to need to see that picture you have of you and your mommy," Miranda said, cutting into what she was afraid the man was about to tell the little girl. "Can you go get it for me, Lily?"

The little girl bobbed her head up and down enthusiastically. "I'll be right back," she stated, and took off.

"I can't promise her I'll find her mother," Colin said in a no-nonsense voice.

"Maybe you could try," Miranda suggested. When she saw his expression darken, she tried to make him see it from Lily's side. "Everyone needs something to hang on to," she pointed out.

Colin looked totally unconvinced. "Hanging on to a lie doesn't help," he told her.

"It won't be a lie—if you find Gina," Miranda countered.

He couldn't believe she'd just said that. The woman obviously had her head in the clouds. "Does your plane ever land?" he asked.

"Occasionally," she allowed, and then, smiling, she added, "To refuel."

Colin was about to say something about the danger of crashing and burning if she wasn't careful, but just then Lily returned, burrowing in between them. The little girl was clutching a five-by-seven, cheaply framed photograph against her small chest.

Planting herself squarely in front of the police officer, she held out the picture for him to see. It was recent, by the looks of it, he judged. The little girl appeared the same in it and she was wearing the dress she had on now.

He caught himself wondering if it was her only dress, which surprised him. Thoughts like that didn't usually occur to him.

"That's us. Me and my mommy," Lily told him proudly. She held the framed photograph up higher so he could see it better. "Miranda says she's pretty," the little girl added. And then her smile faded as she asked, "You're not going to lose the picture, are you? It's the only one I've got."

Colin paused, looking at the small, worried face. "Tell you what," he said, pulling his cell phone out of his breast pocket. "Why don't I take a picture of your photo with my phone?" he suggested. "That way I'll have a copy to show around so I can find your mother, and you get to keep that picture for yourself."

He was rewarded with a huge smile that took up Lily's entire face. "That's a good idea," she told him. Her eyes were sparkling as she added, "You're really smart."

He was about to dismiss that assessment, flattering though it was, when he heard Miranda tell the little girl, "He's a police officer," as if the one automatically implied the other.

"Just seemed like a simple solution," Colin told the little girl evasively. "Now hold up the picture," he said to her, wanting to move on to another topic.

Lily did as he asked, holding the framed photograph as high as she could so that he had an unobstructed view. The moment he snapped the picture with the camera app on his phone and, after looking at the screen, pronounced it "Good," he suddenly felt small arms encircling his waist just below his belt and holstered weapon.

"Thank you!" Lily cried. "And thank you for looking for my mommy."

He was about to say that "looking" didn't necessarily mean finding, but before he did, something made him glance in Miranda's direction.

She was moving her head slowly from side to side, silently indicating that she knew exactly what he was about to say to the little girl, and imploring him not to do so.

Colin blew out his breath impatiently, then compromised and told the little girl, who still had her arms around him, "I'll do my best, Lily."

"You'll find her," she declared. "I know you will." Lily said it with the kind of unshakable belief that only the very young were blessed with.

"Lily, honey," Miranda prompted, "you need to let go of Officer Kirby so he can get started looking for your mommy."

"Oh."

He was surprised and maybe just a bit charmed, he discovered, to hear the little girl giggle.

"I'm sorry," she said, releasing him. "I just wanted to say thank you."

Again he wanted to tell her that just because he'd promised to *look* for her mother didn't mean that he was going to be able to *find* her.

Maybe it was because Miranda was standing so close

to him, or maybe it was all that hope he saw shining in the little girl's blue eyes, but the words he was about to say froze on his tongue, unable to exit. He couldn't bring himself to be the one to force Lily to face up to reality and all the ugliness that came with it.

So all he did was mumble, "Yeah," and then turn on his heel and begin striding toward the shelter's exit—and freedom.

It wasn't until he was way past the front door and standing outside, dragging in air to clear his head, that he realized the woman who had roped him into this was right behind him.

Now what?

Was she going to try to get him to pinkie-swear that he was going to come through on that half promise he'd been forced to make?

"Look, I'll do what I can," he said, before she could open her mouth to say a word.

To his surprise, the woman who was quickly becoming his main source of irritation nodded as she smiled at him. "I know. That's all anyone can ask."

No, Colin thought, as he mounted his motorcycle. The exasperating blonde was asking him for a hell of a lot more than that.

The thing that he *really* couldn't understand, he realized as he rode away, was that for some reason Miranda Steele was making him want to deliver on that vague nonpromise he'd just made to that little girl.

Chapter Five

He absolutely hated asking anyone for anything, even if it involved something in the line of duty. If he didn't ask, Colin felt that there was no chance of his being turned down. There was also the fact that if he didn't ask someone to do something for him, then he wouldn't owe anyone a favor in return.

Again he found himself wishing he had never pulled Miranda over to give her a ticket in the first place. If he hadn't done that, then he wouldn't be faced with the dilemma he was now looking at.

It was the end of his shift and Colin was tempted to just clock out and go home. But despite his desire to divorce himself from the situation, his mind kept conjuring up images of that little girl's small, sad face looking up at him as if he was the answer to all her prayers.

No one had ever looked at him like that before.

It was all that woman's fault, Colin thought grudgingly.

Miranda.

Who named their kid Miranda these days, anyway? he wondered irritably.

It was late, Colin thought as he walked into the locker room. Too late to really start anything today. To assuage his conscience, he decided to come in earlier tomorrow and maybe nose around, see if anyone had any information pertaining to a woman who matched this Gina Hayden's description.

After opening his locker, Colin took out his civilian clothes and began changing into them. He was tired and he'd be able to think more clearly tomorrow morning when he—

"The poor woman was lying there, slumped over by the Dumpster and hardly breathing. I thought she was dead. Really not the kind of thing you'd expect to see around here."

Colin stopped tucking his shirt into his jeans. The conversation that was coming from the row of lockers directly behind his caught his attention. He listened more closely.

"Lucky thing you found her when you did, Moran," a second, deeper voice commented. "Why did you go in that alley, anyway?"

Colin heard a locker door being closed before "Moran" answered the other officer. "I saw two kids running out of there. They looked pretty spooked."

"You think they were the ones who assaulted her?" the other patrol officer asked.

A second locker was closed. The officers sounded as if they were about to leave.

"There was no blood on either one of them," Moran was saying, "and frankly, they looked too scared to have beaten her that way. To be on the safe side, I snapped a picture of them as they took off. They ran into a building across the way. Shouldn't be all that hard locating them if I need to."

Colin closed his locker. What were the odds? he wondered.

At the very least, he needed to check this out.

Making his way to the next set of lockers, he was just in time to catch the two officers before they left the locker room.

"What happened to the woman?" Colin asked.

Officer Bob Moran looked up at him, surprised by the question. They knew one another vaguely by sight, but that was where it ended. They'd certainly never talked shop before.

"I called a bus for her," Moran answered. "The paramedics took her to Mercy General."

"Did you go with her?" Colin inquired.

Moran looked slightly uncomfortable. "No. It was the end of my shift and she was unconscious. I figured she'd be more up to giving me a statement tomorrow morning."

"What happened to her?" Colin pressed.

The fact that he was asking questions seemed to surprise the other two officers. Moran exchanged glances with Pete Morales, the second policeman, before answering. "Looked to me like someone stole her purse. I couldn't find any ID on her—or a wallet."

Colin took out his cell phone and flipped to the picture he'd taken of the photograph Lily had held up for him.

He turned his cell toward Moran. "This her?"

Bushy eyebrows rose high enough to almost meet a receding hairline. Moran appeared stunned. "Yeah, that's her, minus the swollen lip and the bruises." And then he looked at Colin. "You know her?"

He put his phone away. "No."

When he didn't volunteer anything further, curiosity had Moran asking, "Then why do you have her picture?"

Colin scowled. Granted, this wasn't exactly personal, but he still didn't like being put in the position where he had to elaborate. He preferred keeping to himself in general and answering questions only when he had no other choice.

But he didn't see a way out without arousing even more questions. Pausing for a moment, he finally said, "The woman was reported missing from a homeless shelter."

"That her little girl with her?" Morales asked, his demeanor softening as he looked at the child holding up the framed photograph.

"Yeah," Colin answered shortly. "Thanks for the information." Without any further exchange, he began walking away.

"You going to see her?" Moran called after him.

Colin didn't stop to turn around when he replied, "That was the idea."

"I can go with you," Moran volunteered, raising his voice.

Colin almost asked why, but supposed the other man's conscience had gotten the better of him. Or maybe Moran just wanted the credit. In either case, Colin didn't care.

"You've done enough. I'll take it from here." He kept on going, then slowed down long enough to throw the word *thanks* over his shoulder before he left the locker area.

He heard a somewhat confused "Don't mention it" in response.

Colin just kept on walking.

The last person in the world Miranda expected to see walking into the women's shelter that evening was the motorcycle officer she'd managed to talk into looking for Lily's missing mother.

Ordinarily, Miranda would have left by now, but she'd stayed at the shelter today to try to bolster Lily's spirits. Despite her normally upbeat, cheerful nature, it was obvious that the little girl was sincerely worried about her mother. The fact that several of the other children there had told her that her mother had "run away" and abandoned her didn't help any. Lily refused to listen to them.

"My mommy wouldn't leave me!" she'd cried. "She loves me!" The little girl was convinced that something had to have happened to her mom, preventing her from returning.

Miranda had stayed at the shelter until she'd finally managed to calm Lily down and get her to fall asleep.

She was just leaving when she saw the officer coming in.

One look at Colin's grim face had her thinking the worst—and fervently hoping she was wrong.

It was obvious that he didn't see her when he walked in. Miranda cut across the common area like a shot, placing herself in his path.

Trying to brace herself for whatever he had to say, she didn't bother with any small talk or preliminary chitchat. "You found her," she said breathlessly, willing him to say something positive.

Colin hadn't been sure Miranda would still be here, but she managed to surprise him by materializing out of nowhere.

"Yeah, I found her."

Miranda immediately felt her heart shoot up into her throat, making it almost impossible for her to breathe.

How was she going to tell Lily that her mother was dead?

Her mind scrambled, searching for words, for solutions. Maybe she could take Lily in as a foster parent, or maybe—

The woman standing in front of him almost turned white. That was *not* the sort of reaction he was expecting from her.

She also wasn't saying anything, another surprise, he thought.

"Don't you want to know where she is?" he finally asked.

The startlingly blue eyes widened more than he thought was humanly possible. "You mean she's alive?" Miranda cried.

"Well, yeah," he answered, surprised she was asking that. "If she was dead, I would have led with that."

"Dead? Somebody's dead?" an adolescent boy standing within earshot asked, instantly alert.

"Every single nerve in my body, for openers, Edward." Miranda blew out a shaky breath. "That's what I get for jumping to conclusions." She turned toward the police officer, who had just become her hero. Suddenly, tears were filling her eyes, spilling out and rolling down her cheeks. "You really found her," she whispered, clearly choked up.

"We've established that," Colin retorted. And then he looked at her more closely and realized what was going on. "Hey, are you crying?" he demanded, stunned.

Miranda pressed her lips together as she nodded. "Miracles make me do that," she told him hoarsely.

He wasn't sure if the miracle she was referring to was that he had found Lily's mother, or that he had bothered to look in the first place. Either way, he knew he wasn't about to ask her to elaborate. He was determined to keep communication between them to an absolute minimum—or as close to that as possible.

Digging into his back pocket, he pulled out a handkerchief and pushed it into her hand. "You're getting messy," he muttered.

Taking the handkerchief, Miranda smiled at him.

I see through you, Officer Kirby. You're not the big, bad wolf you pretend to be. You're a kind man under all that bluster.

Wiping her eyes, she asked, "What happened to her?"

He'd gone to the hospital to get as much information as he could before coming to the shelter. He knew there would be questions and he wasn't about to turn up unprepared.

Drawing her toward an alcove, he told Miranda, "From the looks of it, someone tried to rob her. When she held on to her purse, the thug decided to teach her a lesson. Doctor said she was pretty badly beaten. She was unconscious when they first brought her in," he added.

"But she's conscious now." It was half a question, half an assumption.

The woman had been just coming around when he'd gone to see her. "Yeah."

"Which hospital is she in?" Miranda asked.

"The paramedics took her to the one closest to where they found her," he answered. "Mercy General."

Miranda nodded, absorbing the information. Lily. She had to tell Lily.

She started to head toward the back, where some of the beds were located, when she stopped suddenly and whirled back around to face Colin again. Hurrying over, she caught him completely by surprise by throwing her arms around him.

Startled, Colin's ingrained training immediately had him protecting himself and pushing the person in his space away. But that turned out to be harder than he'd anticipated. For a rather willowy, dainty-looking woman, Miranda had a grip worthy of a world-class wrestling champion.

The second she'd thrown her arms around him, she'd felt Colin stiffening. She was making him uncomfortable.

Loosening her hold, Miranda took a half step back. "Thank you," she said.

He'd never heard more emotion stuffed into two words in his life.

Colin deflected the tidal wave of feelings as best he could. "I'm a cop. That's just supposed to be part of my job."

The smile on her lips was a knowing one, as if she had his number—which was impossible, because they were practically strangers. Still, he couldn't shake the feeling that his protest was falling on deaf ears.

"The key words being 'supposed to,'" she told him. "I didn't think you were going to look for her," Miranda admitted.

That made no sense. "Then why did you ask me to?" he asked.

Her face seemed to light up as she answered, "A girl can always hope." And then she grabbed his hand and said, "Come with me."

But Colin remained rooted to the spot, an immovable object. "Come with you where?"

"To tell Lily that you found her mother," she answered, tugging on his hand again.

But Colin still wouldn't budge an inch. "You can tell her."

Miranda was nothing if not stubborn. He had done the work and he deserved to get the credit, which in this case involved Lily's gratitude. "You found her. Lily is going to want to hear it from you. And then after you tell her, you can take us to the hospital to see Gina."

She had this all mapped out, didn't she? He didn't like being told what to do. "You're assuming a hell of a lot, aren't you?"

Miranda gazed up at him with what had to be the most innocent look he had ever seen. "So far, I've been right, haven't I?"

"Well, guess what? Your lucky streak is over," he informed her.

But just as he was about to break free and walk away, Colin heard a high-pitched squeal coming from the far side of the room. Looking in that direction, he saw a small figure with a flurry of blond hair charging toward him.

Obviously, someone had woken the little girl and told her he was here. She must have put the rest together on her own.

"You did it!" Lily cried. The next moment, she had wrapped herself around him like a human bungee cord. "You found her! You found my mommy, didn't you?" Tilting back her head so that she could look up at him, Lily gushed, "Thank you, thank you, thank you!"

Utterly stunned, Colin looked at the woman standing behind Lily. "How—?"

"It's not just the walls that have ears here," she told

him, beaming just as hard as Lily. She nodded toward the cluster of children who had been steadily gathering around them as if that should answer his question.

"Can we go see her now?" Lily pleaded. She looked from her hero to Miranda and then back again. "Please, can we? *Can* we?" she asked, giving every indication that she intended to go on pleading until her request was granted.

Looking at the officer's expression, Miranda made a judgment call. The man looked far from eager to go with them and he had done enough.

"Officer Kirby has to go home now, Lily. But I'll take you," Miranda said, putting her hand on the little girl's shoulder.

"And I'll drive," Amelia told them, approaching from yet another side.

The director had been drawn by the sounds of the growing commotion and just possibly by her own pint-size informant. In any case, the woman appeared relieved and thrilled at the news.

"Officer Kirby found my mommy," Lily told the director excitedly.

"So I heard," Amelia replied. Nodding at Colin, she smiled her thanks. "All of us here at the shelter— especially Lily—really appreciate everything you've done, Officer Kirby," she told him.

Colin wanted to protest that he really hadn't done anything. He certainly hadn't gone out of his way to find Lily's mother. The information had literally fallen into his lap and all he had really done was follow up on it.

But something told him that the more he protested, the more gratitude he would wind up garnering. His protests would be interpreted as being modest rather than just the simple truth.

So he left it alone, saying nothing further on the subject.

Instead, he decided that going home could wait a while longer.

Turning toward the director, he addressed her and the little girl who was jumping up and down at his side. "I'll lead the way to the hospital, since I know what floor Lily's mother is on."

He deliberately avoided looking at Miranda, sensing that if he did glance her way, he'd somehow wind up being roped into something else, and his quota for good deeds was filled for the month.

Possibly the year.

Chapter Six

"Wait!"

The order came from the head nurse sitting at the second floor nurse's station.

When the three adults and child continued walking down the corridor, she hurried around her desk and into the hall to physically block their path.

Surprised, Miranda told the woman, "We're going to see Gina Hayden. We won't be long," she promised.

"Clearly," the nurse snapped, crossing her arms over her ample chest. "Visiting hours are done," she informed them in a voice that would have made a drill sergeant proud. "You can come back tomorrow."

Lily looked stricken. "But she's my mommy and we just found her," the little girl protested in distress.

"She'll still be here tomorrow," the woman told her,

sounding detached. It was obvious she wanted them off the floor and wasn't about to budge.

Lily's lower lip trembled. "But—"

"Rules are rules, little girl," the nurse maintained stiffly.

Colin felt Lily tugging on his sleeve, mutely appealing to him for help. He made the mistake of looking down into her worried face.

Swallowing an oath, he took out his badge and held it up in front of the nurse so she couldn't miss seeing it. "But they can be bent this one time, can't they?" It wasn't a question.

The head nurse looked no friendlier than she had a moment ago, but she inclined her head and backed off—temporarily.

"Ten minutes, no longer. Ten minutes or I'll call security," she warned.

"No need," Miranda promised the woman. A small victory was better than none. Taking Lily's hand, she urged the little girl, "Let's hurry."

"She's in room 221," Colin told them gruffly.

They moved quickly. He followed at his own pace.

There were four beds in the room, two on either side. Lily's head practically whirled around as she scanned the room looking for her mother. Seeing her lying in the bed next to the window, she sprinted over.

"Mommy!" she cried happily, and then skidded to a stop as she took a closer look at the woman in the hospital bed.

Her mouth dropped open in surprise. Her mother

was hooked up to two monitors as well as an IV. The monitors were making beeping noises.

The scene was clearly upsetting to the little girl, as were the bruises she saw along her mother's arms and face.

Inching closer, Lily asked in a hushed voice, "Did you fall down, Mommy?"

Gina turned her head and saw her daughter for the first time. Light came into the woman's eyes and she tried to open her arms so she could hug the little girl, but she was impeded by the various tubes attached to her.

"Oh, Lily-pad, I did. I tripped and fell down," Gina told her daughter.

Miranda squeezed the woman's hand lightly, letting Gina know that she understood she was lying for Lily's sake.

"We were all worried about you," she told her. "But Lily never gave up hope that we'd find you."

The expression on Gina's face reflected confusion and embarrassment. "I don't remember what happened," she admitted.

"That doesn't matter right now, darling," Amelia said in a soothing, comforting voice. "All that matters is that you're here and you're being taken care of."

"Officer Kirby found you for me," Lily told her mother excitedly. Taking Colin's hand, Lily pulled on it to bring him closer. "This is Officer Kirby, Mommy," she explained, showing off her brand-new champion to her mother.

Eyes that were the same shade of blue as Lily's

looked up at him. They glinted with sheer appreciation. "Thank you."

"No thanks needed," Colin told her, then explained, "It's complicated."

Miranda suppressed a sigh. The man just couldn't accept gratitude, she thought. She wanted to call him out on it, but this definitely wasn't the moment for that.

"We're out of time," she told Lily, as well as Amelia and Colin. And then she explained to Gina, "We promised the nurse on duty to only stay for ten minutes because it's after hours."

"We'll come back tomorrow, Mommy," Lily promised her solemnly.

Miranda bit her bottom lip. She wouldn't be able to come by with Lily until after her shift at the hospital. She looked at the director, a mute request in her eyes.

Picking up the silent message, Amelia nodded obligingly. "See you then," she told Gina, then patted the young mother's hand. "Feel better, dear."

Colin waited for the three females to file out of the room before he started to leave himself. He almost didn't hear Gina say, "Thank you, Officer Kirby."

Again, he wanted to tell the woman that he hadn't been the one who had located her. But that would take time and the nurse at the station had given every indication that she would come swooping in the second their ten minutes were up. He didn't trust himself not to snap at the nurse, which would undoubtedly upset the little girl, and in his estimation, she had been through enough.

So he merely nodded in response to the woman's thanks and left the room.

"Mommy has to be more careful," Lily said authoritatively as she and the three adults with her headed toward the elevator.

Miranda looked at the little girl as they got on. It wasn't entirely clear to her if Lily actually believed what she was saying, or if she was saying it so as not to let the adults with her know that *she* knew something bad had happened to her mother.

In some ways, she felt that Lily was an innocent girl; in other ways, she seemed older than her years. Only children were often a mixture of both.

"That was a very nice thing you did," Miranda told Colin once they reached the ground floor and got off the elevator. When he stared at her blankly, she elaborated. "Getting the nurse to allow us to see Gina."

The officer said nothing. There was no indication that he had even heard her, except for his careless shrug.

The man was a very tough nut to crack. And she intended to crack him—but in a good way. Miranda smiled to herself. Whether Officer Kirby knew it or not, he had just become her next project.

They split up when they reached the hospital parking lot, with Miranda and Lily going back with Amelia, while Colin headed for his vehicle, a vintage two-door sport car that was a couple years older than he was.

"Goodbye, Officer Kirby!" Lily called after him. When he glanced over his shoulder in response to her parting words, Lily waved at him as hard as she could. It looked as if she was close to taking off the ground.

Colin nodded once, climbed into his car and drove off.

Lily insisted on standing there until she couldn't see him any longer.

"He's a hero," she told the two women when she finally turned around and got into the director's car.

"Yes, he is," Miranda agreed.

A very reluctant hero, she added silently.

"Hey, Kirby, there's someone here who's been waiting to see you for some time now," the desk sergeant told Colin when he came into the precinct and walked by the man's desk.

It was past the end of his shift and Colin was more than tired. It had been two days since he'd led that little safari of females into the hospital and he'd assumed—hoped, really—that Miranda was now a thing of the past.

But the moment the desk sergeant said there was someone waiting to see him, he knew in his gut that it had to be *her*. Granted, it could have easily been anyone else; Bedford wasn't exactly a minuscule city and it felt as if the population was growing every day. But somehow he just *knew* it had to be the woman he had made the fatal mistake of pulling over that day.

The annoyingly perky, pushy woman he just couldn't seem to get rid of. She was like a burr he couldn't shake loose.

"Where?" Colin growled.

"Need your eyes checked, Kirby?" the desk sergeant asked. "She's sitting right over there." He pointed to the bench situated against the wall fifteen feet away.

Reluctantly, Colin sighed and looked in the direction the desk sergeant was pointing.

Damn it, he thought.

It *was* her—and she was looking right at him. It was too late to make an escape.

He might as well find out what she wanted.

Striding over to the bench, he saw her rise to her feet. The woman appeared ready to pounce on him.

Now what?

Bracing himself for the worst, he skipped right over any kind of a formal greeting and asked, "Something else you want me to do?"

Just as sunny as ever, Miranda thought, more convinced than before that he needed her to turn him around. "No, actually, I brought something for you," she told him, hoping that would get rid of the scowl on his face.

It didn't.

He needed to stop her right there, Colin thought, instantly on guard. "I can't accept any gifts," he told her. "The department frowns on its officers taking any sort of gratuities in exchange for services rendered, either past, present or in the future."

He sounded so incredibly uptight, Miranda thought. They'd crossed paths not a moment too soon.

"This isn't a gratuity," she assured him, trying to put his fears to rest.

He wasn't about to stand here exchanging words with her. For one thing, she was far better equipped for a verbal battle than he was. For another, he didn't have time for this.

"Whatever you want to call it—gratuity, gift or bribe—I can't accept it." He concluded in a no-nonsense voice, thinking that would be the end of it.

He should have known better. The woman had shown him that, right or wrong, she wasn't one to back off.

And she was clearly not listening to him but was reaching into the large zippered bag she'd picked up from the bench. Extracting something from inside it, she held up what appeared to be an eleven-by-fourteen poster board for him to look at.

It was a drawing.

"Lily drew this just for you," Miranda told him. She pointed to the blue figure in the center of the page. It was twice as large as the four other figures present. "In case you don't recognize him, that's you."

And then she proceeded to point out the other people in the drawing. "That's Lily, her mother in the hospital bed, Amelia, and that's me." Miranda indicated the figure in the corner, who was almost offstage, appearing to look on.

Colin couldn't help staring at the central figure. "I'm a giant," he commented, surprised that the little girl would portray him that way.

As if reading his mind, Miranda explained, "That's how she sees you. You are a giant in her eyes. Heroes usually are," she added.

The term made him uncomfortable. "I'm not a hero," he retorted.

"I hate to break this to you, but you are to Lily," she told him.

Colin continued looking at the drawing, still not taking it from her. His attention was drawn to the stick figure the little girl had drawn of Miranda.

"You could stand to gain some weight," he observed, still not cracking a smile.

"That's good," she responded, as if they were having an actual serious conversation. "That means I get to indulge in my craving for mint chip ice cream."

He glanced at her rather than the drawing, his eyes slowly running over her, taking in every curve, every detail.

"You don't look as if you indulge in anything that's nonessential," he told her.

She laughed. It was a melodic sound he tried not to notice.

"You'd be surprised," she told him. When she saw him look at her quizzically—most likely because she *was* thin—Miranda explained, "I do a lot of running around—at the hospital, at the women's shelter and especially at the animal shelter." They had her exercising the dogs, which meant that *she* was exercising, as well.

"Don't you take any time off for yourself?" Colin asked, positive that she was putting him on.

Miranda smiled. The man just didn't get it, did he? "The women's shelter and animal shelter *are* my 'time off' for myself," she stressed. "I like feeling that I'm helping out and doing something productive. It makes me feel good about myself," she explained.

He still wasn't completely convinced. "Did you ever hear the saying 'Too good to be true'?"

She tried to suppress the grin that rose to her lips. "Are you saying that you think I'm good?"

"You're missing the point of the rest of the saying," he pointed out. Taking a breath, he decided that this meeting was over. "Anything else?" he asked her, impatience pulsing in his voice.

"Well, since you asked—have you thought any more about visiting my kids at the hospital?"

She called them 'her' kids, not just 'the' kids. Did she feel as if they were hers? he wondered incredulously.

He should never have asked if there was anything else. "No, I haven't," he answered, upbraiding himself.

Not about to be put off, Miranda asked, "Well, would you think about it? Please?" she added. "Christmas is getting closer."

Why should that make a difference? Christmas had ceased to have meaning for him when he'd lost his mother.

"Happens every year at this time," he answered.

Miranda gave it another try. "Well, like I told you, I think it would do them a lot of good. Their lives are really hard and they don't have all that much to look forward to."

"And my visiting would give them something to look forward to?" he asked sarcastically.

She never wavered. "Yes, it would."

The woman just wasn't going to give up. He didn't like being made to feel guilty.

"I'll think about it," he said, only because he felt it was the one way to get her to cease and desist. And then he looked at his watch. "Don't you have to be someplace, volunteering?"

"Actually, I do," she said, slipping the straps of her

bag over her shoulder. "I promised I'd come by the animal shelter. There's this German shepherd that needs a foster home until she can be placed."

The woman was a relentless do-gooder. "Right up your alley," he cracked.

Miranda smiled at him. He saw the corners of her eyes crinkling. "Actually, it is."

"Then you'd better get to it."

"I will. Oh, don't forget your picture," she prompted. Picking up the poster board drawing, she forced it into his hands.

"Right," he muttered, less than pleased.

He was still standing there, looking down at the drawing, as she hurried out the door.

Chapter Seven

Colin frowned. He needed to have his head examined. He obviously wasn't thinking clearly.

Or maybe at all.

Why else would he be out here, parked across the street from Bedford's no-kill animal shelter, waiting for that overachieving do-gooder to come out?

As far as he knew, he was free and clear, which meant that he could go on with his life without being subjected to any more taxing, annoying requests.

So why the hell was he here, *willingly* putting himself in that woman's path again? Why would he be setting himself up like this?

It wasn't as if he didn't know what Miranda was like. He'd learned that she was the kind of person who, if given an inch, wanted not just a mile but to turn it into an entire freeway.

Colin sighed. Knowing that, what was he doing out here?

Satisfying his own curiosity, he supposed.

A curiosity, he reminded himself, he hadn't even been aware of possessing a short while ago—not until life had thrown that woman into his path and she'd come charging at him like some kind of undersized, stampeding unicorn.

Damn it, go home, Kirby, he ordered himself, straightening up beside his vehicle. *Go home before anyone mistakes you for some kind of stalker and calls someone from the department on you.*

He'd talked himself out of being here and was just about to open his car door when he heard the sound of metal scraping on concrete across the street. A second later, he realized that the gates in front of the animal shelter were being opened.

Someone was coming out.

Colin's suspicions were confirmed a heartbeat later when he heard someone calling his name.

"Officer Kirby, is that you?"

He froze.

You should have been faster, he upbraided himself. Better yet, he shouldn't have been here to begin with.

Caught, he turned around, to see Miranda hurrying across the street toward him.

She wasn't alone.

She had a lumbering, overly excited German shepherd running with her. Miranda appeared to be hanging on to the leash for dear life. At first glance, it was difficult to say exactly who had who in tow.

Both woman and dog reached him before he had a chance to finish his thought.

Her four-footed companion suddenly reared up on its hind legs and came within an inch of planting a pair of powerful-looking front paws against his chest.

"You sure you can handle him?" Colin asked, far from pleased and moving back just in time to escape the encounter.

"Her," Miranda corrected, tugging harder on the leash. "It's a her."

That, in his opinion, was not the point. Whether the animal was too much for her was.

"Whatever." He never took his eyes off the dog. "You look like you've met your match," he told her as he took another step back.

"Down, Lola," Miranda ordered in an authoritative voice. The mountain of a dog immediately dropped to all four legs, resuming her initial position. "Good girl," Miranda praised, petting the German shepherd's head while continuing to maintain a firm hold on the leash with her other hand. Her attention shifted to Colin. "You're not afraid of a frisky puppy, are you, Officer?"

Colin continued eyeing the animal cautiously. "That all depends on whether or not that 'puppy' is bigger than I am."

"Don't let Lola scare you," Miranda told him. "She was just excited to see you." She petted the dog again. Lola seemed to curl into her hand. "I think she sees everyone as a potential master."

"Uh-huh." He wasn't all that sure he was buying this. Colin continued to regard the dog warily.

"Heel, Lola," she ordered, when the dog started to move in Colin's direction again. When Lola obeyed, Miranda looked at the police officer, wondering what he was doing here. This was not his usual patrolling area, and he was out of uniform. "Were you waiting for me, Officer Kirby?" she asked.

The expression on her face was nothing short of amused. A week ago, seeing an expression like that, seemingly at his expense, would have been enough for him to take offense, but for some reason now, he didn't.

Instead, he let it ride. Reaching into the back seat of his car, he took out the drawing she'd given him the other day at the precinct. "I came by to give you this."

Lola's ears perked up and the animal looked as if she was debating whether or not the drawing he was holding was something to eat.

Miranda pulled a little on the leash, drawing the dog back.

"That's not for you, Lola," she informed the eager German shepherd. Her eyes shifted back to the police officer. "Why are you giving it to me?" she asked. "Lily drew it for you. She wanted you to have it. It was her way of saying thank you."

Colin shrugged. "Yeah, well, I don't have anyplace to put it," he told her, still holding out the drawing.

He kept one eye on the German shepherd to make sure Lola didn't grab a chunk out of the poster board. He didn't want it, but there was no reason to let it be destroyed.

Holding the dog's leash tightly, Miranda made no effort to take the drawing from him. Instead, she looked at the tall, imposing police officer. The solemn expression in his eyes convinced her more than ever that the man needed fixing.

"You don't have any closets?"

"Of course I have closets," he retorted. What kind of question was that? Did she think he lived in a public park?

"Well, you could put the drawing in one of your closets," she suggested helpfully. "That is, if you don't want to hang it on your refrigerator."

Still not taking it from him, she glanced at the drawing. Thinking back, Miranda could remember producing something like that herself when she was younger than Lily. Hers had been of her parents and herself—and Daisy, her father's beloved Doberman. That had stayed on display on the fridge for almost a year.

"Most people put artwork like that on their refrigerator," she added, smiling encouragingly. This was all undoubtedly alien to him. "You must be new at this."

Colin furrowed his brow in concentration as he wondered what made this woman tick—and why she seemed to have singled him out like this. "I guess I'm new at a lot of things," he observed.

Her smile turned almost dazzling. "Hey, even God had a first day."

He thought of the last few days since he'd run into this sorceress. She made him behave in a manner that was completely foreign to his normal mode of operation. Exactly what was this secret power she seemed to have that caused him to act so out of character?

"Not like this," he murmured under his breath.

He heard Miranda laugh in response. The sound was light, breezy, reminding him of the spring wind that was still three months away.

For some reason, an image of bluebells in his mother's garden flashed through his mind, catching him completely by surprise. He hadn't thought of his mom's garden for more than twenty-two years.

He shook his head, as if to free himself of the memory and the wave of emotion that came with it. Colin felt as if he was getting all turned around.

"Is something wrong, Officer?" Miranda asked, concerned.

"You mean other than the fact that I should be home nursing a beer, instead of standing out here trying to make you take back this drawing?" Colin asked, exasperated.

"It's not my drawing to take," Miranda reminded him. "Lily wanted you to have it." And then she abruptly switched subjects. "Seriously? A beer?" she asked. "What about dinner?"

Colin stared at her. "Is this mothering-smothering thing of yours just something that spills out without warning, or do you have to summon it?" he asked.

She ignored his question. Instead, she made a quick judgment call.

"Tell you what," she said. "I owe you a dinner. Why don't you come on over to my place and I'll make it?"

"What?" he cried, dumbfounded. There was no way he could have heard her correctly.

"I'd offer to come over to your place and make dinner there—you know, familiar surroundings and all that to keep you from getting skittish—but I've got a feeling the only things in your refrigerator, now that we've established the fact that you have one, are probably half-empty cartons of ten-day-old Chinese take-out. Maybe eleven days."

He continued to stare at her, as close to being overwhelmed as he had ever been.

When she finally stopped talking for a moment, he jumped in and took advantage of it. "You done yet?"

"That depends," she answered, lifting her chin as if getting ready for a fight. "Are you coming?"

"No," he said flatly.

"Then I'm not done." Glancing at the dog by her side, she added, "I have a very persuasive companion right here who could help me make my argument. All things considered, I'd suggest that you avoid her attempts to convince you to see things my way and just agree to come along to my place."

Damn it, this was insane. But he could actually feel himself weakening. He really *did* need to have his head examined.

Colin put on the most solemn expression he had at his disposal. "You know, there're laws against kidnapping police officers."

Rather than back away, Miranda leaned forward, her eyes sparkling with humor. "Not if, ultimately, that police officer decides to come along willingly."

Then, as if on cue, Colin's stomach began to rumble and growl. Audibly.

Miranda smiled broadly. "I think your stomach is siding with Lola and me," she told him.

Colin scowled in response. She continued to hold her ground. He had to be crazy, but he found himself actually admiring her tenacity. If he had an iota of sense, he'd jump in his car and get the hell out of here.

But he didn't.

"That dog couldn't care less one way or another," he told her, thinking that might blow apart her argument and finally get her to back off.

She studied him for a long moment. Lola tugged on her leash, leaning forward as far as she could, but Miranda continued regarding the man before her, and seemed practically oblivious to the German shepherd. She was mulling over his response.

"You never had a pet when you were growing up, did you?" she asked Colin.

"Why would you say that?"

Miranda smiled. She had her answer. He hadn't told her she was wrong—which told her she was right.

"Because of what you just said," she murmured. "If you'd ever had one, you'd know that pets, especially dogs, *do* care about their humans."

He had her there, he thought. "I'm not her human," Colin pointed out.

"No, but at least for now, I am, and I care about you," she told him. "Lola picked up on that."

That was all so wrong, he didn't even know where to start.

"First of all, you said you were probably going to take a German shepherd home to give him—*her*—" he corrected, "a foster home. That means you're taking this dog home for the first time. She doesn't know a thing about you and she's not really your dog yet," he stressed. "And second of all—or maybe this should be first—" he said pointedly, "why the hell should you care if I have anything in my house to eat or not?"

Miranda never blinked once during what he considered to be his well-constructed argument. Instead, she looked at him, totally unfazed, and when he was done she asked, "Why shouldn't I?"

"Because we're *strangers*, damn it," he muttered in exasperation. "You don't *know* me," he added for good measure. Why didn't this woman *get* that?

In a calm voice, she went on to quietly refute his argument.

"You pulled me over to give me a ticket, then didn't after I explained why I went over the speed limit and where I was going." She paused for a moment, then told him what she felt in her heart had been his crowning achievement. "And then when I told you that Lily's mother was missing, you found her."

He felt like he was hitting his head against a brick wall. No matter what he said, she kept turning it into something positive.

"That wasn't my doing," he told her, repeating what he'd said the other day. "That all happened by accident."

Despite the fact that he had raised his voice, the woman just didn't seem to hear his protest. Or if she did, she wasn't listening. Instead, she went on to make her point.

"You came to the shelter to tell Lily her mother was at the hospital—when you didn't have to—and then you went out of your way to go with us to the hospital—when you didn't have to."

"Damn it, you're twisting things," he shouted.

At the sound of his raised voice, Lola pulled forward, as if to protect her.

"Stay!" Miranda ordered, stilling the anxious dog. And then she looked at Colin. "Why are you so afraid of having people think of you as a good guy?"

"Because I'm *not*," he insisted.

She inclined her head. "I guess we'll just have to agree to disagree on that point," she told him philosophically.

"*We* don't have to do anything," he retorted impatiently.

She smiled at him knowingly. "I think that you might see things differently on a full stomach. Here's my address," she told him, pausing to take a card out of her shoulder bag and handing it to him. "You might find it easier to just follow me," she suggested.

"I might find it easier to just go home," he contradicted.

About to cross back to her vehicle, Miranda stopped and sent him a smile that seemed to corkscrew right through his gut.

"No, you won't." She said it with such certainty, she stunned him. And then his stomach rumbled again. "See?" she said. "Your stomach agrees with me. Just get in your car and follow me. And after dinner, you're free to go home. I promise."

Heaven help him, she made it sound appealing. And he *was* hungry. Involved in a car chase this afternoon, he'd wound up skipping lunch, and his stomach was protesting being ignored for so long.

He shifted gears, going on the attack. "You know, it's dangerous to hand out your address like that," he told her.

Miranda smiled again, running her hand over Lola's head and petting the dog. "I'm not worried," she answered. "I have protection."

Colin decided to keep his peace and made no comment in response. He'd already lost enough arguments today.

Besides, he *was* hungry.

Chapter Eight

Colin nearly turned his car around.

Twice.

However, each time, he wound up curbing his impulse and talking himself into continuing to follow Miranda. He knew that if he didn't show up at her place for that dinner she seemed so bent on making for him, she would show up at his precinct tomorrow just as sure as day followed night. Probably with some sort of picnic lunch or something like that.

That was the last thing he wanted or needed.

Colin muttered a few choice words under his breath and kept going.

He might as well get this over with, and then maybe the book would finally be closed: he had done a good deed in her eyes and she paid him back with a dinner she'd made for him—hopefully not poisoning him in the process.

Caught up in his thoughts, Colin missed the last right turn Miranda took.

Watching his rearview mirror, he backed his vehicle up slowly, then turned right. When he did, he saw that her car was halfway up the block in front of him. Idling.

Miranda was obviously waiting for him to catch up.

Once he came up behind her, she started driving again.

His gut told him that he'd been right. There was absolutely no way this woman would have allowed him to skip having this payback dinner with her.

Her house turned out to be two residential blocks farther on. It was a small, tidy-looking one-story structure that seemed to almost exude warmth.

He caught himself thinking that it suited her.

Miranda parked her vehicle in the driveway. He parked his at the curb. It allowed for a faster getaway if it wound up coming to that, he thought.

She got out of the car, then opened the passenger door for the dog she'd brought home. Lola jumped down onto the driveway and they both stood at the side of her vehicle, waiting for him to come up the front walk.

"Don't trust me?" Colin asked, just the slightest bit amused, when he reached her.

"We just wanted to welcome you, that's all," she told him, nodding toward the German shepherd, which had somehow become part of this impromptu dinner.

Leading the way, Miranda went up to her front door

and unlocked it, then walked inside, still holding on to Lola's leash.

She threw a switch that was right next to the door. Light flooded the living room.

"Welcome back to your home, Lola," she cheerfully told the dog. After bending to remove the leash, she dropped it on the small table that was just a few feet beyond the entrance.

"She's been here before?" Colin asked. From what she'd said earlier, he thought Miranda was bringing the dog home with her for the first time.

"A couple of times," Miranda answered. "It was kind of a dry run to see how she fared in my house."

"And how did she?" he asked, shrugging out of his jacket as he walked into the house.

Miranda smiled. "Well. She fared well."

Colin was about to make a flippant comment in response, but he'd just glanced around and his attention had been completely absorbed by what he saw.

There was a Christmas tree in the center of the room. Not just a run-of-the-mill Christmas tree but one that looked to be at least ten feet tall. Overwhelming, the tree appeared to only be half-decorated.

The rest of the Christmas ornaments were scattered all over the room—in and out of their respective boxes—waiting to be hung up.

"It looks like a Christmas store exploded in here," he commented, scanning the room in total disbelief.

"I haven't had a chance to finish," Miranda explained. "I don't have much time left over every night to hang up decorations," she tossed over her shoulder as she made her way to the kitchen. "I'm usually pretty beat by that time."

Miranda was back in less than a minute with a dog bowl filled with fresh water and set it down in a corner by the coffee table.

"There you go, Lola, drink up," she told the animal. "Dinner will be coming soon."

Despite himself, Colin was surprised. "You've got a dog dish."

She paused for a moment to pet the dog's head. She viewed it as positive reinforcement. "Like I said, this isn't her first time here. And I believe in being prepared."

Obviously, he thought. Colin looked back down at the decorations that covered three-quarters of the living room floor space.

"Are these all your decorations?" he questioned incredulously. He'd seen Christmas trees in shopping centers with less ornaments on them than were scattered here.

"Well, if I'd stolen the decorations, it'd be pretty stupid of me to bring a police officer into my house to see them, wouldn't it?" she asked. Not waiting for a response, she told him, "Half these ornaments belonged to my parents. I've just been adding to the collection over the years."

"And the ten-foot tree?" Colin asked, nodding toward the towering tree. Most people opted for a smaller tree, if they had one at all. He couldn't remember the last time he'd put up a tree for the holidays.

"That was theirs, too. I inherited it. My mother decided that she needed to scale back and get a smaller tree. I couldn't see throwing away a perfectly good tree," she told him. Since he was asking about the tree, she said, "You can help me hang up a few of the ornaments after dinner if you like." Seeing the wary look on his face, she added, "But you don't have to."

The next moment, she turned back toward the kitchen.

"If I'm going to make that dinner I promised you, I'd better get started," Miranda announced. And then she caught him off guard by asking, "Would you like to keep me company?"

Thinking that she might ask him again to hang up ornaments if he chose to remain in the living room, he said, "Yeah, sure, why not?"

Miranda grinned. "That's the spirit. How are you at chopping vegetables?" she asked, moving toward the refrigerator.

"Depends on how you want them chopped," he answered drolly.

"Into smaller vegetables," she answered, her eyes sparkling with amusement. "I just want to be able to cook them faster."

Placing a cutting board and large knife on the counter in front of the police officer, she took three kinds of vegetables out of the refrigerator and deposited those in a large bowl. She put the bowl next to the cutting board.

"Have at it," she told him.

Colin regarded the items on the counter. "You didn't mention that I'd have to make my own dinner," he said.

"Not entirely," Miranda corrected. "It's just a little

prep work," she explained. "I figured you'd want to join in."

Cooking was something he usually avoided. Takeout and microwaving things was more his style.

"And exactly what made you 'figure' that?" he asked.

"Easy," she answered. "You don't strike me as the kind of person who likes standing around, doing nothing while he's waiting."

"I wasn't planning on standing, I was planning on sitting," he told her.

"You'll be sitting soon enough," Miranda promised cheerfully—in his opinion, *nobody* was this damn cheerful. What was wrong with her?

Turning away from the counter, she opened the pantry on the side and took out a medium-sized can from the bottom shelf. He assumed that whatever was in the can was going to be part of dinner. He watched her placing the can under a mounted can opener. Once the can was opened, he was surprised to see her emptying the can's contents into a bowl that was beside Lola's water dish.

She was feeding the dog.

"I take it that wasn't part of our dinner," he quipped drily.

Picking up the large knife, he made short work of the carrots he found in the large bowl.

She grinned at him. He deliberately looked away. "Not unless you have an insatiable fondness for ground up turkey liver."

"I'll pass," he told her.

"Hopefully, Lola doesn't share your lack of enthusiasm," she said, glancing over her shoulder toward the dog. The dog was eating as if she hadn't been fed for days, a fact that Miranda knew wasn't the case. She smiled as she watched. "Looks like she doesn't."

Lola was making short work of the liver that had been deposited in her bowl. Within seconds, the liver was almost completely gone.

A moment later, licking her lips, Lola looked up at her. She made no noise, but it was obvious what the dog wanted.

"Sorry, that's it for now, Lola," Miranda told her, walking away. "Play your cards right and you might get something later after we have our own dinner."

"If I were you," Colin commented as he went on chopping vegetables, "I'd consider myself lucky if she didn't destroy half those ornaments you have strewn all over the floor."

Miranda looked unfazed. "Lola's a good dog. She doesn't destroy things. Her philosophy is live-and-let-live," she told the policeman, taking out a large package of boneless chicken breasts from the top shelf in the refrigerator.

"How do you know that?" he challenged.

"I can just tell," Miranda answered, sounding a great deal more confident than he would have been, Colin thought.

Opening the package, Miranda proceeded to cut each of the individual breasts into tiny pieces with the shears she'd taken out of the utensil drawer. The pieces fell into a big pot that she'd put on the larger of the two front burners.

Watching her, Colin came disturbingly close to cutting one of his fingers with the knife that he was wielding. Sustaining a nick, he pulled back his finger just in time and then, swallowing a curse, he asked, "What are you doing?"

"Getting dinner ready," she answered simply, turning up the burner beneath the pot. Turning, she saw the tiny drop of blood. She took a napkin and attempted to dab at it, but he was not about to cooperate. "Do you want a Band-Aid?"

"No. I'll live." Taking the napkin from her, he wrapped a small piece of it around his finger only to keep the blood from mingling with the vegetables. "What *is* dinner?" he asked.

"Stir-fry chicken and vegetables over rice—unless you'd rather have something else," she offered, dubiously watching his injured finger.

The chicken pieces were already beginning to sizzle in the pot. "Seems a little late for that now," he told her.

Undaunted, Miranda shook her head. "It's never too late."

Colin got the distinct impression that the woman actually believed that—and that she applied it to life.

"Stir-fry chicken is fine," he told her. He was not about to have her start something from scratch. Who knew how long *that* would take?

His response was rewarded with a smile that reminded him more and more of sunshine each time he saw it.

The fact that it did bothered him to no end because he wasn't used to having thoughts like that. His was a dark world and he had gotten accustomed to that. This new element that had been introduced into his world disturbed the general balance of things and he wasn't sure what he was going to do about it if it persisted.

"Good," Miranda responded, stirring the chicken so as to make sure that both sides were browned. "Because that means that we're more than halfway to getting dinner on the table."

There was that word again.

"We."

He wasn't in the habit of thinking of himself as part of a "we."

Granted that he was part of the police department, but he was a motorcycle cop, which meant by definition that he operated alone. He was a loner and didn't worry about having anyone's back. "We" brought a whole different set of ground rules with it and he wasn't comfortable with those rules.

Coming here had been a bad idea, Colin thought. And yet, he wasn't abruptly terminating his association with this living embodiment of Pollyanna, wasn't walking out of her kitchen and her house. He was still standing here, in that kitchen, chopping vegetables like some misguided cooking show contestant.

Something was definitely wrong with him, Colin thought, exasperated.

"Perfect!" Miranda declared.

Taking the large bowl filled with the vegetables he'd just chopped, she deposited the entire contents into the pot. She stirred everything together, then poured in a can of chicken broth, followed by several tablespoons of flour.

Stirring that together, Miranda proceeded to drizzle a large handful of shredded mozzarella cheese into the mixture and added a quarter cup of ground up Parmesan cheese.

Watching her, Colin frowned. "That isn't stir-fry chicken."

"That's *my* version of stir-fry chicken," she clarified and then told him, "Give it a try before you condemn it."

"I'm not condemning it," he retorted. "I'm just saying that it's…different."

"And that's what makes the world go around," she told him with a smile.

Stirring the pot's contents again, she lowered the heat under the pot and turned her attention to making the last additive: the rice.

Measuring out two cups of water and pouring them into a small pot, she told Colin, "I do have a can of beer in the refrigerator. You're welcome to it and you can retreat into the living room if you like."

He glanced toward the living room and saw the German shepherd she'd brought from the shelter. As if on cue, Lola raised her head. He felt as if the dog was eyeing him, waiting for him to step into the room.

To what end?

He wasn't afraid of the dog, but why borrow trouble?

The next moment his mind came to a skidding halt. *Why borrow trouble?* That was a phrase he remembered his aunt used to like to say. He felt something pricking his conscience. He hadn't been to see his aunt for several months. He supposed he should stop by and pay the woman a visit. After all, it was getting close to Christmas and Aunt Lily *was* the reason he'd moved back to this city in the first place.

His aunt would probably approve of all this, he realized.

She'd approve of the decorations lying all over the living room, of the animal shelter dog hovering over the empty dog dish—and most of all, she'd probably *really* approve of this do-gooder-on-steroids who was fluttering around the kitchen, preparing some strange concoction that very possibly might just wind up being his last meal.

"Colin?" Miranda asked when he made no response to her suggestion.

Aware that he had just drifted off, he blinked and focused his attention on Miranda. "What?"

"Would you like that beer?" she asked again, nodding toward the refrigerator.

He glanced over his shoulder toward the living room again. The German shepherd was still looking straight at him. Colin shrugged indifferently.

"No," he answered. "I can wait until dinner's ready."

"Well, guess what?" she said, looking very pleased. "Your wait is over. Dinner is ready and about to be served."

Good, he thought, blowing out a breath. The sooner it was served, the sooner he could leave.

Chapter Nine

Miranda waited for what she felt was a decent interval but the silence continued to stretch out as she and Colin sat opposite one another at the small dining room table.

It was giving every indication that it would go on indefinitely. Even Lola remained quiet, sitting under the table close to her feet.

Finally, feeling the need to initiate some sort of a conversation between them, Miranda looked at her incredibly quiet guest and said a single word.

"Well?"

Colin glanced up at her and then back down at the meal he was presently eating. He assumed she wanted him to make some sort of a comment about the dinner she had served.

"Not bad," he told her.

"Coming from you, that's heady praise," Miranda

commented, amused. "But I wasn't asking if you liked the dinner."

"Seemed like it," he answered. And then Colin put down his fork and gave her his full attention. For a supposedly easygoing woman, she certainly didn't make things easy, he thought. "Then what *were* you asking?"

"I wasn't asking about anything specially. I was just asking for *something*—anything you might want to talk about. You know, most people make conversation when they eat."

He had no interest in what "most" people did. "I usually eat alone," he told her.

"It shows," she answered.

Okay, this had gone far enough. He'd let her feel as if she'd paid him back for the debt she'd mistakenly thought she owed him. But now this was over. It was time for him to go.

Putting the napkin on the table, he began getting up to leave. "Look, I—"

Miranda cut into whatever he was about to say and gave in to her curiosity by asking him, "Why'd you become a police officer?"

The question came out of the blue and caught him off guard.

He stared at her for a long moment, trying to make heads or tails of what was happening here. Was she actually asking him that or was there some kind of other motivation at work here?

"Is this an interview?" he asked sarcastically.

"I'm just curious, that's all," Miranda answered. "Being a police officer is all about 'protecting and serving,'" she said, referring to the popular credo. "You don't look all that happy about protecting and you just don't seem like the type who wants to serve."

He would have said the same thing, but life had a strange way of taking twists and turns. "What I am is someone who doesn't want to be analyzed," he told her curtly.

"I'm sorry, I didn't mean to sound like I'm invading your space, I'm just trying to understand you."

Her answer made no sense to him. "Why?" he challenged suspiciously.

"Because I'd like to be friends and friends understand each other."

"Friends?" Colin echoed, stunned as he stared at her. "We're not friends."

"Not yet," Miranda pointed out in her easygoing manner.

"Not ever," Colin corrected sharply.

He was resisting. Well, she hadn't thought this was going to be easy. "Everyone needs a friend," she told him.

He didn't appreciate the fact that she thought she had his number. She didn't. And if she believed that she did, she was way out of her depth.

"I don't," he snapped. Storming to the front door, he yanked it open.

"Yes, you do," she persisted softly.

If he stayed here a second longer, he was going to wind up saying things that he'd regret saying once he calmed down.

So he bit off, "Thanks for dinner," and left, letting the door slam behind him in his wake.

Miranda stood there, looking at the door for a long, long moment.

Maybe she'd pushed too hard. He was a man who needed to be eased into new situations, into accepting that being alone wasn't the answer.

About to turn away from the door, it occurred to her that she hadn't heard the sound of a car starting up—or pulling away, for that matter.

Curious, she opened the door and found herself looking up into the face of a man who was struggling to come to terms with the fact that maybe he had allowed his temper to flare and then spin out of control much too quickly.

Frowning, Colin mumbled, "I forgot to finish my beer."

"I didn't clear the table," she told him, then asked, "Would you like to come back inside?"

He inclined his head and rather than say "yes" he just followed her back into the house.

Still not ready to apologize or say that he shouldn't have just stormed out the way he had, Colin just asked, "Anyone ever tell you you're too pushy?"

Miranda pretended to consider his question as she walked back into the dining room.

"No," she answered. "Not that I know of."

He snorted shortly. "Then you're either not listening, or you're dealing with people who don't want to hurt your feelings."

"But you don't have that problem," she guessed, a smile quirking her lips.

Colin scowled. "My only problem seems to be you."

"I'll work on that," Miranda promised. And then she nodded toward his empty dish. "Would you like some more?" she asked.

"No, just the beer," Colin responded, sitting down again.

But Miranda wasn't finished being his hostess. "I have some ice cream in the freezer if you'd like to have dessert," she offered.

"Just the beer," he repeated.

"Just the beer," Miranda echoed, backing off for the moment. She smiled at him as she sat down again opposite him.

Colin shook his head. He'd just yelled at the woman and she was smiling at him. He just didn't get it. Blowing out an annoyed breath, he sat back and regarded her in silence for a long moment.

Then, still frowning, Colin forced himself to apologize.

"I'm sorry I lost my temper and yelled at you." This was a first for him. He wasn't used to apologizing.

"It's in the past," Miranda told him cheerfully.

He stared at her, trying to make sense out of what she'd just said. "Yeah. Five minutes in the past." Which meant, as far as he was concerned, that it wasn't in the past at all.

But he realized that wasn't the way Miranda obviously looked at things because she said, "Still the past.

And I'm sorry if you felt that I was invading your space. That wasn't my intention."

"Right. I know. You want to be friends," Colin responded, unable to fully cover up the exasperated edge in his voice. It frustrated him that he couldn't figure her out, couldn't get a handle on the woman.

Who talked like that? Or thought like that? Just what was her angle? There was no way all of this was genuine.

"Would that be so bad?" she was asking him. "Being friends?"

He felt like he was trying to get a sticky substance off his hands—and failing miserably no matter how hard he tried.

He tried one more time to make her understand. "Look, lady, we don't have a thing in common," Colin pointed out. "Not a single thing. You seem to see the world as this wonderful, shining place and I see it the way it really is."

"And how's that?" she asked him, wanting to hear what his answer was.

He never hesitated. "A dark place where everyone's out for themselves."

"I'm not," she told him.

He frowned. He had a feeling that she would say that. "Well, maybe you're the exception."

She'd expected him to say that and she was ready with a response. "And maybe there are more exceptions."

"Pretty sure you're the only one."

"What about your Aunt Lily?" she asked Colin pointedly. "Wouldn't you say that she's one?"

He eyed her sharply. "How do you know what my aunt's like?"

"Easy," Miranda answered. "When you asked me why I was speeding and I told you about being late for Lily's birthday, you said that you had an aunt by that name. One look on your face immediately told me you cared a great deal about that aunt."

"So now you're into face reading," Colin said mockingly.

"Not exactly," she corrected him. "You might say that I'm more into reading people."

Colin drained the last of his beer from the can and set it down on the table. He knew if he lingered, he was going to regret it. The woman was getting to him—and nothing good could come of that.

"I've got to get going," he told her, standing up.

Miranda rose to her feet, as well. Following her lead, Lola came to attention.

"Sure I can't talk you into hanging up a few ornaments with me?" Miranda asked. She was fairly certain that she knew his answer, but she wanted to ask just the same.

"Sorry. I'm totally out of practice," he told her as he started walking out of the dining room for a second time that evening. "I'd probably just wind up breaking them."

The way he said it had her drawing conclusions. "You don't have a Christmas tree?" Miranda asked.

"Not for a long, long time," he answered. "Thanks for dinner—and the beer."

She smiled as she walked him to the door. "My pleasure."

He shook his head. By all rights, she should be relieved he was leaving. He hadn't exactly been the kind of guest that a hostess kept asking to come back—and yet she was acting as if she'd enjoyed his company.

"You are incredible," he murmured.

Miranda's smile widened. "If I was incredible, I'd be able to talk you into coming to the hospital ward to visit my kids."

"You just don't give up, do you?" he asked in disbelief.

"What's the point of that?" she said. "If you give up, nothing happens. This way, there's always a chance that it might."

He made no comment on that. Instead, Colin merely shook his head. "There's such a thing as spreading yourself too thin, you know," he told her, trying to get her to be realistic.

There was that smile again, he noted. The one that told him she knew something that he didn't—and was pleased by it.

"Hasn't happened yet," she told him.

"Doesn't mean it's not going to." It was his parting shot.

He had every intention of going straight home. Heaven knew he'd earned it. Spending time with that chipper do-gooder had really tired him out. Hell, it had all but wiped him out, actually.

But it had also started him thinking. Not about Miranda and what was starting to sound like her endless tally of good deeds. What it had gotten him thinking about was the fact that he hadn't been to see his aunt since…well, he wasn't all that sure when the last time had been, exactly.

So rather than going home and having that beer that was waiting for him in his own refrigerator—a beer that would still be waiting when he finally did get home, he reminded himself—Colin rerouted his path and drove over to his aunt's house.

Of course, his aunt might be out, he told himself as he made his way there. But it was the middle of the week and Aunt Lily wasn't exactly the carousing type.

Colin pulled up in her driveway. If it turned out that she wasn't here, well, he'd tried, and according to that Pollyanna who had insisted on making him dinner tonight, trying was what counted.

After parking his car, he got out and walked up to the front door. It could use some paint. Maybe he'd come by and paint it for her over the holidays. He had a lot of time accrued because he usually didn't take any days off. There wasn't anyplace he wanted to go as far as vacations went, and staying home just meant he'd be alone with his thoughts, which was why he'd rather be working.

Colin rang the doorbell and waited.

He'd give it a total of ten minutes, and if Aunt Lily didn't come to the door by then, well, at least he'd—

"Colin?" The small, genteel woman standing in the doorway was looking at him in utter surprise. "Colin, is anything wrong?"

"No. Why would you think something was wrong?"

"Because it's Wednesday," she said. "I mean, because it's the middle of the week and you never come by in the middle of the week."

"Yeah, well, I don't really come by much at all," Colin admitted, feeling somewhat guilty about that. Especially since Aunt Lily never complained that she didn't see him.

"I know," she responded. Then, obviously realizing how that had to sound, she amended by saying, "I mean..." Reaching up, she touched his face lovingly. "You're sure nothing's wrong?"

"I'm sure." He laughed, shaking his head. "The only thing that's wrong is that I haven't been by much to see you."

"I understand, sweetheart. You've been busy," Lily told him. Wielding guilt had never been her way. Tucking her arm through his, she gave in to the sheer pleasure of seeing him. "Come in, come in. Have you eaten?" Not waiting for an answer, she offered, "Can I fix you something?"

"I already had dinner, Aunt Lily," he told her.

She closed the door behind him and then turned to look at her nephew.

"Today? You had something to eat today?" she questioned, then went on to say, "You look so thin."

"The department doesn't like to see fat motorcycle cops, Aunt Lily. It's hard on the bikes."

Lily shook her head. "It's a wonder they can see you at all. Are you *sure* I can't get you something to eat?"

In her own way, his aunt was as persistent as that

do-gooder was. "How about coffee?" he said. "I'll take some coffee."

"How about some banana cream pie?" Lily offered, preceding him to the kitchen. "You used to love banana cream pie when you were a little boy," she recalled.

He knew she wouldn't stop until he agreed to have something, and obviously coffee wasn't going to cut it. "Okay, I'll have a piece of pie. But I really just came by to see how you were."

Lily smiled. "I'm wonderful now that my favorite nephew's stopped by."

"I'm your only nephew, Aunt Lily," he reminded her, amused.

"That makes this that much more special.," She gave him one final penetrating look. "You're absolutely certain nothing's wrong?"

"Absolutely," he assured her.

"All right, then come to the kitchen and let's have some of that pie," she told him, hooking her arm through his again. Smiling up at his face, she said, "I've been dying for an excuse to have some—and this is certainly it."

"Glad to help," Colin told her.

Lily merely smiled.

Chapter Ten

Colin realized that he was more on edge and alert than usual. That was because he kept looking around for Miranda to pop up. He told himself that he *didn't* want to run into her. If he saw her coming, he could avoid her.

So he remained vigilant, expecting the woman to materialize somewhere along his usual route, the way she had the day she'd waylaid him about that little girl's missing mother.

He didn't drop his guard when he walked into the precinct, since she'd turned up there, as well.

But she didn't turn up there, nor did she track him down along his route. Not that day, nor the next day. Nor the day after that.

When the third day passed, he told himself he should feel relieved. That maybe "the curse" had been lifted.

But he didn't feel relieved. Instead, he had this uneasy, growing feeling of impending doom. He sensed that the second he let his guard down, Miranda would strike again.

The odd thing was that he felt edgier when she wasn't around than when she was and he was interacting with her.

So after the third Pollyanna-free day came and went, he began to think that something was wrong. Rather than leave well enough alone, he found himself needing answers in order to gain some sort of peace of mind—or a reasonable facsimile thereof.

Maybe she hadn't been around because Lily's mother had taken a turn for the worse. Or possibly that German shepherd Miranda had brought home with her—Lulu or Lola or something like that—had turned on her. It had been known to happen.

Not all German shepherds took after Rin Tin Tin, although Colin was still annoyed with himself for not just being grateful that she wasn't around, but actually seeking her out.

He refused to examine what he was doing, because if he had, he would have labeled himself as certifiably insane. What else would you call willingly leaping out of the frying pan into the fire?

As if in self-defense, he jabbed the doorbell before he could think better of it, get into his car and drive away as if the very devil was after him.

Run, you idiot! Get out of here before it's too late!

But he didn't.

He heard barking in the background the second he pressed the doorbell. Either that canine Miranda had brought home had turned into a guard dog, or she was trying to get his attention because something had happened to her mistress.

Damn it, what the hell was wrong with him? Colin wondered. He didn't *think* this way.

Calling himself a few choice names, he turned on his heel and began to walk away.

"Colin?"

Miranda had the same surprised note in her voice that he'd heard in his aunt Lily's when he'd showed up at her place.

Apparently nobody expected him just to drop in. So why was he doing it?

"Yeah." Colin answered almost grudgingly, half turning toward her. "I just wanted to make sure everything was all right—with Lily's mother," he added belatedly, not wanting Miranda to think that he was here checking up on her.

Knowing the perverse way the woman's mind worked, he'd never hear the end of it if she thought that.

Miranda's surprise gave way to a welcoming smile. "She's doing fine, thanks to you," she told him. She opened the door farther. "Why don't you come on in? Lola would love to see you," she added, glancing over her shoulder to the German shepherd, who was fairly leaping from paw to paw.

As if she knew that she had temporarily taken center stage, the dog barked at him.

Miranda laughed, then told her visitor, "And I've got some more beer in the refrigerator."

When he still made no move to come in, she took

hold of his arm and coaxingly pulled him across the threshold.

He should have made his getaway when he had a chance, Colin thought, allowing himself to be drawn in.

And then he thought of her offer. "Do you even drink beer?" he asked.

"No."

Okay, like everything else that had to do with her, that made no sense. "Then why do you have it in your refrigerator?"

That was easy to explain. She released him. "A few of the women I work with at the hospital and the animal shelter stop by on occasion. I keep the beer on hand for them."

Again Colin told himself he'd made a mistake in coming here. "I can't stay—" he began.

Miranda felt that maybe he needed to be coaxed a little more. "Well, you came all the way over here, so surely you can stay for one beer."

"It's not that far from your place to mine," he protested. His point was that he hadn't gone out of his way all that much—but he realized his mistake the moment the words were out of his mouth. He'd inadvertently given her too much information.

Her next words confirmed it.

"So you do live in Bedford." Not all members of the police department did. "What neighborhood?"

He was not about to compound his mistake. "There are stalking laws on the books, you know."

There was a knowing, amused smile on her lips.

"You're the one who showed up on my doorstep, and at the animal shelter before that," she pointed out.

He was immediately defensive. "Are you saying you think I'm the stalker?"

"I'm just saying it's only fair that I know where you live, since you know where I live." With a wink, she added, "Not everything has a hidden agenda. Sit," she told him. "I'll go get that beer."

When she walked back in, she saw that he was still on his feet and was looking at the Christmas tree.

"Haven't gotten very far decorating it, have you?" he commented.

Miranda handed him the cold can of beer. "Like I said, I only get to hang up a few ornaments every night. I can't seem to convince Lola to hang up any while I'm out." When his eyes narrowed and he looked at her, puzzled, she told him, "That's a joke."

"I never know with you," he admitted drolly.

She would have loved to just sit down beside him and talk, but she had a feeling he might think she was crowding him. It would seem more natural to him if she worked on the tree, so she asked, "Would you mind if I put up some decorations while you're here?"

Colin waved a careless hand. "Don't let me keep you." As Miranda got back to hanging up the ornaments, he took a long pull from the can. Lola had plopped herself next to his feet and looked up at him. The scene was far too domestic for him.

And yet...

"You decided to keep the dog?" he asked, assuming that was why the animal was still here.

"Well, at least until after Christmas," Miranda answered. Arming herself with several decorations, she moved around the tree, seeking out empty spaces. "Everyone who comes to the shelter at this time of year is looking for a cute little dog to give to their kids." She glanced over at the German shepherd and said fondly, "Lola's cute, but she definitely isn't little."

He laughed drily. "That's an understatement." He studied the animal. "She's got to be the biggest female German shepherd I've ever seen. I thought they were supposed to be a little smaller than this."

"Obviously Lola hasn't read the German shepherd handbook," Miranda quipped, stretching to hang up a long silver bell. "But what she lacks in daintiness she makes up for with friendliness. I've been working at the animal shelter for a couple of years now and she's got to be the most docile dog I've ever encountered." Picking up a few more ornaments, she searched for more empty spaces she could reach. "Most dogs freak out when they see a vacuum cleaner, much less when they hear one being operated. Lola, bless her, is completely indifferent to it. I could probably vacuum Lola and it wouldn't faze her in the slightest."

The dog wasn't all that easygoing, he thought. "I heard her barking when I rang the doorbell."

"That's because when she thinks someone is trying to come in, she instantly gets into her protective mode. She's being protective of me," Miranda explained, her voice coming from behind the tree. "Once she sees that I'm okay with you, she's fine."

Colin remained on the sofa, sipping his beer and absently petting the dog as he watched Miranda circling the Christmas tree, hanging up ornaments whenever she found a space.

"Damn," he heard her murmur under her breath. She'd worked her way back to the point where she'd started.

"What's the matter?"

She sighed. "I'm going to have to bring out a ladder from the garage to hang up any more of the ornaments tonight. The tree's beginning to look kind of bottom heavy and I can't reach the higher branches," she explained.

She was doing it again, he thought. Roping him into helping. If he had half a brain, he'd just ignore her.

Sighing, Colin stood up. Leaving his beer on the coffee table, he crossed to her. "Where do you want to hang that?" he asked, nodding at the decoration in her hand.

"Higher than I can reach," she answered.

Taking the decoration from her, he reached up to the branch that she'd obviously targeted and easily hung the ornament on it.

"That looks very nice," she told him, somewhat surprised that he had willingly volunteered to help.

"I wasn't exactly performing brain surgery."

"No," she agreed. "You were performing a service." And then she grinned as she held out another ornament. "You up for another one?"

"Yeah, sure. Why not," he said carelessly, taking the decoration from her and hanging it on the next branch over. Turning to face her, he saw the huge smile on

Miranda's face. "You're grinning like a little kid," he pointed out.

"Why shouldn't I?" she asked. "I've just witnessed a Christmas miracle."

Colin snorted. "Let's not get carried away here."

Her smile only grew; he didn't think that was possible, but it obviously was.

"Getting carried away is fun," she told him. "You should try it sometime."

The thought of doing just that—of getting carried away—popped into his head out of nowhere. It had nothing to do with hanging up decorations or anything even remotely along those lines. In his case getting carried away involved the sudden desire to find out what those smiling lips tasted like.

The thought zipped through his brain like a lightning bolt, daring him to follow through.

Okay, time to go, Colin thought sternly. He didn't know where that thought had come from, but he wasn't about to stick around and risk acting on it.

Turning his back on the tree and the miscellaneous ornaments that still needed to be hung up, he said, "Thanks for the beer—again."

Miranda looked at him in surprise. "You're leaving?"

"Yeah, I shouldn't have stayed this long," he told her. "I just wanted to find out how the kid's mother was doing."

They both knew that was just an excuse, but Miranda nodded as if she wholeheartedly believed what he was saying.

"Thanks for coming by," she said, walking alongside him to the door.

Colin stopped in his tracks. He didn't need an escort. Putting space between himself and the woman was the whole point of his leaving.

"I know my way out," he protested.

"I know that," Miranda answered.

Her tone of voice was friendly but firm, as if to let him know that she *wanted* to walk him to the door and wasn't about to be talked out of it.

As they approached the front door, Miranda began to broach another subject. "Since you're being in such a generous mood…"

Instantly on his guard, Colin looked at her warily. The woman seemed to know just how to get to him. He *knew* coming here had been a mistake on his part.

"Yeah?"

"The kids at the hospital would still love to see you," she told him.

"You just never give up, do you?"

Rather than be insulted or put off by his sharp tone and his question, she smiled as if she'd thought over what he'd asked. "What's the fun in that?"

He scowled. Maybe she thought of this as fun, but he certainly didn't.

He answered her seriously—and hopefully, once and for all. "I can't come to the hospital. We work the same hours."

"That's okay, I'll wait," she answered breezily. "Just tell me what time you can get there."

"Not until my shift is over," he snapped. "By then

you're on your way to one or the other of those two shelters where you volunteer." And that was that.

The next moment, he realized that he really should have known better.

"You know, the good thing about volunteering," Miranda told him cheerfully, "is that it's extremely flexible. There are no hard-and-fast hours for me to maintain."

Colin read between the lines. "I can't get out of this easily, can I?"

"You can." She certainly couldn't force him to come to the hospital. If nothing else, the man was a lot bigger than she was. "But between you and me, I don't think you really want to."

"So you've added mind reading to your list of talents, is that it?" he asked.

"No, no mind reading," she answered. "But as I said before, I can read people pretty well, and despite your bluster and your 'Big Bad Wolf' attitude, I think you're a good guy under all that."

Colin laughed wryly. "I guess it's a good thing you're not trying to earn your money as a mind reader. You'd wind up starving to death."

Her eyes met his—and then she gave him that soul-melting smile of hers. "So then it's a yes?" she asked innocently.

Every fiber of his being was geared up to shout "no" at her, that he wasn't about to be corralled or bullied into agreeing to turn up at a hospital ward like some sort of living, breathing show-and-tell object. He had absolutely nothing to say to one kid, much less an entire ward full of them.

But she was looking up at him with those eyes of hers, those eyes that despite all his attempts to shut them out seemed to get past all his safeguards and burrow right into him, giving him no peace.

"We'll see," he finally growled.

Miranda caught her lower lip between her teeth as if debating what to say next. "So that's a yes?" she asked again.

"No," Colin corrected, holding his ground. "That's a 'we'll see.'"

"Almost as good," she told him with more enthusiasm than he felt the phrase merited. The woman was incredible. She found optimism where absolutely none existed.

The next moment, she joyfully told him, "Thank you!"

With one hand on his arm to steady herself, Miranda rose up on her toes to kiss his cheek in gratitude.

That was the exact moment he turned his head to tell her that he hadn't done anything yet and most likely would not.

He never got the chance to say it, because when he turned his head, her lips made direct contact with *his*.

And just like that, an unexpected, harmless kiss on the cheek turned into something else.

It turned into an actual kiss, and what had started out as fleeting evolved into a great deal more.

Surprised, Miranda began to pull back, but then

paused as their contact blossomed into something far more intense than just a kiss between friends.

Before she knew it, Miranda had her arms around his neck and he had his wrapped around her waist, drawing her closer as the kiss deepened.

He was making her breathless, which in turn was making her head spin.

What was going on here?

And how did she get it to continue?

Chapter Eleven

Colin had no idea what came over him. He had never been one of those men who would size up a woman, biding his time until he could seduce her. It wasn't that he was immune to attractive women. He just felt maintaining any sort of a relationship with one was too complicated, and one-night stands could prove to be troublesome.

He found it easier just to steer clear.

But there was something incredibly compelling about this particular woman that just reeled him in. There was no other explanation as to why he'd sought her out tonight when he didn't have to.

And why else was he even considering showing up at that hospital ward of hers? He'd never thought of himself as someone to take up causes or go that extra mile. Yes, he'd been in the Marines, and yes, he'd become a police officer, but neither had come about out of some compulsive need to help his fellow man. He'd joined the Marines and later the police force because it just seemed like the thing to do at the time. The situations suited him; it was as simple as that.

But although Miranda Steele presented herself as straightforward, there was nothing simple about this woman. And right now, he had an uneasy feeling he was in way over his head. Though he wasn't someone who was ruled by desire, Colin had a feeling there would be no turning back for him if he stayed here a minute longer. And he wasn't all that certain that the road ahead was one he should be venturing onto.

The sound of Lola barking in the background was what finally broke apart the moment—and forced him back to his senses.

Taking a step away from her, he looked at Miranda. Her lipstick was blurred from the imprint of his lips and she looked as dazed as he felt.

He was shaken up inside and it was a struggle not to show it. "Did you do that so that I'd come down to your children's ward?"

That hurt, Miranda thought. Did he really believe she was that kind of person? The kind who physically manipulated people?

"No," she answered, her voice low as she tried to collect herself. "I was just trying to kiss your cheek. *You* were the one who turned his head."

His expression remained stoic and unyielding. "So you're not trying to seduce me into seeing things your way?"

"No, I'm not," Miranda cried, stunned. The moment had shattered and what had seemed so wonderful a second ago no longer was. "Forget I asked you," she told him stiffly.

Damn it, those were tears filling her eyes. He hadn't meant for any of that to happen. He wasn't accustomed to dealing with a woman who didn't have some ulterior motive—except for his aunt.

Hell, he wasn't really used to dealing with women at all, Colin thought, feeling helpless and annoyed at the same time.

Unable to find the right words to express his regret for having hurt her, he marched to the front door, opened it and stepped outside.

He heard the door close behind him. Heard the lock being flipped into place. For just a split second, he considered turning around and knocking on the panel, to apologize.

But words didn't come to him now any more than they had before.

If he tried to say anything, he'd only make things worse, he knew. Communication was not his forte, so instead he walked away.

Numb, confused, Miranda wiped away the tears sliding down her cheeks with the back of her hand. She wasn't all that sure what had just happened here. All she knew was that Colin had taken off like a man who had been ambushed and then suddenly given the chance for a clean getaway.

She heard a car starting up and then taking off.

His car.

She didn't understand. He had given off mixed signals. Why had he bothered coming over in the first place?

Turning away from the door, she sighed. "I really do wish I was a mind reader, Colin. Then maybe I could understand what's going on here."

She realized that she was absently running her fingertips along her lips. She could almost swear she could still feel his lips against hers.

Taste his lips against hers.

She closed her eyes for a moment, trying to focus her brain. She'd never been the type to let a guy throw her, or mess with her mind. But she'd never *felt* what she had felt this evening when he'd kissed her.

"C'mon, Miranda, this isn't like you. Get a grip." Opening her eyes, she saw that Lola was looking at her as if she understood what was going on here.

"You're right, Lola. I don't have time to waste like this. We have a tree to decorate and we don't need anybody's help, right, girl?"

Lola yipped, making her laugh.

"Of course right. So let's get started. I'll hang, you supervise. Deal?"

Lola barked again.

"Deal," Miranda agreed, grinning.

With that, she went to the garage to get the ladder she was going to need in order to reach the higher branches.

Colin did his best to talk himself out of it and he succeeded.

For a day.

But the following day, he did something he had never done before. He called in and told his sergeant that he was taking half of one of his many accumulated vacation days.

The man sounded rather surprised. "Just a half day?"

"That's all," Colin answered.

If he took the whole day, he knew he'd wind up getting roped into spending the entire time visiting sick kids—kids who didn't have the odds in their favor. He didn't like admitting that he wasn't strong enough to face something like that for more than a short amount of time.

It was obvious that Miranda was made of stronger stuff than he was, which was why he was going to the oncology ward as she'd wanted him to. He owed her an apology for the way he'd behaved the other night, and this was the only way he knew how to apologize.

He was probably going to regret this, Colin thought, not for the first time. But if nothing else, he was a man who always paid his debts. It was part of his code.

Miranda peered into one of the few private rooms that were located on the floor. Jason Greeley still appeared to be asleep. His mom had been here with the little boy all night. But the single mother had to go to work, so had left an hour ago. Since then Miranda had been checking on the five-year-old every few minutes. She didn't want him waking up by himself.

Moving closer to the boy, she adjusted his covers. "You usually don't sleep this long after a treatment, Jason," she said, deliberately sounding cheerful. Cheer begot cheer, in her opinion. "Don't turn lazy on me now. Your mama was here all night. She hates leaving you, but she had to go to work. But don't worry, she'll be back soon. And I'll be here all day until she gets here," Miranda promised.

The boy stirred a little, but didn't open his eyes. His even breathing told her that he was still sleeping.

Miranda went on talking as if he could hear every word she said. "I've got cherry Jell-O waiting for you the second you open your eyes. You told me that was your favorite, so I made sure there's plenty. All you have to do to get some is open your eyes. C'mon, baby, it's not that hard."

When he didn't, Miranda sighed. "Okay, play hard to get. But you're going to have to open them some-time. No sense in letting all that cherry Jell-O go to waste, you know."

"How do you do it? How do you deal with this with-out falling apart?"

Startled, pressing one hand against her chest to con-tain the heart that had all but leaped out, nearly cracking her rib cage, she swung around to see Colin, all 6'2" and broad-shouldered, standing just inside the room. He was wearing his police uniform.

It took her a second to find her voice. "What are you doing here?"

"I was in the neighborhood and thought I'd drop by," he quipped. And then his voice lowered. "Besides, I fig-ured after the other evening, I kind of owed it to you."

She wasn't sure if he was referring to the kiss they'd shared or his walking out on her, but felt it best not to pursue the question. He was here, and right now, that was all that mattered.

"You don't owe me anything," she told him. "But these kids will get a big kick out of seeing a real police officer." And then she glanced at her watch. It was early. "Speaking of which, aren't you supposed to be out there, handing out tickets right now?"

"I took half a vacation day." He expected her to ask him why he hadn't taken a full day, followed by a whole bunch of other questions. Instead she just smiled at him, looking pleased.

"That's great," she enthused. "But if you're only here for a little while, we'll have to make the most of it."

He wasn't sure exactly what she had in mind, but he'd come to expect the unexpected with Miranda. "And exactly how are we going to do that?"

Her mind was already racing. "We've got a big recreation room where the kids play games and where we hold their birthday parties. Right now, it's where we put up the ward's Christmas tree."

"But all the kids aren't—"

She knew what he was going to say—that there were more holidays than just Christmas this season. She answered his question before he had a chance to voice it. "That's all right. All kids like bright lights and presents. It helps to cheer them up a little."

"And feel normal?" he guessed. That had to be what she was shooting for.

"They *are* normal," Miranda told him calmly. She had to make him understand. "They just have more than their share of health issues, but you'd be surprised how they bear up to that. It makes me ashamed when I let everyday, mundane problems overwhelm me."

"You? Overwhelmed?" he asked, teasing her. "I don't believe it. Joan of Arc would probably see you as a role model."

That was his idea of a joke, she realized. Her smile widened.

"Mama?" Jason opened his eyes and looked around the room, disoriented, obviously expecting to see his mother there instead of his nurse and a strange policeman.

"Hey, I didn't mean to wake him up." Colin looked contrite as he addressed Miranda. "I'm sorry," he murmured.

She put her hand on his arm to keep him from leaving. "No, this is a good thing," she assured him. "We were waiting for him to wake up." She turned her attention back to the boy. "Jason, guess what? Remember that police officer I told you about?"

"The one who wouldn't give you a ticket," Jason answered. "I remember."

"That's right, he didn't give me a ticket," she repeated, raising her eyes to Colin's for a moment before shifting them back to the boy. Colin looked surprised. "Well, this is him—and he's here to visit," Miranda announced.

"Cool," the little boy said, with as much enthusiasm as he was able to muster, given that he was still trying to come around. Shifting in his bed, he looked to Miranda for help. "I want to sit up."

Colin was about to press a button on the remote control attached to the guardrail on the boy's bed when he saw Miranda slowly shake her head at him.

"You remember what to do, Jason," she prompted. "We practiced."

"Oh yeah." Small fingers pulled the remote a little closer and then pushed one of the arrows. The back of his bed began to rise. He beamed, looking very proud of himself. "I got it right."

"Of course you did." She tousled his hair affectionately. "That's because you're such a smart boy."

Jason's chocolate brown eyes shifted to look at the policeman who had come to visit him. "Is that a real badge?" he asked, pointing toward Colin's chest.

He glanced down and nodded. "It sure is."

Jason looked at him hopefully. "Is it okay if I touch it?"

Colin came closer and leaned over the boy's bed. "Go ahead."

Small fingers reached out and very slowly and reverently traced the outline of the badge.

"Wow," Jason murmured. "When I grow up, I'm gonna be a police officer just like you."

No one had ever said anything like that to him before—since he didn't interact with children—and Colin found himself truly moved, more than he thought possible. Especially since the boy was talking so positively about a future he might not live to see.

"And you'll be a really great police officer. Maybe even a police detective, if you study very hard," Miranda told the little boy. She could see that Colin had been affected. It wasn't that she wasn't as moved as

Colin. She had just learned to handle her own onslaught of emotions so they wouldn't get in the way of her being the best possible nurse she could be for the sake of the children.

"I'll study *real* hard," Jason promised. He sounded sleepy. And then he yawned. "I'm tired, Miranda."

"Well, then I suggest you'd better get some sleep," she coaxed.

It was obvious that he was trying not to let his eyes close. "But then I'll miss seeing Officer Colin," the boy protested.

"Tell you what," Colin said. "I'll come by again and see you before I leave."

"And will you be back tomorrow, too?" the little boy asked. It was clear that he was losing his battle to keep his eyes open.

"Not tomorrow," Colin answered honestly. "But I'll come back soon."

"Promise?" Jason asked sleepily.

"I promise," Colin told him, saying the words as solemnly as if he were talking to an adult.

But the boy was already asleep again.

Miranda moved the covers up higher on Jason's small body. "That was very nice of you," she told Colin with genuine warmth.

He shrugged. "I didn't do anything out of the ordinary."

"Jason might argue with you about that—if he could argue," she added, looking at the boy with affection. She glanced at her watch. "C'mon, we need to spread that charm of yours around before your coach turns into a pumpkin."

Colin shook his head, mystified. "I never understand half of what you're talking about."

Miranda laughed. "You might just be better off that way."

He inclined his head in agreement. "I was thinking the same thing."

But Miranda didn't hear him. She was on her smartphone, busy summoning the other nurses.

Chapter Twelve

In less than three minutes after Miranda finished making her call, the hallway outside Jason's room was alive with activity.

As Colin looked on in amazement, nurses and orderlies pushed children in wheelchairs and patiently guided others who were using walkers, crutches or braving the way to the recreational room on their own under the watchful eye of an aide or a parent.

To Colin, it looked as if an organized mass evacuation was having a dry run. The whole thing seemed incredible to him, given the average age of the children. However, rather than leaving the building, everyone was going to the large recreation room that currently held the Christmas tree.

Glancing back, Miranda realized that the "guest of honor" directly responsible for this mass migration was still standing just outside Jason's doorway. Determined to change that, she took Colin's hand in hers.

"C'mon," she coaxed.

The expression on his face was rather uncertain as he took in the masses. "That's an awful lot of kids," he told her.

She gently tugged on his hand. "They don't bite," she said cheerfully. "And having them all together in one place means you won't have to repeat yourself. You can say things just once."

The uncertain expression deepened. "What things?"

Miranda had nothing specific to offer, but she was confident that issue would be resolved naturally.

"It'll come to you," she promised. "And the kids'll probably drown you in questions once they get started. C'mon," she coaxed again, drawing him down the hallway. "You're not afraid of a bunch of little kids."

She said it as if she believed it, Colin thought. And it wasn't the kids he was afraid of; he was afraid of inadvertently saying something that might wind up hurting one of them.

But now that she had started this parade of hospitalized children, like some sort of modern-day Pied Piper, he couldn't very well hang back and watch from the sidelines. The sidelines had virtually disappeared in any case, as Colin found himself surrounded on all sides by children streaming into the rec room.

"Kids," Miranda said in a slightly louder voice, when the commotion had died down and the children had all settled in. "This is my friend Officer Kirby. When I told him that some of you had never met a policeman or seen one up close before, he insisted on coming by to say hello." Turning to look at Colin over her shoulder, she grinned at him and said, "Say hello, Officer Kirby."

On the spot and feeling decidedly awkward, Colin murmured, "Hello."

The moment he did, a cacophony of "Hellos," mostly out of sync, echoed back at him.

Pattie, a little girl with curly red hair seated in a wheelchair in the front row, was the first to speak up. "Are you really a policeman?" she asked.

"Yes." And then, doing his best not to sound so wooden, Colin added, "I am."

The two extra words seemed to open up the floodgates. Suddenly he heard questions coming at him from all directions.

"Do you have a gun?" one boy in the back asked.

"Do you shoot people?" a boy beside him added.

"How many bad guys have you caught?" a little blonde girl ventured, while a smaller girl with almost violet eyes shyly asked him if he was "a good cop."

Taking pity on him, Miranda spoke up, hoping that the piece of information she told them would somehow help the children to get a better image of the kind of police work he did. "Officer Kirby rides a motorcycle."

A dark-haired boy with crutches beside his chair cried, "Cool!"

A little girl to Colin's left asked, "Can you do a wheelie?"

"Did you ever fall off your motorcycle?" one little boy wearing a brace asked. "I fell off my bicycle once and broke my neck bone."

"Your collarbone," Miranda corrected gently.

"Oh yeah, my collarbone," he amended. He was still waiting for an answer. "Did you ever fall off?" he asked again.

"No," Colin answered. "I never have."

"Did it take you a long time to learn how to ride your motorcycle?" a little girl sitting near the Christmas tree asked.

As he began fielding the questions a little more comfortably, more and more came his way. Before he knew it, Colin found himself immersed in a give-and-take dialogue with approximately twenty-five children of varying ages, confined to the hospital ward for a number of different reasons.

He was surprised, given the relative seriousness of their conditions, how eager the children all seemed to hear about his job and what he did on his patrols.

Some asked run-of-the-mill questions, like how long it had taken him to become a police officer. Others wanted to know what he thought about while he was out on patrol. Still others asked totally unrelated questions.

The queries came one after another, some voiced eagerly, others shyly, but there were no awkward silences. Everyone had questions, usually more than one. Or two.

Pleased, Miranda stood back, happy to see the children so caught up in their visitor. She kept a watchful eye on Colin, as well, ready to step in if it got to be too much for him. But as the minutes went by, she was fairly certain that he was doing fine. He didn't need her to bail him out.

When the motorcycle officer answered a little girl

named Shelly's question if he'd ever had a pet hamster—
he hadn't—Miranda finally decided he'd had enough
for one day and stepped in.

"I'm afraid Officer Kirby is going to have to be
going," she told the children. The news was met with
youthful voices melding in a mournful "Oh," tinged
with surprise as well as disappointment.

"Can he come back?" the girl with the curly red hair,
Pattie, asked. Then, not waiting for Miranda to reply,
she took her question straight to the horse's mouth. "Can
you, Officer Kirby?"

"If I get the chance," Colin answered diplomatically.

Progress, Miranda thought. She'd expected him to
make an excuse outright. The fact that he hadn't, that
he'd said something half hopeful in response, made her
feel that he was beginning to come around and see the
light.

He was starting to see the children as people.

"When?" A persistent little boy wearing a wool cap
over his bare head looked at his new hero hopefully.

"When his sergeant can spare him again," Miranda
told the child, grasping at the first handy excuse that
came to her. The look in Colin's eyes when their glances
met assured her she'd come up with a good one. "Now,
everybody, say goodbye to Officer Kirby."

A swell of voices, more enthusiastic since the kids
had gotten to spend some time with him, chorused
loudly, "Goodbye, Officer Kirby," while others added,
"Come back soon!"

Putting her hand on Colin's elbow, Miranda took
control of the situation. She gently guided him out of

the room. They swung by Jason's room and he spent a little time there.

After that, Miranda walked him to the elevators.

"Well, you survived," she observed happily, offering him a pleased smile.

"I guess I did, didn't I?" There was no missing the relief, as well as the surprise, in his voice. Colin paused, looking back over his shoulder in the general direction of the rec room. "Are all those kids...you know...?"

Somehow, even though he'd spent more than an hour talking with them, Colin couldn't get himself to say the word. Saying it made it that much more of an evil reality.

Miranda seemed to know exactly what he was trying to ask her. If the children were terminal.

"Treatments have greatly improved over the last five years. A lot of those kids have more of a fighting chance to beat the odds and get well, or at least have their diseases go into remission. Meanwhile, every day they have is special to them, and we all have to make the most of it.

"They really enjoyed having you come," Miranda went on. "Thank you for letting me bully you into coming to the hospital to talk to them."

"Is that what you call it?" he asked, amusement curving his mouth. "Bullying?"

"No," she admitted honestly, raising her eyes to his. "I don't. But that's what I figure you'd call it, so I thought I'd put it into terms that you could relate to more easily."

Her eyes were at it again, he thought. Doing that funny little laughing, twinkly thing that captivated him.

The elevator arrived and he put his hand against one of the doors to keep it from closing. He searched for words to answer her and finally said, "Maybe I'll let you bully me into it again soon."

There was no other way to describe it but to say that he saw joy leap into her face. "Just say the word," she told him.

Doing his best not to stare, Colin nodded. "Maybe I will," he said.

Stepping inside the elevator, he dropped his hand. Her smile was the last thing he saw before the doors shut.

During the remainder of the day, after he returned to the precinct and went on duty, Colin tried to tell himself that the heat he was experiencing radiating through his chest and his gut was nothing more than a case of heartburn. But he had a strong suspicion that even if he consumed an entire bottle of antacid tablets, that wouldn't have any effect on the warmth that was pervading him.

He should have been annoyed. That pushy woman had invaded his world and messed with his routine. She'd completely messed up the natural order of things.

But somehow, try as he might, he couldn't drum up the slightest bit of irritation. To make matters worse, he caught himself thinking about her.

A lot.

Thinking about her and wondering if he wasn't inadvertently sealing his own doom if he just happened to stop by her place and see her again sometime in the near future.

Like tonight.

Telling himself that it was the holiday season and that everyone was guilty of experiencing some sort of generosity of spirit—why try to be different?—he didn't go home after his shift was over. Instead, he hung around the precinct for a while, killing time by catching up on the paperwork that was the bane of every police officer's existence.

And when he was finished and he'd made sure to file all the reports before leaving, Colin decided to play the odds. For this to work out, Miranda needed to be home instead of one of the two places she volunteered.

He had less than a fifty-fifty chance of finding her there, but he went and picked up a pizza anyway.

With the tantalizing aroma from the pizza box filling the interior of his vehicle, Colin made one more quick stop, at a pet store that was along the way, and then drove on to his final destination, Miranda's house.

He wasn't aware of holding his breath that last half mile until he found himself releasing it.

Her car was parked in the driveway.

Apparently, Miranda was done doing good deeds for the day, Colin thought happily as he parked his vehicle at the curb and got out.

When he passed her car on the way to her front door, he felt heat coming from her engine.

She must have gotten home just minutes ago, he thought with a faint smile.

Juggling the extra-large pizza, Colin rang the doorbell. Inside, Lola instantly began barking. The familiar sound was oddly comforting, though he couldn't begin to explain why. He was afraid that if he thought about it too much, he'd turn right around and go home. Coming here like this carried many implications, and he wasn't sure he was ready to face them.

The best way to deal with those implications at the moment was just to ignore them. Ignore them and focus on the hungry feeling in the pit of his stomach. The one that involved not having eaten.

When Miranda opened the door she was obviously more than a little surprised to see him.

"Hi, what's up?"

"Um, I thought that since you made me dinner that other time, I should reciprocate." Rather than continue— because he felt himself about to trip over his tongue—he held up the cardboard box. "Pizza," he added needlessly, since the aroma—as well as the shape and the label— clearly gave away what he had brought.

"You made me a pizza?" Miranda asked, amused.

Her question threw him for a second. "What? No. I picked this up on the way over here. I guarantee you wouldn't want to eat any pizza that I made," he told her with a self-depreciating laugh.

"Oh, it couldn't be all that bad," she stated, ushering Colin in and then closing the door behind him.

Lola came bounding over the moment he walked in. The animal's attention was totally focused on him and, more specifically, the aromatic box he was carrying.

Miranda caught the dog's collar to keep the German shepherd from knocking Colin over. "She's happy to see you."

Colin harbored no such illusions. "She smells the pizza," he said.

"And you," Miranda added. "Dogs have incredibly keen senses of smell—and they can separate one thing from another. The pizza's the draw," she agreed. "But Lola clearly *likes* you."

Colin made no acknowledgment of that statement one way or the other. Instead, he took a small paper bag out of his jacket pocket. The sack had the insignia of a local pet store chain embossed on it. Thinking ahead, he had stopped to pick up several doggie treats before coming by. At the very least, he'd wanted to be able to distract the dog for a few minutes so that he and Miranda could have their pizza in peace.

"I brought these for her," he announced, passing the bag of treats to Miranda.

Opening it, she looked inside and then smiled broadly at him.

"I think that before the evening is over, Lola is going to be madly in love with you."

Lola had begun to nudge the paper bag with her nose before Miranda finished her sentence.

"I was just hoping to distract her long enough for us to eat the pizza," Colin explained.

Miranda laughed. "In that case, you should have bought out the entire pet shop. Have you ever watched a dog eat? It's like watching a furry vacuum cleaner. The treats'll be gone before we have a chance to sit down.

"But that's okay," she assured Colin. "I've been

working with her and she's getting to be a little more well behaved than she was." Her grin widened as she added, "We might even get to eat an entire slice apiece before she starts begging for a bite—or ten. The trick," Miranda told him with a wink, "is not to give in."

Easier said than done, Colin thought. The dog was already looking up at her with soulful eyes.

Chapter Thirteen

"I see you finished decorating your Christmas tree," Colin commented as he followed her into the kitchen.

Miranda nodded cheerfully. "Yes, finally. All those boxes and ornaments were starting to make the living room a real obstacle course, not to mention pretty messy. So I made up my mind that I wasn't going to go to bed until I had hung the last ornament on the tree.

"The next day I happily put all the boxes away." She looked down at the dog, who was eyeing the pizza box as if expecting to see slices come leaping out. "This way Lola has a little more room to move around, don't you, girl?"

"She doesn't strike me as the type to be put off by a bunch of boxes," he observed. "I can see her plowing through them."

"She kind of does plow through things when she wants to get somewhere," Miranda agreed.

He set down the pizza box and watched her take a couple plates from the cupboard. She placed them on either side of the box. "I thought you said she was becoming more obedient."

"I said we were *working* on it," she corrected. "Right now," Miranda told him, patting the German shepherd's head, "she's a work in progress."

There was no missing the affection in the woman's voice. "You seem kind of attached to her," Colin observed.

"It's hard not to be." Taking out a bottle of beer, she set it next to Colin's plate. "She's very affectionate and lovable." She saw the confused way Colin was looking at the beer. "I just replaced the can you drank the other day," she explained.

"Uh-huh," he responded, taking her explanation at face value. He waited for her to sit down opposite him. "What are you going to do when someone adopts her?" he asked.

"Be happy for her," she answered.

Her response sounded rather automatic to him. Miranda probably meant that on some level, because she was a selfless person. But on another level, he had a feeling she would miss the German shepherd a great deal if the dog was placed in another home. "Why don't you adopt her?"

Taking a large slice of pizza, she bit into it. And then laughed softly. "If I adopted every dog I fostered, I'd wind up being cited by the police for having way too many dogs in my house. This area isn't zoned for kennels," she reminded him.

He shrugged. After all, she probably knew what was best for her. It was just that there seemed to be a bond between her and the dog she was fostering. But then, he hadn't known Miranda all that long and most likely she was like this with all the dogs she took care of—just like she was with all the children she looked after at the hospital.

"This is really good pizza," she commented. Looking at the box, she read the name written across the top. "Rizzoli's." She shook her head. It didn't ring a bell. I don't think I'm familiar with that chain."

"That's because it's not a chain," he told her. He was finishing up his second slice and then slid a third one onto his plate in between washing them down with beer. "It's this little hole-in-the-wall of a place in the next town. Easy to miss," he told her. "It's been there for about twenty years. I discovered it when I moved back to Bedford."

"The next town?" Miranda repeated. "That's a long way to travel for something that's available in practically every shopping center in Bedford."

Colin shrugged and then his eyes met hers. "Sometimes quality is worth going the extra mile or so."

Miranda grinned. Leaning over, she took her napkin and wiped away a dab of sauce from the corner of his mouth. Maybe it was her imagination, but she could have sworn a spark of electricity zapped through her. "I'm glad you think so."

What was she up to? he wondered, and why was he

so captivated by her? Why wasn't he just walking out instead of sitting here across from this do-gooder?

"Why do I feel like I'm being set up for something?" he asked Miranda.

"Because you're a cop and you're naturally suspicious," she replied with a warm laugh. "You're not being set up for anything," she told him, and heaven help him, he believed her. "Besides, setting you up would be an awful way to pay you back for bringing over this really great pizza."

Lola had been whimpering since they'd started eating. Her whimper was growing louder by increments. Obviously antsy, the German shepherd had moved from Miranda's right side to her left and then back again, watching her with big brown eyes that seemed to grow larger each time she moved.

Upping her game, Lola dipped her head and slipped it under Miranda's arm, nudging it.

Miranda laughed. "Okay, okay, I surrender." Tearing off a piece from her slice, she held it out to the dog. Less than half a second later, the piece was gone, disappearing between Lola's teeth.

"Hey, you could lose a finger that way," Colin warned, instantly alert.

"No, she's very careful," she assured him. "For a dog with such big teeth, Lola's incredibly gentle when she takes food from my hand."

He knew that in Miranda's place, he would have flinched, hearing those teeth click shut. But she had remained completely unfazed. "I take it this isn't the first time she's eaten out of your hand."

"No, it's not," she confirmed. "Lola likes to kibitz when I'm having dinner."

"You're spoiling her," he told her. There was disapproval in his voice.

It was Miranda's turn to shrug. "Lola's been through so much, I figure she's entitled to a little spoiling." As he watched, Miranda's expression darkened. "Her last owner chained her up in the backyard, then beat her and starved her. He didn't give her any water, either."

"How did Lola wind up at the shelter?" Colin asked her.

"A neighbor heard her whimpering and looked over this guy's fence. Lola was half-dead. Horrified, he called the police. They arrived just in time. Another couple of days and Lola would have died," she told him fiercely. "Needless to say, they took her away."

Colin had set his beer down when she started telling him about Lola's background. "What happened to the owner?" he asked.

Every time she thought about the incident, Miranda was filled with anger.

"He got off with a fine. If it were up to me, I would have had him drawn and quartered in the town square and made an example of." She saw Colin looking at her incredulously. She wondered if she'd set off some alarms in his head since, after all, the man was a police officer. "What?"

"I've just never seen you angry before. I didn't think you were capable of it," he confessed.

"Oh, I'm capable of it all right," Miranda assured him. "Cruelty of any kind gets me very angry—especially when it comes to children or animals." She saw his re-action. "Why are you grinning?"

For once his poker face failed him. "You look kind of…I don't know…*cute* when you get angry like that. You don't exactly fit the part of an avenging angel, that's all."

Miranda pressed her lips together, but her anger was abating. Her eyes did narrow a little, though. "You're making fun of me," she accused.

"No, not really." He polished off yet another pizza slice. "It's just nice to know that you have this darker side to you. Up until now," he admitted, "I wasn't sure you were human."

"I'm all too human," Miranda told him. She pushed away her plate. "I'm also stuffed."

Colin doubted it. "You only had two and a half slices," he pointed out.

"And I'm stuffed," Miranda repeated.

"How?" he asked. He nodded at the dog, who was still circling the table. "Lola could probably eat more than you just did."

"Undoubtedly," Miranda agreed with a laugh. She watched the dog for a moment "She burns it all up run-ning around in the backyard."

Colin snorted. "And you, of course, just lie around like a slug."

Tickled, Miranda grinned at his assessment. "I don't need much fuel."

He nodded at her empty plate. "Obviously."

Her attention shifted toward the open pizza box. There were several slices still in it. "Speaking of which, why don't you take what's left home with you when you go? You can do it more justice than I would. And if you leave it here, I'll only wind up giving it to Lola when she starts begging."

He sighed, shaking his head. "You're going to have to learn how to say no."

Amusement curved her mouth as she raised her eyes to his. "I'm working on it."

For just a moment, he wondered if Miranda was putting him on some kind of notice—and if she felt she needed to. Which in turn led him to wonder why. Was she afraid that he thought bringing over pizza entitled him to make a move on her?

Where the hell had that come from? Colin silently demanded. He was here because he was paying her back for the dinner she'd made him, nothing more. He certainly wasn't thinking of her in any sort of a romantic light. Just because they'd accidentally kissed didn't mean he wanted to capitalize on it—even if it *had* been a memorable kiss.

Damn it, he upbraided himself, he was overthinking the whole thing. Maybe he *should* go home now.

As he wrestled with his thoughts, Miranda rose and took her plate to the sink.

He still had part of a slice—his fifth one—on his plate. Making a decision, Colin picked up what was left of it and lowered his hand to Lola's level.

On cue, the German shepherd quickly rounded the table to his side. Colin hardly saw her open her mouth. Just like that, the pizza was gone.

"Now who's spoiling her?" Miranda asked with a knowing laugh.

Colin's shoulders rose and fell in a careless shrug. "I don't like seeing food go to waste," he told her.

"Neither do I," she replied. "Of course, if I keep this up with Lola, she is definitely going to wind up being a blimp."

He looked at the dog, who seemed to know that no more slices were coming her way tonight. With a satisfied yawn, she stretched out at his feet.

This was far too domestic a scene, Colin thought uneasily. He really should be on his way home.

But somehow, he remained sitting where he was. "I don't think there's much chance of that," he told Miranda. "She looks pretty lean to me."

"Hear that, Lola?" Miranda asked. She finished drying her hands and left the towel hanging on the hook next to the refrigerator. "The nice police officer just paid you a compliment."

Hearing her name, Lola barked in response.

Miranda's eyes crinkled as she suppressed a laugh. "She says thank you," she told Colin.

"You didn't tell me you can communicate with dogs." But to be honest, it wouldn't have surprised him if she said she did.

"You don't have to speak the language to be able to communicate," Miranda answered. Rather than sit down at the table again, she paused and glanced toward the rear of the house. "Oh, by the way, I have something for you."

"What do you mean by 'something'?" he asked warily, on his guard.

"Don't look so worried. It's not a bribe," Miranda teased. "It's harmless. Wait right here." With that, she hurried out of the kitchen. "I got it on my lunch break," she called, raising her voice so that it carried back to him.

Minutes later, Miranda returned to the kitchen, carrying a two-foot potted fir tree. The tree was decorated with a string of lights and tiny silver and blue Christmas balls.

"This is for you," she told him, setting the tree on the table. "I took a chance that you still hadn't gotten a Christmas tree."

"I didn't," he answered.

Colin was about to add that he had no plans to get one and that he *never* got a tree at Christmas time. The last time there'd been a Christmas tree in his house, he was living at his aunt's and the tree in question had been hers, not his.

But something stopped him from telling Miranda any of that, at least for now.

"I was going to get a bigger tree, but I didn't think you'd want it, so I settled for this small, live one," she explained.

He didn't want one at all, but since she'd gone to the trouble of going out and buying it for him, he bit his tongue and refrained from saying that.

Instead, curious, he asked her, "Did the tree come with decorations?"

"Not exactly," she confessed. "But to be honest, I

didn't think you'd decorate it if I handed you a naked tree, so I did it for you. It was kind of fun, being able to deck out a Christmas tree in half an hour." Her momentum picked up as she added, "And when the season's over, you can plant it in your backyard."

"Just one problem with that," Colin told her. He broke off a small piece from one of the remaining pizza slices. Out of the corner of his eye, he saw Lola come to attention again. "I don't have a backyard."

Miranda never missed a beat. "Or you can transplant it into a larger pot as it starts to get bigger." Second-guessing Colin's objection to that suggestion, she offered, "I could do that for you if you're too busy."

"Because you have so much time on your hands," he said with a touch of sarcasm. He felt his conscience taking him to task. Miranda was only trying to be nice, he reminded himself. "Sorry, I didn't mean that the way it came out."

"No offense taken," she told him. "Besides, haven't you ever heard the old saying 'If you want something done, ask a busy person to do it'?"

"No, I haven't. But I'll take your word for it." He looked at the tree with its dainty ornaments and the bright red foil wrapped around its base. "Thanks. It's a nice-looking tree." He left it standing on the table for now. "But you really didn't have to get me one," Colin stressed.

"Let's just say it makes me happy doing so," she told him. "I couldn't stand the idea of you not having at least a little tree—so I got you one."

It was little, but he would have preferred an even smaller one—or better yet, none at all.

Colin pinned her with a piercing look. "But why would that bother you?" he couldn't help asking. "Not having a tree doesn't bother me."

"I know, but it does me." She could see they could go on dancing endlessly around the same point, so she tried something else. "It's a reminder of goodwill toward one another."

It took a lot to suppress the laugh that rose to his lips, but somehow, he managed. "Maybe if everyone thought the way you do, there'd be no need to be reminded. It would just be a given," Colin mused.

"That's the nicest thing anyone ever said to me," she told him, her eyes misting.

"If it's so nice, why are you crying?" he asked. If he lived to be a hundred and fifty, he would never understand women.

Miranda shrugged. "I guess I'm one of those people who cries when she's happy."

Colin shook his head. "Talk about mixed signals," he murmured.

He needed to leave.

He could feel barriers weakening within him, walls being breached and beliefs he'd held as hard and fast truths dissolving like cotton candy left out in the rain.

This woman was turning him inside out without lifting a finger, he thought grudgingly. If he didn't leave now, he didn't know what sort of mental condition he'd be in by the time he *did* leave.

"Okay," he said, rising. "I'd better be going." Belatedly, he remembered the little Christmas tree on the table. "Thanks for the tree."

"Thank *you* for dinner and for coming to the hospital today," she told him. "The kids just couldn't stop talking about you after you left. You were definitely the highlight of their week."

He had no idea how to respond to that. Being on the receiving end of gratitude was totally new to him. "Yeah, no problem."

"Oh, I think it was a problem for you, which was why having you come was so special—for everyone," she added meaningfully.

"You included?"

Now why the hell had he just said that? Was he *asking* for trouble? Colin silently demanded.

Miranda took a breath before answering. "Me most of all."

Chapter Fourteen

The moment, wrapped in silence, stretched out for a long time. He didn't know how to respond to what she'd just said.

Me most of all.

Finally, he stumbled through an awkward answer. "Oh, um, good to know."

Miranda felt sorry for him. Colin looked completely out of his element. Deftly, she changed the direction of the conversation.

"I'll walk you to your car," she offered.

"No," he said, perhaps a little too forcefully. All he wanted to do now was to get into his vehicle—quickly—and drive away. "You don't have to," he added.

She nodded at the things still on the table. "You can't carry the Christmas tree and the pizza box at the same time."

The German shepherd presented herself right next to him, a plaintive look on her face. He read between the lines.

"Um, I think that Lola would probably prefer if I left the pizza here."

Miranda pushed the pizza along the table so it was closer to him.

"Which is exactly why you're taking it with you. Too much people food isn't good for her and you've already seen what a pushover I am around Lola."

He wasn't accustomed to women who owned their shortcomings. He found himself smiling at Miranda in acknowledgment. "That's something you're going to have to overcome when you have kids."

He'd just said *when*, not *if*, Miranda noted. Was that just a careless slip of the tongue on his part, or did Colin really see her as a mother?

She rather liked the idea that he did. Of course, that would have to mean she'd have to slow down long enough to actually *have* a child.

Miranda took the pizza box, leaving the Christmas tree for him to carry. When he picked it up, they began to walk to the front door.

"Disciplining is something that I think I'll delegate to my husband," she told him, adding, "He'll probably be the strong and masterful type."

Colin's laugh was dry as he thought over her comment. "He would have to be."

Miranda cocked her head, trying to decide how he meant that. "Was that a compliment or a criticism?" she asked, curious.

He was talking too much, Colin decided. That had never been a problem for him before he'd met this woman.

"Take it any way you want," he answered, thinking that being vague was the safest way to go right now.

Miranda felt Lola trying to crowd her, attempting to push her way outside.

"No, girl, you have to stay in. I'll be right back," she promised.

Tucking the pizza box under her arm, she cringed slightly as she both heard and felt the remaining slices sliding together.

With her free hand, she gently steered the dog back into the house. Then, trying not to drop the box, she pulled the door closed behind her.

Looking on, Colin said with approval, "You're making progress."

"Well, I had to," Miranda told him. "You were watching me."

"So if I wasn't here…?" He left the end of the sentence up in the air and waited for her to finish it.

She did, but not as he expected. "…I wouldn't have pizza to keep away from her in the first place."

Colin shook his head, impressed despite himself. "I've got to say, you really do know how to dance around a subject."

"I've learned from the best," she said, grinning. She watched his brow furrow as he looked at her over his shoulder, perplexed.

Miranda hadn't meant for it to sound cryptic. Following him to his vehicle, she explained, "Kids. They can spin tales that'll make you dizzy."

Stopping beside his car, Colin looked at her pointedly. "I know the feeling."

He took his keys out of his pocket. Unlocking the doors, he put the potted Christmas tree on the floor in the rear. Taking the pizza, he placed the box on the passenger seat, then turned to face her.

"Well, thanks for your help with the pizza. And thanks for the tree," he added belatedly.

He watched as a smile filled her eyes. "Don't mention it. It's the least I can do after all that joy you brought my kids."

Her thanks made him feel awkward again. "I just showed up," he insisted again, not wanting to make any more out of it than that. But with Miranda he should have known better.

"You did a lot more than that," she insisted. "You brightened up their day. Their parents come as often as they can—and that's a good thing," she assured him. "But having you come to their ward was something out of the ordinary. Something special," she said with feeling.

He opened his mouth and then shut it again. When he saw the curious look on her face, he told her, "Well, I'm not going to argue with you, because I'm beginning to get the feeling that no one stands a chance of winning an argument with you."

"Sure they do," she declared, although, offhand, she couldn't think of a single example to cite.

"Uh-huh." His response as he started to go reeked of skepticism.

"Oh, and Colin?" Miranda called after him, raising her voice.

Colin was about to round the hood to get into his side of the vehicle, but stopped. "Yes?"

"Promise you won't forget and leave the tree in the car. It's a hardy little thing, but if you leave it in the car indefinitely, it'll wilt and lose all its needles."

Indulging her, he promised, "I won't forget."

"Oh, and drive carefully," she called after him.

Colin paused again. He should feel annoyed or insulted that, given the nature of his work, she still felt the need to say something like that to him. And yet this whole scene just made him smile. He had no idea why.

Waiting, he turned around. "Anything else?"

Miranda knew that she was pushing her luck to the absolute limit, but then nothing ventured, nothing gained, right?

Taking a breath, she forged ahead. "Well, there's a Christmas Eve party, if you'd like to come."

He hadn't expected her to say that; he'd just assumed she'd have more trivial slogans to send his way. "At the hospital?"

He'd done his part at the hospital and she was now focusing on the other two places where she volunteered her time.

"Well, yes, there, too," she allowed. "But I was thinking of the shelter."

She still wasn't narrowing it down, he realized. "Homeless or animal?"

"Homeless. Although, now that I think about it, we are having a party at the animal shelter, too," she told him. "It's an adoption party. There's one every month, but there's an extra push to find the animals a home just before Christmas."

"Of course there is." Listening to her, he shook his head. It was a wonder the woman didn't just fall over and collapse. "When do you have time for *you*?" he asked.

"All of this is for me," she responded. Seeing the doubtful look on his face, she insisted, "I derive pleasure out of seeing the animals find new homes and the kids getting better and going back to their families. And the women at the shelter taking stock of their situation and finding a way to create new lives for themselves and their children."

Saints have less to do, he thought. Colin shook his head again, but the corners of his mouth had curved ever so slightly.

"All of this is for you, huh?" He watched as she nodded with feeling. "I don't think I've ever met anyone like you before, Miranda Steele," he told her in all sincerity.

"Is that a good thing?" she asked.

"I'm thinking on it," he answered, remaining deliberately vague.

She couldn't read his expression, and her curiosity was getting the better of her even though she knew it shouldn't. "Let me know what you come up with."

"I have a feeling you'll be the first to know."

Colin suddenly found himself fighting the urge to pull her into his arms. If he didn't leave now, he might wind up doing something stupid, and as unique as this woman was, he didn't need any complications in his life.

He'd already gotten too involved with her as it was.

He needed distance, not closeness, Colin insisted silently.

So why wasn't he getting into his car and leaving? Why was he turning around and crossing back toward the woman?

Miranda was standing at the curb, ready to wave at him as he pulled away.

When instead of leaving, he approached, she looked at him uncertainly, slightly confused even while she felt her heart climbing up into her throat.

Her breath was backing up in her chest. "Did you forget something?"

"Yeah," he muttered. "My sanity."

Her confusion mounted. "I don't know what that means."

Colin didn't respond. At least not verbally. Instead, he took her into his arms just the way he'd told himself not to, and kissed her the way he *knew* he shouldn't.

The way every fiber of his being felt that he just *had* to.

Confusion ran rampant all through Miranda. One moment she was standing at the curb, getting ready to watch Colin drive down the street and disappear; the next moment she found herself smack in the middle of an old-fashioned twister, being sucked up into its very core and whirling around so hard she couldn't breathe. She certainly couldn't think or get her bearings.

But then, bearings were highly overrated, she decided.

Standing up on her toes, Miranda dug her fingertips into his shoulders in a desperate attempt to anchor herself to something solid before she was swept so completely away she would never be able to find her way back again.

This *wasn't* a kiss. She'd been kissed before, kissed by faceless, unremarkable men who faded from her memory before they had a chance to even walk out the door.

But this—*this* was an experience. A mind-blowing, incredible experience that she would remember to her dying day even if she lived to be a hundred and ten.

Colin fought the urge to deepen this kiss and take it to its natural conclusion. Fought the urge to sweep her up into his arms and carry her back inside her house so that he could make love with her. Make love with her until they were both too exhausted to even breathe.

He came within a hair's breadth of giving in to that urge, that desire.

And then a last sliver of sanity rose up, stopping him.

He couldn't do this, he silently insisted, couldn't make love with her. Because if he did, he would be willfully bringing his darkness into her world.

She was a bright, shining ray of light, bent on bringing happiness to everyone and everything. If he took this to its natural conclusion, he would be guilty of if not extinguishing that light, then at the very least dimming it considerably.

He couldn't be responsible for that, couldn't do that to her and all the other lives that Miranda would wind up touching.

Although every fiber of his being fought it, trying to keep him from following through, he separated himself from Miranda. He removed her arms, which she'd wound around his neck, and pushed them down against her sides, held them there for a long moment—until he could collect himself.

"I've got to go," he told her hoarsely.

Then, without another word, Colin got into his car and turned on the ignition. He pulled away from the curb without a single backward glance.

Then, unable to help himself, he looked in the rearview mirror.

Miranda was still standing there at the curb where he had left her.

A pang of regret seized his very being.

Colin struggled with the impulse to turn the car around and head back to her. Instead, he pushed down hard on the accelerator, determined to put more and more distance between them.

"Count yourself lucky," he said, addressing the figure that was growing progressively smaller and smaller in his rearview mirror. "You don't need someone like me in your life."

He had a very strong feeling that if he had given in to himself tonight, if he had weakened and made love to Miranda, he wouldn't have been able to walk away from her, short of being sandblasted away.

That would be a very bad thing.

For her.

Miranda had a sinking feeling as she watched Colin drive off that he could very well be gone from her life for good.

There'd been something about the set of his shoulders, about the foreboding expression on his face as he had removed her arms from around his neck and stepped away, that made her think of an iron gate coming down, separating the two of them.

Cutting her off from him.

But even so, she kept watching for him every time she looked up, every time her attention was drawn to something—a noise, a flash of light out of the corner of her eye.

Every time she raised her eyes, she was looking for Colin.

And every time she did, he wasn't there.

He wasn't leaning in the doorway of any of the hospital rooms belonging to the small patients she attended, wasn't standing across the street from the animal shelter, waiting for her to come out. He wasn't walking into the women's shelter, wasn't ringing her doorbell and standing on the front step until she opened the door.

He wasn't anywhere in her life—except in her mind, and there he had set up housekeeping, big-time.

If she was going to function properly, she was either going to have to purge him from her mind and forget all about him, or else beard the lion in his den, Miranda thought in a moment of madness.

Get hold of yourself, she silently lectured.

She was far too busy for this, far too busy to mentally dwell on a man who—a man who…

In the middle of her rounds, Miranda abruptly came to a dead stop. She'd initially been drawn to the tall, dark, silent police officer not because he could kiss like nobody's business and set her soul on fire. She'd been drawn to him because of the sadness she saw in his eyes. She remembered thinking that Colin needed someone to brighten his world, to help him find hope and hang on to it.

He needed *her*, and somehow, she had lost sight of that.

But not anymore, she vowed. She was back on track and determined to strip that sadness, that darkness out of him until Officer Colin Kirby found a reason to smile of his own accord.

He could keep those lips to himself. That wasn't what was important here. What she wanted was his happiness.

And she was determined to help him find it if it was the last thing she did.

Chapter Fifteen

Despite his resolve, he couldn't seem to get Miranda out of his head. Not that day, nor the next. The harder he tried, the less success he had. His thoughts turned to the bubbly nurse over a dozen times a day. More, if he was being honest with himself.

For the first time in his adult life, Colin's laser-like focus completely failed him.

He couldn't get himself to concentrate exclusively on his work. Images of Miranda's face kept materializing in his mind's eye at the worst possible times, impeding him at every turn.

Colin had never been one to throw in the towel. He struggled to regain control over himself and his thoughts. He'd triumphed over the racking pain of losing his parents—especially his mother, who he'd been so close to—and managed to keep going during his tour overseas when more than half his platoon had been wiped out all around him.

And though they hadn't been close, guilt had skewered him when he'd lost his partner, Andrew Owens, while on the job.

But he'd managed to rise above all that, erasing it from his mind and functioning as if his insides hadn't been smashed into a thousand pieces. He did it to survive, to continue putting one foot in front of the other and moving on the path he found himself on.

But this—this was completely different. For some mysterious reason, he'd lost his ability to isolate himself, to strip all distracting thoughts from his mind.

He'd lost the ability to continue, and he knew he had to resolve this if he had any hopes of functioning and moving on with his life.

He just had to figure out how.

How had this happened? It felt as if Thanksgiving had been only yesterday, then somehow she'd blinked, and now Christmas was a week away and Miranda had more than enough to keep not just herself but half a dozen people busy.

To paraphrase Dickens, it was both the best time of the year and the worst time of the year, mainly because of all the things that were associated with the season. The shelters as well as the hospital needed her more than ever, and there was enough for her to do thirty-six hours a day if she could somehow find a way to create that many hours out of thin air.

But even with everything she had to handle, she

couldn't stop thinking about Colin. Worrying about Colin. It was interfering not just with her ability to devote herself to her work as a nurse, but also as a volunteer—in both areas that used her services.

She needed to talk to Colin, she decided, and she needed to do it face-to-face, not over the phone. Any other means would be far too impersonal.

Because of the hectic pace this time of year generated, taking time off from the hospital was not an option. The only thing she could do was try to shave a little time from her volunteer work. The pace there was hectic, as well, and there were a great many demands on her time whenever she had any to spare. But she *had* to do this. Because not talking to Colin was unthinkable.

The problem was, since she still didn't know where the man lived, the only place she could hope to find him was along the route he patrolled or at the precinct before he went off duty.

However, both conflicted with her shift at the hospital.

Still, maybe if she played the odds and really hurried— and hopefully he was getting off late—she might be able to catch Colin before he left work for the day.

Miranda felt stressed because even if she was lucky enough to catch him, she'd have to talk fast because the women's shelter's Christmas party, the one she'd helped organize for the children, was scheduled to begin the minute she walked through the door.

She was exhausted already.

As Miranda dashed to her car, all set to take off for the precinct, her cell phone rang.

Please let it be a wrong number, she prayed as she took it out of her purse and then quickly put in her password.

The caller ID that came up belonged to the homeless shelter. Specifically, to Amelia.

Maybe the director was just checking in with her, Miranda thought, mentally crossing her fingers as she answered.

"Hi, Amelia." She used her free hand to buckle her seat belt. "What's up?"

"We've got an emergency," the woman said, without even bothering to return the greeting. "I just hung up with Santa Claus. He called to say he's stuck in traffic in LA and he's not going to be able to get here in time."

Miranda knew the director was referring to the man she had hired to play Santa for the kids at the shelter. Thinking of the children's disappointment, she felt her heart sink.

The words came out before she could stop them. "But the kids are expecting to see Santa Claus."

"I know. I know," the director answered. "The toys are here, but they're going to feel really let down that Santa Claus couldn't make it to hand them out."

Her mind going in all directions, Miranda searched for a solution. And then she thought of something. "Do you still have that old Santa suit from last year?"

"I think so," Amelia answered. "The last time I saw it, it was in the storage room, shoved behind some cans of paint. Why?"

"Find it," she told her. "I'll be at the shelter as soon as I can get there," Miranda promised, terminating the call.

So much for waylaying Colin today, she thought, dropping her phone into her purse.

"Looks like you've gotten a reprieve, Officer Kirby," Miranda murmured under her breath, starting up her vehicle and then peeling out of the hospital's parking lot.

She was going to need padding. Lots and lots of padding if she had a prayer of pulling this off. She'd have to have Amelia round up a whole bunch of pillows.

Miranda was still trying to figure out exactly what she would do as she pulled into the women's shelter's parking lot. If she hadn't been so lost in thought, she would have seen him.

As it was, she didn't.

Not until after she'd jumped out of her car and run smack-dab into him, so hard she all but fell backward. Only Colin grabbing her by the arm kept her from meeting the concrete skull-first.

Stunned, for a split second Miranda thought she was hallucinating—until her brain assured her that she really wasn't conjuring Colin up.

He felt much too real for that.

"Colin?" she cried, shaken. "What are you doing here?" Miranda still wasn't a hundred percent sure that she wasn't just imagining him, putting his face on another man's body.

The police officer released her slowly, watching her intently to make sure she was all right.

"I guess I'm not as noble as I thought," he answered with a self-depreciating shrug.

Maybe she *had* hit her head, Miranda thought,

blinking. She didn't understand what he was telling her. "Why?"

"Because," he confessed, "I was going to stay away from you."

Miranda continued staring at him. He still wasn't making any sense to her.

"Why is staying away 'noble'?" she asked.

He might have known she'd want an explanation. This wasn't easy for him to say. "Because I would only bring you down, and you don't need that."

Miranda thought of the kids in the shelter. She was still in a hurry, but the emergency would have to wait, at least for a couple minutes. This needed to be cleared up, and it needed to be cleared up *now*.

"First of all," she told him, "I do have free will and a mind of my own. I'm not just some ink blotter that indiscriminately absorbs whatever happens to be spilled on it—"

"I'm not saying that you're an ink blotter!" Colin protested.

"I'm not finished," she informed him crisply. "And second of all, I can make up my own mind whom I want or don't want in my life. That's only up to you if you don't want to be in my life because you can't abide being around me."

Colin stared at her in astonishment. How could she even *think* that, much less *say* it?

"You know that's not the case." Angry at how the situation was devolving, he had to rein himself in to keep from shouting the words at Miranda.

"Well, then there's no problem, is there?" she concluded. Turning on her heel, she started to walk toward the building.

Before he could think better of it, Colin caught her by the arm to keep her from leaving. "Oh, there's a problem, all right."

Her desire to resolve this warred with her sense of responsibility. She was going to be cutting it very close, Miranda thought. For all she knew, Amelia might not have located the Santa suit yet.

"Walk with me," she requested. When Colin fell into step beside her, she asked him to elaborate on what he'd just said. "Do you want to tell me just what *is* the problem?"

Colin tried to smother his frustration. He felt as if he was talking to a moving target, but then, that was part and parcel of who this unique creature was.

He thought of waving away her question, or just telling her flatly, "no." But he had started this and had to be man enough to own up to it.

Colin forced himself to say, "I can't get you out of my head."

Miranda's eyes were shining. She spared him a smile as they came up to the shelter's double doors. "Still not seeing the problem."

"But you will," Colin predicted.

She highly doubted that. "Then we'll put a pin in this now and talk about it later. Right now, I have an emergency to deal with," she told him as she reached for the door's brass handle.

So she wasn't just running from him, Colin thought.

Taking charge, he nudged her hand away and opened the door for her. "What sort of an emergency?"

She glanced at her watch. "The Christmas party starts in less than half an hour and Santa Claus is still in LA, stuck in traffic."

Okay, this was convoluted, even for her. "You want to run that by me again? And this time, try to speak slower than the speed of light."

Miranda took a breath. "Amelia hired this professional Santa Claus for the party, and now he can't get here in time because he's stuck in traffic. These kids have been disappointed an awful lot in their lives. I'll be damned if I'm going to let it happen again if I can do something about it."

"Just what is it you have in mind?"

"Amelia said there's an old Santa suit here at the shelter. If we can find it, I'm going to play Santa Claus."

Colin looked at her for a long moment. And then he laughed. Hard. It occurred to Miranda that she had never heard him laugh out loud like that before, but now wasn't the time she wanted to hear it. "You got a better idea?"

It took him a second to collect himself and stop laughing. "Sorry, Miranda, I don't mean to laugh at you, but you just don't look like *anyone's* idea of Santa Claus." He paused again, thinking. And then he nodded. "And yes, I've got a better idea."

She thought she knew what he was going to say and she shook her head, shooting down his idea.

"Just handing out the gifts to the kids isn't going to be enough. These children want Santa Claus giving them those gifts. They want to be normal and see Santa Claus, like every other kid this time of year. They've got a right to that," she insisted passionately.

Just seeing her like this nearly undid Colin. "That wasn't the idea I had," he told her. "Let's go see if we can find that Santa suit. I've got a better chance of pulling this off than you do."

It didn't happen very often, but Miranda found herself practically speechless. When she did recover, she cried, in astonishment, "Really?"

Colin nodded. "Really."

Miranda continued staring at him, waiting for some sort of a punch line. When none came, she had to ask, "You're going to willingly play Santa Claus without having me twist your arm?"

He really did like surprising her.

"Without bending any of my body parts," he assured her. "Now are we going to go on standing here talking about it or are you going to take me to wherever you think that Santa suit is stashed so we can get this show on the road?"

Her response to his question sounded incredibly like a squeal. The next second, Miranda had grabbed his hand and was dragging him through the shelter's main room.

Before they had crossed it, Amelia approached them.

"Did you find it?" Miranda asked breathlessly. "The Santa suit?"

"It's in my office." The director seemed a little surprised by the man Miranda had in tow. "Officer Kirby, it's so nice to see you again. Are you going to be join-ing the party?"

Before he could answer, Miranda cried, "Definitely!"

Turning on her short, stacked heel, Amelia followed Miranda and the policeman to her office.

Still somewhat bewildered, the woman sounded un-certain as she asked Colin, "You're not going to be playing Santa Claus for the children, are you, Officer Kirby?"

Glancing her way, Miranda answered the question for him. "It's a real Christmas miracle, isn't it?"

The dignified director was smiling so hard she was practically beaming. "It most certainly is. The suit's going to be a little big on you," she warned Colin. "So I found some pillows." She gestured to some stacked on the battered, secondhand easy chair that stood in the corner of her small office.

Colin briefly glanced at them. "They'll work," he told her.

Looking pleased, Amelia said, "Well, I'll give you some privacy…" And she eased herself out of her office.

"And I'll go get the sack of toys ready so you can hand them out," Miranda volunteered. "I'll meet you back here in Amelia's office. If you finish dressing be-fore I return, wait for me. You don't want to go into the main hall empty-handed."

No matter how much Miranda had built up the im-portance of Santa Claus making an appearance, he knew that the toys were the main attraction. "Not a chance," he assured her.

But as he turned to look at her, he found that he was talking to himself. Miranda had already hurried off.

"That woman's got way too much energy," he murmured as he began to change.

Chapter Sixteen

Miranda turned around when she heard the office door behind her opening. About to tell Colin that she'd gotten the bulging sack of toys for him to hand out while he'd been changing into his costume, she instead wound up saying, "Wow."

"Does it fit all right?" He glanced down at himself critically.

"You look just like Santa Claus," Miranda declared. "I wouldn't have known it was you if I hadn't handed you the costume." She circled him, then nodded with approval. "Laugh."

He eyed her warily. "What?"

"Santa's jolly, remember? You're going to have to go 'ho, ho, ho' at least a few times, so let's hear it."

"Ho, ho, ho," Colin said.

"You're frowning under that beard, aren't you?" she

guessed. "Never mind," she told him when he started to answer. "The beard covers it. But put some gusto into it. And here's your bag of presents." She indicated the sack next to her.

Taking hold of it, he began to swing it over his shoulder. Then his eyes widened. "You carried this here?"

"Dragged, actually," she admitted. "It's kind of heavy."

"That's an understatement," Colin muttered under his breath. "Okay, let's get this over with."

"A little more 'ho, ho, ho' spirit," she advised.

"I'm saving myself," he responded, following her back to the main room.

"Hey, look, everybody! Look who's here," Miranda called out to the children the moment Colin walked into the common area.

The space was filled with kids of all sizes who had been anxiously waiting for the legendary elf to make his appearance. As they turned almost in unison in his direction, their faces lit up with delight, Colin saw.

"It's Santa!"

"Santa's here!"

"Santa!"

A chorus of excited voices called out, creating a cacophony of eagerness and joy blended with disbelief that Santa had actually come to the shelter—and he'd made it ahead of Christmas Eve, as well.

The next second, Colin found himself surrounded as children eagerly rushed up to him.

Miranda took control. Raising her voice, she told the children, "Okay, give him a little space. We don't want to overwhelm Santa. He's still got a lot of places to visit before the holidays are here." Waving the little ones over to her side, she instructed, "Line up, kids. You'll all get your turn, I promise."

As Colin watched in surprise, the children obediently lined up as ordered and patiently awaited their turn.

His eyes shifted in Miranda's direction. This was definitely a new side to her, he thought in admiration.

"That's your cue to get started," she prompted.

"Oh, right." Colin set down his sack and opened it.

To his relief, Miranda stayed by his side the entire time and helped him hand out the gifts. As each child came up to him, she very subtly fed him his or her name to personalize the experience for the child.

Any doubts or uncertainty he'd harbored about volunteering to play Santa vanished within the first few minutes. The excitement, gratitude and awe he saw shining in the eyes of the children who surrounded him managed to create nothing short of an epiphany for Colin.

He began to understand why Miranda did what she did. Being there for these children brought about an incredibly warm feeling that he'd been unacquainted with prior to today.

He really got into the part.

Colin continued digging into the sack and handing out gifts until the very last child in line cried, "Thank you, Santa!" and hurried away, clutching her present against her.

It took him a second to process the fact that there

was no one left in line. Turning toward Miranda, he asked, "Is that it?"

"Yup. You saw every last kid in the place," she told him happily.

The sack sagged as he released it, and it fell to the floor. "Good, because there's only a couple of gifts left. I would have hated to run out of presents before you ran out of kids," he told her. He saw the wide grin on her face. "What?"

"Look at you," she said proudly. "All full of Christmas spirit."

He didn't want her making a big deal of it. "There's a difference between being full of Christmas spirit and not behaving like Scrooge."

"Not in my book," Miranda responded. Leaning into him, she whispered, "Lighten up, Santa, and take the compliment."

Colin glanced down at the suit he was wearing. She saw the look in his eyes and took an educated guess as to what he was thinking. "Itchy, huh?"

He lowered his voice. "You have no idea."

"You held up your end very well," she told him. "Let's get you back to Amelia's office so you can get out of that suit." Miranda looked around at the children, all of whom were happily playing with their toys from Santa. Some were still regarding their gifts in awe. "C'mon, the coast is clear," she whispered. "Let's go."

Following her lead, Colin slipped out of the room. When he didn't hear any of the children calling after him, he breathed a sigh of relief and quickly went down the hall to the small office at the rear of the building.

He went in and was surprised when Miranda followed.

"I'll leave in a minute," she promised, "so you can get out of that costume. I just wanted to indulge a fantasy."

"A fantasy?" he questioned, surprised. She struck him as being so squeaky clean, so grounded, and not the type to have fantasies. His curiosity was aroused. "What kind of a fantasy?"

Mischief danced in her eyes. "I've always wanted to know what it was like to kiss Santa Claus," she told him. "Do you mind?"

Was she kidding? He could feel the whiskers in his fake beard spreading as he grinned. "Not at all."

Miranda wasn't certain just what had possessed her to behave like this. Maybe it was the fact that Colin had volunteered—of his own accord—to help, and by doing so, had literally managed to save the day, which in turn had created a really warm feeling within her.

Or maybe it was because the memory of that last kiss was still lingering on her mind, making her long for a replay. Besides, there was something safe about kissing "Santa Claus" here in the director's office, with a building full of people nearby.

Whatever excuse she gave herself didn't really matter. What did matter was that a moment after she'd asked, she found herself being kissed by "Santa."

Or more specifically, by Colin.

And she discovered that the third time around was even better.

This time, her knees turned to mush right along with the rest of her, and she really did have to hold on for dear life as Colin/Santa deepened the kiss by soul-melting degrees until her mind slipped into a black hole.

Only the sudden awkward noise in the doorway kept the kiss from totally engulfing not just her but both of them.

"Oh, I'm sorry, I—I didn't mean to interrupt," Amelia stuttered, obviously embarrassed about having walked in on them like this. Averting her eyes and addressing the nearby wall, she said, "I just wanted to thank you, Officer Kirby. You really made all those kids extremely happy."

The director turned her head slowly, as if to make sure it was safe to look at them. She breathed a sigh of relief to see that neither was annoyed with her for the accidental intrusion.

"Well, I've said my piece," she added, "so I'll leave you two alone. Thank you again, Officer Kirby."

"Um, yeah. Don't mention it. I got a kick out of it," Colin confessed.

"I'll wait for you out here," Miranda told him, quickly slipping out of the room right behind Amelia. She closed the door in her wake.

When he came out less than five minutes later, the director was nowhere in sight. However, true to her word, Miranda was standing out in the hall close by, waiting for him.

"I'm leaving the suit on the chair in the office," Colin said, nodding toward the room.

"That's perfect," Miranda assured him. "Amelia'll put it away until next year."

He'd already forgotten about the costume. His mind

was on something more important. He searched for the right words.

"Are you going home?" he asked.

Miranda nodded. "Lola's waiting for her dinner. She's probably right in front of the door."

"So she's still with you." It wasn't really a question. He'd just assumed that the dog had become more or less of a fixture at Miranda's house, even though she'd called the situation temporary.

Miranda smiled as she nodded. "Still with me. And I have to say that I'm really getting used to having her around."

"Then why not keep her?"

"It wouldn't be fair," she told him. "Lola needs kids to play with."

He didn't understand why she thought that. "What that dog needs more is love, and you seem to have that covered."

His comment surprised her. It wasn't like him. "I think that Santa suit transformed you."

Colin waved away her assessment. "I don't know what you're talking about. I just say it like it is. Speaking of which…" He let his voice trail off as he framed his next sentence. He didn't want her getting the wrong idea, but didn't want to be so low-key that she turned him down.

When he paused, Miranda cocked her head, waiting for him to finish. "Yes?"

"Would you mind if I came home with you? Just for a while," he qualified a little too quickly. "I feel like I need to wind down a bit after this whole Santa thing."

She laughed. "Too much adulation to handle?" she guessed, amused. This had to be all new to him.

He shrugged carelessly. "Something like that. Is it all right?" he asked, still waiting for her to tell him whether or not he could come over.

"Sure," Miranda replied, wondering why Colin would think that it wouldn't be. "Lola would love to see you."

He laughed drily. Miranda made it sound as if he had some sort of a relationship with the German shepherd. "I'm not so sure about that."

"I am," she said, hooking her arm through his. Thinking he might like to leave with a minimum of fuss, she suggested, "We can take the side door if you want to avoid walking through the main room and running into the kids."

"No, that's all right," he told her. "We can go out the front."

He really had changed, she marveled. And she definitely liked this new, improved Colin. "Maybe you should have put on that Santa suit earlier."

He shrugged. It wasn't the suit; it was what had prompted him to put it on: Miranda.

"Maybe I should have," he allowed casually. "By the way, how was it?"

He'd lost her. "How was what?"

"Back in the director's office, you said you wanted to see what it felt like, kissing Santa Claus," he reminded her. He knew he was leaving himself wide-open, but he was curious about what Miranda would say. "So how was it?"

She smiled up at him and said, "Magical."

He had no idea if she was kidding or not, but they had just entered the common room. Most of the kids were still there and he didn't want to say anything that could draw attention to them, so made no comment on her response.

As they crossed the floor to the front door, he saw the director looking their way. Colin nodded at the woman and she mouthed, *"Thank you."* He smiled in response but kept walking.

"I've got a question for you," Miranda said once they were out the door and in the parking area.

Colin braced himself. "Go ahead."

It was already cold and the wind had picked up. Miranda pulled her jacket more tightly around herself. "How did it feel to save the day? Or is that something you've pretty much gotten used to, being a police officer and all?"

Colin laughed to himself, shaking his head. She was serious, he realized. "Miranda, I'm a motorcycle cop, remember? I usually ruin people's day, not save it."

"You know, it doesn't have to be that way."

"Oh? And what is it that you suggest?" he asked, humoring her.

"Well, did you ever think about switching departments?" Miranda asked.

Colin grew solemn. "I *was* in a different department when I worked in LA."

"What happened?"

His expression grew grim as he remembered. "My partner got killed. On the job," he added. Confronted with that information, she would surely drop the subject. But he'd obviously forgotten who he was dealing with.

"All right," she said slowly, processing what he'd just told her and extrapolating. "Bedford's got a canine unit. You could ask to be transferred there," she told him. She thought of the way he interacted with Lola. "You'd be really good at it."

"We'll see," Colin answered, just to get her to stop taking about it.

But Miranda was on to the way he operated. "Just something to think about," she told him. For now, she tabled the subject. Pointing to her vehicle, which was farther down the lot, she said, "I'm parked over there. Do you want to follow me home?"

"I do know where you live, Miranda," Colin reminded her.

Miranda's smile widened as she inclined her head. "Then I'll see you there. I'll make dinner," she added.

He didn't want her to feel obligated. "You don't have to—"

"I've got to eat," she told him. "And I've seen you eat, so I know that you do, too." She gave him a knowing look. "You don't have to turn everything into a debate, Colin."

He supposed he was guilty of that—at least part of the time. "You do have a way with words."

She grinned. "As long as you know that, everything'll be fine."

He wasn't sure about that, Colin thought, as he walked over to his car. Ever since he'd met Miranda, he'd been doing things completely out of character.

Getting into his vehicle, he started it up and pulled out of the parking lot.

His simple routine of eat, sleep, work, repeat, had gone completely out the window. Ever since he'd moved back to Bedford, he hadn't socialized, even remotely. But since he'd crossed paths with Miranda, he found himself entertaining strange thoughts. He *wanted* to socialize. How else could he explain what he had done today?

Never in his wildest dreams would he have thought that he'd put on a Santa suit, much less wear it for more than two hours the way he'd done, while handing out toys to a whole bunch of kids. Even letting those kids crawl onto his lap, and not just putting up with having some of them hug him, but actually, deep down in his soul, *liking* it.

It felt as if he'd lost sight of all the rules he'd always adhered to. Not just lost sight of them but willfully abandoned them.

If he wasn't careful, he would never be the same again.

What "if"? he silently jeered. There was no "if" about it. He wasn't the same now—and did he even want to be?

All these years, he'd been sleepwalking, moving like a shadow figure through his own life—and that wasn't living at all, he silently insisted.

For weeks now he'd kept thinking that if he hadn't crossed paths with Miranda, his life wouldn't have been turned upside down. As if that was a bad thing.

But maybe it wasn't. Maybe it—and she—had actually been his salvation.

And maybe, he told himself as he approached Miranda's house, he'd be better off if he just stopped thinking altogether.

Chapter Seventeen

Colin never got a chance to ring Miranda's doorbell. The front door flew open the minute he walked up to it.

Seeing the surprised look on his face, Miranda explained, "Lola heard your car pulling up and she barked to let me know you were here. I looked out the window and saw she was right."

Walking in, Colin paused to pet the German shepherd's head. He didn't really have much of a choice since she was blocking his path into the house.

"She let you know it was me," he repeated incredulously.

Moving around them, Miranda smiled as she closed the door. "She has a different bark when a stranger comes."

"I'm flattered, Lola." In response, the dog jumped up, placing her paws against his chest. He had a feeling he knew what she was after. "I'm sorry, girl, I don't have anything for you this time. I came straight here from the shelter."

"Don't worry," Miranda said. "I'm always prepared." To his surprise, she reached around the dog and slipped something into the front pocket of his jeans. "I'm not getting fresh," she told him. "I'm just giving you a couple of treats to give her. What?" she asked, when she saw the amused expression on his face.

"I don't think I've ever heard that phrase—getting fresh—outside of an old movie from the sixties, maybe earlier. No offense," he added quickly. "I think it's kind of cute."

"None taken—now that you've redeemed yourself," she added cheerfully. "C'mon, dinner's on the table."

Colin stared at the back of her head, stunned, as he followed her to the dining room. "How did you manage to get anything ready so fast? You couldn't have gotten here more than five minutes ago."

"Ten," she corrected. "I know a shortcut. And I really didn't have to cook. Those are leftovers from yesterday." She gestured at the covered tureen in the center of the table. "Nothing fancy. Just some chicken Alfredo over angel-hair spaghetti."

"Leftovers," Colin repeated, nodding. "That makes more sense. I didn't think even you were *that* fast."

She dished out the spaghetti, then the chicken Alfredo, first on one plate, then the other.

"Am I being challenged?" she asked him, the corners of her mouth curving.

"I didn't mean it that way," he said, then qualified, "Unless you wanted me to."

All she wanted right now was to sit down to a peaceful dinner with him.

"Eat," she prompted. "Dinner's getting cold. And, you," she said, looking down at Lola, who had presented herself at the table. "Let the man eat in peace, girl. He already gave you a bribe."

He was amused by the dog's antics. "I think she's expecting more."

Miranda sighed. "You were right. I have been spoiling her. But her new owner is going to do a better job of making her toe the line," she said.

Surprised, Colin lowered his fork. "New owner? Lola's been adopted?"

Miranda nodded, looking oddly calm to him. He would have expected her to be more upset. "Her papers were all put through and her fee was paid."

"Fee?" he questioned. He had no idea how pet adoption was conducted.

"Every dog and cat that the shelter takes in gets all their shots and they're neutered or spayed, depending on the animal's gender. When they're adopted, the new owner is charged a nominal fee for those services. It's to ensure that the next homeless animal can be taken care of."

Something didn't make sense to him. "If Lola's been adopted, why is she still here?" he asked.

The surge of disappointment he was experiencing over the news of the adoption really caught him off guard. He realized with a pang that he was going to miss Lola once her owner picked her up.

"That's rather a funny story," Miranda answered. "I'll tell it to you once we finish eating."

Colin filled in the blanks: they were going to be taking Lola to her new owner right after dinner. That was why Miranda was holding off telling him the story until later.

He honestly didn't know if he wanted to go with her. Watching the German shepherd being handed over to someone else wasn't something he wanted to witness.

But then it occurred to him that maybe Miranda was asking him to come along because *she* was going to need some moral support for this. He knew that she had gotten close to the animal. She'd said as much herself. What surprised him was that he had, too.

Picking up his fork again, Colin continued to eat, but he was no longer tasting anything and twice had to rouse himself because he'd missed what Miranda was saying.

"You're awfully quiet," she noted, finishing her dinner.

"I'm just thinking," Colin told her without elaborating.

"Okay," she announced, rising from the table. "Let's do this."

He looked at the empty plates on the table. She was leaving them where they were. "You're not going to do the dishes first?"

"They can wait," she told him loftily. "I'll do them later."

That wasn't like her. Giving up Lola and taking her to her new owner was undoubtedly hard on Miranda, he thought. He wanted to shield her from this, but had no idea how.

"Okay, let's get it over with," he told her.

Responding, Miranda took his hand and led him into the living room.

"Aren't you forgetting something?" he asked, nodding at Lola. Miranda hadn't stopped to put a leash on the dog. In fact, she'd left her in the dining room, gnawing on a bone that she had given her.

"I don't think so," Miranda answered innocently.

Instead of walking to the front door, she stopped in front of the Christmas tree. Bending down, she picked up a flat, rectangular box sporting shiny blue wrapping paper and held it out to him.

"Merry Christmas," Miranda declared. "A little early."

"What is it?" he asked, perplexed.

When he didn't take it from her, she gently shoved the box into his hands. "You could open it and see."

She was being very mysterious about this, Colin thought. Still not opening it, he told her uncomfortably, "I didn't get you anything."

"You've given me more than you think—and you were Santa Claus for all those kids," she added. "Now, are you going to open that? Or are you going to just keep looking at it?"

He would have preferred going with the latter, but knew that wouldn't be fair to her, especially after she had gone through all the trouble of not just getting him something but wrapping it, as well.

Colin made his decision. "I'll open it."

"Good choice," she told him with approval. Watching him do so, she could only marvel. "You tear off wrapping paper slower than anyone I've ever seen." Finally, he finished removing the wrapping paper to reveal a decorative gift box beneath. "Now take the top off the box and see what's in it," she coaxed.

When he did, Colin found paperwork. Specifically, paperwork that belonged to Lola, saying that she'd received her rabies vaccination as well as a number of other vaccinations. There was also confirmation of a license registration with the city of Bedford that was good for one year. The certificate stated that her name was Lola Kirby and that she belonged to—

Colin's head jerked up. "Me?" he asked, stunned. "I'm Lola's owner?"

Nodding, Miranda told him, "I didn't know what to get you for Christmas and then it came to me. You needed to have a friendly face to come home to, and Lola needed a home. It seemed like the perfect solution."

"But I can't take care of her," he protested. "I'm never home."

"Sure, you can take care of her. And when you need to take a break, you can leave her with me. I'll dog-sit Lola for you," she volunteered cheerfully.

He was as close to being speechless as he had ever been in his life. Shaking his head, Colin muttered, "I don't know what to say—you're crazy, you know that?"

"I would have accepted 'Thank you, Miranda. It's just what I wanted,'" she responded. Then, growing serious, she told him, "I saw it in your eyes, you know. The way you felt about Lola."

Moved, he came closer to her. So close there was hardly any space for even a breath between them. His gaze met hers. "What else did you see in my eyes?"

Lola was still in the dining room, working away at her soup bone. Except for the sound of teeth meeting bone, there was nothing but silence in the house.

Silence and heat.

"What else was I supposed to see in your eyes?" Miranda asked, her voice dropping to barely a whisper. Her mouth suddenly felt extremely dry, even as she felt her pulse accelerating, going double time.

"You, Miranda," he replied softly. "You were supposed to see you."

She could hardly breathe. "I thought that was just wishful thinking on my part," she confessed.

"You're trembling," he said.

She couldn't seem to stop. Grasping at straws, she said the first thing that came to mind. "It's cold in here."

"Then I guess I'll have to warm you up," Colin told her, his voice low and seductive as he took her into his arms.

The next thing she knew, Colin had lowered his mouth to hers.

And then the whole world slipped into an inky, endless abyss. There was nothing left except the two of them.

This time, there was no hesitation, no second thoughts.

For the first time since he'd met her, he felt no need to put on the brakes, or to tell himself that being with her like this was a mistake.

He wanted her.

Wanted her more than he wanted to breathe.

Because he had come to understand that this woman was what made his existence worthwhile. Just by being herself, she had brought happiness into his life. She'd taken his dark existence and illuminated it, bringing color into his world.

Color and warmth and desire in such proportions they completely overwhelmed him.

And humbled him.

He kissed Miranda over and over again, each kiss more soul-stirring than the one that had come before it. And then, just as she was about to utterly succumb to the passion that was making her head spin, he drew back for a moment.

Miranda felt confusion taking hold.

Oh Lord, he wasn't stopping again, was he? She didn't think she could bear it if he stopped.

Colin drew in a shaky breath. He needed to make his intention clear to her. He didn't want Miranda to look back on this later and feel that he had somehow used the madness of the moment to take advantage of her.

He wanted to be sure—and most of all, he wanted *her* to be sure.

"Miranda, I want to make love with you."

A laugh escaped her lips, a laugh of relief. "It's about time."

And then suddenly, just like that, everything felt right.

He kissed her with more eagerness than he thought he could possibly possess. His lips never left hers as desire surged through him, guiding him.

Controlling him.

He didn't remember undressing her, but he remembered every smooth, tempting curve of her body once her clothing had been stripped away. Remembered the thrill of passing his hands slowly over her silky skin. Remembered the rush he felt as he mentally cataloged every part of her, making it his.

Passion grew to incredible proportions, demanding an appeasement that couldn't be reached, because each time he drew closer to the peak, it moved that much further out of reach, tempting him to kept going, to keep taking refuge in all parts of her, in everything she had to offer.

The sound of her breathing, growing shorter and more audible, drove him wild.

He wanted to take her now, this moment. Wanted to bury himself in her. But with iron control, he reined himself in.

For her.

He wanted Miranda to remember this night, to remember him, and for that to happen, he needed to slow down. To make this all about her—and that, in turn, would make it about them, which had become so very important to him.

Sweeping her up in his arms, he carried her to her bedroom. He closed the door with his back, automatically creating their own private little world. Carrying her over to her bed, Colin placed her down on it gently.

His heart was hammering in his chest and echoing in his head as he lay down beside her. Demands collided within him, making it increasingly difficult to hold himself in check, to not give in to the ever-mounting desire just to take her.

Somehow, he managed to pace himself, but it was the hardest thing he had ever done.

Trailing his lips along Miranda's body, he anointed every part of her, thrilling to the sight and to the feel of her growing more and more excited. She was twisting and turning beneath him as if trying to absorb every sensation that he was creating for her.

With her.

When she ran her hands up and down his torso, when she turned the tables and mirrored all his movements, spiking his desire to unbelievable heights, Colin came exceedingly close to losing total control. But again, at the last moment, he caught himself, vowing to go one more round before he surrendered and made them into one joined being.

He feasted on her lips, the hollow of her throat, working his way down to her belly and farther. Her unbridled gasp when he brought her to her first climax reverberated within his chest, exciting him so much that he tottered on the very edge of restraint.

And then, fearing he couldn't hold on for even another heartbeat, Colin worked his way back up along her damp body, with Miranda rising and twisting against him as he went.

Suddenly, he was over her, his eyes meeting hers, his fingers entwining with hers.

Her legs parted beneath him, issuing a silent invitation he welcomed with every fiber of his aching being. When he entered her, they instantly moved together as if this was the way it was always meant to be. The tempo increased, the rhythm grew to demanding proportions that neither of them was capable of resisting.

Passion wrapped heated wings around them as they raced to the very top of the summit. To the very end of their journey.

When the explosion finally came, fireworks of majestic dimensions showered over them.

And Colin clung to her as if she was his very salvation.

Because she was.

Chapter Eighteen

A myriad of feelings vied for space within Colin as the heated, comforting glow of euphoria he'd been experiencing slowly began to recede. Feelings he wasn't able to completely sort out just yet.

Feelings that had been missing from his life for more than a decade.

As fierce passions settled down, he drew Miranda to him, happy just to have her here next to him on the bed. Contentment, something he was unfamiliar with up until now, washed over him.

He felt like a different person.

Colin wondered if there was a way he could remain here like this indefinitely, her breath mingling with his, the scent of the light, flowery body wash she used filling his senses.

He came close to drifting off when a noise caught his attention.

Moving his head to hear better, Colin couldn't quite place the sound. "You hear something?" he asked Miranda.

She turned her face toward him, managing to rub her cheek against his chest. He could literally feel her smile on his skin.

Raising her head just a little, she looked at him. "You can't tell what that is?"

"So then you *do* hear something." He was beginning to think that he was imagining it.

"Sure. That's Lola scratching against the door," she murmured. "I guess she finished gnawing on that bone and decided to track you down."

"Me?" he questioned. "Why me?" It didn't make any sense to him.

"My guess is that she wants your attention." He could feel heat beginning to travel through his body again as every inch of Miranda seemed to be smiling at him. "Why don't you open the door and let her in?"

"In here?" he asked, surprised.

Miranda didn't see why he would hesitate. "Why not? She's got the run of the place already."

"But we just, um…" Colin seemed to trip over his tongue.

She hadn't thought that he could be this incredibly sweet, so delicate that he didn't know how to go about saying that they'd just made love. She came to his rescue and glossed right over his meaning.

"Which is why she probably tracked you down," Miranda told him. "Lola knows that you're the alpha male and she wants to be the alpha female."

Colin stared at the woman in his arms, stunned as well as confused. "This is getting way out of hand. I don't understand any of it."

Miranda laughed. "Don't worry," she said, patting his chest. "I'm here to talk you through this if you need help. Just think of Lola as a fuzzy child. She needs discipline, a firm hand and lots of love—just like any child."

Colin sat up, looking at the door. The scratching continued.

He dragged a hand through his hair, trying to think, and feeling totally out of his element. "Taking care of a dog is a lot of responsibility."

"Yes, but it has a lot of compensation, too. Like boundless love."

He still looked uncertain. "I don't think I'm ready for this."

Since he wasn't getting up, Miranda did, wrapping the sheet around her.

"Not ready for being on the receiving end of boundless love? Sure you are," she exclaimed, making it sound as if she knew him better than he knew himself.

But he was thinking of the responsibility part. "No, if I'm going to be her new owner, I'm definitely going to need help," he said, looking at Miranda pointedly.

Meanwhile, she had opened the door and Lola came flying in. In two steps the German shepherd went from standing out in the hallway to standing on the bed. She came close to knocking Colin off the mattress in her enthusiasm and then started licking his face.

"Lots and lots of help," Colin declared, doing his best to sit up again and gain some semblance of the upper hand over the dog.

Miranda laughed as, still wearing the sheet like a Roman toga, she climbed back into bed. Lola was between them and was acting as if this was some sort of new game. Her head practically spun as she looked from one of them to the other, as if to say that she didn't know the rules to this game yet, but was more than willing to play.

Watching her, Miranda stated, "I think she wants you to pet her."

Stroking the animal, he looked over Lola's head at Miranda. "Now you see, I'm going to need that sort of insight to help me navigate through this pet ownership thing."

She was certainly on board with that, Miranda thought. "Like I said, you can give me a call anytime you need help."

"I appreciate that," he told her. "But then you'd have to find the time to come over, or I'd have to come over to you and bring the dog. That would consume an awful lot of downtime and we're both pretty busy as it is."

She knew she'd taken a chance when she'd decided to make him Lola's owner, but she'd thought he would last longer than a few hours.

Miranda took a breath, resigning herself to the inevitable. "You're saying you don't want the dog." She gave it one more shot, taking Lola's muzzle in her hands and turning the dog's head in his direction. "How can you say no to this face?"

"I'm not saying no," Colin told her. "I'm saying we need a different solution."

She took the only guess open to her. "You're saying you want her to stay with me."

But Colin shook his head. Stroking the dog's back—Lola had settled down and was now lying in the bed, content to have one of them on either side—he said, "That's not it, either."

At a loss now, she asked, "All right then, so what is it?"

Nerves all but got the better of him. This was brand-new territory for him and he didn't know how she would receive what he was about to say. "If you stop making guesses and just listen, I'll tell you." The moment the words were out of his mouth, he knew he'd sounded short with her.

"Okay." Miranda crossed her arms, waiting for him to go on.

The sheet slipped down just enough to give him a tantalizing glimpse of what he'd availed himself of earlier. Thinking about that, Colin found he had to struggle to keep his mind on what he was trying to say.

"So talk," she prompted, when he remained silent.

Here went nothing, Colin decided.

"I thought that we could move in together," he told her.

He was surprised that the words came out as easily as they did.

Miranda's mouth dropped open. But not a single sound emerged.

She was speechless, he realized, and he didn't know if that was a good thing or a bad one. Was she trying to find the words to turn him down gently, or was she so shocked that she'd lost the ability to talk?

"Move in together," she said, repeating his words.

"Yes," he confirmed, then went on to elaborate. "You could move in with me. But my place is small. It's an apartment and it might be kind of crowded for you, especially with Lola. Or I could move in here," he said, watching Miranda's face intently for her reaction.

"Move in together," she repeated again. "For the sake of the dog." The last words were uttered in semi-disbelief.

"Well, yes," he agreed. Something was off and he felt like a man trying to walk across a lake on very thin ice. He could feel the ice cracking beneath his feet with every step he took, yet he had no choice but to forge on. "You were the one who gave her to me, so I figured you'd want to do what was best for her."

"You want to move in together because of the dog," she said, as if trying to wrap her mind around what he was telling her.

"Well, that's one reason," he agreed. He was having a devil of a time getting the words out.

"Oh, so there's another reason?" she asked innocently.

Feeling awkward and totally inarticulate, not to mention afraid of being turned down once he told her the real reason behind his suggestion, Colin seriously thought about throwing up his hands and just abandoning the whole idea, lock, stock and barrel.

But then something egged him on.

It was all or nothing.

If he didn't say anything, he'd already lost, so there was nothing to lose by speaking up.

Frustrated, he shouted at her, "Of course there's another reason."

Lola instantly sat up, a canine barrier intent on protecting whichever one of them needed protecting.

"It's okay, Lola," Miranda said soothingly, rubbing the tip of the animal's ear, a trick she'd learned to calm a dog down. "It's okay. Lie down, girl."

After a moment, the dog obeyed.

"Okay," Miranda said, turning her attention back to him. "You were saying there was another reason…" She trailed off, waiting for him to pick up the conversation.

"You know there's another reason," he told her. When she continued silently looking at him, waiting, he blew out a breath. "You're going to make me say this, aren't you?"

"I'm afraid so." The corners of her mouth curved ever so slightly. "I need clarification, Colin. What's the other reason you want us to move in together?"

Exasperated, he raised his voice again. "Because I love you, damn it."

She struggled not to laugh. "Is that one word?"

"Miranda…" He sounded very close to the end of his rope.

Once again she came to his rescue. "I love you, too, damn it," Miranda said, mimicking his exact intonation. And then she asked, "Are you sure about this?" She would hate for him to look back with regret because it had all come about in the heat of the moment.

"Sure that I love you?" he questioned. "Yes, I'm sure. I just didn't want to have to say it. Putting myself out there is hard for me," he told her. "It's not something I do."

Reaching over the dog, who appeared to be close to falling asleep, she touched Colin's face and smiled. "I was talking about moving in together, but what you just said was very nice."

"Just 'very nice'?" he asked in surprise, mimicking *her* intonation.

There was humor in Miranda's eyes as she told him honestly, "I'm afraid if I say any more, I'll scare you off."

"After everything I've just been through, that is *not* going to happen," he stated.

"Since words are so difficult for you—" Miranda rose up on her knees, allowing the sheet to fall away and pool around her thighs "—why don't I just show you how I feel about what you said?"

She was about to lean into him when Colin put a finger to her lips, stopping her. "Hold that thought."

The next moment, he got off the bed, coaxing the dog to do the same. Holding on to Lola's collar, he guided the animal to the bedroom's threshold.

"C'mon, girl," he told her, "you need to go back into the other room for a few minutes."

"Just a few minutes?" Miranda pretended to question him.

"Maybe an hour—or two," he amended.

After taking Lola out, Colin was gone for a couple minutes. Returning, he made sure to close the door behind him.

Miranda cocked her head, listening for a moment for scratching noises.

Or whining.

She heard neither.

"Nothing," she said. "You really are good at disciplining." She wove her arms around his neck as he joined her.

Rather than say anything in response to her compliment, Colin murmured, "I hope you didn't have any plans for that other soup bone in the refrigerator."

So that was why the dog was so quiet. Miranda could only laugh. "You're as bad as I am."

"I really hope so," he told her.

And with that, there was no more talk. About anything. He had far better things to do than talk, and was more than eager to get started.

Epilogue

"Ladies, I think that it's pretty safe to say this is quite possibly the most unique wedding venue we have ever attended," Maizie told her two friends as she sat on the white folding chair between Theresa and Celia.

There was row after row of folding chairs in the hospital rec room, in the same area of the children's ward that just a few months ago had housed the giant Christmas tree.

The large room was all but filled to capacity with small patients from the ward, a great many women and children from the shelter, and several volunteers who worked with Miranda at the animal shelter.

"Thank goodness Miranda's mother and Colin's aunt were here early to make sure the altar was set up before it got so crowded in here," Theresa commented.

She and her catering team had arrived early, as well.

Working quickly, they had prepared everything for the reception that was to follow immediately after the ceremony.

"If they knew there was going to be this many people attending, why didn't they just opt for someplace bigger?" Celia asked.

"That's simple enough to answer," Theresa told her. "Miranda didn't want the children here missing the wedding. A lot of them aren't able or well enough to leave the hospital—and all of them are very attached to her. Miranda wouldn't dream of leaving any of them out."

Maizie nodded, pleased. "You ask me, Colin's getting a hell of a girl," she said to her friends. "There aren't many young women who are that thoughtful."

Theresa was beaming as she kept her eyes peeled for any sign that the bride was about to enter. "I really think that we outdid ourselves with this particular match, girls."

"Well, none of this would have happened if Maizie hadn't charmed that desk sergeant into rescheduling Colin's regular route so that he'd be right there when Miranda whizzed by," Celia commented. She turned toward Maizie. "How *did* you know that Miranda would be driving too fast?"

"And how did you really get that sergeant to change Colin's schedule with the other police officer's?" Theresa asked.

Maizie merely smiled, remaining tight-lipped, at least for now. "A girl's got to have some secrets, ladies," she told them with a wink.

"Not at this stage she doesn't," Celia told her life-long friend.

"Shh, they're starting to play the wedding march. You don't want to miss any of this," Maizie said.

Those who could rose to their feet. The rest of the attendees remained seated, anxiously anticipating the entrance of the bride.

Miranda was standing just outside the recreation room's closed doors, holding on to her bouquet of pink and white carnations and willing the sudden burst of butterflies in her stomach to go away.

"Nervous, darling?" Jeannine asked her daughter.

"A little. Mostly just afraid of tripping before I reach the altar," Miranda answered, a small smile curving her lips.

"You won't," Jeannine said confidently. "You're the steadiest person I ever knew."

Miranda took a breath, pressing one hand against her stomach as if that would get the butterflies to settle down.

"I wish your father was here," Jeannine said in a soft whisper. "He would have loved to see you in your bridal gown."

"He's here, Mom. I can feel it." The music swelled. Miranda took a breath. "That's our cue."

"I love you, Miranda," Jeannine told her.

"And I love you." She looked at her mother. The woman's cheeks were wet. "Please don't cry, Mom. You'll get your contacts all foggy."

Jeannine laughed, brushing the tears away. "Don't worry, I'll get you there. I promise."

The doors parted, drawn open by two of the orderlies. Miranda saw a sea of faces turning in her direction, but they all blended together before her eyes. Looking out at them, she could make out only one face in that enormous crowd.

The only face that mattered to her right at this moment.

Colin's face.

He was standing at the altar, looking incredibly handsome in his black tuxedo and dark gray shirt. She had half expected him to come in his police uniform. She wouldn't have cared what he wore, as long as he came.

"Ready, darling?" Jeannine asked.

Her eyes not leaving the man she had never expected to come into her life, Miranda answered, "More than ready, Mom."

They made their way up the makeshift aisle until they reached the minister, who was standing in front of the altar, waiting to say the words that would join her to Colin.

"Who gives this woman?" the man asked when she came before him.

"I do," Jeannine replied, her voice trembling. And then she withdrew so that the ceremony could begin.

"You look beautiful," Colin whispered to Miranda.

"You do, too," she told him.

He nearly laughed. It was a good feeling, he couldn't help thinking. Miranda had brought laughter into his life and into his heart.

More than a few of the children giggled as they

watched Lola trot up the aisle next, the wedding rings tied around her neck with a navy blue bow.

"We can begin," the minister announced.

Colin never thought he would ever be this lucky. When he looked at Miranda, just before they began to exchange their vows and their rings, he realized that she was thinking the same thing.

He could see it in her eyes.

They really were meant for one another, he thought. And he for one would always be eternally grateful for that.

* * * * *

MILLS & BOON

THE HEART OF ROMANCE

A ROMANCE FOR EVERY KIND OF READER

MODERN

Prepare to be swept off your feet by sophisticated, sexy and seductive heroes, in some of the world's most glamourous and romantic locations, where power and passion collide.
8 stories per month.

HISTORICAL

Escape with historical heroes from time gone by. Whether your passion is for wicked Regency Rakes, muscled Vikings or rugged Highlanders, awaken the romance of the past.
6 stories per month.

MEDICAL

Set your pulse racing with dedicated, delectable doctors in the high-pressure world of medicine, where emotions run high and passion, comfort and love are the best medicine.
6 stories per month.

True Love

Celebrate true love with tender stories of heartfelt romance, from the rush of falling in love to the joy a new baby can bring, and a focus on the emotional heart of a relationship.
8 stories per month.

Desire

Indulge in secrets and scandal, intense drama and plenty of sizzling hot action with powerful and passionate heroes who have it all: wealth, status, good looks…everything but the right woman.
6 stories per month.

HEROES

Experience all the excitement of a gripping thriller, with an intense romance at its heart. Resourceful, true-to-life women and strong, fearless men face danger and desire - a killer combination!
8 stories per month.

DARE

Sensual love stories featuring smart, sassy heroines you'd want as a best friend, and compelling intense heroes who are worthy of them.
4 stories per month.

To see which titles are coming soon, please visit

millsandboon.co.uk/nextmonth

MILLS & BOON
True Love

Romance from the Heart

Celebrate true love with tender stories of
heartfelt romance, from the rush of falling
in love to the joy a new baby can bring,
and a focus on the emotional
heart of a relationship.